A Woman's Heart

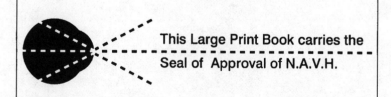

This Large Print Book carries the
Seal of Approval of N.A.V.H.

A WOMAN'S HEART

JoAnn Ross

Thorndike Press • Waterville, Maine

Published in 2003 by arrangement with Harlequin Books S.A.

Thorndike Press Large Print Romance Series.

The tree indicium is a trademark of Thorndike Press.

The text of this Large Print edition is unabridged.
Other aspects of the book may vary from the original edition.

Set in 16 pt. Plantin by Christina S. Huff.

Printed in the United States on permanent paper.

Library of Congress Cataloging-in-Publication Data

Ross, JoAnn.
 A woman's heart / JoAnn Ross.
   p. cm.
  ISBN 0-7862-4983-8 (lg. print : hc : alk. paper)
 1. Ireland — Fiction. 2. Widows — Fiction. 3. Large type books. I. Title.
PS3568.O843485 W66 2003
 813′.54—dc21   2002075031

To my agent, Damaris Rowland, who believed in this story from conception.

To all my pals who kept me writing during the tough times — especially the wonderfully supportive members of RWA On-Line; the Romance Group on AOL, who provided a fun place to hide out; the wise and witty Stars, who've come to mean so much to me; and most particularly, Patty Gardner Evans, who always knows exactly when to let me whine.

To my son, Patrick, his wife, Lisa, and Marisa-the-Wonder-Toddler, a brilliant ray of sunshine who can brighten even the darkest of days.

And last, but certainly not least, to my beloved Jay, who changed my life that fateful morning so long ago and continues to make every day an adventure.

PROLOGUE

It was twilight, that mystical time when the world seems suspended between day and night. The remote lake, carved by glaciers into the surrounding folded green hills, glimmered with the reflection of the ruins of the twelfth-century castle that had given the Irish town of Castlelough its name.

As the sun sank lower and lower in the cloud-scudded sky, six-year-old Rory Fitzpatrick sat in his secret wishing place and related the events of the day to his best friend.

"Johnny Murphy stole communion hosts. And not just ordinary bread ones, either, but the special holy hosts in the tabernacle that were already blessed. You know, the ones Father O'Malley takes to shut-ins.

"And Johnny even passed them out on the playground. A lot of kids who haven't had their first communion yet and didn't know better ate them. But I didn't."

The Lady didn't answer. She never did. But Rory sensed her unspoken approval.

7

"He got in a lot of trouble. Sister Mary Patrick paddled him, and he's not going to be allowed to go on the father-and-son trek."

He sighed, drew his knees up to his chest and wrapped his thin arms around them. Across the reed-fringed lake, the stone castle seemed to brood in the gloaming.

"I think I'm going to pretend to get sick that day. Father O'Malley says you don't need a da to go, and Cousin Jamie says I can share his, but it's not the same thing. And besides, his da's drunk a lot. And mean even when he's not. So I wouldn't want to be sharing him, anyway."

Rory put his chin on his bent knees and looked out over the darkening blue water. "I wish I had a father."

Beside him, Maeve, the gray, white and black Irish wolfhound his aunt Kate had given him, whimpered. Rory might have thought she was feeling sorry for him, but the dog whined all the time. His mother said poor Maeve was the most fearful beast ever born in all Ireland. Or probably anywhere else, for that matter. Rory figured she was probably right. Which was why it was strange she'd never seemed afraid of the Lady.

"Great-grandma Fionna says that God always answers our prayers. But you know how I've been praying forever. Ever since I was a little kid. And Aunt Kate gave me a special rock she said is just like one the druids used for making magic —" he pulled the rune with the marks scratched into its surface from the pocket of his jeans and showed it to her "— but I still don't have a da."

Another sigh. "If I had a da, maybe Mam would stop crying."

The Lady's bright eyes, which were exactly the color of Rory's favorite aggie marble, asked a silent question.

"Oh, she never cries when anyone's around," he said quickly. "But sometimes, late at night, when I have to get up to go to the bathroom, I hear her. I think she's worried she's going to have to take the job working for that businessman in Galway."

He'd been telling the Lady all about this for a month. A month during which his mother had been pretending nothing was wrong.

The mountains were changing colors in the shifting light. Rory knew if he didn't get home soon, she'd worry.

And didn't his Mam already have cares enough without having to wonder where he was always taking off to? He could practically hear his aunt Mary scolding.

"If we had a father," he said to the Lady, "we'd have more money. And then we wouldn't have to leave Castlelough." *And you.* The unspoken words hung suspended on the soft moist air between them.

"Grandfather rented a room to one of the Americans who are coming to Castlelough tomorrow," he reminded her unnecessarily.

The Lady never forgot anything Rory told her. That was only one of the reasons she was his best friend. Another was that he could share anything and everything with her. Things he couldn't even share with his mother.

"The American is paying a lot. Maybe it'll be enough." Rory's throat closed up the way it always did whenever he thought about having to move away from the farm. He swallowed painfully. Maeve nudged his hand, coaxing it onto her huge head; Rory absently stroked her while he battled with his unruly feelings.

"I guess you'll be staying out of sight while the Americans are here." As much as the family needed the money, Rory hated this idea.

The Lady slowly nodded her head. Although it could have been a trick of the light reflecting off the water, Rory thought he saw the shimmer of tears in her gentle golden eyes. It made him want to cry himself.

"It's only a month." It seemed like for-ever. "And after they're gone, I'll come back." If he wasn't living in Galway by then.

Rory wiped his burning eyes with the sleeve of his sweater. He hated the way his voice, all thin and shaky, sounded just like some stupid crybaby.

"I'll come back." He made his voice stronger, as if saying the words out loud could make them true. Beside him, Maeve thumped her tail.

Of course you will.

Rory's blue eyes widened with surprise. It was the first time the Lady had ever spoken to him! Oh, the words weren't really out loud, they were inside his head, but he heard them just the same.

The sun was setting behind the mountain in a blinding flare of ruby light. It made the Lady's green scales glitter like emeralds. His spirits lifted, his hopes renewed, Rory watched as the ancient lake creature gave one last flick of her tail, then disappeared beneath the cobalt water.

CHAPTER ONE

Nora

The news came to Castlelough as if riding on wisps of early-morning fog, winding its way from Donal's gift shop on the tidy medieval square, to The Irish Rose pub on Gaol Road, to Molly Lee's Confectionery at the top of the ancient steps, from which visitors made a breath-stealing descent down the towering limestone cliffs to the sea.

From schoolyard to church to cottage to manor house to the post office — where Elizabeth Murphy was quick to announce whenever another red, white and blue overnight express letter arrived from America — the question was always the same:

"Did you hear? The movie people are coming."

By the time Nora Fitzpatrick arrived in the village on the day the movie people were due to arrive, the whispers and murmurs had risen to a near clamor.

Although the sunshine yellow gorse was blooming vividly in the hedgerows and the taste of late spring rode faintly on the soft wet sea air, the day had turned chilly and threatening.

Nora dropped into O'Neill's Chicken and Chips for a cup of tea, to warm up after her long ride from the farm, and watched the oldest O'Neill daughter flirt with the handsome boy delivering an order of canned lemonade. Feeling a great deal older than her twenty-five years, Nora left them merrily laughing at some joke the boy had made.

As she crossed the stone bridge over a river rushing its way toward the Atlantic, it occurred to her she'd been jealous of eighteen-year-old Brenda O'Neill.

"Not jealous," she amended out loud. "Perhaps just a wee bit envious." The sight of the carefree couple had brought back thoughts of when her husband, Conor, had been courting her. She sighed at the memory, which was both pleasing and sad at the same time.

Conor Fitzpatrick, who'd grown up on the neighboring farm, had matured into a man as handsome and bold as an ancient king. Nora doubted any woman would have been able to resist falling in love with him. After spending time on the continent, he'd literally burst back into her life and eased the grief she'd been suffering so at the time. And for that she'd always love him.

She pushed her bicycle up the steep narrow cobblestone street. In the distance she could see the lake, carved out by a glacier thousands of years ago, limpid against mountains tipped with silvery fog. On the far bank a pre-Christian ring of stones appeared to be silently awaiting a solstice ritual fire. The sap had begun to flow in the birch trees, turning the winter brown twigs a brilliant eye-pleasing purple.

It was spring when Conor had first made love to her — their wedding night — and Nora hadn't even thought to be afraid, she'd trusted him so. The bittersweet memories were as preserved in her mind as fossils captured in amber.

"I had a 'dream' about your mam the other night," Nora's sister-in-law had told Nora just the week before. "She thinks you need a new man in your life."

Nora was not particularly surprised that Kate would be claiming to be in communication with Eleanor Joyce. The fact that her mother had been dead for years had certainly not stopped *Nora* from talking to her. Since the conversations were a source of comfort, she never bothered to wonder if others might think her a bit daft. Besides,

Nora often thought she'd probably go daft if she weren't able to talk things out with her mam. But although her mother never actually answered her back — except in Nora's own mind — she suspected it might possibly be quite a different case with Kate.

Ever since childhood, Kate had been able to "see" things. Like when she was five and saw the black wreath on Mrs. Callahan's door two months before the old woman dropped dead of a heart attack while weeding her cabbage patch. Or the time they were teenagers and had been picnicking on the beach with a couple of boys and Kate saw little Kevin Noonan floating facedown in the surf seconds before a white-crested wave swept the wandering toddler off his feet — but soon enough to warn his mother, thank God.

When her sister-in-law had brought up the subject of men the week before, Nora had reminded Kate — and her mother, in case Eleanor Joyce had been eavesdropping from heaven — that she already had enough males in her life. "There's Da," she'd said. "And, of course, Michael and John."

"I don't think your mam was talking about your father or brothers," Kate had argued. "She thinks you need to marry again. You need a husband."

Nora had grown up in Castlelough. As a child she'd run barefoot in the meadows with boys who'd grown up and were now the county's eligible males. She knew them all, liked most of them well enough, but there wasn't a single solitary one whose boots she'd want to put beside her bed.

"Well, then," she'd said with a soft laugh, "since there's none handy around here and I'm too busy taking care of the farm and the children, along with trying to keep Da on the straight and narrow, to go out and find myself a proper husband, I guess you'll have to tell mam to pull some strings up there and send me one."

"I suspect that may be what she has in mind to do," Kate had answered. "But I doubt she has a proper one in mind. What would be the challenge in that, after all?"

What indeed? Knowing her father's quicksilver nature all too well, Nora suspected Eleanor Joyce had certainly had a great many challenges in her own life. As did Kate. And most of the other married women of her acquaintance. Irish men, while charming, unfortunately did not always make the easiest of husbands, she thought as she stopped in front of her destination.

The sparkling windows of Monohan's Mercantile were filled with treats designed to lure the passerby inside — colorful tins of biscuits, bags of saltwater taffy, tidy rows of Cadbury chocolates, jars of skin creams and bath lotions made from the carrageen moss still gathered by hand from the rocky western coast and bunches of perky golden daffodils displayed in dazzling white pots.

A paper banner, handpainted kelly green on white, welcomed the cast and crew of *The Lady of the Lake* to Castlelough. Bordered with blatantly touristy shamrocks, the banner also featured an imaginative rendition of the creature rising from the water. Nora guessed it had been drawn by the Monohans' twelve-year-old daughter, Margaret, a talented young artist who always won, in her age group, the summer's Sea Safety poster contest.

Beneath the sign was a collection of miniature sea monsters for sale, ranging from cheap plastic ones to sparkling crystal serpents hand-blown by local artisans. A towering pyramid of hardcover novels claimed the center spot of honor in the gaily decorated window.

A small brass bell tied to the Dublin blue door signaled Nora's arrival in the shop.

"So, today's the big day, is it?" Sheila Monohan asked, looking down from the top rung of a ladder where she was replacing a burned-out fluorescent tube. "The day your movie man arrives."

"Mr. Gallagher is a writer." Nora repeated what she'd already told Mrs. O'Neill.

She glanced at the pyramid of books. From this vantage point, the author photo on the back of the dust jacket seemed to be looking right back at her. Scowling at her, actually, which she didn't believe was the best expression to encourage people to buy his book. Still, even with his glower, Quinn Gallagher didn't appear old enough to be so successful. Perhaps success, like so many other things, came easier in America.

"I don't read horror novels," Sheila confessed. "There are so many things to worry about in the world. I'd much rather settle down at night with a nice love story. But I hear many consider him quite a fine writer."

"John certainly thinks so." Nora's youngest brother had stayed up all night reading the American horror novelist's latest book. "Kate sings his praises, as well. But it still strikes me as odd the way everyone's behaving. You'd think a bunch of Americans arriving in Castlelough was as important as the Second Coming."

After all, Americans weren't an uncommon sight. Even perched on the far west coast of Ireland as it was, Castlelough received its share of tourists. Still, Nora hadn't seen so much excitement since the time it was rumored — erroneously, it turned out — that the pope was coming to visit the rural county.

"People figure the movie folk will liven up the place," Sheila said.

"We're already lively." When the older woman lifted a jet-black eyebrow at the outrageous falsehood, Nora shrugged one slicker-clad shoulder. "Well, we may not have the bright lights of Dublin, but that's the point. Some of us appreciate a quiet life."

"If it's a quiet life you're seeking, Eleanor Rose Joyce Fitzpatrick, you should have stayed in that Dublin convent.

"Besides —" Sheila nodded, appearing pleased with herself when the light flickered to life "— you know as well as I do there's not much opportunity in a small village like Castlelough. Tourism or emigration, that's our choice, my Devlin always says."

Even as her heart took a little dive at the depressing prospect of having to leave Castlelough, Nora couldn't resist a smile at the mention of Sheila's son, the man who once, in what seemed like another lifetime, had taught her to French-kiss, even as she'd worried for her immortal soul.

19

Sister Mary Augustine had taught all the girls in her class that letting a boy put his tongue in your mouth was one of the vilest of mortal sins.

"And don't forget, girls, every sin you commit is another thorn in our Lord Jesus' side." Sister had glared like Moses standing atop the Mount at the group of tartan-clad adolescents. "French-kissing debases a girl. And makes the devil smile."

Although Nora certainly hadn't wanted to make Satan smile, three years after that memorable sex-education lecture, Devlin Monohan's kisses had proved so thrilling she'd recklessly risked hell on more than one occasion during that idyllic summer of her first love.

"How is Devlin?" she asked now.

"Fit as a fiddle. He rang up last night, as a matter of fact, to say he's been offered a position at the National Stud."

"That's wonderful!" Graduating from veterinary college and working at the National Stud had been Devlin's dream. He'd talked about it a lot between kisses.

"Isn't it just? I'll have to admit I'm guilty of the sin of pride at the idea of my son helping to breed the best racehorses in the world."

"It's no sin to be proud of a son." On this

Nora had reason to be very clear. Nora wondered if her mother knew this latest news about Devlin and decided she probably did. Not much had ever slipped by Eleanor Joyce.

The woman who might have been Nora's mother-in-law climbed down from the ladder and brushed her dusty hands on her apron, which, like the poster, bore a fanciful image of the lake creature — which, in a way, was the source of all this uproar.

If those old myths hadn't existed, Quinn Gallagher wouldn't have written the book, Hollywood wouldn't have bought the film rights and the movie people would have stayed in Hollywood.

"We were all surprised when you went off to become a postulate," Sheila said suddenly, as if that life-altering Sunday morning were only yesterday and not eight long years ago. "Everyone expected you and my Devlin would get married."

"I thought we might, as well. For a time." After all, Nora wouldn't have risked hell for just anyone. "But I truly believed I had a vocation."

"Just because you could memorize all the prayers and catechism answers faster than any girl at Holy Child School," Sheila said, "didn't necessarily make you a candidate for the convent." She was only pointing out

21

what Nora's own mother had told her as they'd loaded her suitcase — filled with the muslin sheets, black stockings, black shoes and white cotton underwear the nuns had instructed she bring to the convent — into the family car.

"I would have eventually realized that." Nora wondered briefly if this out-of-the-blue discussion might be no coincidence. Her mother had supposedly told Kate she might be sending Nora a husband. Could she be trying to get the two childhood sweethearts back together again?

"As it turned out, you didn't have time to make up your own mind," Sheila said with a regretful shake of her head. "What with your poor mam dying giving birth to Celia and you having to leave the order."

It had been the second-worst time of her life. "Someone had to tend to the house and children." And Da, she thought, but did not say.

"I've always said it was too much responsibility for a young girl. A child raising children was what you were. Lord knows Brady, as good a man as he is in his way, couldn't take care of himself, let alone those babies.

"Considering how lonely you must have been, it's no wonder you fell head over heels for Conor Fitzpatrick when he came back from the continent with all those flashy trophies."

"I loved Conor," Nora stated firmly.

Her love for her dashing husband — who'd held the promise of becoming one of the world's greatest steeplechase riders — had been the single constant in Nora's life during that time. And if she hadn't married Conor, Rory, the shining apple of her eye, wouldn't have been born.

And then Conor had been killed in a race, which had been the worst time of her life.

"He's been dead for five years, Nora. It's not good for a woman to be alone. Especially a woman with children to raise."

"I manage."

"Of course you do, dear." Sheila paused, giving Nora the impression she was choosing her words carefully. "Devlin had other news."

"Oh?"

"He's engaged. To a young woman he met in veterinary school."

The older woman's gaze had turned so intent Nora felt as if she were standing at the wrong end of one of those telescopes all the lake-monster trackers inevitably carried.

"I'm so happy for him," she said. "You'll have to give me his address so I can write him a note."

"You don't mind?"

"Of course not. It's been over between Devlin and me for a long time. I'm pleased he's found someone to share his life with."

So much for her mother's perceived matchmaking.

"Here's my list." Not wanting to discuss her love life — or lack of it — any longer, Nora handed the piece of paper to the storekeeper. "I hope you have some of those Spanish oranges. Rory loves them, and they're so much better for his teeth than sweets or biscuits."

"You're a good mother, Nora Fitzpatrick," Sheila said. "And no one can fault the job you're doing with the children. But it's easier on a woman to have a man around the house. Sons, especially, need a father's firm guiding hand."

As the older woman began plucking items from the wooden shelves, Nora almost laughed as she thought how much Sheila Monohan sounded like her mother. Which made sense, she decided, since the two women had been best friends.

"Brady brought in your eggs this morning, in case you're wondering," Sheila offered as she began adding up Nora's purchases on her order pad. "I gave him a credit."

Nora had worried her father might have forgotten to sell the eggs before heading off to the pub for a day of storytelling and gossiping. She was also grateful Sheila hadn't paid cash for the eggs. Da could make coins disappear faster than the magician she'd seen at last year's Puck Fair in County Kerry.

"Thank you."

"No thanks necessary. They were good-size eggs, Nora. A lot bigger than Mrs. O'Donnel's. We'll get a good price for them."

Nora smiled at that. "John says it's the Nashville music he's started playing in the henhouse. Perhaps I ought to write a letter to Garth Brooks and ask if he'd be interested in paying me for a commercial endorsement."

Although Nora still refused to believe that the piped-in tunes had any effect at all on the hens, she couldn't deny that since her seventeen-year-old brother's latest science experiment, they'd begun laying more — and larger eggs.

"Brady said you were thinking of joining the cheese guild," Sheila said after laughing at Nora's suggestion. Her sentence tilted upward at the end, turning it into a question.

"I'm considering it. The man from the guild assures me I could increase my profits by twenty percent. He suggested Cashel blue."

"That's one of our most popular cheeses," Sheila agreed. "And a twenty-percent profit increase is certainly nothing to scoff at."

"I know. And it's not as if we couldn't use the money."

Which was, of course, the only reason Brady had arranged to rent out her bedroom. Her father had informed Nora — after the fact — that the American novelist, Quinn Gallagher, would be staying in their house, and Nora had no option but to agree. Besides, the man was paying an amazingly generous price for a bedroom, shared bath, and morning and evening meals.

She'd almost resigned herself to moving the children to Galway and taking that job as a bookkeeper to a land developer, a former schoolmate who'd become wealthy refurbishing the bay waterfront for tourism. Now she could allow herself to think she might actually be able to turn down the offer.

"Money's always something we could all use more of," Sheila said with a sigh.

Yes, Nora thought, it wasn't easy resisting the lure of the city with its high-paying jobs.

And traffic congestion, and polluted air, and so many people a body couldn't take a breath without invading the private space of her neighbor.

Nora knew that her brother John and her sister Mary longed for the bright city lights, but she supposed that was natural when you were seventeen and sixteen. Not that she herself ever had. Conor, who'd certainly enjoyed the fast life, had accused her of having the green fields and rich black peat of the family farm in her blood. Nora had never denied it. It was, after all, true.

CHAPTER TWO

Forty Shades of Green

From the air, Ireland was a panorama of field and hedgerow, patchwork valleys set amidst abrupt mountains. Quinn Gallagher thought he'd never seen so many shades of green in his life — sage, olive, beryl, jade, emerald, malachite, moss, sea green, bottle green — the list seemed endless.

"Christ, it looks just like a postcard," he murmured as he looked out the window of the Aer Lingus jet.

"It looks like a gigantic bore," his seat-mate in the first-class cabin countered. "We haven't even touched down yet and I'm ready to go home."

Home. The word had never had any real meaning for Quinn. Home was a place you wanted to go back to, a place where people would take you in. Welcome you. The roach-infested apartments and ramshackle trailers where he'd spent his hardscrabble early years certainly didn't fit that description.

Neither did the succession of brutal foster

homes until, weary of working on farms from sunup to sundown and being beaten for his efforts, he'd run away at sixteen, lied about his age and joined the navy. And while the navy had, admittedly, represented the most stability he'd experienced in his life, the ships on which he'd sailed around the world certainly hadn't been home.

The sun reflecting off the water below was blinding. Quinn shaded his eyes with his hand as he took in the sight of the farmhouses looking like tiny white boats floating on a deep green sea.

"Boring's relative. I think it looks like God's country." As soon as he heard himself say the words, Quinn wondered where the hell they'd come from. He also immediately regretted having said them.

Laura Gideon's trademark sexy laugh revealed she was every bit as surprised by his statement as he was. "Strange words from a card-carrying atheist, darling."

Quinn forced a reluctant laugh as something indefinable stirred inside him, something that resisted his writer's need to analyze and label.

"Okay, so I overstated. But you have to admit, it does look beautiful."

"Of course it does," the actress agreed. "You said it yourself. The quaint little scene looks like every postcard of Ireland you've ever seen. Heaven help us, I have a horrible feeling that the entire country might turn out to be a living cliché."

Shuddering dramatically, she linked her fingers with his, a familiarity that came from being a former lover.

"Perhaps it's something else." She turned toward him, her eyes gleaming with the wicked humor Quinn had always enjoyed. "Perhaps it's your 'auld sod' roots calling to you."

"I strongly doubt that." He might be one of the hottest horror writers in the business, but even Quinn couldn't think up a more terrifying idea.

"Roots tie you down, Quinn, baby," he remembered his mother saying. "They wrap around your ankles so bad you can't never get free."

It was the only thing Angie Gallagher had ever told him that Quinn had taken to heart. Twenty-four hours after making that boozy proclamation, Angie was dead. Quinn had gone to her funeral in the company of the Elko County sheriff and his tearfully sympathetic wife, watched the rough-hewn pine coffin being lowered into the unmarked grave and wondered if his rambler of a mother had known she was fated to spend the rest of her life in Jackpot, Nevada, population five-hundred and seventy, not counting the cows.

The memory, which he usually avoided revisiting, was not a pleasant one. Quinn fell silent as he watched the verdant landscape rush closer. Laura, busy repairing her makeup before facing the press at Shannon Airport, didn't seem to require further conversation.

The wheels touched down with a thud. As the jet taxied toward the terminal, Quinn felt his entire body clench — neck, shoulders, chest, legs.

Enter, stranger, at your own risk, an all-too-familiar voice hissed in some dark lonely corner of his mind. Anxiety coiled through Quinn like a mass of poisonous snakes, twining around phobic pressure points, reminding him of that awful endless summer of his ninth year when he'd slammed the secret doors on his psyche — and his heart — and nailed them shut to keep out the monsters.

He forced a vague unfocused public smile, heard himself exchanging farewells with the first-class flight crew, even watched himself sign an autograph for the captain's seventeen-year-old son who was, the silver-haired pilot assured him heartily, his "number-one fan."

It would be all right, Quinn told himself firmly. He would be all right.

But as he walked toward the light at the end of a jetway that had suddenly turned claustrophobic, the raspy little voice belonging to Quinn's personal bogeyman whispered another warning: *Here there be dragons.*

"I still can't believe that real-estate agent's screwup," Laura complained while they waited for their bags in the terminal. "How on earth could she have forgotten to book you a room in town?"

"She explained that. My name somehow got left off the list of crew members."

"You're not just any crew member. You're the screenwriter, for Christ's sake."

"With the emphasis on writer. The only reason I agreed to write this screenplay in the first place is because I'm tired of the way Hollywood screws up my books."

"If you feel that way, perhaps you ought to stop selling them to Hollywood."

"I may be a control freak, sweetheart, but I'm not crazy enough to turn down the big bucks."

His accountant had assured him he'd passed the millionaire mark three books ago. But Quinn couldn't quite make himself stop running from his old demons that continued to pursue him. There were still times when he'd awaken in the middle of a hushed dark night, drenched in sweat, deafening screams ringing in his ears.

"Besides," he said, "things probably worked out for the best. I'm playing with an idea for a new story, and it'll be easier to think about it if I go home to the Joyce farm at the end of the day, instead of partying every night with all of you."

"I can remember when you liked partying with me," Laura pouted prettily.

Her blatant flirting succeeded in banishing the lingering chill. "Those were fun times."

"And could be again." She laughed when he didn't immediately answer. "Good Lord, darling, you remind me of a wolf sensing a trap. Don't worry, I'm not trying to rope you into any long-term affair. I just thought, since we're both going to be stuck in this Irish backwater for four long weeks, we may as well try to make the best of it."

Quinn liked Laura. A lot. She was smart, witty, easy to look at and a tigress in bed. But he'd always subscribed to the theory that when something was over, you moved on. And didn't look back.

"I don't think that'd be a very good idea, sweetheart." His eyes, rife with a practiced masculine look of appreciation, swept over her. "Not that I'm not tempted."

She laughed again, a rich throaty sound designed to strum sexual chords. "That is undoubtedly the nicest rejection I've ever had. I've known a lot of men, Quinn, but none of them have perfected the art of hit-and-run relationships better than you," she said without rancor.

"This from a woman who's been engaged four times." And broken it off every time.

"So I'm a slow learner." She grinned up at him, seemingly unapologetic about behavior that had provided the tabloid press with more than a few headlines. "That's why we're so good together. Neither of us has any wide-eyed expectations about the other, and we don't harbor any dreams of a rosy until-death-do-us-part romantic future. You and I are two of a kind, Quinn."

There was no arguing with the accusation. Besides, it was a helluva lot better than the one he'd heard too many times to count — that his heart was little more than a dark pit of ice water covered with a crust of snow. Quinn merely muttered something that could have been agreement as the baggage carousel rumbled to a start.

After retrieving his bags and clearing customs, he found his way blocked by a phalanx of reporters. Laura, damn her, had ducked into a rest room, leaving him to face the horde alone.

"Mr. Gallagher, do you believe the Castlelough lake creature exists?" a red-haired man wearing a rumpled wool sport coat and holding up a small tape recorder called out.

"I've always believed in the existence of monsters. I know you call her the Lady, but technically she's still a monster."

A murmur of interest from the reporters.

"Do you expect to see the Lady while you're in Castlelough?" a bald man wearing thick-framed black glasses asked.

"That would be a plus since it would undoubtedly save a fortune in special-effects costs if we could get her to perform for us," he answered, drawing the expected laugh.

"Do you plan to research your Gallagher-family roots while you're in the country?"

"No." His tone was curt. His eyes turned to frost. "If there are no more questions —"

"I have one." This from a winsome young woman. Her hair was jet, her thickly lashed eyes the color of the Irish sea, and her skin as pale as new snow. The invitation in her bold-as-brass eyes was unmistakable.

"Ask away."

"Is the female protagonist in your story

based on a real woman? Perhaps someone you met on a previous trip to Ireland?"

"Actually this is my first visit to your country. And Shannon McGuire was an entirely fictional character."

The heroine of his most recent novel was unlike any real woman Quinn had ever met. Unrelentingly optimistic, softhearted, ridiculously virtuous and brave as hell. And even knowing her to be a product of his imagination, Quinn had been fascinated by her.

Usually, by the time he finished writing one book, his mind was already well on to the next, and so he was more than glad to get rid of the characters he'd begun to grow bored with. But the widowed single mother had been strangely different. He'd found her difficult to let go.

"And speaking of Shannon," he said, turning toward Laura, who'd finally decided to make an appearance, accompanied by Jeremy Converse, the film's producer/director who'd taken the same transatlantic flight from New York, "of course you all recognize the lovely Laura Gideon. She'll be playing Shannon McGuire in the film."

Quinn practically pushed her forward. "It's show time, sweetheart," he murmured. As the reporters all began shouting out questions to the sexy blond actress, he made his escape.

Since he wouldn't be staying in town with the crew, Quinn had arranged to rent his own car. He found his way to the Hertz booth where he rented a four-door sedan from a tartan-clad beauty who was a dead ringer for Maureen O'Hara. Quinn decided he must be suffering from jet lag when he found her directions difficult to follow, but she willingly took the time to draw the route to Castlelough on his map. How difficult could it be? he asked himself as he headed out of the airport.

How difficult, indeed. At first Quinn was entranced by the scenery — the stone fences, the meadows splashed with purple, white and yellow wildflowers, and the mountains — the rare times the sun broke through the rain — streaked with molten gold. Here and there stood whitewashed cottages with thatched roofs. Little grottoes featuring statues of the Virgin Mary — many adorned with seashells — seemed to have been built at nearly every crossroad, and every so often he'd pass a small statue of the Madonna standing in the center of a white-painted tire, perky plastic flowers surrounding her bare feet.

The road seemed to go in endless circles.

And the myriad signs, many written only in Irish, hindered more than helped.

Ninety minutes later, when he realized that the cemetery with the high stone Celtic crosses he was driving by was the same one he'd passed about an hour after leaving the airport, Quinn was forced to admit he was hopelessly lost.

"I'll make you a deal, Lord," he muttered, conveniently forgetting he'd given up believing in God a long time ago. "If you just give me a sign, I promise to stop at the first church I see and stuff the poor box with hundred-dollar bills."

He cast a look up at a sky the color of tarnished silver, not surprised when the clouds didn't part to reveal Charlton Heston holding a stone tablet helpfully etched with a proper map to Castlelough. So much for miracles.

Then again . . . When he suddenly saw an elderly woman wearing a green-and-black-plaid scarf and blue Wellingtons weeding the grave nearest the gates, Quinn told himself she must have been there all along.

He pulled over to the side of the road and parked, then climbed out of the car and walked over to her. The rain had become a soft mist.

"Good afternoon."

She stopped raking and looked up at him. "Good afternoon to you. You'd be lost of course."

"Is it that obvious?"

"You passed by earlier. Now here you are again. Isn't that certainly a sign you've lost your way?"

"I'm trying to get to Castlelough."

"Well, you'll not be getting there driving circles around the Holy Name Cemetery, will you now?"

The merry laughter in her dark eyes allowed Quinn to keep a curb on his temper. Although he wasn't accustomed to being laughed at, especially by a woman, he couldn't deny that it was probably one of those situations he'd look back on and laugh at himself. A very long time from now.

"I thought I had the directions clear —" he held out the wrinkled map with the fluorescent green marker outlining what the rental clerk had assured him were the proper roads "— but they turned out to be more confusing than expected."

"Americans always get lost," she said. "But then again, haven't I known native Irishmen to have the same problem from time to time? Especially out here in the west." She shot a look at the car — the only

Mercedes in the Hertz inventory when he'd arrived — and then another, longer look up at him. "You'd be one of those movie folk," she guessed.

Quinn decided there was no point in denying it. "Yes." He prepared himself for the usual barrage of questions about the so-called fast life in Hollywood.

"I thought so." That settled, and seeming less than impressed by his exalted status, she took the map from his hand, making a clucking sound with her tongue as she studied it.

"Ah, here's your problem. You should have taken the second left at the roundabout right before you got to Mullaghmore."

Quinn had suspected all along that one of the many roundabouts — the Irish answer to eliminating four-way stops — had been his downfall. "Could you tell me how to get back there?"

"That's not difficult at all. The first thing you need to do is turn around and go back in the direction you just came from. Then keep driving until you see a sign pointing off to the right that says Ballybrennan."

"Ballybrennan?" The name sounded like several he'd already passed by.

"Aye, Ballybrennan," she repeated with a

nod of her scarf-covered head. "Now, mind you don't take that road —"

"I don't?"

"Oh, no. You'll be wanting to take the one that comes a wee bit after it. To Mary's Well. You'll not miss it. There's a lovely statue of the Virgin standing right beside the sign. Follow that road straight through and you'll be finding yourself in Castlelough in no time."

Considering how many virgins he'd spotted, Quinn wasn't certain the landmark was going to be a very big help, but didn't quibble. "Thanks. You've been a great help."

" 'Twas no trouble at all," she assured him with a nearly toothless grin. He was almost to the car again when she called out, "Of course, the sign might not say Mary's Well, mind you."

Biting back a flash of irritation, he slowly turned back toward her. Having always been a direct-speaking kind of guy, Quinn was beginning to realize that the land of his ancestors may prove more of a culture shock that he'd suspected.

"What might it say?" he asked mildly.

"It might be in Irish — *Dabhac a Mhaire*."

He was having enough trouble untangling the woman's thick west-country brogue. There was no way he was going to attempt to translate this incomprehensible language.

Quinn had known that Castlelough was located in a *Gaelact* area of the county, where, despite the penal laws enforced by the British government, the Irish language had never been allowed to die out. At the time, he'd thought it might add quaint color to his story. He'd never, until now, worried he might be unable to communicate with the natives.

Thanking her again, he climbed back in the car and headed off in the direction he'd come. Quinn considered it another near miracle when he found the turnoff. Although the rest of the directions weren't quite as simple as the woman had promised — the road split into different directions a couple of times and he had to choose — he felt of flush of victory when he finally viewed the sign welcoming him to Castlelough.

CHAPTER THREE

Weather the Storm

By the time Nora finished her weekly errands, forced at every step to listen to more talk about the movie people, the gathering gloom had darkened the sky over Castlelough, making her wish she'd insisted her father leave her the car. A stiff breeze from the Atlantic whipped her hair into a wild tangle that kept blowing across her eyes.

She could of course cycle over to The Irish Rose and retrieve the car, but that would leave *him* to walk or cycle home in the rain. Although her father often drove her to distraction, she'd never forgive herself if he came down with pneumonia.

"It's only five kilometers," she reminded herself optimistically. "If you hurry, you might get home before the rain starts."

She was grateful Quinn Gallagher wasn't expected to arrive until early this evening, which would give her time to fix a proper supper. She didn't want anyone saying Nora Fitzpatrick wasn't a good hostess.

Nora stuffed her purchases into waterproof canvas bags, then fit them into the wire baskets that hung on either side of the bicycle's rear wheel. She'd barely begun to pedal down the road when the sky opened up. Ten minutes later she'd just about decided to take the children and emigrate to a sheep ranch in sunny west Australia — where her eldest brother Finn served as a parish priest — when the blare of a car horn almost made her crash into the stone edging the roadway.

Swearing beneath her breath, she moved closer to the shoulder, trying not to get bogged down in the thick mud.

Instead of passing, the car pulled up beside her. Rather than the compact usually seen on Irish roads, this was a huge whale of an American vehicle from the gilded era of excess chrome and overgrown tail fins. That alone would have made it unique in a country with such narrow winding roads and expensive petrol.

But what truly made it one-of-a-kind were the pink-cheeked cherubs and gilt-winged angels cavorting amidst the orange rust spots on the thirty-five-year-old lemon yellow body. And then there was the mural — depicting the Virgin Mary, arms outstretched and halo gleaming, riding a puffy white cloud to heaven — painted in bright primary colors on the hood.

Nora knew that inside the car a rosary blessed by Pope John XXIII himself hung from the rearview mirror; also, although the Vatican had repossessed his sainthood, a plastic statue of Saint Christopher continued to ride shotgun on the padded dashboard.

The enormous gas-guzzling Cadillac came to a stop with a protesting squeal of wet brakes; there was an electric hum as the passenger window slowly rolled down and a head as brightly red-gold as Nora's popped out.

" 'Tis only a fit day for fish, ducks and lake creatures," Fionna Joyce declared. "Put your bicycle in the back, darling. And get yourself in out of the rain before you catch your death."

After stowing her bicycle and groceries in the vast cavern of a trunk, Nora opened the angel-adorned door and settled into the tucked and pleated heavenly sky blue leather seat of her grandmother's ancient miracle-mobile.

The heat blasting from the vents in the padded dash immediately began warming the chill from her bones. The Cadillac might be a ridiculous car for Ireland, or anywhere else for that matter, and it might be large enough for a family of four to live in, but Nora couldn't fault its heater.

Fionna Joyce was a small wiry woman with a complexion ruddied by the suns of more than eighty summers and weathered by the winds that blew from coast to coast. Despite her age, her dark eyes were bright as a sparrow's and her hair was a vivid red-gold.

"You should have dragged Brady from the pub and gotten him to drive you home," Fionna said.

"It's not that far," Nora argued. "And I didn't want to disturb him."

Fionna sighed as she fingered the tiny crucifix with Jesus' feet crossed modestly at the ankles that hung from a gold chain in the vee of her pink wool cardigan. The lapels of the heavy sweater were adorned with religious cameos.

"I dearly love my youngest son, but he's an incurable dreamer. Just like his father before him."

"And you're not?" Nora's smile took the sting of accusation from her words.

"Of course not!" Fionna seemed honestly shocked by the idea. "Women don't have time to be dreamers, Nora. Shouldn't you, of all people, know that?"

46

"Wouldn't you consider your Bernadette crusade just a wee bit fanciful?"

"There's nothing fanciful about getting dear Bernadette canonized, darling. And, heaven knows, don't those red-skirts in the Vatican owe us a saint after taking Saint Philomena away from us?" She paused. "And speaking of Bernadette, I have a line on a new tale."

Fionna had been attempting to get Sister Bernadette Mary — a Sister of Mercy nun who'd worked tirelessly to bring about peace during the Anglo-Irish War for independence and had been killed by the Black and Tans for her efforts — declared a saint for the past decade. Since an important part of the juridical process was to document the candidate's life, holy works and, most importantly, provide proof of at least two miracles, Fionna had been relentless in her search for evidence of a miraculous event done in the young woman's name.

Nora had begun to worry that such religious obsession might be a sign of senility. Then again, considering her own close conversational relationship with her long-dead mother, she decided perhaps all the Joyces were more than a little fanciful.

"How did your trip to Eniscorthy go?" she asked.

Fionna sighed. "I suppose it depends on whether or not the Holy Father would consider the curing of a mare's colic a miracle."

Nora repressed the smile tugging at the corners of her mouth. Fionna found nothing humorous about sainthood. "I'd suspect the owner was happy. But I doubt such an event would pull much weight with the bishop."

"The only way that man would be impressed would be a modern-day repeat of the wine-at-the-wedding miracle. If Bernadette could make whiskey flow out of the bishop's water tap, he'd recommend her before you could say Bushmills malt."

Bishop McCarthy had steadfastly refused to pass along any of Fionna's documents to the Vatican's Congregation for the Cause of Saints. Nora knew her grandmother believed that such an unrelenting lack of cooperation was proof of the bishop's sexism.

"It's bad enough, in his mind, that the evidence is being compiled by a mere female, instead of a priest, as is usually done," Fionna muttered. "It's obvious he has no intention of adding another female saint to the religious roster."

Like her Irish Volunteer forefathers who'd refused to give up a good fight, Fionna refused to surrender what she'd come to view as a holy war.

She slanted Nora a look. "If I die before the Vatican comes through, you'll have to carry on."

"You're going to live forever," Nora said quickly. Firmly.

"No one lives forever, dear," Fionna said mildly. "Not in our mortal form, at any rate." Then, as if understanding Nora's reluctance to discuss the subject, she returned the topic to its earlier track. "I'm off to Derry to hear another story next week. Is there anything you'd like me to get for you?"

Although the prices were often lower in Northern Ireland, Nora wasn't at all eager to hear that her grandmother would be traveling there. But she also knew the futility of arguing.

"My Sunday blazer is getting too holey even for church, thanks to the moths dining on it," Nora said. "Perhaps, if you have time, and find one on sale . . ."

"On sale or not, it's yours."

"Remind me to give you the money before you go."

"That's not necessary. And it's not a gift," the older woman insisted before Nora could argue the point. "Consider it payment. For continuing my work after I'm gone," she tacked on slyly.

Knowing when she was bested, Nora

didn't even try to protest. As she watched the mist-shrouded landscape flash by the window, she wondered if the American writer would expect dessert every night after his supper.

Nora heard the wails before she even got to the kitchen door. Since her older brother, Michael, was away in Kerry, selling his wool, her younger brother, John, had been stopping by Michael's farm after school to tend to the milking. Which had left the younger two children in Mary's hands this afternoon.

Despite the fact that her sister suffered the usual mood swings that came with being sixteen, Mary was, for the most part, a good dependable girl.

"Another boy crisis," Fionna guessed.

"You're probably right." Nora hoped that whatever it was that was making her sister keen like a banshee was not as serious as it sounded. She felt guilty when the first thought that came to mind was an unplanned pregnancy, but then again, Nora knew all about teenage desires.

And wasn't Mary's best friend, Deidre McMann, about to become a mother? The father was a college boy Deidre had met at a fair in Limerick.

"Jack broke Mary's heart," Rory ran up to

announce, his wolfhound at his heels, as always. Blue eyes, the deep-sea shade of his father's, held seeds of worry. His dark hair, again so like Conor's, had fallen over his forehead.

Feeling a familiar rush of love for her son, Nora brushed the hair back. "I'll tend to Mary. Meanwhile, why don't you go finish your chores? I brought Maeve a nice juicy bone," she said, handing him a package tied with a string. "She can chew on it while you feed your rabbits."

"Thanks, Mam!" He was off like a shot, seemingly relieved to leave matters of the heart to the female members of the family. Uncharacteristically, Maeve, emboldened by the smells emanating from the waxed white paper, began barking excitedly and nipping at his heels.

Enjoying the carefree sight of boy and dog, Nora said a quick prayer that she wouldn't have to take her son from the life here that fit him so well. Then, unable to avoid this latest problem any longer, she went with Fionna into the house. She put the grocery bags on the wooden counter and turned to her sister. "So. What did Jack do now?"

Since her mother had taught her there were very few problems that couldn't be solved by a cup of tea, Nora put a kettle of water on the stove to boil.

"He broke my heart!" Mary wailed, echoing Rory's explanation.

"And how exactly did he do that?"

"He asked Sharon Fitzgerald to the May Dance."

"Is that all?" Fionna asked.

"You don't understand! Everyone's already coupled up. I won't have a date!"

"You could always go to the dance alone," Fionna suggested.

"Grandmother!" Mary shot a desperate look at Nora. "Would you please explain that these days only the wretched homely girls destined for spinsterhood go to dances alone?"

"I doubt you're destined for spinsterhood," Nora replied mildly as she noted the black trails of mascara running down her sister's cheeks.

While she understood a teenager's natural impulse for rebellion, she did wish that Mary hadn't taken to emulating what had become known in Dublin as the Gothic look. The black tortured-artist's clothing, white Kabuki-dancer powder and maroon-painted lips Mary favored on weekends away from school detracted from her natural beauty.

At least the nuns had forbidden the fluorescent green or orange spiked hair sported by the city teenagers. And, needless to say, body piercing was out of the question. Nora decided to be grateful for small favors.

"I realize it hurts," she tried again. "But it's not the end of the world, darling. There are still three weeks until the dance, and perhaps Jack will change his mind —"

"He's not going to change his mind," Mary sniffed. "Because the only reason he dropped me for Sharon is 'cause she puts out. She's probably slept with half the boys in school."

There it was again. That ever-threatening sex issue. Lately, Nora had finally come to understand all too well why her mother had worried so during the days *she'd* been stealing off to hidden meadows with Devlin Monohan.

"A man won't buy the cow when he can get the milk for free," Fionna said sagely. "You're right to hold on to your virginity, Mary, dear. When you're with your husband on your wedding night, you'll look back on this day and be glad you held firm."

"I'm never going to get married!"

"Of course you will." Nora handed her a tissue.

"No, I'm not." Mary blew her nose with a

loud unfeminine honk. "I've decided to become a nun."

"You've certainly got the wardrobe for it," Fionna muttered, casting a derisive look at the flowing black skirt and ebony tunic sweater.

"You can't be a nun," seven-year-old Celia, who was coloring in a book of Irish Grand National winners, piped up. "You have to have a vocation. Then you go off to be a missionary in the Congo."

The kettle whistled, allowing Nora to turn away to hide her smile. *The Nun's Story* was a perennial favorite on television, broadcast every season during Lent.

Mary turned on the youngest Joyce sister. "That's just a stupid movie."

"I know that." Celia lifted her small pointed chin. "But Sister Mary Anthony is reading us the lives of the saints, and they all had vocations. Like Saint Theresa who walked on thorns and didn't flinch. And Joan of Arc who was burned at the stake and never even cried."

"And let's not be forgetting Saint Maria Goretti who died rather than submit to a man," Fionna said pointedly. "She didn't even lose courage when her attacker started stabbing her with his dagger. Now *that's* a vocation."

"I didn't say I was going to be a bloody saint!" Mary's palm hit the kitchen table with enough force to send crayons rolling off onto the floor. "I said I was going to be a nun."

"There's no need to swear." Nora put the teapot on the table.

"You just don't understand!" Mary jumped up, knocking over her chair with a loud clatter. "None of you understand!" she cried as she ran from the room.

There was the sound of footfalls on the stairs. Moments later the slam of a door reverberated through the farmhouse, causing the calendar from Monohan's Mercantile, with the lovely photograph of wildflowers, to tilt on the wall like a drunkard.

Appearing unfazed by the histrionics, Celia returned to her coloring, carefully filling in the lines of a flowing mane with a crayon that was nearly the same color as her russet braids. "When I'm a teenager, I'm not going to have anything to do with boys," she vowed.

"I, for one, would be very grateful if you stick to that decision," Nora said, even though she knew it would never happen. Boys and tears were just part of growing up.

Wanting to calm things down before the American writer arrived, Nora followed the pitiful sound of sobbing upstairs. Although she tried her best to sympathize with Mary's upsets, it was difficult when they occurred so often. Granted, Jack's behavior was just cause, but usually Mary's bleak moods were triggered by far less.

But then again, Nora reminded herself, *she* hadn't lost her mother at the tender age of nine as Mary had. She'd been all of eighteen and had had Conor to offer comfort and love during that sad time.

As she rapped on the closed bedroom door, Nora thought that Sheila Monohan had definitely been right about one thing. Raising her mother's three children along with her own — not to mention worrying about her father, who was little more than an overgrown child himself — was far from easy.

Nora lifted her eyes upward, which, unfortunately made her notice the new brown water stain on the ceiling. She really was going to have to get the roof rethatched.

"It would certainly be nice, Mam," she murmured, "if you could give me a little help with this one."

CHAPTER FOUR

Smoke and Strong Whiskey

As Quinn drove past the butcher shop, the rows of meat and dressed chickens displayed in the storefront window reminded him of how many hours it had been since he'd eaten. Spotting the hanging sign across the square advertising The Irish Rose pub, he decided to stop.

"Some food and a couple cups of coffee should stave off jet lag." And ease the headache that had begun to throb while he'd been driving around in circles.

This would also give him an opportunity to ask directions to the Joyce farm. He'd been assured by the rental agent who handled the transaction that the farm was on the road directly out of Castlelough. However, having already discovered the vagaries of the Irish roadway system, Quinn feared the agent's assurances would prove to be overly optimistic.

He allowed himself a smile when he read the words burned into the piece of wood nailed to the pub door: Here when we're open. Gone when we're closed.

The interior of The Irish Rose could have been lifted directly from the set of *The Quiet Man*. Quinn suspected it had looked much the same when the town of Castlelough had been founded more than five hundred years earlier.

The dark-paneled walls had shelves filled with bottles of whiskey gleaming like a pirate's bounty in the light from the brass-hooded lamps. Behind the bar, a mirror advertised Guinness in fancy gold script.

A turf fire burned in the large open hearth at one end of the room, warding off the chill; a cloud of smoke hung in the air. Wooden tables had been crowded onto the hand-pegged floor and heavy benches resembling church pews had been placed along the wall. The only anachronism was the television, bolted above the bar and currently tuned to a hurling match.

When his eyes adjusted to the dimness, Quinn could see three men seated at the bar, more men scattered around at the tables smoking pipes and reading newspapers, and a pair of teenage boys playing darts. A man and woman were eating a late lunch of pub grub while a pair of carrot-haired toddlers Quinn took for twins happily munched on crunchy chips.

All eyes immediately turned toward him as he crossed the floor and sat down on a stool in front of the scarred wooden bar.

"Lovely day," a small spry leprechaun-like man remarked.

"A bit chilly," Quinn replied. Only yesterday he'd been basking in the California sun.

"Aye." The man nodded. "Though myself, I don't care for it when it's warm. Then you've got nothing to complain about, after all. It's no good for the talk . . ." His words trailed off. Abruptly he said, "You'd be Quinn Gallagher."

"That was either one helluva guess or you're psychic."

"Now, there have been some who've accused me of that over the years, but it's not how I knew you." A smile brightened the apple-cheeked face; still-young blue eyes twinkled merrily. "I recognized you from the photograph on the back of your books. Hasn't my youngest son, John, read them all? He especially liked the one about the banshee."

"That was one of my favorites, as well." It was his first published novel, written during a blaze of inspiration the likes of which

59

Quinn had never experienced since. His muse was a fickle mistress.

"Brady's seen a banshee," the second man, who appeared to be nearing the century mark, revealed. His bulbous red nose suggested he'd spent several of those many years indulging a fondness for the bottle.

"Brady?" It was undoubtedly a common enough name, Quinn told himself.

"Brady Joyce, at your service," the first man said. "And isn't this the divil's own luck, you stopping by The Rose on your way out to the farm?"

"It's quite a coincidence."

"Not so much of one," the second man alleged. "The Rose is the only pub this side of the river. It's also the first one on the road into town, which made it likely it'd be the one you chose to stop at.

"And whenever The Irish Rose is open —" he took a long drink of the dark beer in front of him and wiped the creamy tracing of foam off his top lip with the back of his hand "— isn't it sure you'll find Brady Joyce sitting right on that very stool, spinning his tales. He's the finest *seanachie* in the county."

"Oh, I'm not nearly as fine a storyteller as Mr. Gallagher," Brady said with what Quinn suspected was more than a little false modesty.

"That may be the case, indeed, but the banshee story is a grand fearful tale," the old man countered. "It never fails to give me gooseflesh." He cast Quinn an appraising look. "You'd be one of those movie people."

"I am."

"Brady was telling me about you staying at the farm. We were thinking you might want to make a movie outta one of his tales."

"Oh, it was Fergus here who was thinking that," Brady said quickly. A bit too quickly, Quinn thought. "I told him it was foolishness."

"Getting a movie made is a real long shot," Quinn said carefully, afraid of offending his host by suggesting he might not consider Brady Joyce's stories worthy of consideration.

The rest of the cast and crew was already booked into every spare room in the village; if Joyce decided to welsh on the rental agreement, Quinn would have no choice but to take Laura up on her offer. A situation he was determined to avoid.

"And isn't that just what I was telling Fergus?" Brady nodded. "A long shot."

"And wouldn't one consider getting a movie made about a lake creature in a small

Irish town few have ever heard of a long shot?" the man named Fergus suggested slyly.

"Good point . . . So, you've actually seen a banshee?" Quinn asked Joyce. Although he'd enjoyed writing the story of the keening fairy woman, he considered such a thing on a par with the Easter Bunny, Santa Claus and the tooth fairy.

"Aye, that I have," Brady agreed cheerfully. "I've also seen the lovely Lady who brings all you movie people to Castlelough. But those are tales for another time. First we need to get you something to drink.

"Publican, a pint for my guest," he called out robustly to the man who was drying glasses not two feet away. "I'll stand a round for the room, as well. And bottles of orange for the boys.

"And while Brendan pulls your pint, you can tell us all about yourself," Brady invited, turning back to Quinn.

"There's not that much to tell." Never one to talk about his past, Quinn was definitely not eager to discuss it here, among strangers.

"Of course there is. As a storyteller yourself, you should know there's no one else like you. No story like your own. And there's always the fact that," Brady tacked on impishly, "if you don't tell us, we'll have no choice but to make things up."

Before Quinn could respond to that, a large man at the end of the bar abruptly stood and announced, "I'll not be drinking to the likes of him."

The room suddenly went deathly still. Glasses lowered to wooden tables.

"Now, Cadel," Brady said cajolingly, "is that any way to be talking to a visitor?"

"Did I ask him to come here?" His hands were curled at his sides. The meaty fists and the murder in his dark eyes reminded Quinn of a heavyweight boxer. "I don't recall inviting any focking Yanks to Castlelough," the man growled. He shot a lethal glare Quinn's way. "Why don't you bloody Americans stay home where you belong?"

Quinn decided the question was a rhetorical one, designed to start a fight. And although he'd gotten into his share of bar brawls in his younger days, he had no intention of allowing himself to be baited now.

When Quinn didn't answer, his red-faced challenger turned back to Brady. "And aren't you're just as bad, Brady Joyce, letting this focking rich tourist into your house for the price of a few pounds? The bloody foreigners are overrunning this country, flashing their Yank money, buying up our land, destroying tradition. Ireland's a beautiful woman. And some people —" his hard-as-stone eyes raked both the old man and Quinn "— are focking pimps."

That said, he tossed back the rest of his whiskey and strode from the pub, slamming the heavy oak door behind him. A thick silence lingered in his wake.

"Now don't be paying any mind to the likes of Cadel O'Sullivan," Brady advised Quinn with unfailing cheer. "He's been in a sour mood for most of his thirty-three years."

All the men in the room laughed on cue. The tension dissolved.

A tall glass was placed in front of Quinn. Brady raised his own. "*Slainte!* To your health!" he translated helpfully.

"*Slainte,*" Quinn returned the toast. As the hum of conversation resumed, he took a long swallow of the lacy-headed, velvety dark brew and felt the headache that had escalated during the brief confrontation with Cadel O'Sullivan begin to ease.

Brady next launched into a long introduction of his drinking mate, Fergus, that went back several generations and included an ancestor alleged to be a silkie — one of the seal women of Irish myth. Quinn listened, surrendering to the alchemy of the Guinness.

Although she was not a worrier by nature, Nora grew concerned when the evening passed with no sign of Quinn Gallagher or Brady. She wasn't all that surprised about her father; after all, the pub didn't close for another hour. But most of the Americans she'd met over the years appeared wed to the clock. It seemed unlikely that the writer would be so late without at least trying to notify her.

Rory and Celia had gone to bed some time ago. Mary, who'd finally stopped her weeping, seemed to have fallen asleep, as well, and the faint sound of music drifting from John's room suggested that her brother was studying, as he did late into every night.

She'd finally taken the stew off the stove and put it in the refrigerator, and now she was pacing the floor of the small front parlor, stopping every so often to peer through the rain-streaked window at the well of darkness surrounding the farmhouse.

"His plane landed hours ago," she told Fionna after she rang the airport. "And Ellen down at Flannery House said that several of the Americans who arrived at Shannon on the same flight checked in this afternoon."

Fionna glanced up from her knitting. "Perhaps he went sight-seeing."

"Perhaps." Nora frowned and wondered if she should put more peat on the fire or just go upstairs to bed. "But you'd think that he would notify us if he'd changed his plans."

The click of needles didn't stop as the older woman continued working on the thick sweater destined to go to university in the fall with John. The sound provided an accompaniment to Waylon Jennings's deep voice coming from the radio upstairs, the steady tick-tick-tick of the mantel clock as it counted off the minutes and hours, and the rat-a-tat-tat of wind-driven rain against the windowpanes.

"The man is certainly starting off on the wrong foot," Fionna allowed. Her expression turned thoughtful. "Do you think he could have had an accident on the roadway? After all, Americans aren't accustomed to driving on the left-hand side of the road, and what with all this rain . . ."

"I hadn't thought of that." A tiny shiver of icy fear skimmed up Nora's spine. "I wonder if I should ring the hospital?"

"Or the Garda, perhaps," Fionna suggested.

Although Nora was not at all eager to involve the police, she was headed for the phone again when she saw a flash of head-lights through the leaded front window.

"Finally!" She ran to open the front door. The porch light cast a yellow, rain-shimmered glow on the white car with black markings parked in the driveway. "It's Sergeant O'Neill."

Fionna tossed her knitting aside and hurried to stand beside her. "I'm certain it's nothing, darling. The sergeant probably found the American broken down alongside the roadway and —"

"It's Da." Nora watched Brady stagger from the back seat of the police car.

"Oh dear. It's been a while since he drank too much to drive," Fionna said with a sigh.

"I hope he didn't crash the car." It would take more eggs than even her musically stimulated hens could lay to buy a new one.

"Good evening to you, Fionna." The sergeant touched his fingers to the brim of his dark hat. "Nora. My cousin Brendan was working the bar at The Rose and rang me up to say that Brady and his friend needed a ride home."

"His friend?"

"The writer. As I told Brendan, I was happy to oblige. We wouldn't want a famous Yank crashing his car his first day in the country, now, would we?"

Nora watched as a second man climbed out of the back seat. Straightening his back, he began walking toward the house with the exaggerated care of someone who was drunk to the gills.

"No," she agreed faintly, "we certainly wouldn't want that." How in the name of heaven had the American and Brady met up? "Thank you, Gerry, for bringing them home."

"No problem, Nora." Gerry O'Neill put the bags he'd fetched from the American's car inside the open door. "I was just doing my job. Good night, all." Touching his hat again, the policeman folded his tall lean body into the car, backed up and drove away into the night.

"Evenin', Nora darlin'," Brady greeted his daughter. He laid a hand on her shoulder and bestowed a sloppy kiss on her cheek.

Then he grinned at Fionna. "Evening, Mam."

"Don't 'Evening, Mam,' me," Fionna shot back, her hands on her hips. "Not when you come home from the pub weaving like a salley tree in the wind."

"Would you not have me properly welcome our guest to the land of his ancestors?" Still using Nora for ballast, Brady waved his free hand toward the much taller man who'd come up beside him. "This fine fellow is none other than the famous American writer, Quinn Gallagher. Quinn, may I present my sharp-tongued but endearing mother, and my darling lovely daughter, Nora."

"It's a pleasure to finally meet you, Mr. Gallagher," Nora said politely to her guest — her *paying* guest, she reminded herself.

Only an alert listener would have been able to detect the note of irritation in her voice. To think that he hadn't been lying near death in some hospital emergency ward, that after all her worrying he'd merely been getting drunk in The Irish Rose pub with her father!

"We were concerned you may have driven off the cliff on the way here from Shannon."

"I'm sorry." Quinn's words were far more slurred than Brady's. "I never meant to cause anyone any concern." His gaze moved from daughter to grandmother. "And I have no excuse for my inconsiderate behavior. Other than the fact that I lost track of the time."

"That's likely enough, once my son begins spinning his tales," Fionna allowed. "At least you had the good sense not to get behind the wheel."

With those words of absolution, Fionna turned and went back into the house. If

Nora's nerves hadn't been so frazzled, she might have enjoyed watching the two men follow as meekly as newborn lambs.

When she joined the three in the sitting room, Nora studied Quinn Gallagher more closely. Despite his appropriately contrite words, she thought that he was a hard, tough man. His face — all sharp angles and lean hollows, narrowing down to a firm un-yielding boxer's jaw — could have been roughly chiseled from stone. Too harsh to be considered lived-in, it revealed an arro-gance and a remoteness that were in de-cided contrast to his outwardly penitent tone. A faint white scar on his cheek added a menacing touch.

His deeply set eyes were as dark and unrevealing as midnight. Despite his glower, the photograph on the back of the book covers in the window of Sheila Monohan's store had made the novelist appear intelli-gent and sophisticated. However, there was nothing sophisticated about this man.

He was rangy, like a long-distance runner, all sinew and lean muscle clad in black jeans, a black T-shirt and black leather jacket. She'd known larger men, but none so physically imposing. The sense of tightly coiled male energy emanating from Quinn Gallagher and the way, even as inebriated as he obviously was, he made a woman all too aware of being female, had Nora suddenly wanting to throw him out of her house.

Kate's earlier remark about Nora's mother sending her a husband suddenly seemed more threat than promise.

Tell me this isn't your doing, Mam, Nora begged silently as nerves tangled themselves into a knot inside her stomach.

If Eleanor Joyce had searched the entire world over, she couldn't have found a more unsuitable husband and father candidate than this man clad all in devil's black.

For a fleeting moment Nora envisioned the writer as an old-time gunfighter, standing on some dusty Western street with six-shooters drawn, facing down a gang of train robbers at high noon. It was a scene she'd seen a hundred times in American movies — with one difference. This time, in her mind's eye, it was Quinn Gallagher who was wearing the black hat.

Dear Lord, she was getting every bit as fanciful as Fionna and Brady!

"You'll be wanting to go directly to bed, I imagine." Nora was pleased when her calm voice revealed none of her inner turmoil.

As if giving up his attempt to stand erect, Quinn leaned back against the white plaster wall. She forced herself to hold her ground as his dark eyes swept over her again.

"Now there's an idea," he murmured for her ears only. His voice was like silk, wound through with a thread of sarcasm. Wicked intent gleamed in his gaze and played at the corners of his mouth.

"As drunk as you are, I suspect even the idea would be more than you could handle, Mr. Gallagher," she said under her breath, grateful that her father was currently distracting Fionna with the story of how he and the Yank had happened to meet up.

"I wouldn't bet the farm on that, sweetheart."

He was too brash. Too dangerous. Too male. How in the name of all the saints was she going to put up with this arrogant man in her house for four long weeks? Reminding herself she'd already spent the generous deposit the rental agent had forwarded to repair the smoking chimney, Nora gathered up her scattered composure and managed, with effort, to hold her tongue.

Wanting to get the man out of sight and mind as quickly as possible, she glanced over at Brady, who'd collapsed in his easy chair. Since he was obviously too unsteady on his feet to escort their boarder up the steep set of stairs, it appeared Nora was stuck with him.

"I'd best be showing you to your room." Then, since the writer appeared nearly as unsteady as Brady, she had no choice but to put her arm around his waist to help him balance. "Before you pass out and end up spending the night on the floor."

"It wouldn't be the first time."

Oh dear. She wondered what Brady had gotten them into, renting a room to a man accustomed to coming home drunk. Despite the much-needed funds he represented, Nora vowed on the spot that if he caused any problem in front of the children, she was going to send the American writer on his way.

"Not the passing-out part," he elaborated, as if reading her mind. "Despite appearances to the contrary, Mrs. Fitzpatrick, I am not a drunk." He spoke slowly and deliberately. Exactly, Nora thought, like a drunk.

"You've no idea how it pleases me to hear that, Mr. Gallagher."

As she began leading him across the room, he glanced back over his shoulder. "Good night, Joyce. Thanks for the welcome. I enjoyed myself immensely. Ma'am, it was indeed an honor." This last to Fionna.

"Good night to you, too, Gallagher," Brady said.

"It was indeed interesting, Mr. Gallagher," Fionna responded. "Pleasant dreams."

"Nice lady," Quinn said to Nora.

He leaned against her and slid his arm around her shoulder in a surprisingly smooth gesture for a man who'd been drinking. The stairs were narrow, forcing them to climb thigh to thigh. Nora had the impression of steel — hard and unyielding.

"Lord, you're soft." Quinn leaned down and nuzzled her neck. "And you smell damn good, too. Like wildflowers and rain."

Nora would bet her prize bull that he said that to all the women. "And you smell like whiskey."

"Unfortunately that's probably true." He frowned. "I don't know what the hell got into me."

"I suspect too much Jameson." She opened the door to the bedroom she'd grown up in and they stepped inside. "You'll have the devil's own head in the morning."

"Undoubtedly true, also. But it was worth it. Your father is one helluva storyteller."

"Aye, he is that. The best in the county. The finest in all Ireland, some say."

"That wouldn't surprise me. I suspect it doesn't hurt to have Joyce blood flowing in his veins."

"No. I imagine not." Nora, who'd been

brought up to be proud of her literary heritage, had often thought that same thing herself. "Still, it's easy for the hours to slip away when he begins spinning his tales."

"So I discovered. The hard way."

Their eyes met and in a suspended moment of shared amusement, there occurred a flash of physical awareness so strong that Nora had a sudden urge to hug herself. With her mind whirling the way it was, she couldn't decide if the desire came from a need for self-protection or an even stronger need to feel the touch of hands on her uncomfortably warm body.

At the same time Quinn seemed to turn strangely angry. His smile vanished and his dark eyes went shuttered, like a pair of windows painted over with pitch.

"You know what I said about going to bed?" He shrugged out of his leather jacket and tossed it onto a nearby chair.

"I don't think we should be talking about this." Nora's unruly heart fluttered like a wild bird as she pulled back the handmade quilt that had been a wedding gift from her sister-in-law. Then she reached up, took hold of Quinn's broad shoulders and pushed him down onto the bed.

"Tough. Because, you see, sweetheart, there's one thing you should know about me. I'm the kind of guy who likes to put all his cards on the table right off the bat."

Nora was not accustomed to men she hardly knew calling her sweetheart. And she definitely wasn't accustomed to having such an intimate conversation with a stranger. Wondering how it was that the man could still appear threatening while lying flat on his back, she nevertheless gave him a go-ahead gesture.

He was, after all, a guest. Besides, it seemed prudent just to let him have his say. Maybe then he'd drop the bloody subject.

"The point I want to make, sweetheart, is that I've decided I'm not going to sleep with you."

Nora's temper flared like a match in the night. "And I suppose you'd be thinking it's your decision to make in the first place?"

Telling herself she didn't care about his damn comfort, that it was only her sheets she was trying to save, she yanked his boots off. They were cowboy boots, which brought her earlier Western-movie fantasy tumbling back.

"If I wanted you, it sure as hell *would* be my decision."

"Do you always get what you want?" It wasn't exactly a challenge. Nora was genuinely curious.

"When it comes to women? Always." His eyes cleared. Nora looked down into those fathomless midnight depths and, feeling like a bog butterfly pinned to a cork, had the impression Quinn was giving her a warning. "But you don't have to worry, sweetheart. You're not my type."

Even as she told herself it was for the best, she felt a prick of feminine annoyance at being so easily dismissed.

"And isn't that a coincidence," she said briskly, throwing the quilt over him. "Since you're not my type, either."

She held her breath, almost expecting God to send a lightning bolt through the thatched roof to strike her dead for telling such an outrageous falsehood. Because unfortunately, from the way her body had grown warm in proximity to his, it appeared that Quinn Gallagher was very much her type.

Quinn arched a sardonic brow, but didn't challenge her lie, which relieved Nora greatly. "Then we shouldn't have any problem, should we?"

"None at all." If only that was true. Nora had the sinking feeling this brash American was going to provide a very large problem indeed. She reached out and turned off the bedside lamp, throwing the room into darkness. "Good night, Mr. Gallagher."

"Good night, Mrs. Fitzpatrick." His deep voice echoed the formality in hers. He'd already begun snoring by the time she reached the door.

She moved down the hall to the small room that, thanks to her father, would serve as her bedroom for the next four weeks. She washed her face and brushed her teeth as quietly as possible in the adjoining bathroom she was forced to share with her boarder.

Since it was chilly in the unheated room, she undressed quickly, changing into a long cream flannel nightgown and a pair of gray-and-white caterpillar-striped wool socks Fionna had knit for her last Christmas. Then, as she knelt beside the bed the way she had every night since childhood, Nora, who was not normally a petty person, derived some small mean satisfaction from the idea that come morning, Quinn Gallagher would be suffering one hell of a hangover.

CHAPTER FIVE

The Devil's in the Whiskey

Quinn awoke to the sound of birds chirping and sheep bleating. He was sprawled on his back on the bed, still in the clothes he'd worn on the plane — which reeked of cigarette and peat smoke — his head pounding like the bass drum in a marching band. Not yet wanting to risk opening his eyes, which felt sandpaper scratchy, he ran his tongue over teeth as fuzzy as moss-covered rocks.

While he might have the mother of all hangovers, the prodigious amount of alcohol he'd drunk last night had not, unfortunately, impaired his memory. He recalled everything about the night before, including the fact that he'd made an ass of himself by hitting on Nora Fitzpatrick.

In between fanciful stories of banshees, warriors and revolution, Brady Joyce had waxed eloquent about his widowed daughter, clearly a man prone to overembellishment. Quinn, upon first stumbling out of the patrol car last night, had discovered that perhaps for the first time in the man's life, Brady had been guilty of understatement.

Nora Fitzpatrick's face, haloed by a wavy cloud of hair as bright as the cozy peat fire burning in the parlor hearth, had brought to mind a pre-Christian Celtic goddess. Her eyes were a soft mystical green that could have washed off the velvet hills of the countryside. And her mouth! At first sight of her lush unpainted lips, he'd felt an instant desire to taste them.

Quinn had no intention of apologizing for experiencing a sexual attraction. His approach, however, had definitely lacked subtlety.

She'd looked somehow familiar, but remembering the tug of recognition he'd experienced when he'd first seen the country from the plane, Quinn had discounted the sensation.

One thing he hadn't been able to discount was that momentary flash of shared sexual awareness, when he'd caught a glimpse of something in her eyes, something he couldn't quite put a finger on. It couldn't be inexperience, since she had, after all, been married. She'd even had a child, he recalled Brady telling him. A son.

Innocence, perhaps?

Whatever it was, even tanked as he'd

been, every instinct Quinn possessed had told him that Nora Fitzpatrick was trouble. With a capital *T*.

"No point in borrowing trouble," he muttered, quoting his mother, who'd always possessed a natural knack for doing exactly that. "The widow Fitzpatrick is off-limits."

He'd no sooner stated the vow when he heard a whimper he first thought might have come from him. Gingerly opening one eye, he came face-to-face with a huge furry gray, white and black muzzle and a pair of limpid brown eyes.

"Either Brady has taken to parking a Buick in the bedroom, or you're the biggest damn dog in Ireland."

The beast whimpered again, a thin sound more suited to some toy breed a tenth its size, then self-consciously looked away.

"You can't be shy."

One ear cocked. But the dog still refused to meet Quinn's gaze.

He reached out, caught hold of the muzzle and turned the fuzzy face back toward him. "Hell, don't tell me I hurt your feelings."

He'd never had a dog. The closest he'd ever come to having a pet was the field mouse he'd captured when he was seven and his family had been living in a trailer outside Apache Junction, Arizona. Using money earned running errands for a local bookie, he'd bought a hamster cage from Kmart, which he hid in a kitchen cupboard. Since his mother had never been one to cook, it had seemed the safest place.

He'd kept the mouse for nearly a week, feeding it limp lettuce from a nearby Safeway Dumpster. Unfortunately his father had discovered it while searching for a carton of cigarettes, cussed him out royally, then whipped him with a belt that had left welts for two weeks. Years later he still had the scars from the buckle to remind him of that day.

The mouse had fared even worse. His father had suffocated it in a plastic bag, then tossed it outside for the feral desert cats to tear apart.

"You realize, of course," Quinn said to the dog now, "you're too big to be such a candy-ass."

The dog rolled brown eyes beneath furry beetled brows.

"I'm not going to hurt you, dammit."

Another whimper. And if a dog could look dubious, this one was definitely pulling it off. Quinn shook his head in disgust, then wished he hadn't when boulders started tumbling around inside.

"Lord, we're a pitiful pair," he muttered, crawling out of the double bed.

Although his legs felt as if he were walking on the deck of a rolling ship, Quinn managed to make his way into the adjoining bathroom, which smelled vaguely of flowers, followed by the wolfhound who trailed a safe three feet behind. One look at the haggard face in the mirror assured him he looked every bit as bad as he felt.

He opened the medicine cabinet, found a bottle of aspirin, poured three of them into his palm and swallowed them dry. He found a new toothbrush and a bar of soap still in its wrapper, realized that Nora Fitzpatrick must have left them for him, and decided the woman, while still Trouble, was a saint.

He brushed his fuzzy teeth, splashed cold water onto his face, then took a long hot shower that filled the small room with steam and smoothed out some of the kinks in his hungover and jet-lagged body. The towel he wrapped around his hips was a far cry from the thick Egyptian-cotton ones he was accustomed to, but it was pleasantly soft and smelled like sunshine.

By the time he'd shaved with the razor he found in the cabinet, he was beginning to feel as if he just might live.

"So what do you think?" he asked the dog,

who was sitting on its haunches watching his every move. "Feel up to some breakfast?"

When the oversize tail began thumping on the floor and the huge pink tongue lolled, Quinn decided he'd just found the dog's weakness.

"Guess that's the magic word." Ignoring the lightning bolts behind his eyes, he bent and rubbed the massive multihued streaked head. "The room's supposed to come with two meals a day. Let's go see what's on the menu."

Fearing he'd have to wear yesterday's clothes, which could definitely use an airing, Quinn was gratified to see his luggage lined up just inside the bedroom door. Apparently the friendly police officer who'd arrived to take Brady and him to the farm had rescued the suitcases from his rental car. As he pulled on a pair of clean briefs, Quinn decided a donation to the local police benevolent fund was definitely in order.

He made his way down the stairs; the dog, appearing a bit more emboldened, stayed close on his heels, nails clicking on the wood.

The kitchen could have appeared on the cover of some country-living magazine: a bright blue-plaid oilcloth covered the round table, and the unmatched wooden chairs surrounding the table had been painted school-bus yellow. The window had been left open to admit moist air that carried the fragrance of freshly mowed grass and the distant scent of the sea; white lace curtains swayed in the early-morning breeze.

He found an old-fashioned aluminum percolator sitting on the stove. The note taped to it informed him that the family was at mass and would be home by ten o'clock at the latest.

"I'll be making breakfast," the neat convent-schoolgirl script assured him. "But if you wake before I return, there's porridge on the stove, a tin of coffee on the counter, and you're welcome to anything you find in the icebox." It was formally signed, Nora Fitzpatrick.

Quinn glanced up at the round-faced wooden clock on the wall. If he had to wait another forty-five minutes for coffee, he just might die, after all.

"Looks as if we're on our own, sport." The oatmeal, kept warm in a double boiler and too reminiscent of youthful farm days, held little appeal.

When he opened the refrigerator door, the dog grinned. "How about some bacon?" Quinn took the white-wrapped bundle from the meat compartment and a blue bowl of speckled eggs from a wire shelf. "Do you prefer your eggs scrambled or fried?"

The dog barked eagerly.

"Yeah, me, too," Quinn said. "Fried it is."

The bacon was thick and spicy, more like ham than the bacon Quinn was used to back home. Both he and the dog agreed it was delicious. The oversize eggs might have ended up a little crispy at the edges, but neither of them was in a mood to complain. Quinn ate three, enjoying the sweet taste of the butter he'd fried them in; the dog inhaled two.

The only failure was the coffee. It was as thick as the black peat bogs Quinn had passed on the way to Castlelough.

"Peat would probably taste a damn sight better," he told the dog, whose morose expression seemed to be offering canine sympathy.

Although he usually drank his coffee black, he tried cutting it with the rich cream he found in the refrigerator, then tossed in a heaping spoonful of sugar. He took another tentative sip, decided it wasn't going to get any better, but in desperate need of caffeine, downed it in long swallows, anyway, like bitter-tasting medicine.

The caffeine clicked in almost instantly, putting a slightly sharper edge on the fog surrounding his brain. Quinn decided some fresh air might do the rest.

"So how about giving me a tour?" he suggested to the dog after he'd washed and dried the dishes and put them away.

Filming didn't begin for another two days, and since he'd left the rented Mercedes outside the pub, Quinn figured he was stuck here until the family returned and someone could drive him into Castlelough to retrieve it. Then again, he reconsidered, from what he remembered of last night's drive, it wasn't that far into town. He could probably walk there. Later, after he felt more human.

When he opened the door that was split in two Dutch-style, the dog raced out ahead of him.

The house he'd only glanced at last night was a basic two-story farmhouse with a rounded yellow thatched roof. It was in need of a fresh whitewash, but the baskets of crimson flowers hanging on either side of the blue door added cheerful splashes of color. Several red hens pecked in the gravel in front of the house, green herbs jostled for space in a small garden, the white sheets on the clothesline fluttered in the morning breeze, and a rutted dirt driveway led to a wooden gate.

Last night's rain had stopped, leaving the

sky clear save for the wisps of blue smoke coming from the chimney and a few clouds that meandered overhead looking like shaggy lambs. The land folded out in green fields where herds of white-faced cows and flocks of sheep grazed. The heads and shoulders of the sheep had been marked for identification with various Day-Glo colors, and the blue, orange, chartreuse and scarlet gave the shaggy animals the look of punk rockers.

Since the nearby barn brought back more memories of those harsh foster-care days he was determined to forget, Quinn went back into the house to unpack.

Nora stood outside the gray stone church, surprised to discover that by allowing one of the Americans into her house she'd become a celebrity of sorts herself. Everyone, it seemed, wanted to know what the famous Mr. Quinn Gallagher was like.

"We didn't have much opportunity to talk," she replied evasively to Father O'Malley's inquiry regarding her boarder. The priest was a young man with a tall, asparagus stalk-thin body. The first time Nora had watched the father cutting peat, she'd realized the cleric was far more vigorous than his bookish ascetic appearance suggested. "He arrived late."

"I heard he spent the evening at The Rose. Do you think he has a drinking problem?" the priest asked with a frown.

Since it was obvious that the men at the pub had been telling tales, Nora decided there was little point in trying to avoid the question. "I worried about that. But Mr. Gallagher assures me it was an aberration. And he was, after all, with Brady."

"That does explain a great deal," the priest allowed. "However, if he gives you any trouble, Nora, I could always find room for him at the rectory."

"Thank you, Father. That's very kind. But I'm sure he won't be any problem." With that lie stinging her tongue, she smiled and drifted away, hoping she could gather up the family and get back to the farm before the troublesome American awoke and demanded his breakfast.

Yesterday's storm had passed, leaving behind a brilliant blue sky that seemed like a benediction. As she drove back to the farm, Nora decided to take the glorious day as a sign that her next encounter with her boarder would go more smoothly.

Quinn finished putting away his clothes in the old oak chest and had returned to the kitchen to take another stab at coffee making when he heard the crunch of car tires on the gravel outside.

Moments later the door burst open and two children — a boy and a girl who appeared to be about the same age — ran into the room, followed by a pair of teenagers, then Fionna and Brady. Bringing up the rear and backlit by a sun that turned her hair to flame, was Nora Fitzpatrick.

She was wearing a high-necked heather-hued dress that stopped just a bit above the knee and a well-worn blazer the color of rain. If the skirt had been a few inches longer, she could have been a nun. When she shrugged out of the blazer to hang it on a wooden hook beside the door, Quinn discovered that the widow Fitzpatrick's body, which last night had been hidden beneath a bulky sweater, was far more curvaceous than he'd first thought. And the softly clinging dress was anything but nunlike.

A face of a convent girl and a body built for sin. It was, he was discovering, a perilous combination. The woman wasn't merely trouble. She was pure TNT.

And Quinn felt as if he'd just been handed a lit fuse.

She greeted him with a hesitant smile. "So you're up," she said. Her scent, which made him think of making love in a meadow of wildflowers during a soft summer rain, had entered the kitchen with her.

Deliberately, to prove to himself — and to her — that he could, Quinn aimed cool dark eyes at her exquisite face. "I woke up about an hour ago."

"I'm sorry I wasn't here to fix you breakfast."

When she didn't look away from what other women had assured him was a quelling stare, Quinn decided she might just be tougher than she looked.

"The dog and I managed."

"The dog?" She glanced down at the beast, who was lying beneath the table, head on its forepaws, looking adoringly up at Quinn. "Isn't that amazing." She tilted her head and studied him. "You're obviously a miracle worker."

"Maeve's afraid of everyone but my aunt Kate, my mam and me," the younger boy volunteered.

He had a shock of dark hair, blue-black eyes and a scattering of freckles across his face. But even with the difference in coloring, Quinn had no difficulty in recognizing him to be the grandson Brady had boasted about.

"Her name is Maeve?" Quinn asked.

"After the warrior queen of Connacht

from the old stories. It was Mam's idea. She thought being named after such a powerful person might help give Maeve courage."

"Sounds reasonable to me," Quinn said with a sideways glance at Nora. Her face curtained by her hair, she began taking cups down from the open shelf. "She seems like a great dog."

Admittedly, he might have been a bit of a bastard when it came to Nora. But Quinn didn't have it in him to be cold to a child. Especially one forced to grow up without a father. Not that having a father was any real guarantee of happiness.

"I assume you're Rory."

"I'm sorry. I should have introduced you to everyone," Nora said before her son could answer. "Rory, this is Mr. Gallagher." She went on to introduce the other children.

"I have all your books, Mr. Gallagher," offered the tall gangly teenage boy with the serious eyes she'd introduced as her brother John.

"Call me Quinn." Being called Mr. Gallagher reminded him uncomfortably of his father. "And thanks for the support. Your father said your favorite is *The Night of the Banshee*."

"That was my favorite. But I think I like *The Lady of the Lake* best now. And I especially like that you set it right here in Castle-lough."

"Perhaps you'd like to come watch some filming."

"Could I? Really?" It was such a small thing. And offered without thought. But it obviously meant a great deal to John Joyce.

"How about me?" This from the younger girl with the bright nest of Orphan Annie curls. Celia, Quinn remembered. Which would make her the child Brady's wife had died giving birth to. "May I come, as well?"

Nora lit the stove, then shot a stern warning look over her shoulder as she filled a kettle from the tap. "That's enough, now," she said. "I won't be having you all pestering Mr. Gallagher. He's here to work on his movie and is to be left alone."

"I don't mind," Quinn lied. Although he was not usually diplomatic, he could be when necessary.

Nora gave him a look that said she didn't believe him for a moment. "You're a paying guest. Don't you have a right not to be pestered to death?" Her voice lilted with the soft cadence of the Irish west. "Would you be wanting some tea?"

"Of course he'll be wanting tea," Brady said, entering into the conversation. He looked hale and hearty, revealing not an iota of hangover. Yet further proof, Quinn considered grimly, that life wasn't fair.

"Nora makes the best tea in the county," Brady assured Quinn. "Stout enough to trot a mouse across, it is."

"Now there's a thought," Quinn murmured, watching as his words caused the corners of her mouth to curl in a faint smile. "Tea sounds good. I tried making coffee, but I couldn't get the knack of boiling it."

"Didn't I tell you we should have bought one of those Mr. Coffee machines, Nora, darling?" Brady said.

"Really, tea's fine," Quinn insisted.

Everyone but Nora was watching him again, as if he were some sort of unique animal. A unicorn, perhaps. Or the creature in the lake.

"I knew a Donovan Gallagher when I was a girl," Fionna said. "He had family in Donegal. Would you be knowing of them?"

"No."

She tilted her head and studied him. "You have the look of the boy I knew. Perhaps while you're in Ireland, you might be wanting to take a visit to Donegal and —"

"No." Realizing he'd snapped at her, Quinn softened his expression. And his tone. "I'm afraid I'm going to be very busy working on the film. I doubt I'll have time for sightseeing."

"Ah, isn't that a shame, now?" Fionna's direct gaze told him that she suspected there might be more to his refusal than a scheduling problem. "To come all this way from America and not see your family . . . perhaps next time," she suggested.

"Next time," he agreed. Wanting to move the conversation away from himself, Quinn turned back to Rory. "So, what grade are you in?"

"Oh, I'm in first form."

Quinn remembered attending three different schools in three different states during his first-grade year. He also remembered the broken arm his father had given him when he hadn't fetched the bottle of Coors fast enough that September they'd lived in Boulder. "Do you like school?"

"Aye." The small freckled forehead creased. "But I'm not so sure about next year."

"Why not?"

"Because when you're in second form, everything changes. You have to learn cursive, and start learning about the lives of the saints, and you become culp . . . culp . . ."

"He's trying to say culpable," Celia broke

95

in with a toss of her head that suggested feminine superiority.

"Culpable?"

"You get reason," Celia explained. "It means you become responsible. You can't say you didn't know any better because by the time you're in second form, you're supposed to know the difference between good and evil. So all your sins go against your permanent record."

"I can see where that might be a worry." Quinn decided he didn't ever want to get a look at *his* permanent record. "But I can't believe you could have all that many sins," he assured Rory.

"Everything's a bloody sin." Mary spoke up for the first time, her dark kohl-lined eyes flashing. Seeing through the makeup the girl had spread like Spackle on her face, Quinn realized she was going to grow up to be a real beauty. "Everything pleasurable, that is."

"And what kind of words are those from a girl who's decided to become a nun?" Fionna demanded.

"I'm not going to be a nun."

"Yesterday you said you had a vocation," Rory reminded her.

"That was yesterday. Can't a girl change her mind?"

"Mary wanted to become a nun because Jack asked Sharon Fitzgerald to the May Dance," Rory informed Quinn.

"Sounds like Jack's loss." Quinn's complimentary words caused color to flood into the teenage girl's pale face.

"That's what I told her," Fionna said.

"Sharon sleeps around," Celia volunteered. "Which is why Jack asked her to the dance, instead of our Mary."

That was all it took to make the teenager burst into tears and run from the room.

"Don't be minding the girl's histrionics," Fionna said matter-of-factly. "She's at an age, don't you know."

"It's difficult being a teenager," Quinn agreed. Realizing he was wading once more into murky conversational waters, he was relieved when the kitchen door opened again and an ebony-haired woman accompanied by two children entered the room.

"Good morning, all." While the greetings the others returned were cheery enough, Quinn thought he detected a sudden tension in the kitchen. Nora, especially, seemed to be studying the newcomer carefully.

"I'm Kate O'Sullivan." She held out a friendly hand. Her flesh was pale, her grip strong, her smile warm. "And you'd be Quinn Gallagher. And these two are my daughter and my son. I enjoy your books. Even if they are marketed all wrong."

"Oh?" Just what he needed. Another critic.

If she heard the faint warning note in Quinn's voice, Kate ignored it. "You don't write horror of course."

"I don't?"

"Surely you know you don't? You write social commentary. In fact, your stories remind me, in many ways, of Jonathan Swift."

"I'm flattered."

"Why should you be when it's the truth? It doesn't take a degree in literature to understand that *The Lady of the Lake* is an allegory about prejudice, the overreach of science and the paranoia that can so easily run rampant in small isolated villages such as our own."

Quinn laughed, liking her immediately. "The woman's obviously a genius. So how would you like a job as my Irish publicity rep?"

"I think you'd be in trouble," she countered. "Being that there's many in these parts who wouldn't buy a book just because I recommended it."

"Aunt Kate's a witch," Rory explained.

"A druid witch," Celia tacked on.

Quinn was amused by the faint challenge that rose in Kate O'Sullivan's blue eyes at this revelation. "As it happens, I've been playing with the idea of writing a witch heroine," he said mildly. "Perhaps you'll make time to consult with me while I'm here."

It was her turn to laugh. "And wouldn't that start tongues wagging?" Her smile was warm, belying the stereotype of the wicked witch of fairy tales. "Of course I'll consult with you, Mr. Gallagher, if only to make certain you get it right."

"There you go again." Nora smiled with affection at her sister-in-law as she placed a flowered teacup in front of Quinn. "Stirring things up again."

"The gods gave us all unique talents, Nora. Unfortunately stirring things up seems to be what I seem to do best." Kate gave a slight sigh, then pulled out a chair across the table from Quinn, picked up her little red-haired daughter Brigid and plunked her on her lap.

Unlike the gregarious Rory Fitzpatrick, Kate O'Sullivan's son, standing almost behind his mother's chair, reminded Quinn vaguely of Maeve.

"Hi." Quinn held out his hand. "My name's Quinn. What's yours?"

The boy shot a quick wary look up at his mother.

"Answer the man, darling," Kate coaxed gently.

"Jamie." He stared down at the floor. "Jamie O'Sullivan."

The surname, which he hadn't paid all that much attention to when Kate O'Sullivan had introduced herself, rang a bell. It was a common enough name in Ireland certainly, but Quinn knew without a single doubt that the bad tempered, foulmouthed drunk in the pub was this little boy's father. He also knew that the reason Jamie refused to shake his hand was not so much because he was shy. He was afraid.

And why not? Quinn thought grimly, knowing all too well how painful a man's big rough hands could be.

He glanced up at Nora and read the regretful answer in her eyes. And in that suspended moment of shared concern for Kate O'Sullivan and her children, Quinn — who'd spent his entire life deftly avoiding involvement — felt as if he'd just taken a fatal misstep into quicksand.

CHAPTER SIX

In Fortune's Hand

Intending to retrieve his car, Quinn had put on his jacket and was headed for the front door when Brady called to him.

"From the looks of you, you'd be going out somewhere."

"I thought I'd walk into town." Quinn entered the book-filled room, which looked out over green rolling pastures and the distant sea beyond. The sun was brighter in this country renowned for rain than Quinn had expected. "I'm going to need my car to get to the shoot at the lake tomorrow."

"Oh, you can't be doing that, my boy." Brady put down the book of Gaelic folktales he was reading on a nearby table. "It's much too far to be walking. I'd offer to drive you myself, but I've a great deal of paperwork to do. The bills don't pay themselves, don't you know. And poor Nora, as lovely and sweet as she is, has never had a head for figures."

He pushed himself from the overstuffed

chair and began rummaging around in an old desk, finally locating a green ledger book.

"It's no problem," Quinn said. "The walk will do me good." Especially after the unusually large breakfast he'd shared with Maeve.

"Truly, there's no need for you to be doing that," Brady said quickly. "Nora will be more than happy to drive you back into the village to fetch your automobile."

"I don't want to disturb her Sunday."

"You won't be disturbing her at all," Brady assured him. "Aren't you a guest? She wouldn't be having you walk all that way into Castlelough."

Quinn decided not to mention that he ran longer distances on a daily basis back home.

"Thanks for the suggestion."

"You're more than welcome." Brady looked up from sharpening a yellow pencil with a penknife and beamed his approval. "Enjoy your Sunday drive, now."

Quinn was on his way to the kitchen when he passed the parlor and saw Fionna sitting in front of the lace-covered window, knitting needles clacking.

"I expect you'll be wanting a ride into the village to fetch your automobile?" she called out to him.

He paused in the doorway. "Actually I was planning to walk. Brady suggested Nora, but —"

"And isn't that clever of my son to think of her?" Fionna's smile, which echoed Brady's, set internal alarms blaring. "Our Nora's an excellent driver. And you couldn't have a better tourist guide."

"Surely your granddaughter has better things to do than chauffeur me around."

"Now don't you be worrying your head about that." The knitting needles continued to clack with the speed of dueling rapiers in an old Errol Flynn movie. "The family can take up her chores for this one day." With a brisk nod of her bright red-gold head, Fionna declared the subject closed.

It crossed Quinn's mind that Nora's father and grandmother seemed awful damn eager to get the two of them alone together. He wondered idly if they could actually be setting a trap for him, the rich Yank.

It wasn't as if such schemes hadn't succeeded before: get an American to marry you so you can get a green card to live legally in the States, then bring over your entire family on the next boat. Or plane, these days, he supposed.

The idea almost made him laugh. Fionna and Brady Joyce could set all the snares they chose. But in this case their prey was far too wary to be captured.

He'd planned to sneak out the kitchen door without being noticed, but found Nora where he'd left her earlier. The O'Sullivans had apparently departed and she'd changed from the dress she'd worn to church into a pair of jeans, a creamy sweater and a white apron.

She was kneading bread. The warm smell of the yeast coupled with the sight of her slender arms elbow deep in the mound of dough made Quinn's gut twist with something indefinable.

"May I help you?" She glanced up at him with a smile, but her eyes were guarded. As well they should be, Quinn thought grimly. The widow Fitzpatrick was obviously intelligent enough to realize he was way out of her league. "Would you be liking a cup of tea? Or, perhaps, some coffee?"

"Nothing, thanks. I need to go into town to get my car. Brady suggested you'd be able to drive me, but I assured him I can walk."

"Of course I'll be taking you." Again, her smile was pleasant, but self-protective barriers remained firmly in place in her eyes. "If you don't mind waiting until I get this bread in the pan."

"I don't mind at all." He turned a chair around, straddled it and leaned his arms on the top of the seat back. "I've never seen bread being made."

She laughed at that. "What a deprived life you've led, then, Mr. Gallagher."

"I'm beginning to think you might be right, Mrs. Fitzpatrick." The movement of her hands pushing at the elastic white dough was both homey and sensual at the same time. "I really hate to intrude on your day."

"You're no intrusion at all. I enjoy driving. And it's a lovely day, after all."

"Your father said he'd take me if he wasn't so busy with his ledger book," Quinn said conversationally.

"Ledger book?" Nora's hands stilled for a moment, and she glanced at him in surprise. "The farm account book?"

"That's what it looked like."

"Well." She shook her head and began pounding harder at the dough.

"Something wrong?"

"Wrong?" She was refusing to look at him, her voice had taken on a sharp edge, and she'd begun attacking the dough as if she bore it a personal grudge. "What could be wrong with a man tending to business?"

What indeed? Quinn wondered. But

something definitely had her ire up. Electricity was practically radiating from every pore.

"Well, that's done for now." She turned the dough into two oblong pans, covered them with a cotton dish towel, then brushed her palms together to dust off the flour. "It'll just take me a few minutes to wash up and —"

"I'll do that," a voice offered from the doorway. Both Quinn and Nora turned to see Mary.

"You're volunteering to do dishes?" Nora's eyes narrowed. "Saints preserve us," she said with an exaggerated brogue that reminded Quinn of her father's. "Ring up Father O'Malley right away, because it's sure we're witnessing a miracle."

"I've done dishes before. Lots of times," Mary countered with a toss of her dark head. "Gran sent me in to finish washing up so you and Mr. Gallagher could leave for the village."

"And isn't that thoughtful of your grandmother," Nora said dryly. She washed the remaining bits of dough off her hands beneath the tap, dried them on her apron, then took it off and hung it on a wooden hook on the wall. "If you're ready, then, Mr. Gallagher." After plucking a set of keys from another hook, she walked out the kitchen door, leaving Quinn to follow.

"What the hell is that?" He stared at the huge garishly painted old Caddy sitting in the driveway where earlier red-feathered chickens had scratched.

Nora arched a brow. "Are you telling me you've never seen a miracle-mobile, Mr. Gallagher?"

"This is a first. Is it yours?" He assured himself that he'd survived far worse in his lifetime than being seen by any of the crew in what looked like an amateur artist's rendition of the Sistine Chapel ceiling.

"Don't worry, it's Fionna's. Mine is the blue one parked behind it. We fetched it from the pub after mass this morning."

Thank God. "Nice car," he murmured.

Nora laughed in a way that told him she knew exactly how relieved he was feeling. "Thank you. It's a wee bit boring compared to Fionna's. But I like it."

The car, like most he'd seen in Ireland, was a compact sedan that could probably fit into the rear of the Chevy Suburban parked next to the Porsche in his three-car garage back in Monterey.

"I really am sorry to inconvenience you this way," he said into the well of strained silence surrounding them as they drove through the rolling green hills. It was obvious that her brief humor over his reaction to her grandmother's colorful Cadillac had faded, leaving her still upset about something.

"It's no inconvenience," Nora snapped. Then, as if realizing how brisk she'd sounded, she sighed and rubbed at her temple, as if trying to ward off a headache. "I'm sorry. Truly I don't mind driving you into the village, Mr. Gallagher. It's just that I'm a little put out at my family at the moment."

"For throwing us together."

She shot him a surprised look. "You knew that's what they were doing?"

He watched the color — like wild primroses — rise in her cheeks, tried to remember the last time he'd been with a woman capable of blushing and came up blank. Even as he reminded himself that innocence held no appeal, Quinn found the rosy hue enticing.

"It was pretty obvious."

"I'm sorry." She combed a not very steady hand through her riot of curls. In the midday light her hair glowed like a burning bush. Her wrists were narrow, her fingers slender, her short nails unlacquered, once again bringing to mind a nun. A sensible man would give her a wide berth. Quinn reminded himself he'd always considered himself a sensible man.

"It's not right that you should have to deal with their foolish matchmaking schemes while you're a paying guest."

"I've survived worse."

"But you shouldn't have to, you see."

"Why don't you let me worry about it?" he suggested mildly.

"It's just so . . . embarrassing. And annoying. As if I'm some over-the-hill spinster who can't get a man on my own."

Since she'd practically handed him a gilt-edged invitation, Quinn allowed himself the luxury of an in-depth perusal of the woman sitting so close to him. His eyes, safely hidden behind the dark lenses of his sunglasses, looked her over with slow deliberation, from the top of her fiery head to her sneaker-clad feet, where he found a surprisingly whimsical touch — white cotton socks trimmed with lace. And although he knew his mind had no business going off in such a dangerous direction, he wondered if she was wearing more white lace beneath those jeans and that sweater.

"The gold wedding band on your finger proves you're no spinster. And I've no doubt there are more than a few men in Ireland who'd want you, Mrs. Fitzpatrick."

The color in her cheeks deepened. "I'll be taking that as a compliment, Mr. Gallagher." Although her voice remained steady, her eyes had gotten that guarded look again. "Especially since you've already assured me I'm not your type of woman."

He'd been wondering if she was going to bring that up. "I suppose this is where I apologize for my boorish behavior. Although being drunk's no excuse, I can't remember the last time I got so wasted. Believe me, I usually display a helluva lot more finesse when I'm seducing a woman."

"And are you in the habit of seducing women who aren't your type?"

Quinn gave a harsh bark of laughter. "Hardly. In fact, last night was a first."

"It was probably the drink," she offered helpfully.

"Probably," he agreed, not believing it for a minute. "I suppose that's what I get for trying to keep up with all the toasts."

Quinn had quickly discovered that when anyone in the pub offered to stand for a drink, it was bad manners to refuse. Then, of course, you had to return the compliment. Next it would be someone else's turn. And on and on until he was amazed anyone was left standing at the end of the evening.

"My father doesn't usually drink so much," Nora volunteered, as if needing to defend Brady's behavior. "It's his habit to drink a pint or two and get his enjoyment from telling his tales."

"Alcohol's a slippery slope. Sometimes people can lose their footing."

"True enough." She slanted him another curious glance. "You sound as if you have some personal experience with such things."

"My mother was a drunk." Quinn had never told another living soul about his mother. He wondered why the hell he'd just told Nora Fitzpatrick.

"Oh."

She fell silent. And seemingly thoughtful as she drove down the ribbon of road past hedgerows thick with lacelike flowers. The fruit trees blooming in yards along the roadway looked like pink and white bouquets against the blue sky. The windows of the car were open, allowing in air so fresh Quinn felt almost as if he could drink it.

They passed a donkey-pulled cart carrying ten-gallon milk cans, headed, Quinn supposed, to the creamery in Castlelough; amazingly a small dog stood on the donkey's back. The driver of the cart, an elderly man wearing a tweed suit, billed cap and green Wellies, seemed delighted to see them and waved his hand enthusiastically. Nora lifted a hand to wave back.

"And your father?" she asked Quinn at length. "Did he have a liking for spirits, as well?"

"My father could have been the poster boy for AA. If he'd ever seen fit to attend a meeting, that is. Or go a day without a drink."

She glanced over at him again, her exquisite face grave. "I'm sorry."

"So was I." Quinn hated the sympathy — and worse yet, pity — that seemed to soften her tone.

"And now?"

Out of longtime habit, he shut his mind to thoughts of his father, whose brutal blood tainted his own veins.

"And now I don't think about it." He gave her a hard level look. His curt tone, thick with a tension he didn't bother to conceal, declared the subject closed.

She should just drive Quinn Gallagher into Castlelough, drop him off at The Irish Rose to retrieve his car and return home to finish her chores, Nora thought, biting her lip at his curtness. After all, the bread would need punching down soon, there was laundry to do — the last time Mary had taken on the chore, she'd tossed in one of

Rory's T-shirts and turned all Brady's underwear pink — and, of course, dinner to prepare.

It shouldn't bother her that the man sitting beside her in the suddenly too-close confines of the car seemed to be mired in unpleasant memories of his past. He'd been less than charming since his arrival late last night, and the simple truth was that she'd only rented him a room. She was under no obligation to provide guided tours of the county she loved, concern herself with his brooding or care that he seemed to be filled with dark shadows.

Quinn Gallagher meant nothing to her but a rental fee that would keep the farm afloat for the next few months. Whatever internal demons the American might be fighting meant nothing to her. She didn't care about him or his moods.

The devil she didn't.

Nora sighed and thought once again how useless it was to fight nature. Hadn't she learned that lesson with Conor? Living in the west was living poor, and Conor, born on a neighboring farm where Kate still lived, had been determined to outrun and outride poor.

As for herself, so long as she could keep the bankers at bay, Nora had never minded not having money for the extras Conor had seemed to need. Her husband, who'd set his sights even higher than Dublin, had jokingly called her his little country mouse. Indeed, Nora could more easily imagine traveling on a spaceship to the moon than moving away from the family farm.

Conor had been bold, daring and restless as the wind.

He'd also been a wee bit self-centered. But since that had been part of the cocky confidence that contributed greatly to his charm, she'd never complained. Not even when he hadn't managed to make it home for Rory's birth.

He'd been competing in the Olympic trials at the time. And although she'd understood the importance of the event, Nora couldn't deny that she wished he'd been by her side when she'd brought their only son into the world.

At the time, Kate, who was not nearly as unforgiving of her brother's behavior, had accused Nora of being a natural-born caretaker, always willing to put her own wishes aside in order to concentrate on the whims of others. Nora hadn't argued then, and truth be told, couldn't argue the fact now.

She had, indeed, been a caretaker all of her life, and a caretaker she'd undoubtedly die. Normally the personal rewards made the sacrifices worthwhile. She feared that Quinn Gallagher might prove to be the exception to the rule.

"Shall I show you the lake?" she asked into the prolonged silence.

"The lake?" Appearing to pull himself momentarily out of whatever gloomy place he was wallowing in, Quinn looked over at her with surprise.

"Lough Caislean." She called the lake by its Irish name.

He lifted a brow. "Ah, where the famed monster lurks."

"The creature," she corrected quietly, hoping his words didn't mean the movie people were planning to portray the Lady as some voracious killer from the deep lagoon. Like in those grainy black-and-white Japanese Godzilla films John had been so taken with when he'd been Rory's age.

"Creature, monster." He waved a hand dismissively. "What's the difference?"

Nora thought about that for a moment. "I suppose it's a matter of semantics. And respect."

He laughed again, a rough rusty sound that reminded her of the nearly bald tires of Fionna's miracle-mobile running over a gravel road. It occurred to Nora that Quinn

Gallagher was not a man who allowed himself to laugh often.

"Are you saying you believe the Lady exists?" he asked.

She shrugged, feeling foolish. She dearly wished they'd not gotten onto this topic. "I've never seen her myself. But I respect others' beliefs."

She did not mention that Rory was one of those who insisted he'd not only seen, but talked with the Lady. Since it seemed to give him comfort and she'd had her own imaginary playmate when she was his age, she'd never been overly concerned with her son having the lough beastie for a best friend.

"That's not exactly the same thing."

"I suppose I believe that myths are capable of possessing their own reality. And if there is a Lady in the lake — and I'm not saying I believe there is, mind you —" she shot him a stern look "— she deserves the same consideration we give any of God's creatures. Including a rich and famous American horror novelist."

Having tacked on the last without taking time to censor her words, Nora feared he'd take offense, but he surprised her by flashing a grin that came and went so quickly she thought perhaps she'd imagined it.

"Point taken."

The brief argument, if it could, indeed, even be called an argument, appeared to have burned off his dark mood, like a July sun burns off cold morning fog.

"I think I'd like to see the lake," Quinn said, "if you have time."

Although holding a grudge was nearly a national pastime, Nora had never been able to keep a decent pique going. She smiled, pleased at the opportunity to share one of her favorite places with him. "We have a saying here in Ireland, Mr. Gallagher — when God made time, he made plenty of it."

CHAPTER SEVEN

Whatever You Say, Say Nothing

Less than five minutes later Nora pulled off to the side of the road. "It's a bit of a walk. But a lovely one, just the same."

"I could use some exercise." Once again Quinn figured the fresh air might help banish the remnants of his hangover and jet lag.

"It might help clear away any lingering Jameson fog," she said with a smile, revealing similar thinking.

Quinn started to remind her she hadn't locked the car door, then realized there was probably no need, which left him feeling a lot like Dorothy after the tornado had blown her out of Kansas. Ireland might not exactly be Oz. But it sure as hell wasn't California, either.

They passed a cemetery like the ones he'd seen while driving around in circles, a somber place of high crosses standing like silent sentinels and rounded gravestones covered with pale green moss. A few of the more recent stones had been decorated with arrangements of colorful plastic flowers in domed containers.

The narrow well-worn path meandered through the hills like a tangled fishing line, crossing meadows lush with blue lupine, wild roses and strawberries. After climbing for about ten minutes, they came upon a mound of earth blanketed with yellow poppies and decorated with stones.

"It's a cairn," Nora explained, "built about five thousand years ago. There are quite a few of them around this part of the country."

"It's a tomb, right?"

"Of sorts. There's probably a passage below leading to a central burial chamber. The early ones believed in an afterlife, so they often buried their loved ones with tools, weapons or household goods."

Quinn, who always prided himself on his research, knew about the pre-Christian burial sites. But reading about something in a dry archeological text was vastly different from actually standing right beside it. This place hidden in the green folds of the mountain had gone unchanged for millennia; memories of that long-ago heroic time and shadows of a mysterious faith hovered over the site like ghosts standing guard over an ancient past.

He paused and drank in the atmosphere, breathing deeply of air scented with golden hollyhock and something else he could not quite define. Then he rubbed at the tingling sensation at the back of his neck.

"I don't know if I believe in an afterlife," he said. "But here . . . it sure feels as if some spirits might have lingered on." He could almost hear the eerie sound of ghostly voices floating on the breeze.

Nora gave him a surprised look that quickly turned to pleasure. "Sometimes, you know, I come here and talk to the early ones. I tell them my troubles, and strangely, things seem better when I leave. Although I suspect it's just the telling, getting it off my chest, as you Yanks would say, that lifts my spirits."

"That, or magic," Quinn suggested.

The soft color he was beginning to enjoy too much for comfort rose high on her cheekbones again. "Listen to me, going on so," she protested with that soft cadence that strummed dangerous chords inside him. "You'll be thinking I'm just a foolish *culchie.*"

Quinn lifted a brow. *"Culchie?"*

"It means a country person. Usually a daft or stupid one."

"Ah." He nodded and felt an unaccustomed smile tugging at the corners of his mouth again. "A bumpkin." The breeze was blowing her hair in a wild tangle around her flushed face in a way that put him in mind of a Botticelli maiden.

"A bumpkin." She appeared to consider that. "Is that how you see me, then? As a fanciful and foolish country bumpkin?"

Fanciful she might be. Foolish? Quinn didn't think so. Although a more cautious woman would probably know enough to take off running right about now.

Some errant strands of fiery silk blew across her face. When he reached out to brush them back, she went as still as one of the stone crosses they'd passed earlier.

"I certainly don't consider you a bumpkin. Although I have to admit I've never met a woman who had the imagination to carry on conversations with Stone Age ancestors."

This time the color flamed to the roots of her hair. "We'd best be continuing on if we want to reach the lake before it rains."

Unlike every photograph he'd ever seen of Ireland, there wasn't a cloud to be seen anywhere in the robin's-egg blue sky.

"Good idea," he heard himself saying as she looked up at him, wary, but fascinated, the way one might stare at a pretty, poisonous snake. He watched her exhale a brief shuddering breath. Then, squaring her slender shoulders, she turned away and resumed walking.

They left the trail, Nora scrambling over rocks as nimbly as one of the black-legged sheep he could see grazing in distant meadows. The mountains they were walking over were ancient, headed toward dust. Although they weren't as bold and breathtaking as the jagged mountains he was accustomed to, Quinn found them strangely soothing.

"Aye, they can be a solace," Nora answered after he'd shared his thoughts. "Of course some people view them as prison walls. Keeping them locked into a place, or in a life that's not all they'd like it to be."

Quinn wondered if she might have just given him a little insight into her marriage to that hotshot rider on the European equestrian circuit Brady had told him about. Suddenly they came to a towering hedge ablaze with shocking pink fuchsia. The thick seemingly impenetrable greenery extended in both directions for as far as the eye could see.

"Looks like we've just hit a dead end," he said.

"Oh, there's a passageway that leads to the lough. I like to fool myself that it's my own secret entrance," she added with a soft laugh.

Quinn followed her through the bright fragrant passageway, then stopped dead in his tracks as he gazed down into a valley of unparalleled beauty. The lake, surrounded by feather-crowned reeds that swayed in the breeze, was a splash of glistening sapphire satin on a mottled green carpet.

"It's lovely, isn't it?"

"Lovely doesn't begin to describe it." His voice was hushed, almost reverential, as if he'd entered a cathedral. "It's stunning. And so . . . peaceful."

The only sounds were the soft sigh of the breeze and the buzzing drone of fat bees flying from flower to vivid flower. Quinn could hear himself breathe.

"We have a saying — *ciunas gan uagineas*. It means quietness without loneliness. I'm always reminded of that when I come here."

"*Ciunas gan uagineas,*" Quinn struggled to wrap his tongue around the unfamiliar syllables. "It fits."

"Doesn't it? I suppose you know the legend of how the Lady arrived in the lake in the first place."

"Actually, I don't. I just ran across a mention of her in an article about Irish mermaids and let my imagination fill in the blanks." Besides, when it came to monsters, Quinn figured he had enough lurking in his own mind to keep writing long into old age. "But now that I'm here, I'd like to hear it."

"Oh, it's a lovely tale. And far better told by Da. But I'll try my best not to disappoint you," she said in the soft swaying tones that made him think of fairies dancing in the moonlight.

"The lake was once the site of a splendid kingdom ruled over by a beautiful benevolent queen," she began. "She had long flowing yellow hair that fell down her back in waves and glittered like a leprechaun's gold beneath a full summer sun.

"Because she was as good as she was lovely, the gods had rewarded the people of her kingdom by bestowing upon them a marvelous gift — a sweet spring whose waters brought youth to all who drank of it."

"So this is where the Fountain of Youth's been hiding all these years," Quinn said.

"Aye." Her eyes sparkled with humor. "It's a secret we've kept well to prevent ourselves from being overrun by even more tourists." She paused, then went on, "At any rate, the queen had instructed that the spring be capped every night with a large stone so it couldn't flow out and flood the valley.

"Unfortunately a fairy who lived in the glen fell in love with the queen's husband. But the fairy was as ugly as an old boar, sharp as a brier, and evil as the devil, which, of course, made it difficult for any man to love her in return."

"I can see how all that might prove a problem."

"Aye, a fearsome problem, indeed. But even when the hag turned herself into a beautiful young girl, the noble prince remained steadfastly faithful to the queen and didn't return her affections.

"Well, unfortunately for all, this fairy had a terrible temper, and when the handsome prince rejected her for the third time, she cast a wicked spell on him. That night, during the summer-solstice celebrations, although he'd always been known as a man who could hold his liquor, the prince got drunk and passed out before putting the capstone on the spring.

"So it flowed and flowed, and by morning the entire valley, including the fair city and all its people, were now underwater. But since the water was magic, no one drowned. Indeed, they adapted quite well to their new life beneath the lake, although every so often, the queen, who has sensibly replaced her satin gowns with emerald scales, comes to the surface to gaze upon the hills that she continues to miss after all these many years."

"Nice story." And a helluva lot more benevolent than the dark and threatening one he'd created.

"I've always thought so. There are also fishermen who swear that sometimes on a still summer evening you can look over the edge of your boat and catch a shimmering glimpse of the turrets of the queen's castle and the townspeople busily going about their daily work."

Quinn found the idea of a hidden Atlantis-like city almost as appealing as the magical silent site itself.

"You know," he said, "although this place isn't nearly as wild, it reminds me a bit of my home on the California coast." It was the solitude, he decided. A quietness that was both inspiring and comforting at the same time.

Nora smiled, seeming pleased he was enjoying her gift. "If it's wild scenery you're wanting, Mr. Gallagher, I'll take you to our seacoast on our next outing."

Quinn tensed at her casual mention of another sightseeing trip. Instincts kicked in, the primordial knee-jerk behavior Laura had, only yesterday, teasingly compared to a wolf sniffing out a trap.

He knew he should refuse further excursions before he got in any deeper. "I think I just might like that," he heard himself saying, instead.

In a gesture too natural to be contrived, Nora slipped her hand in Quinn's as they gazed down at the lake.

The crystal-clear sapphire water reflected every cloud, even a passing gull. Two white swans, looking as if they'd just flown in from Sleeping Beauty's castle, floated serenely on the glassy surface.

"I wish I'd seen this before I wrote my book," he said.

"Would you have changed something?"

"Yeah. I would have set the story in Scotland, since they already have Nessie. Or Wales. Or even California." He shook his head. "It almost seems a sacrilege to invade this place with a movie crew."

"It's not a church."

"Not now. But I'll bet that the Celts — and before them, the people who built that burial mound — felt differently."

He shifted his gaze to the ruins of the castle. "It's a strange thought."

"What?"

"Thinking of people once living here. Loving and laughing and warring behind those walls. Lord, the stories those stones could tell if they would talk."

"I believe I owe John an apology," Nora said suddenly.

"John? Your brother?"

"Aye. He's been telling me I should read your books, but I haven't. Oh, I'm sure you're a fine writer," she said quickly, as if afraid she might have insulted him. "But I'll admit to preferring stories that don't give me nightmares."

Having heard that remark countless times, it no longer bothered him. "Horror has its own reality," he said, twisting her earlier words concerning myths.

As a lone cloud came from behind the velvety mountain to move across the sun, Nora looked up at him, studying him in that solemn way she sometimes had. The way that made Quinn feel as if she were seeing all the way to his soul. Not that she'd be able to see anything but darkness, he thought grimly, unable to remember when he'd last believed he even possessed a soul.

"I suspect that's true enough." She reached up as if to touch his cheek, apparently thought better of it and lowered her hand. "But any man who can feel the magic and the mystery of this place is a man whose books I want to read."

She was suddenly too close. Quinn felt in danger of suffocating. "If you're looking for a way in to who I am," he said, sensing she might actually be naive enough to believe she could steal into his sealed-off private places by reading his books, "you'll be disappointed. Because there isn't any." His fingers tightened on the hand he was still holding. "And even if there was, believe me, baby, you wouldn't want to go there."

"And you'd be knowing where I want to go?" Her lilting tone remained soft, but she lifted her chin in an obvious challenge.

"I'd be knowing where you damn well shouldn't want to go," he practically growled. How the hell had they ever gotten on this subject? "It's a dark place, Nora. Teeming with things you could never understand."

She surprised Quinn by smiling. A faint sad little smile that tore at something elemental deep inside him.

"Now there's where you'd be wrong, Quinn."

This time she did touch his cheek, her fingertips feeling like a burning brand against his scarred skin. Then, before he could come up with an appropriate response, she'd tugged her other hand free of his and was headed back the way they'd come.

Cursing, Quinn jammed his hands into

the pockets of his jeans and followed her. Without the warmth of the buttery spring sun, the day had suddenly turned as cold and dark as his mood.

And his heart.

"So, how are you and your handsome boarder getting on?" Kate asked Nora three days later. They'd gone shopping together in the village, taking time for tea at O'Neill's.

"We're not."

Nora pretended grave interest in stirring sugar into her tea. Though she was truly fond of her sister-in-law, she didn't want to admit that she'd actually been a bit depressed by the American's disappearing act after their outing to the lake.

Despite the fact that his rental fee included meals, he left the house every morn- ing before breakfast and returned late at night. If she was still sitting up in the parlor — not waiting for him, Nora told herself, merely working on the account books or mending Celia's jumper or some such necessary task — he'd merely give her a curt nod, a grunt she supposed was meant as a greeting, then go straight upstairs to his room.

"Mr. Gallagher is a source of much-needed income, nothing more."

"So that's why he was looking at you the

other morning as if you were a custard topped with clotted cream."

"He was not! He wouldn't even be staying at the house if Da hadn't gone behind my back and rented out my room. Besides," Nora added, "I'm not his type." Hadn't the man told her that himself?

"You're not his usual type of woman, perhaps." Kate's smile managed to be both smugly knowing and sympathetic at the same time. "But I could tell he fancies you."

"Even if he did — and I'm not saying he does, mind you — nothing could ever come of a romance with the likes of Quinn Gallagher." The tea tasted bitter on her tongue, so Nora added another spoon of sugar. It didn't help. "We're from different worlds."

"Who says anything has to come of it?" Kate argued. "You've been widowed for five long years, Nora. I'd say it's high time for you to be kicking up your heels, so to speak."

Unlike Kate, who'd once been the most sought-after fun-loving girl in the county before her marriage to Cadel O'Sullivan, Nora had never been one to kick up her heels. Not for the first time since Quinn Gallagher's arrival in Castlelough, was she forced to consider how impossible it was to fight nature.

"Are you saying I should just fling caution to the winds and go to bed with him?"

Kate appeared surprised by the question. "Has it already come to that?"

Nora felt the blush — the bane of all red-heads — flood hot as burning peat into her face. "He may have mentioned it the first night. But he'd been drinking, so I didn't pay any heed."

"But you were tempted."

Nora knew better than to lie to this woman who was, in many ways, closer to her than her own sisters. A woman who could see beyond the obvious.

Hadn't she even foreseen Conor's hor-rible accident? Discovering that fact at the wake had strained their friendship for a time, because although Kate had attempted to warn her brother — who'd always consid-ered himself impervious to injury — she'd never uttered a single word to Nora.

"And what would it have done," she'd ar-gued at the time, "but only make you fret more?" She hadn't suggested Nora might talk her hardheaded husband out of steeple-chase racing; they'd both known that would have been impossible.

Eventually the resentment had faded, enough so that now Nora was able to under-stand how difficult it must have been for her sister-in-law to have been burdened with such painful knowledge.

"All right," Nora said now as Kate continued to look at her in her steady knowing way, "I'll admit to a passing thought, just for an instant, mind you, about what it would be like to make love with Quinn Gallagher."

"Mr. Gallagher has the look of a man who'd be a grand lover," Kate said.

"I suspect Laura Gideon would be knowing about that better than I."

She'd seen the photograph of Quinn and the stunningly beautiful actress on the front page of yesterday's *Irish Independent*. The couple had been standing on the bank of the lake, their heads close together in a way that suggested intimacy. They were laughing, obviously enjoying themselves immensely, and his arm had been around her waist in a casually possessive way that spoke volumes.

"Ms. Gideon told the reporter that she and Quinn are merely friends."

"They certainly looked friendly enough," Nora muttered.

"Surely you're not jealous?" Kate's eyes narrowed as she studied her old friend and sister-in-law. "Oh dear. You can't have fallen in love with the man so fast?"

"It's not love." Nora shook her head and swallowed the rest of the too-sweet still-bitter tea. "It can't be love. I don't even know him. Besides, we have nothing in common," she said firmly, wondering who she was trying to convince — herself or her sister-in-law.

"Except lust," Kate suggested.

"Well, there is that," Nora admitted reluctantly.

"Some people might say lust is a good beginning for a relationship."

"Kate O'Sullivan!" Nora hissed, looking around the small tearoom, terrified Mrs. O'Neill or one of the other patrons might have overheard the scandalous remark.

"Just because I'm married doesn't mean I can't appreciate a good-looking man. And remember how exciting — and terrifying — it is to fall in love."

Her tone was suddenly touched with sadness, making Nora wonder, not for the first time, if Kate had ever truly loved Cadel O'Sullivan. Since she didn't want to hurt her lifelong friend, she decided not to point out that illicit lust for that American horse trainer who'd come through Castlelough seven years ago was, in a roundabout way, responsible for Kate's marriage in the first place.

If Kate hadn't gotten pregnant, Nora doubted she ever would have married the man who'd been more enamored with the

Thoroughbred stud farm Kate and Conor had inherited from their father, Joseph Rory Fitzpatrick. The irony was that Cadel proved to have no talent at all for handling horses.

Fortunately Kate's trainer had stepped in, revealing her bridegroom's unnecessarily heavy hand with a whip. It was then Kate had sold a promising stallion to get the money to buy her husband the fishing boat he'd been working until recently.

Nora often thought how ironic — and sad — it was that a woman possessed with the gift of Sight should prove to be so blind when it came to her own life.

"It's not love," she insisted, dragging her thoughts back to the matter of her feelings for her elusive American boarder. It couldn't be. She wouldn't *let* it be.

"Would that be so bad?" Kate asked quietly, proving yet again her unnerving ability to read her best friend's mind. "Falling in love with Quinn Gallagher?"

"Yes. Because if I were to go falling in love with any man, I'd want to marry him."

"And you don't believe your American is the marrying kind?"

"No. He's not. And he's definitely not my American. And while we're on the subject of marriage —" Nora lowered her voice "— how are you and Cadel doing?"

Kate began fiddling with her cutlery. "He's upset about the Americans."

"I'm sorry." Nora could see how the invasion of Americans might remind Cadel that he'd not been the first to bed his wife. Then again, she'd always thought that the horrid man latched on to whatever excuse was handy to justify his bullying behavior.

It was Kate's turn to look away. "I think it's partly envy. They're all so rich. And brash."

"Aye, they are that," Nora agreed, thinking of the outspoken seductive way Quinn had talked to her.

For the first time in her life Nora understood what Kate Fitzpatrick had been thinking — and, more importantly, feeling — that fateful night she'd given her virginity to a stranger she'd known would be moving on in the morning.

Although Andrew Sinclair's name had never been mentioned again since Kate's decision not to write to him about her pregnancy, the man suddenly hovered in the air between them, like an unwelcome visitor who'd come to tea.

Feeling as if she were walking on eggshells, Nora reached across the table and covered her friend's hand with her own.

"You can't go on this way."

"And what would you have me do?"

Kate's eyes brightened with unshed tears. "I can't leave him, Nora. Not after what he did for me."

"Cadel had his own reasons for marrying you while you were carrying another man's child. He might not be the smartest man God ever put on this green earth, but he was surely clever enough to realize that you'd inherit the stud when your da died.

"You said at the time that you were willing to do anything to save your reputation and avoid bringing dishonor to the Fitzpatrick name. Did you ever think that none of your family would have expected such a sacrifice from you? Your reputation isn't worth your life, Kate."

"It won't ever come to that."

"And you're quite sure of that, are you?"

"Of course. I may be a foolish woman, Nora, but I've never possessed a martyr complex."

"If Conor were still alive, he'd kill Cadel for what he's done to you." Heat flashed in Nora's angry tone and in her eyes.

"It's not that bad. Sometimes when he's drinking, Cadel may get a wee bit rough, but he's never really hurt me."

"Have you already forgotten about last winter's sprained wrist?"

Kate unconsciously rubbed the wrist in

question. "I tripped over Maeve. Which is why Cadel suggested we give the dog to Rory."

"You told me at the time that Cadel had pushed you after a night of drinking," Nora countered. "Which made you trip over that poor sorrowful mess of a dog anyone can tell has been mistreated."

Kate didn't even try to argue the point. "I can't leave," she said again. "What would Jamie and Brigid do without their da?"

"Perhaps sleep a bit easier."

"Those are harsh words, Nora." Kate's chin lifted ever so slightly in a way that gave Nora the feeling there just might be a little fight left in her sister-in-law, after all. "I love my children more than life itself."

"I know you do," Nora soothed. "But did you ever think there's a chance that if you separated from Cadel, your son might not be so deathly afraid to shake a man's hand?"

Kate's complexion went as white as the sugar in the pottery bowl. "You noticed."

"Aye." Nora took a deep breath. "He's a wonderful boy, Kate. I remember the night he was born as if it were yesterday. And he was so bright and happy when he was a toddler.

"But then he seemed to lose his joyful gift of laughter. And this past year it's as if he's living under a dark threatening cloud. I hate seeing Jamie this way. I hate seeing you so unhappy."

Kate sighed heavily. Her shoulders slumped. "When it turned out that Cadel didn't have a knack for horses, I'd hoped that fishing might be his salvation. But ever since he lost his boat to those Dublin bankers, it's been difficult for him, being a man dependent on his wife's income."

"And what will it be next year? What will your husband's excuse be when he begins beating his son?"

"How can you say that? You know I'd die myself before I ever let such a thing happen!"

"And don't you realize that's exactly what may happen?"

Rather than answer, Kate looked at her watch. "Where has the time gone? If we don't get to the butchery, that old harridan Mrs. Sheehan will bolt the door and we'll have no fresh meat for dinner."

Realizing she was knocking her head against a stone wall and not wanting to get into a public argument, Nora nevertheless vowed to somehow get her sister-in-law out from under Cadel O'Sullivan's brutal thumb. Before it was too late.

CHAPTER EIGHT

A Man You Don't Meet Every Day

"I hear you have one of those movie people staying at the farm," Lena Sheehan, proprietor of Sheehan and Sons' Victualers, greeted Nora the moment she and Kate stopped into the butcher shop. "Did he bring along his own food?"

Nora blinked. "No. Why would you think he'd be doing that?" She might not be a gourmet chef, like those who were making a name for themselves in trendy Kinsale, but she'd certainly managed to feed her family for all these years without poisoning them.

"I read in a magazine about a Hollywood film star who always had his food shipped in whenever he was filming on location."

The butcher woman's pink face, which had seen too much weather over her sixty-some years, furrowed into a worried frown. Her salt-and-pepper hair was pulled in a tight bun at the nape of her thick neck.

"Well, Mr. Gallagher isn't a film star. He's a writer." And a very good one, too, Nora had discovered. After finishing Quinn's banshee novel late last night, she'd been almost afraid to turn off the bedside-table lamp. Not even Brady could have created a more terrifying tale.

"I still think they should have stayed home where they belong. Aren't the usual monster trackers bad enough?" Mrs. Sheehan asked scathingly. "Witless city folk traipsing across the fields, leaving gates open and letting the cows out to be run down. And all for what? A burning desire to see some creature that doesn't exist in the first place."

She shook her head and went on, "Wouldn't a person be more likely to have the Holy Mother herself appear in one of the hillside bogs, holding her baby boy wrapped in swaddling clothes, surrounded by the flaming tongues of the Holy Spirit, than see Castlelough's Lady of the Lake?"

Nora and Kate exchanged a look. When Kate lifted a brow, Nora had to bite her lip.

"I'd like a rasher of bacon," she said, her voice choked with the laughter that was clogging her throat. "And seven chops. Lean ones, please." Mrs. Sheehan was notorious for her parsimony; why carve away the fat when you could get customers to pay for it?

"Lean you asked for, lean you'll get,"

Dermott Sheehan said around the stem of his pipe as he came out of the back room and selected the leanest-looking chops.

Nora couldn't remember ever seeing the butcher without the briarwood pipe that added a vaguely smoked flavor to the meat bought at Sheehan's. His apron was stained with dark splashes of blood from his day's work.

"And not that I'd be pushing you ladies into anything," he added, "but we've got two nice plump stewing chickens Galen McPheran brought in from his farm. Killed them fresh just this morning, he did."

Nora beamed a smile at the man who never failed to throw in a juicy dog bone for Maeve at no extra charge. "I'll take one, thank you, Mr. Sheehan."

Her own hens were layers, none old enough at the moment to waste to the pot. Well, there was Cromwell, the nasty banty rooster, but he was too skinny to make a decent mouthful. And as mean as he was, there probably wasn't enough sugar in the county to sweeten his bitter taste.

A chicken stew would also be healthier than the pan-fried chops, which, although she'd never admit it to one of the biggest gossips in Castlelough, she'd recently cut back on serving at Dr. Flannery's suggestion.

Nora didn't truly believe the new doctor could be right about her father's increased risk of heart attack. Having married late, like so many Irish bachelors, Brady was certainly no longer a young man. But he seemed as inexhaustible as ever. And didn't everyone in the county always remark that Brady Joyce had the energy of a man half his age?

Still, Nora thought, better to be safe than sorry.

"And I'll take the other hen, thank you, Mr. Sheehan," Kate said, her cheery smile revealing neither her domestic problems nor their earlier serious conversation.

"I'm thinking of getting in some fresh pheasants for the movie folk," Mrs. Sheehan revealed as she wrapped the bacon in white waxed paper and tied it with a string. The announcement was made in a tone that Nora thought should properly have been accompanied by a blast of trumpets.

"Pheasants?" The butcher shop had always featured plain, affordable fare. The kind of cuts favored by the ordinary people of Castlelough. "Gracious. Are they even available this time of year?" Surely Mrs. Sheehan wasn't thinking of sending her husband and sons out to do a little poaching?

"They're dear," the older woman allowed.

"But I can order them from a wholesaler in Cork. Hollywood types like that fancy stuff."

"Next she'll be ordering in Russian caviar," her husband, who appeared less than thrilled by the notion, muttered darkly.

"That's not such a bad idea, Dermott." The sarcasm appeared to slide off Mrs. Sheehan like water off a swan's back. Her face lit up with an avid enthusiasm Nora, who'd first come to the butcher shop as a toddler with her mother, had never before witnessed. "Beluga is the best, isn't it, Nora?"

"I wouldn't know." Nora had never understood why any sane person would want to eat something best used for bait. If Quinn Gallagher expected to be served fish eggs at her table, he was in for a disappointment.

"Beluga," Mrs. Sheehan repeated firmly, answering her own question with a brisk nod of her gray head. "And some of that fancy pâté from France."

"Isn't pâté nothing but goose livers?" her husband pointed out. "And don't we have our own geese right here in Castlelough? Why would you want to be paying to import it?"

"Because no one's ever heard of Irish pâté. Those movie folk are going to want French." Her narrow back went as straight as the handle of a spade as she finished wrapping the chickens and handed them over the top of the counter.

"You'd be paying for nothing more than a fancy image," her husband argued.

"I won't be paying. The movie people will be the ones who pay."

"You don't even know if they like pâté," he said. "We could end up with a bucket of expensive French goose livers rotting in the freezer. And what good will that do us then?"

"We'd best be going." Nora managed to break into the argument when Mrs. Sheehan took an angry breath. She flashed her best smile as she and Kate paid for their purchases, thanked Mr. Sheehan for today's bone, then escaped the shop, leaving the couple to their bickering.

"I wonder if Mrs. Sheehan has ever smiled in her life," Kate mused as they drove back to the farm.

"Brady swears she wasn't always so sour," Nora said. "Once, when I was complaining about her, he told me a story about a summer crossroads dance, when men from all over the county stood in line to dance with the lovely young Lena McDuffy."

"Surely he was making that up!"

"Brady said she was a pretty girl. With a

laugh that always brought to mind angels."

"The dark angel, perhaps." Kate shook her head. "That sounds like another of your da's tall tales."

"I thought so myself at the time." Nora couldn't imagine the dour woman ever laughing. Let alone dancing. Lena Sheehan ran her family — including her husband — the way she ran her butcher shop. In a strict no-nonsense way that brooked no argument. "But Brady swears she was a popular girl and that Dermott was considered a lucky man to win her."

"He must have been talking about some other Lena. Can you imagine that woman ever loosening up enough to have sex?"

"Her sons are proof she must have slept with poor old Dermott on at least five occasions." The four eldest Sheehan boys worked with their parents in the Castlelough victualers and in another one the family had recently opened in Fallscarrig, on the road to Galway.

It had, of course, not mattered a whit that two of the boys had professed a desire to go to Dublin and work in the hotel business. The Sheehans had been butchers going back at least six generations, and once she'd married into the family, Lena McDuffy Sheehan had become determined not to be the first wife to let tradition fall by the wayside.

"Dolan was lucky to escape," Kate said. "I suppose he has the Church to thank for that."

Dolan, the fifth and youngest Sheehan son, had been born with a sensitive nature that had prevented him from being able to saw up a bloody carcass, let alone kill a live animal. He'd miraculously escaped his brothers' fate by joining an order of missionary priests and hadn't returned to Castlelough for more than a decade.

"I always thought Dolan made an intelligent decision," Nora agreed. "Given the choice of living beneath Lena Sheehan's iron thumb or surviving in the jungles of New Guinea, I'd certainly take my chances with cannibals any day."

Kate laughed along with Nora, the tension that had lingered between the two best friends dissolved.

"Have you ever seen anything like it?" a wide-eyed Jamie O'Sullivan asked his cousin as they stared down at the army of people who'd taken over the east bank of the lake. It was midafternoon and they'd come here straight from school after picking up Maeve.

"Never in all my life," Rory said.

"It's bigger even than the carnival that came through Castlelough last summer!" Jamie breathed.

"Aye." Rory lifted the binoculars to his eyes again and scanned the teeming crowd, looking for Quinn Gallagher.

"You're lucky, having the American staying at your house. You get to hear all about the moviemaking."

"Mr. Gallagher's hardly ever there, except to sleep." The truth was, Rory had only caught sight of him one other time after that first Sunday. It had been early in the morning, when Rory had been taking the cows out to the field before going to school. He'd seen the writer practically sneaking out of the house by the front door, as if he wanted to avoid running into the family gathered each morning in the kitchen. "I guess moviemaking is hard work."

"I guess so." Both boys fell silent, enthralled to be watching a piece of Castlelough history unfold before their very eyes. "Shall we go closer?" Jamie asked.

Rory hesitated, mindful of his mother's words not to disturb their boarder. But then again, it wasn't as if they were the only townspeople who'd come to watch the movie being filmed. The hills were covered with onlookers, including, he'd noticed with surprise, that gossipy old Mrs. Sheehan.

"I suppose there'd be no harm in that," he decided.

Ten minutes later they were sitting atop a large rock, watching as a man in a green baseball cap opened the back door of a large truck.

"It's the creature!" Jamie exclaimed as a trio of bulky laborers hired from the village unloaded a huge green fiberglass sea serpent. "Did you think it would be so large?"

It was enormous, nearly the size of three lorries. And as green as emeralds. But it was all wrong.

"It's not the Lady," Rory said with a frown. He knew that movies were only make-believe, but it bothered him that his best friend should be portrayed as being so vicious-looking. This one had a huge yellow snout, like all the dragons in the picture books he'd liked to look at when he was a little kid. "I wonder if they're going to make her spout smoke and fire?"

"Something wrong with smoke and fire?"

The deep voice, coming from behind them, made both boys jump.

"Jaysus!" Jamie exclaimed, ducking his head.

Rory didn't — couldn't — say anything. He felt the heat flooding into his face and wished *he* was at the bottom of the lake.

Maeve, obviously delighted with her new friend's arrival, pushed herself to her huge feet and stretched forward, then back. Then bounded the few feet to Quinn, tail wagging, tongue lolling.

"I — I'm sorry." Rory's apology came out on a croak. His mam was going to kill him if she found out about this! "I didn't mean to offend you, Mr. Gallagher."

"No offense taken." Quinn obligingly rubbed the huge furry head Maeve had stuck beneath his hand. "I suppose I'm just surprised. I would have expected boys your age to enjoy special effects like fire-breathing dragons and explosions."

"Will there be explosions?" Jamie asked, his enthusiasm for that idea overcoming his timidness toward Quinn.

"Toward the end, when the scientists are trying to take the Lady's baby away for their research and the soldiers set charges into the lake to distract her. The director thought it would be dramatic."

"It sounds cruel," Rory murmured.

Quinn took in the furrowed brow and saw Nora in the boy's worried face. "Life isn't always cakes and cream," he said.

"That's true, sure enough," Rory agreed glumly. Beside him, his freckled face far more serious than a small boy's should be, Jamie solemnly nodded. "But I was hoping that the movie Lady might look more like the real one."

"I suppose you've seen the real Lady?" Quinn asked with amusement. Deciding Rory must be a chip off Brady Joyce's block, he folded his arms and prepared to hear a tall fanciful Irish folktale.

"Aye." Rory lifted his chin in a way that once again reminded Quinn of the boy's mother and met Quinn's teasing gaze straight on with nary a flinch. "I have. And she doesn't look at all like your monster."

"Creature," Quinn corrected absently, remembering Nora's distinction. "So . . ." He sat down beside Rory, drew his knees up to his chest and wrapped his arms around them. The wolfhound lay down beside him with a huge sigh of pleasure. "Why don't you tell me a little about her?"

Rory paused, as if remembering his mother's admonition not to bother the American writer.

"Well, in the first place, she looks more like a sea horse than a dragon," he said warily. "But you do have the color right. Her scales are as green and shiny as emeralds."

The ice broken, he began warming to his subject. For the next twenty minutes, Rory rattled on, describing the supposedly mythical creature in amazing detail, and although it went against every logical bone in his body, Quinn began to wonder if the stories could possibly be true.

It wasn't that he didn't believe in monsters. After all, he'd certainly suffered more than his share of them. The difference between him and Rory Fitzpatrick, it seemed, was that his monsters had all worn human faces. And not one of them had possessed as benevolent a nature as the lake creature with whom Rory claimed close acquaintance.

"That's quite a story," he said when Rory finally ran down.

"It's the truth."

"I'm not disputing your word. I'm just rethinking my script."

"You'd not be taking out the explosions?" Jamie asked, openly alarmed by that prospect.

"No. I think the director would ban me from the set if I suggested getting rid of those. They work too well on the trailers."

"Trailers?" Rory echoed. "Like a traveler's caravan?"

"No, the type of trailers I'm talking about are movie previews."

"Ah," Jamie agreed shyly. "The comings. They're my favorite part."

"Sometimes mine, too," Quinn said. "And getting back to our problem with the Lady, perhaps I could make the creature a bit less vengeful."

"I don't know if that's such a good idea." Rory was plucking out handfuls of bottle green grass as he looked down at the fiberglass creature that had cost a small fortune and kept a team of special-effects artisans busy for months. "If the bad scientists are trying to take away her child, she'd probably fight back. My mam sure would."

"Mothers are like that, I suppose," Quinn murmured. Though he'd never shared such maternal devotion firsthand, he had no doubt Nora Fitzpatrick would fight like a tigress for her only son.

"My ma says she'd never let anyone hurt me, either," Jamie said somberly.

Remembering the fear Rory's cousin had displayed on Sunday morning and the bullying behavior of Cadel O'Sullivan in the pub, Quinn suspected that this was a promise Kate O'Sullivan felt she needed to make to her son. Unfortunately, he suspected, it wasn't one she'd be able to keep forever.

"As I said, mothers are like that," he repeated with more certainty than he felt. Experiencing that sinking feeling again and wanting to get off this topic that was suddenly hitting too close to home, he rubbed his hands together and said, "So, although our creature looks more like a dragon than the Lady she is, how would you boys like to get a look at her close-up?"

Needless to say, neither lad needed to be asked twice.

They stayed the rest of the afternoon, enthralled by everything. Not wanting Kate or Nora to worry, Quinn had his assistant phone both mothers, assuring them their sons were fine and he'd be bringing them home later that evening. While neither argued against the plan, the young woman reported back to Quinn that Nora Fitzpatrick had sounded less than pleased.

Rory displayed interest in every detail, asking a continual litany of questions. His cousin remained far more reserved, and once, when Quinn absently placed a hand on the O'Sullivan boy's shoulder, Jamie had frozen in obvious fear. Understanding that response all too well, rather than take his hand away, Quinn had allowed it to linger another significant moment. The next time Jamie had merely flinched. Then, as the strong male hand proved harmless, he'd relaxed. By the end of the day, he seemed almost willing to trust Quinn, and while not nearly as outspoken as his cousin, he'd begun asking his share of questions, as well.

"It's going to be a grand movie," Rory enthused as the trio drove home. It was twilight and the air was soft and still. The only sound was the light snoring coming from Maeve, asleep in the back seat.

"If it isn't, it won't be for lack of trying," Quinn said. "Unfortunately, unlike westerns or thrillers, which have clearly defined good and bad guys, horror has always been difficult to do on film."

"My mam says the things we imagine are always scarier than real things." Rory wasn't about to admit that when he'd been little, he'd made his mother check under the bed every night for monsters before he'd let her turn off the light.

"Your mother is a wise woman."

"Aye, Grandda always says she's the smartest girl in the county," Rory agreed with renewed enthusiasm. "She's pretty, too."

"She is that," Quinn agreed.

"Great-grandma Fionna says there are lots of men in Castlelough who'd give their eyeteeth to marry her."

"I don't doubt that for a minute."

"But maybe there'd be those who might not want to get married to someone who already has a son."

Hearing the obvious question behind Rory's question, Quinn slanted him a glance. "I'd say any man worth considering would find a son a bonus."

"Would that be true?" The little face brightened.

"Absolutely." Suspecting he knew where this conversation was going and wanting to head it off at the pass, Quinn decided he was going to have to be totally honest. "If I were interested in getting married, I think I'd like the idea of getting a ready-made family."

"But you're not? Interested in getting married, I mean?"

"No." Quinn's tone was friendly but firm. "I'm not."

"Oh."

When Rory fell silent and took a sudden interest in the misty fields flashing by the passenger window, Quinn felt like the lowest kind of jerk. But he also knew that holding out false hope would be even crueler.

He slowed down as a collie dashed out of a break in the hedgerow up ahead. He'd already discovered that this time of day, whenever you saw a dog, a herd of cows on their way from the pasture to the milking barn were close behind.

"My father died when I was a kid," Quinn

said into the lingering silence. He did not add that Jack Gallagher had been in prison at the time of his death, or that Quinn had practically done cartwheels when the authorities had telephoned his mother with the news. "So I know how hard it is sometimes not having a dad."

"Like for the father-and-son trek," Rory agreed glumly.

Quinn braked, allowing a boy only a bit older than Rory to pass in front of the car. He was leading a herd of white-faced black cows, while the collie ran back and forth, seeming to keep cows and boy in a close-knit bunch.

"The father-and-son trek?"

"Yes. It's put on by the school and it's for a weekend," Jamie piped up. "All the boys will be going. My da's even taking me." The uncensored joy in his expression was a distinct contrast to the shadow that had moved over Rory's young face at the subject of the upcoming trip.

"Perhaps Brady could take you, Rory?" Quinn suggested hopefully.

Damn. He wasn't going to fall into this trap. After all, hadn't he done enough, giving the kids the grand tour today? Why should he be surrogate dad to the world's fatherless boys?

"Grandda said he would. But my mam said he's getting too old for such things." Rory bit his lip and looked steadfastly out the front window. "I don't mind. I'd just as soon catch up on my chores, anyway."

Quinn wondered why none of the myriad books he'd read about Ireland while trying to research *The Lady of the Lake* had bothered to mention that the damn emerald isle was covered with quicksand. Buckets of it. Everywhere a guy stepped. Or spoke.

"When is this trek?"

"A couple of weeks from now," Jamie said. "It goes from Saturday morning to Sunday evening. We even have a dispensation from Father O'Malley to miss mass."

"Imagine that. It must be a big deal."

"It is," Jamie assured Quinn. Rory didn't say a thing.

"Does the man have to be a member of the boy's family?"

"Oh, no." Jamie shook his head. "In fact, I told Rory we could share my da, but —"

"How about me?"

"What?" That captured Rory's attention. He turned toward Quinn, his eyes filled with that same guarded hope Quinn had witnessed in Nora's during the brief stolen interlude at the lake.

"It's been a long time since I've been on a

camping trip. Sounds like fun," he said with a casualness unlikely for a man who could feel the quicksand closing in around him.

"You'd come? With me? Like a da?"

"Like a friend," Quinn corrected, wanting once more to get this essential point straight. "And sure, I'd like to come. If you'll have me."

Dark blue eyes glistened suspiciously, and for a moment, Quinn feared he was going to have to deal with a flood of tears. But apparently Rory Fitzpatrick was, like his mother, made of sterner stuff.

"Thank you, Mr. Gallagher," he said formally. Only the merest tremor in his voice hinted at suppressed emotion. "I'd very much enjoy having you come on the trek with me."

"Well, then, it's settled."

As the boys began excitedly making plans for the upcoming adventure, Quinn was surprised that he didn't find the prospect of an overnight camping trip with Nora's son all that hard.

Here there be dragons.

Oh, yes, Quinn thought with grim irony, remembering how that thought had struck momentary dread in him right before he'd entered the Shannon terminal. Dragons were indeed alive and well in Ireland. He'd just never expected one of them to have taken on the benign appearance of a freckle-face six-year-old boy.

CHAPTER NINE

Oft in the Stilly Night

The moon had risen high in the cloud-darkened sky when Nora stood outside Quinn's room, listening to the faint tap-tap-tap of computer keys that told her he was still awake and working. She knew he'd been avoiding her ever since their time at the lake, and although she found his behavior faintly vexing, she'd also been grateful that he'd stepped back from what she kept telling herself would have been a dreadful mistake.

Oh, Jesus, Mary and Joseph, Nora could almost hear her mother complaining in her head. *Isn't that all I need, a coward for a daughter?*

Although Kate might be a believer in talking with those who'd passed on, Nora had always felt her little chats with her mother were more a case of her mind simply tapping into what she knew Eleanor Joyce would probably say in any given situation.

"Shut up, Mam," she muttered now, just in case her mother truly could be listening to her. She really was in no mood for an argument tonight, imaginary or not.

After returning from the village this afternoon, her day had taken a sharp downhill slide. John had remained late at school working on some end-of-term science project, forcing her to go out to the fields and bring in the cows herself. Mary was in the throes of yet another teenage funk, and Fionna, undeterred by the threat of more violence that had been reported on the news today, was still planning her trip to Derry.

Her father, never one to be counted on to pitch in with farm work, had outdone himself, arriving home from McLaughlin's Stoneworks inordinately pleased with his new purchase: a marble headstone.

"What in the name of all the saints were you thinking?" Nora had lost her temper and shouted at him. "Spending hard-earned money for such a thing?"

"The American has provided us with a profitable little windfall," Brady had reminded her without heat. "Surely you wouldn't begrudge your poor old da a proper stone for his final resting place."

Of course she wouldn't. But that wasn't the point. Her recent conversation with the doctor concerning her father's heart made the idea of someday losing the man who'd always remained a bit of a child too painful to contemplate.

"You won't be needing a headstone for years and years," she'd insisted.

"Ah, but it makes me feel better, knowing it's taken care of," he'd responded.

It was not such an unreasonable thing. Nora knew that the Irish need to have some funds put aside for a pleasant final resting place in the church cemetery and, for those lucky enough to afford it, a proper headstone, dated back to the days of the Famine. If the admittedly lovely piece of fog gray marble etched with an ornately carved Celtic cross made Brady feel more secure, she had no right to begrudge him the purchase. Just the same, it had put a pall over an already trying day.

Then, if all that hadn't been vexing enough, when she'd finally finished up in the milking shed, she'd spotted sparks coming from behind the barn and had discovered that Celia and her best friend, Peggy Duran, had wrapped a Barbie doll in burlap, tied her to a stake and set her on fire, reenacting the martyrdom of Saint Joan.

With the acrid scent of melting plastic still in her nostrils, Nora had one more problem to deal with before she could drag herself off to bed. The business of Rory's trek.

She took another deep breath, fought the anxiety that was flapping huge wings in her stomach, then rapped on the plank door.

"It's open," the deep male voice called out. "Come on in."

Nora paused in the open doorway, her heart tumbling in a wild series of somersaults at the sight of Quinn sitting in bed — her bed, mind you! — bare to the waist. And even perhaps, she feared, beyond.

It had turned cool and wet after sundown, the spring weather predictably unpredictable. He'd lit a fire, and the light from the glowing peat made his tanned skin gleam copper.

"I'm sorry." Nora told herself she should look away, but like a starving child gazing at hand-dipped chocolates in the sweet-shop window, she couldn't. She took another deep breath meant to calm. "I don't mean to be interrupting your work."

"No problem. Just a minute." He tapped a few more keys on his laptop. "Sorry, I just wanted to save the new stuff about the Lady."

"Rory said you're changing the story." That had surprised her. But then again, everything about the American had proved a surprise from the beginning.

"Actually I'm turning her back to the way

I originally depicted her in the book."

"Oh." Since Nora still hadn't read the novel that was responsible for Quinn living beneath her roof, there was nothing she could say to that. "I should be thanking you for giving him such a wonderful day."

"It was my pleasure. He's a great kid, Nora."

"Aye. I believe so, too. Although I shouldn't be so boastful. After all, what mother doesn't think the sun rises and sets on her child?"

He laughed at that, causing her romantic heart to skip a beat. She wondered if he had any idea how appealing he was when he put aside his usual grim demeanor and allowed those little crinkly lines to fan out from his midnight eyes. His smile was surprisingly warm for a man who seemed unaccustomed to using it.

"You're too hard on yourself, Mrs. Fitzpatrick. Since it's obvious you've done a great job with the kid, you shouldn't feel the need to qualify the issue. Most women I know are better at accepting compliments."

"I've no doubt of that." She would not blush, Nora vowed firmly. No matter what the man said. Or how he looked at her. "However, I believe we've already determined that I'm not like most women of your acquaintance." His kind of woman, she tacked on mentally.

"Point taken." The smile faded, and the shutters slammed closed over his teasing dark eyes. "What can I do for you? From the lines in your forehead when you walked in, I'd suspect you didn't risk confronting me in bed just to thank me for giving your son the VIP treatment today."

"No." The way he'd folded his arms drew her gaze back to his bare California-dark chest and made it even more difficult to concentrate. Nora considered asking him if he'd put on a shirt, then realized she'd only be letting him know exactly how much he unsettled her. Which, she thought on an inner sigh, he probably already knew. "It's about the trek."

"Ah." He arched a dark brow. "Are you about to suggest you don't trust Rory with me?"

"Oh, not at all." Her first thought was shock that he'd even consider such a thing. Her second was a faint wonder why she was so certain that, despite his cautionary words to the contrary, Quinn Gallagher was, deep down inside, a good man. A man she could easily trust with her only child. "It's just that I can't be having him imposing on you in such a way."

"It's not an imposition. If you think I volunteered to take your son on a hike in order to win points with you —"

"Oh, I wouldn't be thinking that!"

"Good. Because I know how tough it can be to miss out on all that father-and-son stuff. Besides, I haven't seen that much of the country since I arrived. This will give me a chance to do some sight-seeing."

"And of course sight-seeing with eleven six- and seven-year-old boys is your lifelong dream."

She couldn't resist the pleasure she felt when she made him laugh again. Yes, Quinn Gallagher was a hard man to know. But somehow, Maeve and Rory seemed to have found the way beyond the barricades he'd erected. And, although she knew it was the most dangerous thought she'd had yet concerning her boarder, Nora wondered what it would take to send those barricades tumbling altogether.

"All right," he allowed. "If the truth be told, given a choice, I'd rather go trekking with you, since despite what I said about you not being my type, the idea of sharing a sleeping bag with you beneath the stars has its appeal.

"But don't go looking for ulterior motives, Nora. I'd never use a kid to get to his mother."

"I know you'll be thinking of me as just a backward country girl, but —"

"Ah, we're back to you accusing me of accusing you of being a *culchie*."

"Well, it's true, isn't it?" Making Quinn laugh was one thing. Nora hated the way she seemed to be a continuing source of amusement for him even when she was trying her hardest to be serious. Growing more self-conscious by the moment, she went to the window, put her hand on the cold rain-wet glass and looked out into the blackness beyond.

"I've no doubt that any number of women in America would willingly tumble into your bed without a second thought." When he didn't bother to respond to something that was so obviously true, she glanced at him over her shoulder. "But I can't escape the way I was brought up. I can't take such things casually."

"Now, why doesn't that surprise me?" When he pushed aside the quilt, Nora was both vastly relieved to discover he was wearing jeans and shaken by how the sight of that open metal button at the low-slung waist had her fingertips practically tingling with the need to touch.

In two long strides he was standing in front of her. Too close. She took a tentative step backward and realized those steady dark eyes missed nothing.

"You're right to back away." His voice was deep and low, like the rumble of distant surf. It also drew her as a silkie was inexorably drawn back to the sea. "After all, a woman like you would be crazy to get mixed up with a man like me."

"You don't know anything about me." Unnerved but determined not to show it, Nora lifted her chin.

How could he possibly know what type of woman she was, she wondered, when she didn't know herself? Ever since this man's arrival in Ireland, she'd felt as if a stranger had slipped beneath her skin and taken over her mutinous body. A stranger whose wicked thoughts alone undoubtedly shattered more commandments and church tenets than Nora had ever dreamed of breaking.

"Just as I don't know anything about you," she added.

Quinn narrowed his eyes, then reached out his hands and thrust his long fingers through her hair, splaying them at the back of her head, holding her hostage to his steady gaze. Then he moved closer, trapping her between the cool glass and the heat of his body.

"And that would be important to you," he said.

It was not a question, but Nora answered it, anyway. "Aye." The single soft word sounded frail and shaky. Once again she considered how foolishly old-fashioned and parochial she must appear to this sophisticated American. "I told you, I can't take —"

"Sex casually. I know." He continued to look down at her for a long thoughtful moment. Just when Nora's tightened nerves were on the verge of screeching like a wild banshee on a November eve's *Samhain* night, he backed away.

"It's late." His voice was gruff and distant. "I know from experience that a farm day begins ridiculously early. You'd best be getting to bed."

Any other woman might have been stung by such a curt dismissal. But Nora took heart from the realization he'd just given her a clue about his past. From the looks of him, she never would have guessed Quinn Gallagher knew anything about farming. But apparently he did.

Which meant, she thought with a burst of optimism, that perhaps the two of them had something in common, after all.

Sweet Mary, you're a hopeless romantic,

Nora Joyce Fitzpatrick, she imagined her mother's scolding tone.

Aye, Mam, I fear you're right.

Although life had taught Nora that leading with one's emotions could lead to heartbreak, such behavior had also allowed her to experience a great deal of joy, as well. Just looking at her son's face over the breakfast table every morning or gazing down at him asleep in his bed each night was enough to make her heart sing.

"Good night, Quinn." His given name, which she was using for the first time, tasted as rich and sweet as freshly churned cream.

He'd backed away, granting her easy access to the door. Before leaving, she glanced over her shoulder. "Will we be seeing you for breakfast?"

There was more than the offer of porridge and scones in her question. Nora knew it. And obviously Quinn knew it, too. She could practically see the stone barricades going up around him again.

He rubbed his night-stubbled jaw. "I can't promise anything."

Once again Nora understood they were not talking about breakfast.

"We'll leave things nice and easy, then."

Because her fingers itched to rub at the lines bracketing his tightly set mouth, because she felt an unruly need to soothe the tension from his brow, Nora gave him a smile she hoped appropriate for an inn-keeper to share with a boarder. Then she left the bedroom before she got herself into more trouble than she could handle.

Quinn couldn't sleep. His mind was tangled like the woven Celtic-knot tapestry hanging on the wall opposite the bed. He tried working on the outline for his new novel, but Nora kept intruding herself into the story.

Instead of being a dark-haired fey creature, his druidic witch possessed hair as bright as a California sunset and eyes the sparkling hue of polished emeralds. The one thing that didn't change was the way the heroine be-witched the hapless hero, casting a spell on him that drew him to her like iron filings to a magnet. And even though his fictional witch-hunter knew her to be the most dangerous woman he'd ever met, he was powerless to re-sist her charms. A feeling Quinn, unfortu-nately, could readily identify with.

Finally, sometime after midnight, needing to cool off from the sexual images writhing in the dark depths of his mind, Quinn dragged himself out of the tangled sheets, dressed and went outside.

The rain had passed on, leaving a clear night sky studded with stars glittering as icily as diamonds on black velvet. A white ring encircled a full moon that floated overhead like a ghost galleon.

He looked up at the darkened window he knew to be Nora's and told himself he was just imagining the way the lace curtains seemed to have moved ever so slightly. The damn woman had gotten beneath his skin and into his mind and he was beginning to suspect that the only way he was going to exorcize her was to take her to bed. Then, his sexual hunger satiated, he could get on with his life. As he always had in the past.

Even as he told himself that, Quinn suspected it would not be so easy. Wishing he still smoked, he was trying to decide which would be more satisfying, throttling Nora for messing with his mind this way or bedding her, when he heard the squeak of the kitchen door opening.

At first he thought it might be her. But the girl who slipped stealthily out of the house into the shadows was too tall and too slender to be Nora.

"Isn't it a bit late to be going out?" he asked.

Mary obviously hadn't noticed him. She jumped like a startled doe at the sound of his voice.

"Mr. Gallagher? Whatever are you doing out here?"

"I couldn't sleep. I guess you were having the same problem."

"Aye." He heard her sigh. A not entirely comfortable silence settled over them. "Have you been out here long?" Mary asked.

"A while." He folded his arms and leaned back against the fender of the rented Mercedes. "It's a nice night. I believe I'll stay out a bit longer," he said, answering the unspoken question he suspected she was dying to ask.

"Oh." The disappointment in her tone told him he'd guessed right.

"You know, I remember a few times, when I was growing up, when I'd sneak out of the house to meet my girlfriend," he offered casually. It was, of course, a lie. By the time he'd been Mary's age he'd been on his own, and no one had given a damn what he did or with whom.

Another sigh. "I was going to meet Jack," she admitted.

"The guy who decided to take someone else to the dance?"

"Aye." She looked away, pretending vast interest in the starry sky.

Quinn told himself he should just stay out of whatever problems Nora Fitzpatrick's

174

sister was having with her unfaithful high-school Lothario.

"You know," he heard himself saying, "it's none of my business, but if this Jack guy makes having sex a condition to dating, I'd say he's not good enough for a bright pretty girl like you."

"I'm not pretty." She dragged her hand through her hair in a gesture that was a visual echo of her sister. Then again, Quinn thought, too damn much these past days reminded him of Nora Fitzpatrick. "I'm too tall. And too thin."

"Most people consider that fashion-model material. And even if you weren't going to grow up to be a beauty like your sister — which I'm sure you will — you shouldn't feel you have to sleep with a guy to get him to like you."

"Nora is beautiful," Mary said, latching on to the wrong part of his statement. The part he'd never meant to admit out loud. "She was already the prettiest girl in the county when she married Conor. And she was barely two years older than I am now."

Quinn wasn't pleased at how much he didn't want to think about Nora having been married to some hunk athlete who looked good on a horse.

"You've plenty of time to be thinking

about marriage," he said, trying to return this already uncomfortable conversation back to the topic of celibacy. Or, at the very least, safe sex.

"That's what Nora says." This sigh was deeper than the earlier ones. "But Nora doesn't understand. She was a virgin when she married Conor."

Quinn was not the least bit surprised by that little news flash. "There's nothing wrong with saving virginity for marriage."

"Not in her time, perhaps," Mary allowed, making her sister sound far more ancient than her mid-twenties. "But things are different these days."

"Are they?" It was his turn to pretend to study the stars. Quinn stuck his hands into his pockets and rocked back on his boot heels. "I'm not so sure about that. I'd suspect boys have probably been trying to talk girls into doing things they might not be ready to do since caveman days."

It hadn't been that way in his case. He'd lost his virginity in the back of a pickup truck to the oversexed adulterous wife of one of the potato farmers he'd been sent to work for when he was fifteen.

At first he'd thought he was the luckiest kid in the entire state of Nevada. By the time his sixteenth birthday rolled around, he'd begun to feel dirty and used. He'd also been terrified of being discovered by the woman's beefy brutal redneck husband.

Other women had followed. More than he could count. But none of them had ever been virgins. Nor had any of them been as innocent as Nora.

"Jack says boys are different," Mary argued. "They have certain needs."

"Not every need has to be acted on." Hell, Quinn was living proof of that. If he'd acted on his own personal hungers, he'd be upstairs in bed with Mary's older sister right now.

"I read one of your books," she revealed. "The one about the banshee. John's right. It was very good."

"Thank you."

"And didn't the man and woman in your story make love? And they weren't married."

He heard the challenge in the question and tried to answer it honestly. "They were a lot older than you. And besides, it was just a story. Not real life."

"In real life would you still be interested in a girl if she wasn't ready to have sex with you?"

The frankness of the teenager's question surprised Quinn. But not as much as his own answer. "Absolutely." It was, he realized, thinking of Nora again, the truth.

Another silence settled over them, this one a bit more companionable. In the star-spangled stillness of the night, Quinn could practically hear the wheels turning in the teenager's head.

"I have a literature test tomorrow," Mary said finally. "It's an essay exam on *The Children of Lir*, in Gaelic, and the sisters like us to use plenty of quotations. I suppose I should be getting my sleep if I want to score well."

"That's probably an excellent idea. You'll want to keep your grades up if you plan to go to college."

"I was thinking of becoming a teacher. Like Nora was going to be before she had to leave the convent."

"Your sister was in a convent?" Somehow, when he'd been listing his daughter's numerous charms, Brady had neglected to mention that salient little fact. Quinn reminded himself that it might not be how it sounded. After all, convent schools were common in this country.

"She was going to become a nun," Mary revealed.

Hell.

"But then our mam died and Nora had to

leave the order and come home to take care of us. Then she married Conor and had Rory, and she said she was happy she hadn't taken her vows. But then Conor was killed in that riding accident."

Quinn wondered what type of bastard he could be to be jealous of a dead man. "Sounds as if she hasn't had an easy time of it," he said with a great deal more casualness than he was feeling.

"She hasn't. But it's not in Nora's nature to complain. Doesn't Gran say she's a natural-born caretaker?"

From what he'd seen, Quinn figured Fionna Joyce was right. He also reminded himself that he wasn't in the market to have anyone take care of him. He'd been doing just fine all by himself for most of his thirty-five years.

"Well, good night, Mr. Gallagher," Mary said. "And thank you."

"The name's Quinn," he reminded her. "And you don't owe me any thanks, Mary. I enjoyed our conversation."

He watched her cross the yard and slip back into the house. First Rory. And now Mary. If he wasn't careful, Quinn warned himself grimly, the damn emotional quicksand he'd stumbled into was going to close in over his head and suffocate him.

★ ★ ★

Unable to sleep a wink with thoughts of Quinn tumbling through her head like abandoned seashells in a stormy surf, Nora heard Mary slip out of her bedroom and make her way down the stairs with all the stealth of a thief in the night.

Remembering all too well how she'd stolen away to meet Devlin when she'd been Mary's age and fearful that Jack wouldn't be nearly as protective of her sister as Devlin Monohan had been of her, Nora went to the window and pulled the curtain aside, expecting to see the teenage boy who'd been causing Mary such distress.

But instead, she saw Quinn standing in the shadows. When, as if somehow sensing her presence, he glanced up at the window, Nora jumped back, realizing a moment later that with the bedroom light off, he wouldn't be able to see her.

Knowing that, and feeling free to observe him undetected, she watched as his presence obviously startled Mary. They talked for a while — about what, Nora couldn't imagine — but from time to time each seemed fascinated by the starry night sky.

Then Mary returned to the house. As she heard her sister coming back upstairs, Nora guessed that somehow Quinn had succeeded in deterring the teenager from her original romantic tryst.

And when later she looked back on this night, Nora would realize that this was the exact moment she'd fallen in love with Quinn Gallagher.

Her first instinct was to wait until tomorrow morning to confront her sister. But the usual rush to school allowed scant time for conversation of any kind, let alone the intimate kind Nora knew she and Mary should have.

Coward, she thought as she paced the floor, listening to the footfalls outside her bedroom door. A moment later she heard Mary's door close.

It would be so easy just to go to bed, pull the covers over her head and ignore the problem, but that was like an ostrich sticking its head in the sand. Nora knew that problems ignored had a way of escalating, and she hated to think that her own cowardice might put her sister at risk.

Sighing, she pulled on her quilted flannel wrapper and left the room. The few feet down the hall to Mary's door seemed like a hundred kilometers.

Mary opened the door at Nora's first light rap. Guilt rose hotly in the girl's cheeks like a sunset before a storm. "Nora?" she asked with an innocent air that was in direct contrast to the guilt in her eyes. "Is something wrong?"

"Not really," Nora said, hoping it was true. "I was just having trouble sleeping and thought I heard you up, as well. So I wondered if you might want to join me in a cup of tea."

"It's not like you to be up so late."

"True enough. Which is why I'd like some company in the kitchen. If you don't mind?" It was more order than request, and both sisters knew it.

Mary gave her another long look, then shrugged. "I suppose a cup of tea might be nice," she said with a decided lack of enthusiasm.

Neither spoke until Nora was pouring the tea into two of the everyday cups.

"So," Nora asked as she placed a basket of dark bread on the table, as well, "how are things going with the May Day celebrations?"

"All right, I suppose." Mary busied herself by adding sugar and milk to her tea. "Sister Mary Augustine says I'm under consideration to be May queen."

"Why, that's wonderful!" Nora didn't have to feign her enthusiasm at this news. She hadn't been expecting to be able to begin the conversation on such a positive note.

"It's not wonderful at all." Mary's eyes glistened with moisture. "Because if I am selected, I'll probably be the only May queen in the history of Castlelough who didn't have a date for the dance."

"I doubt that," Nora murmured, dearly hoping her sister wouldn't burst into tears before they could get to the meat of the subject.

"That's easy enough for you to say. Since you were going out with Devlin when the sisters chose you to be queen."

"Aye." Nora had to fight against the smile that threatened at the memory of dancing in Devlin's strong arms. And the kisses they'd shared after the dance. "But it's better to be without a man than to be with the *wrong* man."

Mary frowned. "Now you're speaking of Jack."

"I suppose I am." Nora dragged her hand through her hair. "I don't want to interfere in your life, Mary darlin' —"

"Then don't."

If only it were that easy, Nora thought with an inner sigh. She paused again, selecting her words with care. "I know you feel as if you're all grown-up, but —"

"I'm nearly as old as you were when you married Conor."

"I didn't realize Jack was talking marriage."

"He's not." Mary's shoulders slumped. She looked absolutely wretched. Nora would have given anything to save her sister the heartache she knew she must be suffering. "At least, he hasn't yet. But I know that if only . . ." Her words drifted off.

"You're thinking if you go to bed with him, he might become more marriage-minded."

Mary didn't answer, but her silence spoke volumes. Feeling a rush of affection for the miserable girl who was trying to feel her way over that rocky ground between the world of a child and adulthood, Nora reached out and covered her sister's hand with her own.

"I'm going to be frank. I think going to bed with Jack would be a horrible mistake. But I also realize that there's little I can do to stop you, if it's what you truly want to do. But there is one thing I'd like you to keep in mind while you're making your decision.

"When a man sincerely loves a woman, the forever-after kind of love we all hope for, the kind I wish for you, Mary, he puts her feelings before his own. He wants to protect her. And he'd never ask her to do anything she wasn't ready to do."

Another silence settled over them. Mary finished off the rest of her tea, then stared down at the bottom of her now-empty cup as if trying to read her future in the dark leaves that had settled there.

"John's offered to take me to the dance," she said at length.

Knowing how shy her studious brother was in social situations, Nora made a mental note to thank him first thing in the morning. "There're worse things than being seen in public with your older brother."

"Aye. And the girls all think he's good-looking."

"Really?"

"Denise Brennan has had a crush on him forever," Mary surprised Nora by revealing. "And Kathleen Ryan is always trying to sit next to him on the bus to school, but his head is always so buried in his stupid schoolbooks, he never notices." She sighed. "He's a terrible dancer, though."

That was one point Nora wasn't even going to try to argue. Their brother had many talents, but dancing definitely wasn't one of them.

"That shouldn't prove a problem since, once you arrive, you'll undoubtedly have all the unattached boys standing in line for the privilege. More than you would if you'd had

Jack hovering over you all night."

Feminine speculation rose in Mary's previously bleak eyes. "Jack was the jealous sort, even though he felt free enough to look at other girls."

"Like Sharon."

"Aye." Nora knew they'd turned a corner when her sister didn't burst into tears at her rival's name. "Can we afford a new dress?"

"Absolutely." Even if the income from the room rental hadn't filled the family coffers and Brady had spent a good chunk of it on a headstone, if a new dress would lift Mary from the doldrums and keep her from Jack's clutches, it was well worth it. "And shoes, as well. Foolishly impractical ones with high heels that will show off your lovely long legs."

"Quinn says that I'm model material."

"He should know. Being a man of the world and all."

"That's what I was thinking."

With the crisis seemingly over, they went back upstairs. A while later Nora heard Quinn return to his room, too.

And as the farmhouse finally settled down for the night, Nora lay alone in the dark, wondering how many glamorous long-legged supermodels her rich American boarder was personally acquainted with.

CHAPTER TEN

The Rising of the Lark

Pleasure was like a lark, singing its sweet morning song in Nora's heart when Quinn entered the kitchen the following morning.

"Well, if it isn't our mystery boarder," Fionna said, lifting her teacup in welcome. "And hadn't I just begun to think you were a figment of my imagination?"

"And a good day to you, too, Mrs. Joyce." He glanced past the lace curtains to the gray drizzle streaming down the window glass. "I decided there wasn't any point in leaving too early. Since we can't shoot until the rain stops."

Not a single soul in the room mentioned the salient fact that it had rained during the early hours nearly every morning since Quinn's arrival.

"It's a soft rain." Nora placed the steaming mug of coffee she'd brewed, just in case, in front of him. "It should clear in time for you to get in a good day's work."

"One can always hope. The director told me yesterday we're already in danger of running over budget."

He neglected to mention that Jeremy's explosion of temper had come after Quinn's suggestion that they might consider changing the looks of the creature — making it more the benevolent sea-horse Lady than the smoke-breathing dragon that had cost the studio a small fortune.

Forgoing the cream and sugar already on the table, Quinn took a drink of the black coffee and felt the welcome jolt of caffeine. "This is terrific."

"Oh, our Nora's a wonderful cook," Fionna said with a meaningful look toward her granddaughter. "You should try her scones. They're sweet enough to make a host of angels sing." She pushed an ivy-sprigged plate piled with golden-topped biscuits toward him.

"Gran," Nora warned softly.

"And isn't the man paying for two meals a day?" Fionna asked with exaggerated innocence. "He might as well be getting his money's worth, after all."

Steam burst forth in a fragrant cloud as Quinn cut the top off the currant-studded scone. One bite was all it took to convince him that, matchmaking aside, Fionna wasn't exaggerating her granddaughter's culinary talents.

"Delicious."

"And didn't I tell you?" Fionna nodded her head.

Feeling the now-familiar matchmaking noose tighten ever so slightly around his neck, Quinn turned toward John, who was seated across the table, nose buried in a thick textbook.

"That doesn't exactly look like light reading."

Serious blue eyes lifted from the pages. "It's advanced biology. We're having a test today on the skeletal system. It's in preparation for our Leaving Examination."

"Our John's the top student in the class," Celia informed Quinn with the pride of an adoring younger sister. "When one of the barn cats died last winter during a snow, he wired its skeleton together. After boiling the flesh off the bones first of course. Brother James, who's taught the sciences practically forever, said it was the best senior project he's ever seen."

"Certainly the least acceptable to discuss at breakfast," Fionna warned sharply.

"The university admissions committee was also very impressed," Nora said as she refilled Quinn's cup. Obviously Celia was not the only proud sister in the family.

"So, you'll be headed off to college in the fall?"

"Yes, sir. Trinity."

"There was a time when a Catholic boy wouldn't have been allowed to walk those hallowed Protestant halls," Fionna said huffily before taking a long drink of bark brown tea.

Quinn saw John stiffen, then watched Nora lay a calming hand on her brother's shoulder. "Times change," she said mildly.

"And isn't the university at Galway good enough?"

"It's a fine university, Gran." John's tone remained measured. Respectful. And definitely at odds with the frustration in his eyes. "But Trinity's medical school is one of the best in the world."

"You want to be a doctor?" Quinn asked.

"I *intend* to be a doctor," John corrected politely, but firmly. He stood up. "I'd best be getting down to the crossroads before I miss the bus."

"You haven't eaten," Nora said worriedly.

"I'll take a scone with me." He grabbed one from the plate. "Wish me luck."

As Nora reached up and brushed a shock of dark hair from his forehead, Quinn caught the pair's familial resemblance. "You don't need luck," she said fondly to her brother. "But I'll be wishing it, anyway. Since you asked."

Watching the grin brighten the usually serious thin face, Quinn was impressed by the way she'd soothed the teenager's rising frustration with merely a touch. Even the obviously strong-minded Fionna appeared to acquiesce to Nora. He understood that while she may no longer carry the Joyce name, Nora Fitzpatrick was the heart of this family. Which was, of course, one more reason to keep his distance.

His relationships with women had always remained uncomplicated, based mostly on sex, with mutual respect and sometimes, as with Laura, even a bit of humor thrown in. But never had they involved more than the two people who found enjoyment, if only for a brief time, in bed together.

Nora Fitzpatrick, Quinn warned himself, came with more baggage than he cared to deal with. From what he'd been able to tell during his brief time in Castlelough, her life was just one big complication after another.

Celia pulled on a tomato-hued slicker and followed her brother out the door. Quinn heard the clatter of shoes on the stairs, and a moment later Mary rushed through the kitchen, calling out a goodbye as she grabbed up a slicker and umbrella from the row of hooks by the door. For a girl who'd been considering surrendering her virginity only a few hours earlier, she looked remarkably prim and conservative in her schoolgirl uniform — starched white blouse and plaid skirt.

Quinn watched as she joined the others, including Rory, who'd run from the barn, the hood of his jacket flapping down around his shoulders. When Mary bent to tug the hood up, tying the cord beneath his chin, Quinn found himself wishing he had a camera so he could freeze the Hallmark-commercial family scene he'd never believed in on film.

"Would you be liking some bacon and eggs, Mr. Gallagher?"

Last night, alone in his room, she'd called him Quinn. Now apparently they were back to formalities. "Thanks, but the scones are fine."

"If you're certain."

"Positive." She'd gotten that now-familiar concerned look in her eyes again. Quinn wasn't accustomed to anyone taking care of him and wasn't sure he liked the idea. "Your brother's a bit on the serious side."

She sighed, poured herself a cup of tea, stirred in some sugar and, as if deciding to abandon her role of innkeeper, sat down in the abandoned chair across the table from him.

"He wasn't when he was a child. Of all of us, John was probably the most like our father. But our mother's death changed him."

"Death changes a lot of things." Quinn's mother's death had sure as hell changed his life. Which hadn't been any great shakes before Angie had been murdered by a violent man she'd made the mistake of bringing home from a honky-tonk one fatal night, he reminded himself grimly.

"Doesn't it just," she agreed, making Quinn think about what Mary had told him about Nora giving up the convent life to return to Castlelough to take care of her family.

They fell silent. Lost in their own thoughts, neither noticed Fionna leave the kitchen, a satisfied smile on her face.

Quinn could have stayed in the cozy kitchen with Nora all day. Which, of course, made it imperative that he leave. He was almost to his rented Mercedes when the kitchen door opened and Nora dashed out into the rain that had, as she'd predicted, softened to mist.

"I thought you might be liking some biscuits for your afternoon tea," she said, holding the brown paper bag toward him. "Or, as you Americans say, cookies. I hope you like oatmeal raisin."

"Who doesn't?" Never, in his entire life, had a woman ever baked him cookies.

"They're Rory's favorite. And Celia's, as well." She hesitated. "Mary prefers chocolate."

"I've found most women do. Not that she's quite a woman yet, but —"

"No," Nora interrupted on a little rush of breath. "And I believe I may have you to thank for that."

So she *had* been watching him last night. "It wasn't that big a deal."

"Perhaps not to you. But it would have been to Mary if she'd gotten herself pregnant."

"It takes two," Quinn reminded her.

"Aye. And I worry that Jack's far too willing to do his part." Her eyes momentarily darkened with that professed worry. Fascinated by the way her face revealed her every thought, Quinn watched the clouds of concern get chased away by the sunny warmth of her smile.

"Someday, hopefully a very long time from now, when she does make love with a husband who adores her, she may look back on last night and remember another man who cared enough to take the time to talk to a confused young girl."

Appearing to act on impulse, she went up on her toes, intending to brush his cheek with a quick kiss. But Quinn proved faster, turning his head and capturing her mouth.

Oh, Lord! The taste of her was as potent as Irish whiskey, slamming into him like a fist in the gut, then hitting his bloodstream with a force that sent his head reeling and nearly buckled his knees.

He tangled one hand in her hair while the other skimmed down her back, cupped her bottom, clad again in those snug blue jeans, and lifted her off her feet.

As he deepened the kiss, Quinn heard a faint ragged moan and wondered if it had escaped her throat or his; he felt trembling and wasn't certain which of them it was. It had to be her, he told himself as he nipped at her satiny lower lip and drew a sound remarkably like a purr.

Women had made him ache; they'd made him burn. But no woman had ever made his body pulse and vibrate with a need so strong it made him feel as weak and powerless as the "before" guys in those bodybuilding ads in the back of the comic books he'd filched when he was a kid.

Her hands were in his hair. Beneath the

onslaught of his mouth her lips opened like pink rosebuds to the sun. Her breasts were crushed against his chest so tightly there was no way a single raindrop could slip between them.

Quinn couldn't think. Could barely breathe. When he realized he was actually considering ripping the car door open and taking her on the leather seat, where anyone — her father, her grandmother, a passing neighbor — could see them, he knew it was time to back away.

He lowered her feet to the ground, but unwilling to release her just yet, skimmed his mouth up her cheek. "You taste like rain."

"So do you." She sounded every bit as shell-shocked as Quinn felt.

"Perhaps. But I'll bet it tastes better on you." When he touched his tongue to the slight hollow between her bottom lip and chin, she sighed with ragged pleasure, then closed her eyes and tilted her head back, offering her throat.

Quinn willingly obliged, nipping lightly, seductively, at the pale flesh. "Another minute of that and we would have been the ones in need of a safe-sex lecture."

Her answer was somewhere between a laugh and a sob. "I don't understand any of this."

She needn't have said the words. As soon as she'd opened her eyes again, he'd read the confusion — along with a lingering unwilling desire — in those swirling sea green depths.

"That makes two of us." Because he still wanted her, dammit, still needed her, he took his hands off the body he'd dreamed of claiming and bent down to retrieve the brown paper bag that had fallen unnoticed to the ground at their feet.

"There'll be nothing left but crumbs," she said.

She was nearly right. He dipped into the bag, pulled out a decent-size piece and popped it into his mouth.

"Best crumbs I've ever tasted." Knowing he was playing with fire, but unable to resist, he traced her lips with a fingertip. "Almost as sweet as the taste of the cook."

His words earned the intended smile. "I do believe you've been kissing the Blarney Stone, Quinn."

"The only thing in Ireland I want to kiss is you, Nora. Again and again." He skimmed a glance over her. "All over."

Her expressive eyes turned somber again. "You don't sound very pleased about that."

"You're right." His finger glided down the slender throat he'd tasted earlier. Quinn felt the little leap in pulse beneath his touch, experienced a similar leap himself, then continued tracing her collarbone out to her shoulder. "Having always prided myself on my control, I'm not wild about the way something I've worked so hard to develop could disintegrate the way it does whenever you get within kissing distance."

"I feel the same way. Which, I have to confess, worries me. Since I have Rory to think of," she reminded him. And herself.

"There's no reason he should enter into it. We're two adults, Nora. If anything were to happen between us, it wouldn't have any effect on your son."

"But don't you see?" She dragged her hand through her hair. "If I get involved with you —"

"Don't look now, lady, but it's too damn late. Because whether we like it or not, whether we planned it or not, we are involved."

"Aye. I'm afraid you're right." She sighed. "Which confuses me, because I'm not accustomed to responding so recklessly to a man."

She was so damn earnest. So sweet. God help him, he was beginning to actually like her. The idea of relating to a woman on some basis other than sex was something

Quinn was going to have to think about. After he got away from here and his blood cooled and his head cleared.

"That's the idea," he said, flashing her another of the rare grins that seemed to please her so. "I expect women to throw themselves at me. It's this uncharacteristic urge I keep having to grovel whenever I'm alone with you that's got me feeling on edge."

Nora laughed. "I can't imagine you ever groveling."

"Join the club, darlin'. Because I couldn't imagine it, either — until I came to Castlelough and met you." Wondering when he'd become addicted to self-torture, he lightly touched his lips to hers again and watched her eyes go opaque.

"I'll see you this evening," he said after he'd ended the brief kiss all too soon.

"You'll be home for supper, then?"

Home. He was no longer that young boy for whom the four-letter word defined fear and pain. He was no longer the wild rebellious teenager who'd discovered that the happy homes depicted on television programs were nothing but a cruel Hollywood myth. It was only a damn word; there was no reason for him to suddenly feel as if he were suffocating.

"It depends." Because he needed space to

breathe, to think, he jerked open the driver's door. "What were you thinking of fixing?"

"Leg of lamb." There was no way Nora would admit she'd been thinking more along the lines of veal stew when she'd first gotten up this morning. It had been five years since she'd looked forward to cooking for any man other than her father and brothers. Which made this an occasion worth celebrating.

He climbed into the car and put the bag of oatmeal-raisin cookie crumbs on the passenger seat beside him. "You damn well don't fight fair, Mrs. Fitzpatrick."

She laughed again, feeling unreasonably young and lighthearted. She felt, Nora realized, almost as giddy as dear reckless Mary behaved whenever that troublesome handsome-as-sin Jack came calling.

"Neither do you, Mr. Gallagher." She touched a finger to her lips and imagined she could still taste his stunning kiss.

She watched his eyes darken as his gaze settled on her thoroughly ravished mouth and knew he truly hadn't been lying when he'd admitted he was as drawn to her as she was to him.

It was, Nora considered, a start. Of what, she didn't know. But having grown up on a farm, where so much depended on the whims of Mother Nature, and having learned the hard way the futility of controlling her life, she was far more willing than Quinn to go along with the flow.

She stood in the driveway, oblivious to the light rain as she watched the silver car drive away. She thought about dinner as she finally returned to the house. A cobbler would be nice. Perhaps topped with ice cream. She remembered Sheila Monohan mentioning last summer that the visiting American tourists did so like their ice cream.

She'd have to make a trip into town. As she went upstairs to change into dry clothes, Nora uncharacteristically decided to splurge on one of those pretty bottles of cologne she'd seen in the front window of Monohan's Mercantile.

Later that afternoon, her trip to the village and shopping completed, a bottle of ridiculously expensive French perfume safely wrapped in white tissue paper and tucked away in a pink-and-green-flowered shopping bag, she drove to Kate's. Now she was leaning against the open half door of Emerald Dancer's box, watching her sister-in-law groom the mare.

"So which of the two of you don't you

understand?" Kate asked, after listening to Nora's halting admission that she was confused about her budding relationship with Quinn. She was giving the horse a sponge bath from a bucket of water. "Your Yank novelist? Or yourself?"

"Both," Nora decided after a moment's thought. "I've never felt this way before."

"And how's that?"

"Confused. Conflicted. Anxious."

The mare, who'd supposedly been responsible for Kate's broken collarbone last year, stretched her head out, blew gently and bussed Nora's cheek, as if offering sympathy. Despite her distress, Nora smiled and rubbed the horse's seal brown muzzle.

"Sounds like love to me," Kate diagnosed as she wrung out the sponge then took out a pick and began cleaning the horse's hooves.

"Oh, it can't be! Surely I'd recognize love."

"You've only been in love twice in your life," Kate reminded her. "That doesn't exactly make you an expert on the subject."

"I know I loved Devlin with all my heart. As much as a young girl can love," Nora qualified. It had also been an easy love. Growing as naturally as the wildflowers in springtime.

"And Conor?"

"Swept me away," Nora answered

promptly. When she scratched Emerald Dancer behind the ear, the mare rolled her liquid brown eyes with pleasure. "I literally adored him."

"My brother was certainly dashing enough," Kate allowed. "But I think it was more a case of the way he took your mind off your troubles than true love."

A lot had indeed happened then, what with poor little Celia being born, her mam dying, Nora having to leave the security of the convent. And just when she'd been at the lowest point of her young life, Conor had come riding his big white horse across the fields, looking for all the world like one of those storybook knights in shining armor. Nora couldn't have resisted him if she'd tried. Which she hadn't.

"I'm not certain I was capable of coherent thought during that time."

"And isn't that exactly my point?" Kate swore as she scratched her finger on a nail. "Conor treated you like some fancy porcelain doll to be put on the shelf."

"That's not true!" Uneasy talking about her husband while thoughts of Quinn were making her feel vaguely unfaithful, Nora began to pace in front of the stall door. "If anything, Conor complained I wasn't fancy enough for his fast city friends."

"So perhaps I used the wrong description. My point is, though, that you and my brother fell in love at a time when you were in a vulnerable needy state. He never treated you like an adult woman."

That stung. Partly, Nora admitted secretly, because it was so close to the truth. She'd always felt inferior to the dashing experienced Conor Fitzpatrick. For the first time in her life, she was forced to seriously consider that her husband might have manipulated her insecurities to his own advantage.

"And would you be saying that my husband shared every intimate aspect of our private lives with you?"

Nora hated the idea of Kate knowing about their arguments. And the making up afterward. Something that had occurred less and less after Rory's birth.

"Of course not." Kate moved on to another hoof. Watching the mare obediently lift her front leg for grooming, Nora knew there was no way this sweet-tempered animal had ever thrown its rider. Especially one as experienced as Kate. In a land known for Thoroughbred breeding, she'd never seen anyone with such a talent for understanding horses as her sister-in-law.

"But I have eyes, Nora," Kate continued.

"I could see that Conor always thought of you as the child that had surprised him by growing up while he was away riding his bloody horse all over the continent. But he didn't want you to be too grown-up. Because then he'd risk losing his power over you."

"Why are we talking about my deceased husband?" Nora asked. Having told herself for the past five years that her volatile marriage would have worked — she would have made it work — she wasn't comfortable examining it under a microscope now. Especially since such examination would prove fruitless. "The problem is Quinn Gallagher," she reminded her sister-in-law.

"And how he makes you feel."

"Aye." Nora sighed. "It's bad enough that I don't understand what I'm feeling. The man is an expert at hiding his emotions, Kate." Unlike Conor, who'd always been remarkably vocal about his likes and dislikes. "I can't get behind that wall he's built around himself." Nor read his thoughts in those coffee-dark eyes.

"That's simple. If you want to understand Quinn Gallagher, all you have to do is read his books."

"I read the banshee story."

"And?" Emerald Dancer's hooves polished, Kate began smoothing tangles out of the glossy black tail.

"And it scared me half out of my wits." Enough so that she honestly hadn't wanted to subject herself to another of his novels.

"You obviously just skimmed the surface. You need to reread the book, Nora, and realize what it's really about."

"What's to realize? It's a tale about a young boy who ignores the advice passed down from his elders and looks into the face of a banshee, who, just as the legend predicts, attacks him and leaves him permanently scarred."

It was a popular folk story. Didn't Brady tell it himself? But somehow Quinn had managed to strike a dark dread deep into Nora's very core, leaving her feeling unsettled.

"Exactly." Kate nodded her satisfaction as she switched ends and began pulling the comb through the animal's long silky mane. "The scar's the key, of course."

"Surely you're not suggesting that the scar on Quinn's cheek comes from a midnight meeting with a banshee?"

"Of course I'm not. Jaysus, you can be so literal, Nora. If you'd paid more attention during literature lectures, instead of memorizing all those prayers and quotations that won you honors and holy cards in religious class, you'd understand that the scar on the boy's face in the story is obviously a metaphor for the damage done to his heart. And perhaps his psyche."

Nora thought about that for a moment and decided that as improbable as it had first sounded, Kate was maybe on to something. "The article in the *Independent* said his mother had died tragically when he was young. Do you think it's possible —"

"That he witnessed her death?" Kate broke in. "I'd say, given the tone of his later books, which all deal in some edgy way with the subject of parents and children, that it's highly likely.

"A young boy saw something he shouldn't. Something beyond the pale. And it left him scarred for life."

Kate nodded, apparently satisfied by her thumbnail psychological profile. "If you want to understand your inscrutable American, Nora, all you have to do is read his books," she repeated.

"If you're right about Quinn's past," Nora mused, "then perhaps I'd be wise to keep my distance. Perhaps whatever happened to him is too terrible to allow him to ever be able to open up to a woman." To open up to *her*, Nora thought. To trust *her*.

Kate paused while gathering up the grooming equipment and slanted her a knowing look. "You know the old saying — Love heals all wounds."

"How can I begin to know if I love him? When I don't know who he is?"

"I told you —"

"I know." Nora blew out a frustrated breath, ruffling her tawny bangs. "Read his books."

"I'd not be knowing how a writer's mind works," Kate admitted. "But if it's true that a novelist writes about what he knows, then Quinn Gallagher has obviously experienced more than his share of monsters."

"Then the man who wrote *The Night of the Banshee* definitely isn't one to settle down with a wife and ready-made family," Nora said, conveniently overlooking the fact that her relationship with Quinn Gallagher, such as it was, hadn't even neared the point of either of them making a commitment.

"True enough. But mind you, that was his first published book," Kate pointed out. "And although he might not have realized it himself yet, the man who wrote *The Lady of the Lake*, a story about the ultimately fatal sacrifice a mother — even an inhuman one covered with green scales who lurks at the bottom of a rural Irish lake — is willing to make to save her child, is literally starving for the love of family."

And here, from John's description, Nora had thought it merely another gory monster tale to be read with the lights on. "Perhaps I should read it."

Kate grinned. "And isn't that just what I've been saying?"

CHAPTER ELEVEN

The Vacant Chair

The Irish Rose was packed to the rafters. Some of the drinkers — like Brady and his friend Fergus — were regulars, some were members of the film crew, looking for a congenial place to pass the evening after a long day of work, and still others appeared to be locals drawn to the pub in hopes of mingling with the rich and famous.

Although Quinn had already observed the Irish to be less likely to fawn over fame, he'd nevertheless signed several paper napkins and even a few books, which the owners, upon finding him in The Rose, had returned home to fetch.

It was getting late and Quinn knew that Nora would be putting dinner on the table soon. Just the thought of what the woman could undoubtedly do with a tender leg of Irish lamb was enough to make his mouth water. Although he'd taught himself to cook, Quinn was more accustomed to nuking a frozen dinner in the microwave every night.

Which made Nora's culinary inducement nearly impossible to resist.

But he continued to sit in this noisy bar with the ceiling lowered nearly a foot by the cloud of blue-gray smoke, listening to Brady spin tale after entertaining tale, because it wasn't merely the promised meal that was proving to be such a siren's call.

What he wanted, Quinn realized, as he picked at a basket of chips with scant interest, was to sit down at the old pine table with Nora and tell her about the hellish day he'd had. A day when neither Laura or her costar, Dylan Harrison, had been able to make their way through a single scene without at least a dozen retakes. A day when the on-and-off again drizzle disrupted shooting, causing an already testy Jeremy Converse to turn downright dictatorial. Which, needless to say, only made the actors more tense and the camera crew screw up the few scenes Laura and Dylan didn't blow.

And then there'd been the problem with the mechanical creature. Some malfunction was causing the Lady to emit a deep humming noise, which might have worked if she'd been a llama. But the tuneless drone tended to take away from her ferociousness when the time came for her to fight back, to protect her infant from the treacherous scientists.

Quinn wanted to tell Nora all this. And then, after she'd displayed the proper sympathy — which he knew he could expect from such a warmhearted woman — he wanted to hear all about her day.

Although he realized that he had no idea how she actually spent the hours he was away from the farm, the images that came to mind were seductively domestic. He pictured her kneading bread dough, imagined her feeding the red chickens their cracked corn and tending to the cows, like some rosy-cheeked milkmaid from an old painting. He wanted to bathe in the soothing warmth of her smile as she returned from gathering wildflowers in the meadow, wanted to kiss her inviting lips and feel the cares of his day melt away.

If it were only that simple, Quinn figured he could still deal with it. He didn't need a novelist's gift for characterization to know that Nora was the quintessential earth mother, so different from his own mother that the two women could have been born on different planets. So it was only natural for him to be drawn to her, he kept telling himself.

But, dammit, there was more. He also wanted to hear that John had aced his science exam; he wanted to find out how Mary had done on her Gaelic test and whether the foolish Jack had come to his senses and realized the pretty teenage girl's true worth. He wanted Rory to tell him more about the Lady, he wanted to look down into Celia's young face, surrounded by that wild cloud of fiery hair and wonder if Nora had looked like that when she was a little girl.

And, God help him, he was even willing to put up with more of Fionna's sly matchmaking.

And because he wanted all that — so much it terrified him all the way to the bone — Quinn was determined to stay away from the farm tonight.

Brady had launched into an old folktale about a beautiful Irish maiden kidnapped by a Norman king. He was a natural orator; his lilting rhythm, timing, phrasing, extravagant gestures, as he related his tales of battles, courtships, tragedies, saints, hermits, fairies and magic, all harkened back to the ancient days when the ability to spin a tale earned a man property, privilege and a seat at the table with the king.

The recital of the king's attack of lust when he'd first caught sight of the young woman while riding through the countryside reminded Quinn of his own reaction to Nora.

He liked looking at her. What man wouldn't? He wanted her. Again, what man with blood stirring in his veins wouldn't? He wanted to make love — have sex, he corrected swiftly — with her all night long. So what?

That only proved he was a normal healthy male.

Unfortunately everything about the lissome widow Fitzpatrick defined permanency, while his life was anything but. There was, after all, certainly nothing permanent about sex. Nothing constant about his career, which right now was burning as bright and hot as a star. But Quinn understood all too well how stars could explode and turn themselves into black holes. Even his house on the Monterey coast was leased, with a thirty-day out clause that allowed him to pull up stakes anytime he wanted.

It wouldn't be difficult to win Nora's warm and generous heart. She'd already let him know, in so many ways, that it could be his for the taking. But didn't she understand that when he left Ireland — and her — he'd be handing it back to her in tatters?

Of course she didn't, Quinn decided. Because, although the necessity of running a farm and keeping her family on the straight and narrow required her to be practical, the fact remained that the woman was a starry-eyed romantic to the core.

That idea reminded him of something Laura had said to him in the airport. Something about their being two of a kind. Not expecting happily-ever-afters. Realizing he'd just found the perfect hideout, Quinn downed the last of this latest Guinness and left the bar, then headed the two blocks down the street to the Flannery House Hotel.

"Well, well." Laura's smile, as she opened the door to him, reminded Quinn of a cat who'd just caught sight of a dish of cream. "This is a surprise."

"I was in the neighborhood and thought I'd drop in." Belatedly realizing that she was dressed — just barely — for bed, he glanced in the direction of the closed bedroom door. "If I'm interrupting anything . . ."

"Don't be an idiot." She took hold of his arm and urged him expertly across the threshold. The fingernails on his sleeve were uncharacteristically unpainted, as her role of Shannon McGuire demanded. Like too much else these days, they reminded him of Nora's. "I just got out of the tub and was thinking of going to bed with a good book." Her eyes handed him a gilt-edged invitation. "I'd much rather go to bed with a good man. Or even better, a bad one."

Quinn stopped midway across the living room. "Do you have a minibar in here?"

"Of course." She eyed him with what appeared to be actual concern. "Are you sure you want anything else to drink?"

"I don't recall hearing your joining the temperance police." His tone warned her to back off.

"Darling, you know I've never been a fan of temperance in anything." She lifted a hand to his cheek, in much the same way Nora had at the lake, but surprisingly, Laura's touch stirred not a single need to touch in return. "I just didn't want you to be disappointed."

"You've never disappointed me, Laura."

"Well, of course I haven't." Blond waves that had spent most of the day covered by an auburn wig bounced as she shook her head. "I'm merely concerned that if you add any more alcohol to your bloodstream, you might have difficulty . . . well, you know . . ."

"Performing?"

"Exactly." Her smile reminded him of the gold stars his third-grade teacher in San Antonio used to put on his spelling papers.

"You've never had any complaints before."

"You've never shown up at my door three sheets to the wind before."

True enough. Back home, in what Quinn had come to consider his "real life," the most he ever drank was an occasional beer or glass of wine with dinner.

"Why don't you let me worry about my performance level?" His tone was mild, but his eyes had hardened to obsidian.

"Whatever you say, darling." Knowing him well enough not to push, Laura flashed the quick smile he'd come to recognize as her professional one.

She opened the bar with a small brass key and bent over it in a way that lifted the hem of her robe to the top of her thighs, just high enough to assure him she wasn't wearing anything underneath the ivory silk.

"We seem to have Guinness, Harp, a selection of Irish whiskeys —"

"Any scotch?" Since his troubles had all begun when he'd landed on this damn green island, Quinn was determined that the rest of the night be a reprieve from everything Irish.

"Let me see." She skimmed a finger over the miniature bottles. "No. But there's some gin."

Quinn hated gin. It was what his mother had always drunk, and even after all these years the smell of juniper berries could make his stomach heave. "That'll do."

When he experienced more anticipation watching her pour the clear liquor into a glass than he did the provocative sight of silk-draped breasts, Quinn knew he was in deep trouble.

After a bit more consideration, she settled on Baileys Irish Cream for herself. Then she crossed the room again with her long-legged stride and settled down beside him on the sofa.

"To old friends." She handed him the glass of gin and lifted her own. "And good times."

"I'll drink to that." He downed the gin in long thirsty swallows like a bitter-tasting medicine, enjoying the burn.

"Gracious. Aren't *we* in a hurry?" She circled the crystal rim of her glass with the tip of her finger. "I do hope that's not a precursor of things to come."

"I told you." Quinn stood up and went over to the bar, pulling out the first bottle within reach. "Why don't you let me worry about that?"

"Well, aren't you the old grouch tonight." She put her drink down on the coffee table and rose in a smooth lithe movement. "What's got into you, sweetheart?"

"I don't know what you're talking about."

The only reason he didn't complain when she took the bottle of Power whiskey from his hand was that he didn't want her to know how desperate he was for the mind-dulling effects of the alcohol.

"I'll bet you're just horny." She looped one arm around his neck and deftly slipped the palm of the other between them, caressing his groin in a way that caused his body to respond exactly as she intended. "I was thinking about you while I was in my bath."

Her voice turned throaty as she looked directly into his eyes. "While I was running the sponge over my breasts, I kept remembering the way you love to lick your way from tip to tip. And when I was washing my legs, I thought about that first time, when we went to that party at Jeremy's house in Bel Air and you dragged me into the bathroom, told me to wrap my legs around your waist and took me right there against the marble sink."

"I was crazy that night." Crazy with lust.

"You were wonderful." Her fingers squeezed his growing erection with a practiced expertise. "I nearly came just thinking about it." Her mouth touched his, warm and oh so willing. "Thank goodness I didn't give in to impulse and start without you."

The kiss was wet and deep and involved a great deal of the tongue action Laura was so good at. The familiar taste, tinged with the sweet Irish Cream, created a curl of lust that sent the blood rushing from his head to other more vital organs.

A very strong part of Quinn — a throbbing primal male part — wanted Laura. Even as he told himself he owed Nora nothing, he knew that to take what the sexy actress was offering would only leave him feeling guilty afterward.

He took his hands from where they seemed to have landed on her hips and captured both of hers. "I can't do this."

"Of course you can, darling." Her smile echoed the feline purr of her voice. "You're doing rather well, so far."

"It's not that." Calling himself every kind of fool, he eased a little away from her. "You know you've always been able to turn me on —"

"Believe me, Quinn, the feeling's mutual."

How the hell was he going to explain the unexplainable? Especially to this woman with the seemingly one-track mind.

"You're going to think I'm nuts."

She surprised him by laughing at that. "Of course you are. That's one of the things I've always liked about you. Most of us run away from our monsters, Quinn. You embrace them, make them part of you, until it's difficult to tell where you stop and they begin. It gives you an edgy dangerous quality not many women can resist."

Quinn had a choice. He could deny her unflattering accusation. Or, since he'd already decided he wasn't going to sleep with her, he could at least acknowledge that there was some truth to her words.

"I never would have suspected you of being a student of human nature."

"A slick shallow woman — an actress — such as myself?" she asked with a careless toss of her blond head.

"I didn't mean —"

"Of course you did. And believe me, you're not the first male to only take the time to look at the surface glitz. But you see, darling —" she slipped a hand free of his and trailed it down his cheek "— that's precisely the point. You're also not the only person in the world who prefers keeping private things exactly that. Private."

It was yet another surprise in a week full of surprises. "And here I always thought I was good at characterization."

"You are. But the one thing you overlooked is that I'm a much better actress than people give me credit for."

And apparently, he thought, a much deeper person. "Hell." Quinn turned away and picked up the bottle of Powers again. He needed a drink and he needed it now. "Now I feel as if I'm just some creep who's been using you."

"Well, of course you have." She plucked the bottle from his hand once more. "You'll thank me in the morning for this," she assured him before returning to the original topic. "We've always used each other." Her sigh caused her breasts to rise and fall in a way that had Quinn telling himself he had to be either a lunatic or a fool to turn down what this woman was offering. "Now I'm afraid we won't be able to do that anymore."

"Why not?"

"Because it's not our little sex game anymore, silly," she said with the trademark pout the cameras — and her legion of male fans — adored. "I have this horrible feeling I'm about to do something really stupid."

"What's that?" Quinn figured that after tonight *he* probably owned the world title for stupid human tricks.

"I'm going to tell you how to seduce your little Irish farmer's daughter."

"What?" Quinn stared at her. "How the hell . . ."

"It's common knowledge, darling. Ever

since you went out of your way to practically adopt the woman's son."

"I don't believe this!" He raked a hand through his hair. "The kid's into sea creatures, like a lot of those dinosaur-loving kids that made *Jurassic Park* such a hit. So I let him hang around while we shot some of the Lady scenes. What's the big deal?"

"How about the fact that you're going on a father-and-son trek with him?"

Damn. Quinn decided he'd have to kill Jeremy Converse. All he'd done was inform the director he was going to be away for a weekend, and the next thing he knew, his life was fodder for location gossip. Hell, next he'd find himself on the front page of the damn tabloids. Undoubtedly with a photo of the mechanical monster accompanying a headline that the Lady of the Lake was pregnant with his love-creature.

"It's just a camping trip," he grumbled. The Guinness buzz was beginning to wear off, the gin had made his stomach roil and he could feel the distant twinges of a hangover beginning to build like a thunderhead behind his eyes.

"Well, I for one think it's very sweet of you. But if you think sleeping on the wet ground with a bunch of first-graders is going to get you an invitation into the boy's mother's bed, you've miscalculated."

"I didn't volunteer to go on any bloody trek to seduce anyone's mother, dammit!" It was the same thing he'd told Nora. It was also the truth.

"You've no idea how relieved I am to hear that, Quinn. Because I'd really begun to fear you were slipping." She returned the miniature bottle of liquor to the bar, closed the door and locked it, slipping the key into the pocket of her robe for safekeeping.

"Nora Fitzpatrick might be different from the women you're used to. But believe me, darling, there's not a female in the world who can resist the Prince Charming treatment."

"Prince Charming?" He had to laugh at that. The one thing no one had ever called him was charming.

"I'm talking grand romantic gestures."

"Aw, Christ . . ."

"Don't scoff. They work. The problem with you is that sex has always come so easily you've never had to work at it like a normal guy. Since you're a screenwriter these days, it shouldn't be that big a leap to think of Bogie and Bacall. Bogie and Bergman. Bogie and Hepburn —"

"Don't look now, sweetheart, but you seem to be stuck in a rut."

"I happen to think Bogart was the sexiest man God ever plunked down on the planet. And believe me, darling, I'm not alone, which, since the two of you are so much alike, has always worked in your favor."

"I've never seen myself as Humphrey Bogart."

"I'm not surprised, since men seldom see themselves clearly. It's one of your sex's most endearing little flaws. And if you can't imagine Bogie, then I suppose Gable will always do in a pinch. Just the thought of Rhett and Scarlett is guaranteed to make any female's heart go pitter-pat."

She gave him a small smile. "Sweep Nora Fitzpatrick off her feet, Quinn, then once you've got her in your arms, carrying her off to your bed will be a cakewalk."

Quinn hated to admit it, but the idea of carrying Nora up a curving antebellum staircase, then spending a long lusty night ravishing her held more than a little appeal.

"I'll think about it."

"Of course you will, sugar." Her voice had turned magnolia sweet, revealing the Confederate roots that had won her the Miss Georgia tiara before she'd packed her Gucci bags and decided to try her luck in Hollywood. "Tomorrow, at Tara."

She patted his cheek again, this time in

the fond way a mother might a child. "Meanwhile, since we're friends now, and everyone knows friends don't let friends drive drunk, you might as well spend the night here. On the couch," she said pointedly.

That was probably the best damn idea she'd come up with yet. Quinn felt on the verge of crashing. "Maybe just a nap."

"You'll spend the night," she repeated. "And don't worry about the widow Fitzpatrick. Even an Irish convent-bred girl isn't immune to the green-eyed monster. You staying away the night is bound to pique her interest."

Quinn wondered if she could possibly be right. Then again, he reminded himself, despite Laura's claims to the contrary, Nora wasn't like other women.

And there he was, he thought later as he lay on his back on the too-short couch and wished like hell his head would stop spinning, right back where he'd started when he'd dropped into The Rose with the stupid cockeyed plan to hide out from Nora Fitzpatrick.

What the hell was the woman doing to his mind?

Chapter Twelve

In Search of a Heart

He hadn't come home. Hadn't been lured by the leg of lamb. Or her. After reading *The Lady of the Lake* last night, Nora realized she'd been foolish to believe he might. Kate had been right when she'd insisted that beneath his horror stories Quinn had, indeed, been writing about families. The problem was, of course, it was also more than a little obvious that his view of a family unit was not a reassuring one.

He'd warned her not to try to get inside his barriers, that she wouldn't like what she'd see. Well, hadn't it turned out that he was right? She'd gotten a glimpse of the man behind the stony facade, but rather than frighten her away, as he'd undoubtedly expected, it had only made her heart ache for anyone forced to go through life so alone.

Quinn was not an easy man to know. He would be an even harder man to love. And in truth Nora still wasn't certain she was falling in love with him. But she did know that if she didn't take the risk — if she didn't reach out to him — she'd spend the rest of her life regretting her fearfulness. For her own sake. And for his.

She was at work pouring grain into individual troughs, thinking that if the roof repairs didn't prove too dear, she'd be able to use the rest of Quinn's rental money to buy that automatic feeder she'd seen at Murphy's Grain and Supply, when Brady entered the milking barn.

"Well, isn't this a surprise," she said. "Good evening."

"And a lovely evening to you, daughter." Brady gave her a peck on the cheek. "I thought I'd drop by to offer my help."

"With the milking?" This was a first. Nora couldn't remember the last time her father had been anywhere near the milking barn.

"Oh, you seem to have that in hand well enough," he said. "Besides, I never have understood these newfangled machines. Now, if you needed someone to milk the old-fashioned way —"

"I'd still have to go out and find John." Her smile took any sting from her playful accusation. "As Kate always says, the gods gave us all our own talents, Da. Yours isn't farming."

"And isn't that the gods' own truth?" He

sighed. "I'm afraid I've been as bad at parenting my children as I've been a farmer."

"No, that's not true at all! You've been a wonderful father."

"I wanted to be." He sighed again, tipped over an empty milk can and perched atop it. "But things got difficult after your dear mother passed on."

"It was a hard time for everyone."

"Aye. But hardest on you. Because I wasn't pulling my weight."

"You were grieving." Nora had almost forgotten how silent he'd gone, barely saying more than two words at a stretch for months.

"My children were grieving, as well. And I was too blind to see it."

Nora wondered what had brought on this uncharacteristic introspection. "It's all in the past now," she said. "We all survived."

"Thanks to you." He took out his pipe, looked around the pristine barn, then, seeming to realize smoking wasn't in order, returned it to his shirt pocket. "I don't believe I ever told you how much I appreciated the way you took charge of the house. And the children have grown up to become a credit to your mothering talents."

"Thank you. But they were good children to begin with. I just gave them a little direction."

Her father had always been lavish with compliments. But they'd been only surface statements, meant to charm. Never had any of them made her eyes grow moist as they did now. She wondered again what had brought all this on, then felt her blood turn to ice as a possible answer came into her mind.

"Are you all right?" she asked.

"Me?" He put a hand against his chest. "Of course I am. Why wouldn't I be?"

"Because it's not like you to be so serious. And because Dr. Flannery —"

"Don't you go paying him any mind. What does he know? He's still wet behind the ears, Nora. Why, the last time I was in there for that examination you insisted on, I took a close look at that fancy Latin medical degree hanging in that fine oak frame on his wall, and do you know what I discovered?"

"What?"

"That the ink was still wet."

She laughed as she was meant to. Then immediately sobered. "I worry about you."

"You worry about the entire world, Nora, darling. It's one of your finest traits. It's also your curse. Because sometimes you care too much."

"I'd like to know what's wrong with not

230

wanting my father to drop dead some morning of a heart attack."

"Now, that's not going to happen."

"Dr. Flannery —"

"Jaysus, don't I wish old Doc Walsh hadn't retired? Ever since that pup Flannery took over his practice, things have gotten depressingly grim down at the surgery."

Nora pounced on his muttered complaint like a barn cat might pounce on a fat field mouse. "So, he *has* told you something."

"Only a bunch of fancy medical words that boil down to the simple fact that while I've always done my best to avoid growing up, I'm not getting any younger. Then he charged me ten pounds to tell me what I already knew." Brady took out the pipe again, but resisted filling it. Instead, he turned it over and over in his hands, as if choosing his words carefully.

"But I don't want to ruin a lovely spring evening talking about Dr. Flannery. Fact is, I've been doing some thinking."

Realizing that she wasn't going to learn anything more about the state of her father's health, Nora decided that since he'd obviously had some important reason for tracking her down, she should at least hear him out.

"Oh?" she responded noncommittally.

"About you."

"I see," she said, not seeing anything at all.

"I was wondering if you ever think about what you've missed, giving up your vocation."

The question came as such a surprise, she couldn't stop the laugh from escaping. "Oh, Da." She went over to where he was sitting, crouched and twined her arms around his shoulders. "I never truly had a vocation. I suspected that was the case even before Mam died. And I was certain when I agreed to marry Conor. And when the midwife placed Rory in my arms, not a single doubt remained that I'd done exactly the right thing in leaving the convent."

"You're a natural-born mother, 'tis true," he agreed, his eyes going bright with unshed tears. "You should have more children."

"I'd like that. Especially now that John and Mary will be leaving home soon. But perhaps it might be best if I were to find myself a husband first."

"Father O'Malley would undoubtedly prefer that order." He gave a quick grin that reminded Nora more of the father that could be both charming and exasperating at the same time. The father she adored. "Did

I ever tell you how your mam and I met?"

"Of course. At the horse fair in Ballinasloe. You were there to tell your stories. And she was the horse trader's daughter."

"The horse trader's beautiful daughter." He gave her a long perusal. "You have the look of your mother. The coloring's different, of course, since you inherited your grandmother Fionna's bright hair and Eleanor's was jet-black. But you favor her around the eyes. And your mouth's just the same . . .

"There are times, when you smile, that my foolish heart skips a beat because it gets confused and believes Elly's come back to me."

"There are times when Rory reminds me of Conor in that same way," Nora admitted quietly. A cow mooed impatiently, reminding her that if she wanted it to stand still for the milking, she'd best be hurrying up with the feeding.

"Aye." He fell silent for a time. Understanding that this conversation was far more personal — and thus more difficult — than any of the stories that tripped so easily off his tongue, Nora waited him out again. "Your grandfather Noonan didn't want your mother marrying me."

"Really?" Her only memory of her mother's father, who'd died when she was younger than Rory, was the scent of horse and leather clinging to his clothes, and the peppermints he always carried in his shirt pocket for her.

"They were from Dublin. City folk, from south of the Liffey. Oh, he wasn't about to let his only daughter take off to the west with some poor farmer who was scarcely more secure than a traveler. A man who'd never be able to buy her all the knickknacks and doodads women like."

"Mam was never interested in possessions," Nora assured him. "She cared about people. About family."

"Aye. That's what she tried to tell her father when I asked for her hand, but he was a hard and stubborn man, and not one given to compromise."

"Yet you were married."

"Only because of the kidnapping."

"What?" Nora stared at this man she thought she knew so well. "You actually dared kidnap my mother?"

"Well, she wasn't your mother at the time, mind you," he said. "And besides, 'twas her own idea. So her father would have to permit the marriage."

"I don't understand."

"Well, of course, things are different now, what with young people living together right out in the open without even bothering to stop by the church to exchange vows along the way. But in those days, if a young woman spent the night with a man, no matter how innocent the occasion . . ."

"Her reputation would be ruined if they didn't get married," Nora guessed. Despite Mary's accusations about Jack's new girlfriend supposedly sleeping around, it wasn't that different even these days out here in the country.

"Aye." He chuckled a bit at the long-ago time. "Your grandda Noonan couldn't get Elly to the altar fast enough. He even tried to bribe the priest into forgoing the usual posting of the bans, because he was fearful she was pregnant and he didn't want people gossiping about his short-term grandchild."

"But she wasn't. Pregnant." Nora couldn't believe she was having this conversation with her father. "Wait." She held up her hand. "Forget I asked that." Nora didn't want to think about her parents' sex life.

"Finn was born nine months to the day of our wedding night. And then Michael. And as much as I love both your older brothers, I have to confess that I wept like a baby the stormy day you came into the world." He rubbed his chin and his eyes took on a faraway look, as if remembering the event in detail. "A man always wants sons. I suppose you could say we even expect them.

"But ah, Nora, when I looked down at you, with that fuzz of me own mam's brilliant hair atop your wee pink head and your wide blue eyes that hadn't yet turned to emerald, I told your mother that no man had ever been so blessed. To have such a perfect wife. And equally perfect daughter."

Nora's eyes filled at the obviously heartfelt revelation. "Now look what you've gone and done," she complained, sniffling back her tears. "You've made me all weepy."

"You should never apologize for weeping, Nora. Didn't God give us tears to help us keep our emotions from getting all bottled up? Even if there are some who won't be understanding that it's better to let those feelings out and fresh air in?"

"Ah." Nora nodded, finally understanding her father's unexpected appearance in the milking barn. "I was wondering if you were going to ask me about Quinn."

"I've seen the way you look at him, daughter — with your heart on your sleeve and shining bright in your eyes. It's the way I remember your mother looking at me."

"And the way you looked back at her?"

"Later on. In the beginning I suspect I had more of the look of how Gallagher looks at you, when he thinks no one is watching." Brady began fiddling with the pipe again. "Men aren't the same as women, Nora. My da once told me that a woman has to be in love with a man to want to make love to him. But a man just has to be in the room."

Even though she was growing nearly as embarrassed as Brady obviously was by the turn the unusually intimate conversation had taken, Nora laughed again. "Is it always that way, do you think?"

"Most cases I know of, aye." He pulled off his cap and dragged his fingers through his curly gray hair. "Jaysus, I wish your mam was here to have this talk with you! It's a mother's duty, after all, to discuss such things with her daughter."

"But I've already been married."

"You were a child. You loved Conor the way a young girl loves an older man who sweeps her off her feet. You were blinded by a bright dazzling sun, Nora, which worried me at the time, but in truth, I was so relieved you were going to marry and take the burden of the younger children from my shoulders that I refused to admit to myself that the marriage wasn't in your best interests."

"I loved Conor. I would have made it work."

"You would have tried," Brady allowed.

"And had your heart shattered in the trying. You weren't the first woman in Conor Fitzpatrick's life, Nora. And although it pains me to say it, darling, you weren't the last."

Oh, God. She'd known that of course. Even as innocent as she'd been, she'd sensed the fact of Conor's infidelity with a wife's intuition of such things. But until now, she'd never so much as allowed herself to state that terrible fear out loud. And if others in Castlelough had known about his other women, which she realized now they undoubtedly had, none, not even Kate, had ever dared say it to her face.

She swallowed, trying to push the words past the lump in her throat. "If it pains you so to tell me this, how do you think it makes *me* feel?"

"I'm sure it's far from easy. But I also notice you're not arguing the point."

Nora turned away and wrapped her arms tightly around herself. It hurt. Heaven help her, it hurt horribly! She didn't want to deal with this. Not now. Not when she was so confused about her feelings for Quinn.

She took a deep breath, then whirled back toward him.

"Why?" she asked on a fractured desperate sound. "My husband has been dead for five years. Why bring this up now?"

"Because I was a selfish bastard when you needed a father's protection. I should have kept you from marrying a man who was so wrong for you."

"There wouldn't have been anything you could have done. After all, you've already told me that Grandda Noonan couldn't stop Mam from marrying you."

"Aye. And he was wrong about what was truly good for his daughter. Because although I tested her temper more often than perhaps I should have, Eleanor was happy in our marriage. But he had no way of knowing I could make her happy at the time, so he did what he thought was best. He fought for her. To protect her."

Brady pushed himself off the milk can with a weariness of body and spirit Nora hadn't witnessed since her mother's death. When he enveloped her in his arms, she remembered him holding her exactly the same way the first time she'd fallen off a horse. At the time, unable to draw a decent breath, she'd been certain she was dying. But it turned out that she'd only had the wind knocked out of her, and later he'd taken her into town for ice cream. Strangely, she felt exactly the same way now.

As she breathed in the familiar comforting scents of hair tonic and tobacco and felt the outline of the pipe he always carried in his breast pocket, Nora wished her current troubles could be solved with a vanilla ice-cream cone.

"If Conor was the sun, Quinn Gallagher is the cold dark side of the moon, Nora. And while I might be able to understand how you'd find yourself drawn to a man who's the exact opposite of your first husband, I'm fearful he's going to hurt you more than Conor Fitzpatrick ever could have."

Nora opened her mouth, prepared to argue. But couldn't.

"You may be right." There wasn't any reason to try to keep fooling herself. She'd already reached the point of no return, whatever happened between her and Quinn during the next three weeks, she'd foolishly let him into her heart. Deep enough that she knew he'd be taking a bit of it with him when he left Castlelough.

Which of course, she reminded herself firmly, he'd be doing. "And I don't mean to quibble, Da. But I seem to remember you throwing Quinn and me together that first Sunday morning."

"Ah, but that was before I knew his true nature." Brady frowned. "Now I suppose you'll be telling me that you can handle whatever the Yank dishes out?"

She met his worried look with a level one of her own. "I'm stronger than I look."

"And don't I know that? But of all the eligible bachelors in Castlelough, why did you have to pick the American?"

"I didn't pick him. Kate believes Mam did. Because he'd be a challenge. As her own husband was."

Brady gave Nora another long look. Then chuckled. "Aye, that sounds just like something your mother would do."

They both began to laugh at the absurdity of it all, which was how Quinn found them, father and daughter, arms wrapped around each other, tears streaming down their faces.

"I'm sorry." Uncomfortable with such an open display of emotion, he began to back out of the open doorway. "I didn't mean to interrupt."

"Don't worry about it, my boy," Brady said, swiping at his wet face with the back of his hands. "I was just about to be on my way into the village. You can take my place helping Nora with the milking."

He left before Quinn could think up a good excuse to escape with him.

"Nice place." He looked around the remarkably clean barn and decided open-heart surgery could be performed on the spotless concrete floor. "I guess I expected something a bit more primitive."

"Ah, there you go again, Mr. Gallagher," Nora said with an impertinent toss of her head that, if Brady had witnessed it, would have reminded him again of her mother. "Trying to fit everyone into tidy little boxes." She poured the last of the grain into the final trough. "I'm disappointed. I would have expected a famous writer such as yourself to have more imagination."

There was something different about her. It was as if she'd let down her guard and was giving him his first glimpse of the woman who'd been brave enough to take on a ready-made family before she was even out of her teens.

"Sometimes it helps to be able to pigeon-hole people."

"Stereotype, you mean." She went back down to the beginning of the row and began attaching the inflations to the cows' swollen udders. "Let me guess, if you'd given the matter of my milking any thought, which I doubt you have, you would have pictured me doing the work by hand, while sitting on a three-legged wooden stool, wearing a dirndl."

"And a scooped-neck cotton peasant blouse to show off the tops of your milky white breasts," he finished for her. The fantasy of unlacing that white blouse had tortured him during the more pastoral of his erotic dreams concerning this woman.

"I'm sorry to disappoint you."

"That's the one thing you couldn't do, sweetheart." Starting at the other end of the line, he began attaching the octopuslike hoses to the teats of the feeding cows. "You frustrate me, frighten me, turn me on, but —"

"Surely you're not serious? I frighten you?"

"You're right. *Frighten* isn't the right word."

"I didn't think so."

"Actually, Mrs. Fitzpatrick, you scare the living bejesus out of me."

Surprised that he'd make such a startling admission in such an easy tone, Nora glanced up, then stared at the sight of Quinn doing what to her had become routine. "What are you doing?"

"Helping out like Brady suggested."

"But you know what to do."

"I told you I knew a bit about farms."

"Well, knowing a bit about farms and knowing farmwork are two very different things."

Quinn shrugged. "I worked on a few when I was a kid. After my mom died. Mostly plowing, haying, milking. I didn't much like it."

"Oh." That wasn't the most encouraging news, Nora thought. It reminded her that Quinn was not the type of man to be happy living a country life. "If you don't like the work, you shouldn't have to do it. After all, you are a paying guest and —"

"Hey, having your guests do the work is the latest thing in the States. Believe it or not, out West, guys actually pay big bucks to get their butts beat up sitting on a horse all day playing cowboy."

"I saw that movie." She thought it important that he realize that Castlelough wasn't entirely the back of beyond. "I thought it was very sweet when the wee calf was born. But to tell you the truth, I don't think taking it back to the city was a very good idea."

"That story was a fantasy written for city slickers who don't want to think about the fact that cows are nothing but Big Macs on the hoof. After the movie finished shooting, that big brown-eyed bovine Billy Crystal supposedly delivered undoubtedly ended up between two sesame-seed buns."

She inclined her head, studied him to see if he was serious and realized he was. "Has anyone ever told you that you're a very jaded man, Mr. Gallagher?"

"All the time. And for the record, they're wrong. I'm merely a realist in a world populated with people who want their lives fuzzed up all pretty and soft-focused at the edges.

"Which is why," he continued, returning to his original point, "you should consider making up a brochure touting the pleasures of good, honest work, and how it lowers blood pressure, increases heart capacity and boosts sex drive. You'd make a bundle from rich Americans."

"I'll consider that," Nora murmured as she returned to work. There was no way she was going to touch that remark about boosting sex drive. "You wouldn't want to be giving me an endorsement, would you? For the brochure."

"That depends. Are you going to smack me if I spill any milk?"

Even knowing it was foolish of her, she grasped this latest clue and held it close to her heart, wondering if he'd realized he'd just shared with her something else of his painful childhood.

"I hadn't planned on it," she answered mildly, despite her stirring of sympathy for the boy who'd obviously been mistreated.

"Well, then, I suppose I could be persuaded."

"Of course you won't be able to give a five-star review of my tasty meals. Since you missed the lamb," she added pointedly.

They'd each reached the center of the barn and were now standing side by side.

Quinn cursed softly. "It seems I've spent a lot of time since coming here apologizing to you."

"You don't owe me any apologies, Quinn. After all, you're certainly free to decide where you want to spend your evenings." And your nights, she thought, but did not say.

"I spent the night in the village. With Laura Gideon."

"I see." She'd expected Quinn to hurt her. She just hadn't realized the pain would come so soon.

"No, dammit." He cupped her chin, holding her distressed gaze to his when she would have turned away. "You don't see. I may have gone there for sex. But I didn't do anything but pass out on her couch."

"You were drinking again?"

"Yeah." He shook his head in self-disgust. "When I was a kid, I used to try like hell to outrun my dad. I never could, of course. Looks like I still can't."

"You're not the first man to have too much to drink from time to time. That doesn't mean you're an alcoholic."

"I can count on one hand the number of times I've been drunk in my life. Two of them have been since I came here to Castlelough. That's got to mean something."

"It certainly doesn't say all that much for the relaxing properties of farm life. Perhaps I'd better rethink printing up that fancy advertising brochure."

"I'm serious, Nora."

"That's your problem, Quinn. You take life too seriously. You expect too much."

He laughed at that. A harsh bark of a sound that held not an iota of humor. "Sweetheart, if there's one lesson I've learned from life, it's not to expect a goddamn thing."

"If that were true, you wouldn't have to work so hard to keep yourself from being hurt. You still have hope in your heart, Quinn Gallagher. Even if you won't admit it."

"Perhaps you ought to hang out a shingle — Nora Fitzpatrick, country psychologist. Dammit, weren't you listening? I stood you up for dinner last night because I'd gone to the inn planning to go to bed with another woman. And not just any woman, but a gorgeous, sexy actress that men all over the world fantasize making love to.

"Laura and I always had a good time together. I was tense. Uptight. I wanted to get you out of my mind."

"And did you?"

"Hell, no," he said wearily.

Nora expelled a breath she'd been unaware of holding. "I suppose I should say I'm sorry. But I'm not."

He dragged both hands down his face, then dropped them to his side. When he looked at her again — hard and deep — Nora saw the misery in his eyes and wondered what kind of woman she'd become that she could actually find such pain encouraging.

"I want you, dammit!" He slammed his fist into his palm as the machines hummed and the cows chewed contentedly. "More than I could have imagined. I don't like the feeling. And I sure as hell don't like not being able to decide what to do about it."

"Oh, Quinn." She sighed out his name, wishing there was something she could do to brighten the murky shadows inside him. If she honestly believed that sex would help, she would have ripped off her clothes and given herself to him right here and now.

But she'd come to understand that sex came easily for this man. Too easily, it seemed. And although he'd never admit it, might not even realize it himself, Quinn was hungry for somebody to care about him. To love him.

She lifted a hand to his shoulder and felt

the muscle tense beneath her touch. "You keep making it sound as if I don't have any say in the matter. I may not be as experienced as the American women you're used to," she said quietly. "But I have been married and have given birth to a child. I'm not nearly as naive or helpless as you seem to believe I am. I do have a choice whether or not I go to bed with you."

"That's what you say." He grabbed hold of her upper arms and kissed her in a way designed to make her head spin. Which it did. When he released her mouth, his expression was as grim as she'd ever seen it. "The thing is, baby, I need to make sure *I* have a choice."

His face set in a rigid inscrutable mask, he backed away. Physically and emotionally. Nora wanted to weep as she watched those hateful walls going up again, stone by impenetrable stone.

"I've got some work to do," he said. "Since you seem to have everything under control here, I'd better get to it."

With that curt dismissal, Quinn turned and walked out of the milking barn. He did not look back.

CHAPTER THIRTEEN

Take Her in Your Arms

From the way he'd marched out of the milking shed, Nora had suspected Quinn was probably on his way back to Castlelough. To Laura Gideon, no doubt. Which was why it came as such a surprise to enter the house and find him in the kitchen, with Rory, Celia and Fionna.

And he wasn't just in it. He appeared to have taken it over!

"Quinn's cooking us supper," Celia, who was setting the table, revealed before Nora could ask what he was doing working at the stove.

"He's making curry," Rory said, looking up from chopping onions.

"Indians eat it." This from Celia.

"People who live in India," Rory said as he concentrated on making all the diced onion pieces the same size. "Not the ones from the American movies."

"I know." She'd eaten curry once at a restaurant in Dublin while living at the convent. She'd grown up on basic country fare, and had found it the most exotic food she'd ever tasted. "I also know I didn't have any curry in the pantry."

"I bought it this afternoon in the village," Quinn said. "Mrs. Monohan keeps a well-stocked store."

"Yes, she does." Nora's mind was racing. "You bought it this afternoon?"

He shrugged. "I figured it was my fault you were stuck with leftovers from last night. The least I could do was help you use them up." He glanced at her. "I came out to the milking barn to tell you, but we got . . . sidetracked talking about other things."

"Oh." She'd never, in her entire life, had a man cook for her! Indeed, she couldn't think of any woman she knew who had.

She took her apron from its hook. "Will we be having rice? Because I can start —"

"No." Quinn plucked the white cotton apron from her hand and hung it back where it belonged. "You're not going to do anything but sit down and drink your wine."

"Wine?"

"He bought it in the village, too." Fionna, who was seated at the table watching the proceedings, lifted her glass. "It's French. And very good."

And very expensive, Nora suspected. This

entire scene: a man standing at her stove, looking as if he had every right to be there, her son helping him cook, her grandmother actually drinking something other than communion wine, was like something from one of Quinn's books. It was far more fictional than anything Nora had ever experienced in real life.

She sank onto one of the chairs she'd painted during a gloomy time last winter when she'd thought the bright yellow color might bring a little sunshine into the dark winter days. Quinn poured some wine into a glass and held it out to her.

"*Slainte*," he said. Then, for her ears alone, he murmured. "To apologies. And possibilities."

"*Slainte*," she answered softly. As she lifted the ruby red wine to her lips, Nora thought she didn't need spirits; she was already high.

The next two hours passed in a blur. As she sipped her wine — which not surprisingly was excellent — Nora watched in amazement the ease with which Quinn fit into her family, instructing her son on the importance of a man being able to feed himself, sharing foolish knock-knock jokes with Celia, complimenting Mary, who'd entered the kitchen a few minutes earlier, on a new, paler, more natural lipstick shade, and discussing DNA, of all things, with John, who had come in with Mary.

"I've been telling Quinn about Bernadette," Fionna revealed as they finished up a meal that was even better than the one Nora had paid so many hard-earned pounds for in Dublin. "He's thinking of putting her into his new book."

"Really?" Nora's eyes narrowed suspiciously. Her grandmother took her canonization campaign very seriously. "I thought your next book was going to be about a witch, Quinn."

"It is. In fact, Kate and I are meeting tomorrow to discuss her impression of my heroine. She promised to take me to a circle of stones nearby."

"I know it." The ancient pre-Christian stone circle staggered the boundary line between Joyce and O'Sullivan land. "But how does Bernadette fit into a story about a witch?"

"Fionna has me intrigued. Sister Bernadette Mary is an interesting vital character. If I move the story back a few years, put it at the time of the revolution, fictionalize her enough to make her, perhaps, my heroine's sister . . ."

"You're serious."

"Of course. I'm always serious, Nora. You should have realized that by now."

His tone held a private meaning that had her looking down into her wineglass.

"A movie based on Bernadette's life might just help the cause," Fionna pointed out. "Even if it's a fictionalized account. And then, if it turns out to be a hit at Cannes, perhaps even the Holy Father himself will take notice."

Nora stared dumbstruck at her grandmother. She was certain Fionna hadn't even known about the famed European film festival before the movie people's arrival in Castlelough. Obviously her grandmother and Quinn had been having quite the conversation while she'd been finishing the milking.

"This sounds very different from your other books."

"Not really. Bernadette and the heroine of *The Lady of the Lake* have a great deal in common." He leaned forward to top off her glass before refilling Fionna's, then his own.

"One's a widowed mother. The other is a nun," Nora said. And nuns could not be mothers. Hadn't the inability to have children been one of the main reasons she'd questioned her vocation even before her mother had died?

"That's not such a difference. As you can probably attest to," he said mildly, revealing that someone had told him about her early convent days. "They're both brave women. Willing to give their lives to something they believe in. And I like the duality of the two sisters — one who's embraced a two-thousand-year-old religion and the other who practices a less acceptable one harkening back to ancient pagan gods."

Nora couldn't help noticing that by making the two characters in his new book sisters, Quinn was once again writing about a family. She wondered if he realized that.

And speaking of families . . .

"I liked the way you ended *The Lady of the Lake*. Having Shannon McGuire hide the baby beneath the tarp as she took the boat to Innisfree." Nora smiled at the uplifting memory of the widowed young mother and her son headed out to the island, determined to save the small green creature its mother had died protecting. "After all that sadness and evil, it made me feel hopeful."

"Shannon decided that all on her own," Quinn revealed, surprising Nora. She thought he'd have felt the need to reign absolute over his fictional worlds. "I had an entirely different — and darker — conclusion in mind when I began writing the book.

"But once Shannon took off on her own, joining forces with the creature, I purposely left the ending ambivalent. Most people seem to focus on the fact that the scientists won't give up." It did not surprise Quinn that Nora would choose the more optimistic — and unlikely — possibility.

"If that's the case, most people underestimate Shannon McGuire."

He lifted his glass to her. "You may have a point, Mrs. Fitzpatrick. She was, indeed, a formidable woman."

As he drank in the sight of her lovely earnest face, Quinn realized why Nora had seemed strangely familiar that first night. She was, of course, the brave unrelentingly optimistic Shannon McGuire come to life. The irony of coming across the sea to meet the only character — the only woman — who'd ever possessed the power to fascinate him did not escape Quinn.

"It's going to be light for another hour," he said. At this latitude the late-spring sun lingered lovingly over the land. "Didn't you say something about an excursion to the coast?"

"Oh, what a grand idea!" Fionna actually clapped her hands. "The poor man's been working far too hard since he came to Castlelough, Nora. I think he deserves a sunset walk at the edge of the tide. Relaxing, don't you think?"

That suggestion had Quinn nearly spitting out the drink of wine he'd just taken. Of all the words he might have used to describe his turbulent feelings for Nora Fitzpatrick, *relaxing* would not have even made the top fifty.

"There's still the dishes to do," Nora protested.

"Oh, we can do them," Fionna assured her. "Show the man the seashore, darling. The fresh air will do you both a world of good."

Nora knew there was no point in arguing. Not that she really wanted to. For the prospect of being alone with this man she just might be falling in love with was far too appealing to turn down.

And that was how they found themselves strolling along the hard-packed sand at the edge of the surf, drinking in the tangy scent of the sea. Overhead, gulls wheeled, their cries echoing off the windswept cliffs as the sun sank lower and lower in the cloud-scudded sky. Sandpipers skittered about in the foamy surf on long thin stilt legs while puffins nested on rock formations green with vegetation.

The slanting light cast a trail of fire on the

white-crested ocean waves. Quinn thought of his great-great-great-grandfather, Quinlan Conroy Gallagher, of County Donegal, who had sailed on the infamous "coffin ship" from Cork to America during the potato famine.

The sea on this warm spring day was calm, nearly glassy. Quinn imagined that in the winter the waves would beat against the rocks like invading warriors. A harsh contrast to the tidy green fields and placid sapphire lakes of summer.

In fact, the entire country was one of contrasts. One minute icy rain would be falling from low-hanging pewter clouds, the next the sun would shine from a cornflower blue sky, gilding the rolling landscape, and literally take your breath away.

The land of his forefathers was a place of sad songs, merry wars, the tragedy of the Troubles, the lilt of laughter mingling with the melancholy of a fiddle, both twining through the murmur of a blue-smoked pub. A place where the entire town might turn out to help one of their own cut peat for the winter, yet stubbornly harbor a decades-old grudge about a neighbor's errant cow getting into the corn.

Quinn had always thought of himself as a man who knew his own mind. Who carefully, after much consideration, charted a course and stuck to it. He'd prided himself on his single-mindedness. Until he'd arrived in Castlelough.

"You must think I'm crazy," he muttered.

It was the first words he'd said to her since leaving the house. Nora, enjoying his company and the sun's dazzling farewell to the day, had not felt the need to press for conversation.

"I have a grandmother who drives all over Ireland in a miracle-mobile, harasses bishops and writes impassioned weekly letters to the pope, a father who's survived an encounter with a banshee and lived to tell everyone about it, a sister who looks as if she's an apprentice vampire, a sister-in-law who dances in fairy rings and prays to pagan gods, and a son whose best friend is a mythical creature who lives in the lake."

Humor lit up her eyes, silvered her voice, as she went on, "And I myself have lengthy conversations with my long-dead mother and Stone Age ancestors. How could you think I'd be calling anyone else crazy?"

Quinn looked into the fathomless depths of those green eyes overbrimming with life and wondered how it was that she could make him laugh so easily.

"Point taken."

She returned his faintly abashed grin with a warm open smile of her own. "It's the magic of course."

"And you'd be one to believe in magic." Quinn never had, despite the fact that he wrote books about otherworldly events.

"Aye. While I may not burn candles and cast old Celtic spells as Kate does, I've felt it myself too many times not to know it exists. Obviously you've been feeling it, too, Quinn, which isn't surprising, since the blood of the ancient ones flows in your veins."

Quinn damn well didn't want to ruin a perfectly good sunset by discussing his Gallagher blood.

"I've always been irritated by women who give men mixed signals," he said, in an effort to change the subject. "But it occurs to me that's exactly what I've been doing to you." This was not an appealing realization.

"It's the magic," she said again. "It's obvious it has you feeling uneasy. And a wee bit testy."

"More than a wee bit." Her creamy complexion was framed by a windblown tangle of flame silk. Feeling an overpowering urge to touch, Quinn brushed away some strands that were blowing across her eyes. "I've been a bastard."

"Aye," Nora agreed.

He laughed again at her unfailing honesty and felt a release of tension. "You could argue with me."

She lifted a teasing brow. "And why would I be arguing with the truth, Mr. Gallagher?"

Quinn narrowed his eyes at the exaggerated lilt in her tone.

"Saints preserve us," he drawled on a mock brogue laced with amusement. "And would you actually be flirting with me, Mrs. Fitzpatrick?"

"I believe I just might be, Mr. Gallagher."

Tenderness. As the water carved new curves into ancient cliffs, Quinn felt it and fought against it. "I'm not a man for pretty words and promises, Nora."

"You're underestimating yourself." She lifted a hand to his cheek and felt the ridge of the white scar beneath her fingertips. "It would seem to me that a famous writer such as yourself would have more than enough words at his disposal."

His fingers curled around her wrist as if to pull her hand away. But he didn't. Not yet. "Are you saying you want me to lie?"

"No." Nora thought it sad that a man who was the epitome of self-confidence would seem so unsure of himself when it came to being loved. Although it cost her, she didn't press. "Pretty words can be lovely, Quinn. I know of no woman who doesn't enjoy hearing them." She saw the Aha! look flash in his eyes. "But I wouldn't be needing them."

"That's what you say now. But you're fooling yourself." His fingers tightened in a way Nora knew would leave bruises. "I won't be kind."

Although she'd rather attempt to face down a banshee on a moonless night on the Burren, Nora forced herself to meet Quinn's challenging gaze straight on. "I don't believe that." She was pleased when her voice revealed none of the anxiety bubbling up inside her.

His answering curse was rich and ripe. "Once won't be enough."

Tangled nerves had her laughing at that. "Sure, and I was hoping not," she said, her exaggerated brogue earning another rare genuine smile. Like a fledgling bird making its first attempt at flight, hope took stuttering wing in her chest.

She'd never been a woman to make the first move. With Devlin, their kisses had been a spontaneous shared exploration of youthful emotions. Conor had literally swept her into his arms less than ten minutes after he'd walked into his sister's horse barn and found her sitting on a bale of hay, crying her eyes out over her poor dead mam.

There'd been other kisses from other men, not many, but enough for her to understand that this ache to taste was as unique as Quinn Gallagher himself.

Linking her fingers together at the back of his neck, Nora went up on her toes and touched her mouth to his.

Magic. Quinn felt it in the sizzle of heat as Nora's lips touched his, tasted it in the hot wine flavor of the kiss, heard it in the small sound — a murmur or a moan, he couldn't quite tell over the thunder of the blood pounding in his head — that vibrated beneath his mouth as he took the kiss deeper. Darker.

Passion, restrained for too long, rose like the wind, tearing from him into her. Desire, rich and ripe and hot, flowed from her lips directly into his bloodstream. She strained against him, saying his name in a way that was part plea, part prayer as his mouth roamed her uplifted face, gathering in the taste of salt mist, searing her skin, cooling it, then setting it aflame again.

She was burning. Engulfed in emotions more turbulent than she'd ever experienced before, Nora was vaguely aware of the echo of the incoming tide, the cry of the gulls, the moan of the wind. And then, all those faded into the distance as she heard the lovely music of Quinn calling her sweetheart in a far different way than all those other times he'd practically flung the word at her like a challenge.

She clung to him, as if he were an anchor, a lifeline in a sea of titanic waves. His hands were beneath her sweater, caressing her in a wicked practiced way that left her shuddering.

"I want to make you crazy." His lips skimmed up her throat; he touched the tip of his tongue against the fragrant hollow where her pulse hammered.

"You are."

"It's not enough." He nipped at her lips in painful yet pleasurable bites that had her moving restlessly beneath his hands. "I want to make you as crazy as you've made me. Being with you is almost all I've been thinking about." He kissed her eyelids, which fluttered obediently closed. "Dreaming about."

"I know." Her own hands had sneaked beneath his sweater, allowing her to revel in the feel of the smooth skin and taut muscles of his back. How could such a strong hard man have flesh as smooth as an infant's bottom? Nora wanted to feel him everywhere. Heaven help her, she wanted to taste him everywhere. "I know the dreaming."

"Thank God." His rich laugh held none of

the acid sarcasm or anger she was used to hearing. He took his hands from her hot flesh, leaving her feeling bereft as he tugged the sweater back into place.

"Another minute of that, Mrs. Fitzpatrick, and I would have been dragging you down to the sand and taking you right here and now."

"Another minute of that, Mr. Gallagher," Nora retorted on a ragged breath, "and I would have helped you."

Chuckling again in a very unQuinn-like way, he framed her face with his palms, bent his head and touched his lips to her ravaged ones in a kiss so sweet it nearly made her weep.

"I want to take you to dinner."

She told herself that it was because her head was still spinning that she'd misunderstood. "After that fine meal you made us?"

"No." Another kiss. Longer, sweeter. "Tomorrow night. I want to drive into Galway for dinner in a fine restaurant, with candlelight and wine and a rose in a crystal vase in the center of the table, and perhaps, if we're lucky, even a romantic violinist to serenade you."

"You want to take me out on a date?"

"For starters." He laughed at the enthusiasm for the idea that was emblazoned all over her face. Her lovely, lovely face. "Then,

I figured, we could take things from there."

Nora knew he'd chosen Galway to get her away from home, where everyone would talk about them. Of course, she considered, spending an evening, and perhaps even a night, away with the man more than one Castlelough resident was now referring to as "her American," would be guaranteed to set tongues wagging. In Castlelough, as in most villages, gossip was the coin of the realm. And the Americans were providing a wealth of stories.

"I'd love that." It was not in Nora's nature to play coy. "But Fionna's leaving for Derry in the morning, and even if I could talk Da into staying at home with the children . . ."

"Mary and John are old enough to babysit. And Kate's just a phone call away, on the next farm."

"You're right of course."

Her mind was whirling its way through her closet, wondering if she possessed anything remotely suitable for such a romantic evening, when she heard the sound of her name being carried on the wind. She turned and experienced a jolt of surprise mixed with pleasure.

"Oh! It's Devlin!"

"Devlin?" Quinn didn't like the rich warmth in her tone.

"A boy I knew from school. His mother is Mrs. Monohan, who sold you the wine and curry."

The man walking toward them on a long beach-eating stride was built like an oak tree. Broad and firm and solid. When Nora waved at him, he began running, and when he reached her, swept her up with a bold confidence that caused something hot and lethal to slice through Quinn.

"Jaysus, if you don't get more beautiful every time I see you, wench," Devlin Monohan said. As Quinn was forced to watch, the Irishman kissed her full on the mouth. Nora, Quinn noticed with building fury, kissed him right back. "It's a wonder all the men in Castlelough aren't crippled from walking into stone walls whenever you go by."

"And you're more full of blarney every time I see you," Nora said laughingly. "Next time you'll have to give me warning. So I can dig out my Wellies to wade through your foolish compliments." She banged a palm against his shoulder. "Now put me down so I can be properly introducing you."

"That's always been your trouble, Nora, me love," he said, nevertheless doing as instructed. "You've always been too proper for your own good." His expression was open and friendly as he turned to Quinn, acknowledging him for the first time. "Good evening to you. I'm Devlin Monohan, the man this one drove to distraction once upon a time ago."

The fact that he'd not imagined the familiarity between the two did nothing to lighten Quinn's mood. "Quinn Gallagher." He reluctantly shook the outstretched hand. It reminded him of a bear's paw.

"Of course you are. I'd recognize you even if Fionna hadn't told me that Nora was down here with you. I enjoy your stories, Mr. Gallagher. And admire the affection you portray for animals. The tale about the ghost stallion was particularly well done."

It was difficult for Quinn to hate someone who'd just paid his work a compliment. But the memory of this man's mouth on Nora's made it easier. "Thank you."

"Devlin's a veterinarian," Nora said. "He's just gotten a position at the National Stud." She beamed up at him. "I'm so proud of you!"

"That's very impressive," Quinn said grudgingly. He knew that the Irish stud farm was responsible for the bloodstock of the world's greatest Thoroughbreds.

"It's an honor," Devlin said easily enough. "And one I hope I can live up to."

"Of course you will," Nora said with a fervent loyalty that had Quinn grinding his teeth. "You've always had the magic touch when it comes to horses, Devlin."

"And you've always been prejudiced, love," he countered with a deep laugh. "I suppose Mam told you my other news?"

"That you're getting married? She did, and I think it's wonderful."

"I'm rather fond of the idea myself," Devlin Monohan's rapt expression revealed that "fond" was something of an understatement. "And that's why I've interrupted yours and Mr. Gallagher's sunset stroll. To invite you to a party to meet my new bride-to-be."

"Oh, that sounds wonderful! When?"

"Since I'm due at my new position the day after next, Mam was thinking tomorrow night."

Nora's face fell. "Oh. I'm sorry, Devlin, but I'm afraid I have plans —"

"Nothing that can't be changed," Quinn broke in. "We can go to Galway some other night. You should celebrate with your friend."

She was, Quinn noted, clearly torn as she looked back and forth between himself and the other man.

"I don't want to be influencing you either way, Nora," Devlin said. He looked over at

Quinn, his friendly gaze now measuring. "And of course you'd be invited, as well, Mr. Gallagher."

"I wouldn't want to intrude . . ."

"Oh, it wouldn't be intruding. Besides, wouldn't it give my mother boasting rights throughout the entire county for the next decade having one of the Americans in her house for a social event?"

Quinn knew that Nora would not renege on her agreement to go to Galway with him. He also knew that he didn't want to risk a possible pall over the evening from any guilt she might be feeling from missing the engagement party of an obviously very close friend.

"It sounds like fun," he said, not quite truthfully. Although from his brief meeting with the gregarious Mrs. Monohan in the mercantile, he was sure she'd be an excellent hostess, he'd much rather be wining, dining and making mad passionate love to Nora in Galway. "Please tell your mother I appreciate the invitation."

From the expression on Nora's face as she looked up at him, Quinn realized he'd done the right thing.

"Thank you," she murmured after they'd said their good-byes and were watching Devlin walk back toward the stone steps carved into the cliff. "That was a very generous thing to do."

Quinn shrugged. "I could tell you wanted to be with him and —"

"No. I wanted to be with you. But Devlin's important to me, as well."

"So it appears." Quinn had to ask. "I suppose he was your first lover?" Apparently Mary had gotten the wedding-night story wrong.

"No," Nora said mildly, ignoring his all-too-familiar gritty tone. "My husband was my first lover. Devlin was my first love." She linked her fingers with his and smiled at him in a way that made Quinn feel like an ass. "And you've no reason to concern yourself about him. Even if he hadn't gotten himself engaged to another woman, what Devlin and I shared was over a very long time ago."

"But you're still friends."

"Aye. Perhaps as you and Laura Gideon are."

Quinn had no response for that. Taking pity on him, Nora stopped walking, went up on her toes again and gave him a kiss that, brief as it was, still packed one helluva punch.

"You don't have to worry about me having romantic feelings for Devlin, Quinn."

That may be, Quinn told himself as they

walked back up the steep breath-stealing steps. But the romantic feelings he was harboring for this woman, whose slender hand fit so perfectly in his, were definitely something to worry about.

Chapter Fourteen

Something to Believe In

Kate O'Sullivan had spent a restless night. She'd tossed and turned, then suffered an anxiety attack shortly before dawn that had her heart pounding so hard she'd feared she was having a heart attack. She'd been left feeling as fragile as glass.

It wasn't just because she and Cadel had had another fight. After all, hadn't she learned to expect him to be out of sorts when he spent the entire day drinking whiskey in the pub? The pitiful truth was, that drunk or not, Cadel O'Sullivan was an ill-tempered bully. And by agreeing to marry him when she'd discovered she was carrying Andrew Sinclair's child, she'd made a deal with the devil.

Nora was, of course, right about her needing to do something about her marriage, Kate thought as she waved Jamie off on the bus to school. But fortunately, with her husband having stormed off to stay with his cousin in Dungarven, such decisions could be put off a bit longer.

"Quinn's coming today," she told her daughter, Brigid, as she washed the breakfast dishes. "We're going to go to the stones."

"Stones!" the red-haired toddler shouted gleefully while banging a spoon against a pot lid. "Brigid dance with fairies!"

"Aye." Despite her continuing unease, Kate smiled and thought how wonderful to be of an age when everything was an adventure. Just then there was a knock on the kitchen door. As she went to answer it, she said, "And won't the fairies smile when they see you've come visiting?"

"Fairies will smile. And dance!" Brigid abandoned the pot and spoon and began spinning around the kitchen, looking like a whirling flame-topped daffodil in her bright yellow dress and leggings.

Quinn had no sooner entered the kitchen when he was attacked by a whirling sunshine-bright dervish. "Dance!" the toddler shouted as she spun up to him and grabbed hold of his legs.

"Far be it from me to refuse a beautiful girl." He scooped Brigid up in his arms, breathed in the scents of milk and baby powder, and began waltzing around the kitchen.

"I thought I might drop her off at Nora's,

but we're running late," Kate apologized.

"Didn't you hear, Mrs. O'Sullivan?" He dipped the little girl and made her giggle. "When God made time, he made plenty of it."

Kate hung up the dish towel, then cocked her head, studying him. He'd certainly changed since that first morning she'd met him at the Joyce farm. It could be her imagination, but she'd swear the harsh lines on his face had softened. And his dark eyes had lost their flinty hardness. She couldn't imagine the man she'd met that morning waltzing around the kitchen with a two-year-old.

"Still, I know you're a busy man."

"The day I'm too busy to dance with a beautiful redhead is the day I need to re-examine my priorities."

"Dance with fairies!" Brigid announced loudly.

"I told her we were going to the circle of stones," Kate explained as she took a small white Aran Islands sweater down from the hook beside the door. "It's one of her favorite places. If you don't mind her coming with us, that is."

"I'd like that," he said, meaning it.

He'd never been all that comfortable around babies and little children, but Brigid

O'Sullivan was so outgoing it was impossible not to fall under her cheerful spell. Quinn wondered if Jamie had once been this gregarious. Then wondered how long it would take for Brigid's spirit to be darkened by her ill-tempered father, how long before she'd lose the ability to trust.

And speaking of Cadel O'Sullivan . . .

As Kate retrieved her daughter and managed to get the little girl to hold still long enough to tug her sweater on, Quinn couldn't miss the purplish mark on her cheek. Visions flooded into his head: his battered mother's ugly bruises, her trembling hands, the tears flowing from her sunken eyes. He could hear the rough curses, the raised voices, the screams. Could smell the sickening stench of blood.

Fury clawed at his gut with razor-sharp claws; his vision went crimson with rage. His hands curled into painfully tight fists at his sides, the instinctively violent reaction reminding Quinn that, despite all the fancy trappings of wealth, deep down inside, where it counted, he was still his father's son.

He had no doubt that if he'd known Kate when Cadel O'Sullivan had first confronted him in The Rose, things would have ended differently. Sickened by the evidence of the man's brutish behavior on Kate's face, equally sickened by his own knee-jerk impulse for violence, Quinn jammed his fists into his pockets and tried to decide the best way to broach the subject.

Apparently oblivious to his internal battles, Kate finished buttoning the sweater and stood up. "Well, then, if you're ready?"

"I've been ready since you first mentioned the stones," he said, deciding there'd be time to bring up her husband's abuse later. When his head was cooler and he could more carefully censor his words.

Not for the first time since arriving in Castlelough, Quinn wondered what it was about this place that made him so quick to involve himself in people's lives. How was it that everything got so personal so fast? If he didn't know better, he might think there was something in the water. Or, he mused, perhaps Kate really was a witch and had cast a spell over him.

He followed her over the hilly countryside, where cows grazed in pastures fenced by stones, to an intoxicating breezy trail overlooking the sea. In the pearly light the Atlantic glistened like a precious jewel, the string of islands looking like green humpbacked sea monsters. The sight soothed his senses, and the bracing scent of salt air cleared his mind, temporarily banishing old ghosts.

"It's not far." Kate had been holding Brigid's hand, but picked her up when the trail came dangerously close to the edge of the savage cliff. "It's on the border between a field I share with the Joyces."

That was something Quinn had noticed, that not all a farmer's fields were adjacent to one another.

"Oh, it's a tricky thing," Kate explained when he asked her about it. "The land is handed down to successive generations over the years and gets all broken up. Then, a farmer who owns a field next to mine might not want to sell because it's better land than the field next to his own house. And I might feel the same way about a field next to one of my neighbors. So we all make do, and I can't see it changing anytime soon."

That certainly wasn't a surprise. From what Quinn had seen thus far, change came slowly to the west of Ireland. Which was, he thought, a great part of its charm.

The faint trail was full of wiggles and twists, cutting across headlands, heather-tinted moors and cliffs indented with hidden coves. When they came around one blind turn, Quinn stopped in his tracks.

"Wow." Although he'd seen pictures of

Celtic stone circles, he wasn't prepared for the actual sight. It was staggering. Suffused in the luminous misty sea light were the sixteen man-size *gallans* — standing stones — surrounding a huge recumbent stone in which lines and swirls had been chiseled. They were located in a small grove of ancient oak trees that had somehow managed to escape the ax back when Richard II plundered Irish woodlands for timbers to build the roof of London's Westminster Hall.

"The symbols are ogham," Kate explained, running her fingers over the etchings.

"A bardic alphabet," he said, remembering from his research.

"The letters are symbolic, with each letter standing for a variety of ideas relating to Celtic philosophy."

"Like a secret code, of sorts, to keep the common folk from reading the writings."

"Aye." She sighed at that less than democratic idea. "There are legends of entire libraries written in ogham, where all the ancient stories were preserved. Although the old Greek and Roman chronicles suggest they were mostly used for casting spells."

Since the stones were a good distance from the cliff, she put her daughter back down on the ground. Quinn smiled as he watched the toddler begin to twirl like a laughing dervish.

"She feels the magic," he suggested. Quietly, because he was feeling it again himself.

"I've thought that, as well," Kate said. "She was just a babe, less than six weeks when I brought her here the first time. She was plagued with colic, a poor wee unhappy thing she was, squalling her head off all the way along the cliff. Until I took her into the circle.

"Then she immediately hushed and I watched her looking around, and although I know there's many who'd suggest it was only gas, I watched her smile. And listen. And I knew she was hearing the voices of those who'd come before."

"I probably wouldn't have believed that a month ago," Quinn said.

"And now?"

He'd never seen a woman more in her element than Kate appeared at this moment, watching her daughter dance with fairies. "And now I guess you'd have to call me an agnostic."

She laughed at that. "Ah, isn't the magic getting to you now, Quinn Gallagher." Her voice sounded like wind chimes in a brisk morning sea breeze. "Another few weeks and we'll be making a true believer of you."

Quinn smiled back, feeling none of the tension with this lovely intelligent woman that he experienced with her sister-in-law. "It almost seems as if she's hearing some type of music," he said, watching the toddler spin from rock to rock.

"I suppose that isn't so surprising, since my grandmother on my mother's side was an Early. Which means the blood of Biddy Early flows through her young veins."

"I think I hear a story coming."

"We do like our stories," Kate agreed cheerfully. "Even those of us who aren't *seanachies,* like Brady. Biddy Early was from County Clare. It's from her that Brigid gets her bright copper hair.

"Biddy was a famous healer with the gift of Sight, who outlived three husbands and invited a great deal of local gossip upon herself by marrying a fourth time — to a fine, much younger handsome man — when she was in her eighties. When she died, the parish priest, who, needless to say, did not look with favor upon her practice of white magic, took her fortune-telling bottle from her cottage and cast it into the tarn of Kilbarron, where it remains to this day."

"So now you carry on the family tradition."

"In a way. When people come to me with problems, it's difficult to turn them away. I was baptized into the Church and confirmed, as well, yet I can't help believing, despite what Father O'Malley preaches, that if I wasn't meant to be following the Old Way, I wouldn't have been given the gifts of the ancient ones."

"Makes sense to me." Quinn had never been a fan of any organized religion. "So if it's not too personal a question, may I ask if you inherited Biddy Early's gift of Sight?"

He was almost tempted to also ask if she could see what lay ahead for him and Nora. But not wanting to get into a discussion about a relationship he still hadn't been able to define, he refrained.

"Aye. A bit of it, at any rate. But I never see anything I might need to know myself unfortunately. Mostly it's just shadows." Like the ones that had lingered uncomfortably after last night's dream, she thought, experiencing another fleeting twinge of something she could not quite explain.

Knowing there was no point in forcing a vision, Kate turned her thoughts back to Quinn's question. "There are rare occasions when a vision comes more clearly. I saw my brother Conor's accident, for example, but I had no way of telling when it would happen or where. I tried to warn him, but he was a stubborn man, overbrimming with self-confidence, and would be hearing none of it."

"How did Nora respond?"

"Oh, I didn't tell her. I've never believed it's my place to tell people bad news that can't be avoided. It hurt our friendship for a time, but Nora's a good-hearted person and has never been one to hold a grudge."

When Brigid came running across the circle, Kate scooped her up, braced her against her hip and gave Quinn a serious look. "Nora's not had an easy time of it. And she's in for more pain."

"If you're suggesting I'm going to hurt her . . ."

"Oh, you will, indeed. But isn't that the way with men and women?" Shadows moved across her expressive blue eyes like clouds across the sun. "But something else is going to happen to someone she loves. I haven't been able to see who. Or when.

"The worry has been deviling my sleep, and when I'm awake, it hovers on the edge of my thoughts like the lingering fragments of a dream I can't quite recall. I've even tried coming up here every day, but it hasn't helped.

"But I do know that Nora will be needing

you to stand by her, Quinn. To offer her strength in a trying time."

"I'll do my best." It was time to bring up Kate's own troubles, he thought as they turned away from the stones and began walking back down the twisting path. "Speaking of trying times, perhaps I should have a little talk with your husband."

"Cadel?" Her head spun toward him. "What would you be wanting to talk with Cadel about?"

"How about suggesting that if he lays a hand on you again, as your new friend, I'll have no choice but to beat the living daylights out of him?"

Her face went as pale as glass. "I don't know what you're talking about."

"You're a delightful woman, Kate Fitzpatrick O'Sullivan, but you're a lousy liar."

Because he knew from personal experience that this could well be an issue of life and death, Quinn decided to forget about concealing his harsh childhood and go for broke.

"My father used to beat my mother. I tried to help, but all that ever happened was he'd beat me, too. Then be even harder on her."

Kate looked away, as if unable to bear the pain she could no doubt read in his eyes. "I'm sorry."

"So was I. He got sent to prison for killing a man in a drunken brawl. The jury convicted him of manslaughter. I wasn't old enough to understand the logistics, but I did understand that he wouldn't be coming back for a long time. And when the sheriff called to tell my mother that my father had been fatally stabbed in a prison riot, I was probably the happiest kid in the entire state of Nevada."

"That's so sad," she murmured. "That a boy would be celebrating his father's death. And your mother? How did she feel?"

"I have no idea. I never understood what made her stay with him in the first place. And I sure as hell never understood why she kept bringing home the same sort of violent men." Quinn stared out over the glistening blue-green water that looked so calm on the surface. But he knew, better than most, how deceiving appearances could be. "One of them killed her when I was nine."

"And the little boy who witnessed his mother's death grew up to write *The Night of the Banshee*."

He turned back toward her. "You're a perceptive woman, Kate O'Sullivan. And you deserve better." Although she was not yet old enough to understand his words, Brigid was looking up at him, her blue eyes suddenly as serious as her mother's. As if she was sensing the mood swirling between the two adults. Quinn skimmed a hand over the silky copper curls. "Your daughter deserves better. And so does Jamie."

"I know." Kate absently touched her fingers to her bruised cheek. "Cadel's away right now, gone to stay with his cousin in Dungarven. When he comes back, I'll be telling him there's no place in our lives, or my home, for him any longer."

Quinn wished it was that easy. But he suspected O'Sullivan would not take such news without putting up a fight.

"If you need any help . . ."

"I'll ring up Sergeant O'Neill."

"I'm closer."

Although there was nothing humorous about the topic, Kate laughed. "For a man who likes to keep to himself, you've certainly gotten yourself involved in a great many entanglements since arriving in Castlelough, Mr. Gallagher."

Not bothering to ask how she knew his nature, Quinn laughed, too. "You're telling me. If only I'd met you sooner, perhaps you could have read my palm, or thrown my stones, or whatever you druidic witches do to tell the future, and warned me of all the pitfalls I was going to encounter."

"Warnings are one thing. Behavior quite another entirely. I have the feeling you've seen most of those pitfalls yourself. And walked straight into them, anyway."

"With my eyes wide-open," he agreed, silently vowing to have a little heart-to-heart talk with Cadel O'Sullivan when he returned from sulking at his cousin's.

"I know you and Nora are close," he said, "but I'd like to ask a favor."

"Don't worry. I'll not be telling her about your childhood, Quinn. That's a story for you to share with her. If you choose."

If you choose. The words sounded so simple. But once again Quinn was forced to wonder if he'd had a choice about anything concerning Nora since his arrival in Ireland.

They were back in Kate's kitchen, sipping their way through a pot of tea while Brigid napped, when John came rushing in the door.

"Aunt Kate!" He was obviously winded, giving the impression he'd run across the fields from the Joyce farm. "You have to come." He bent over, put his hands on his knees and drew in a deep draught of ragged breath. "Nora needs your car."

"What's wrong?" Quinn was out of his chair in a shot. "Is it Nora?" His hands curled around the boy's upper arms, pulling him upright. "Has something happened to her?" Myriad pictures of farm accidents he'd witnessed while growing up, none of them pleasant, most grisly, swam to the forefront of his mind.

"No." John Joyce's eyes were wide, his face pale with red splotches riding in his cheeks.

"It's Fionna," Kate said quietly.

"Aye." John seemed unsurprised by his aunt's knowledge. "Nora got a call from the hospital." He paused to take another deep breath, forcing Quinn to rein in his impatience. "There was a bombing at a mall where Gran was shopping in Derry. She's been injured and taken to hospital. Since Nora wanted to keep the phone line open, in case the Garda might call, she sent me to borrow your car.

"Da's in the village with ours, so Nora needs yours to go fetch him. Then she's driving to Galway to catch a flight to the North."

"That's not necessary." It was Quinn's turn to shoot a look Kate's way. "Call Sergeant O'Neill and ask him to pick Brady up at The Rose and bring him home. I'll drive Nora and him to Galway."

"Fine," Kate said. Although she was pale,

her voice and her hand, as she reached for the telephone, were steady. "Shall I be calling the airline to see about flights?"

"That's not necessary, either. I'll arrange a charter to be waiting for us."

"Perhaps I can reach your assistant and have her ring Galway airfield for you."

Thinking she had one of the coolest heads in a crisis he'd ever witnessed, Quinn let go of John, then took hold of Kate's shoulders and gave her a quick kiss that held not a hint of lust. Only heartfelt gratitude.

"Her name's Brenda Michaels. She should be at Flannery House. She's got all my credit-card numbers, so she shouldn't have any problems. Tell her there'll be at least three people, maybe more," he said, remembering that Nora had an older brother, Michael, who lived on a nearby farm.

"I want the largest, most comfortable plane available and I don't care if it ends up being an Aer Lingus jet. Tell Brenda I'll have the cell phone in the car. She's to phone me with any news she can find out." He took a pen and business card from his pocket and scribbled down the cellular number and handed it to Kate.

"Consider it done," Kate said. "And please tell Nora that I'll spend the night at the house to tend to the children."

"You're a pearl among women, Kate Fitz-patrick O'Sullivan. It's too bad your husband's too damn dense to know what a treasure he got when he married you."

Despite the gravity of the situation, Kate smiled. "You do have a way of knowing what to say, Quinn Gallagher. No wonder Nora's fallen head over Wellies over you."

So Nora had talked with her sister-in-law about him. Although that came as no surprise, Quinn was more than a little relieved that at least some of the discussion appeared to have been positive.

Then, putting aside his own problems concerning his luscious landlady, he put a reassuring arm around Nora's youngest brother's shoulder. "Come on, John," he said with a robust tone meant to bestow confidence. "Let's go take care of your sister."

Quinn found Nora in the kitchen with Mary. "There's lamb stew for tonight," she was saying. "And in the morning, make certain Rory and Celia eat something before going off to school. There's porridge —"

"Celia always complains I make it too lumpy."

"Perhaps it's time for Celia to learn that you can't always avoid lumps in life," Nora snapped uncharacteristically.

"Well spoken," Quinn murmured. "But perhaps Celia can learn that little life lesson some other time. Kate's on her way over. She's spending the night, so she can take care of feeding the troops."

Nora had spun toward the door when he'd first spoken. Despite her remarkably steady voice as she'd instructed Mary on the domestic chores, her eyes were filled with panic.

"Oh, Quinn." Acting on impulse, as he'd discovered she so often did, she rushed across the room and practically hurled herself into his arms. "You were at Kate's," she remembered. "So you know."

"Yes." A tide of warm emotions flowed through him, as deep as the Irish sea. "Brady's on his way home, and as soon as he arrives, I'm taking you to Galway. Then on to Derry." He stroked the wild waves of her hair in a gesture meant to calm rather than arouse, then pressed a light kiss to her brow. "Why don't you go toss a few things into an overnight bag?"

She closed her eyes and held on tight for another long moment, accepting the strength he was offering. "Thank you."

Quinn watched her leave the room, then turned to Mary and John. "You're both old enough to be consulted about this," he said, knowing Nora might resent his taking over her duty as head of the household, but feeling that her brother and sister should have the opportunity to make their own decisions. "Do you want to come with us?"

"I'd only be in the doctors' way," John replied. "I think it's best I stay here and help with the younger children."

"And I couldn't bear to see Gran hurt," Mary said with a sniffle. "I'd just start weeping and make things worse for Nora."

True enough, Quinn thought. "I promise to keep you updated."

"Thank you, Mr. Gallagher," John said with his usual serious manner. "We'd appreciate that."

Kate was as good as her word, making the arrangements and showing up at the farm in record time. Since Nora had not yet returned downstairs, Quinn went to see if she needed help.

She was standing in the center of the small room he'd belatedly realized she'd been forced to move into in order to make room for him.

"I can't think." She turned toward him and dragged a trembling hand through her hair. She was pale as a wraith, and her green eyes, circling the room like frightened birds seeking escape, were bright with moisture.

"Heaven help me, I can't think of what to do. What to pack."

Quinn felt a powerful need to comfort her and was both surprised at how right it felt and irritated that he was too inexperienced with such feelings to know how to act on it.

Feeling as if he were crossing a tightrope blindfolded while juggling flaming torches, he began massaging her shoulders. "She'll be all right."

"I didn't want her to go." Her mind was spinning in circles, chased by frantic emotions. "I was so worried, but I kept telling myself she's an adult, after all. That I don't have any right putting curfews and restrictions on her the way I do the children."

"She wouldn't have listened if you'd tried."

"I know." Nora leaned her forehead against his shoulder and sighed. "I'm beginning to hate this bloody Bernadette campaign."

"Everyone needs a mission. Your grandmother could probably have a lot worse ones than getting a brave woman declared a saint."

"Why can't she just stay home and bake soda bread and say her rosary like other grandmothers?"

Nora's heart had been pounding in fear ever since she'd gotten the horrible telephone call from the Derry authorities. Now it crossed her mind that Quinn's shoulder was broad enough to bear heavy burdens. He was a man of many strengths, a man who'd stand by a woman. And though she suspected he'd argue the point, a good and loyal man.

For a woman who'd become accustomed to handling all sorts of problems by herself and felt pride in her ability to take care of her family, Nora might well have been annoyed by his take-charge attitude. But instead, she was discovering how lovely it was to have someone ease the burden for once.

"Fionna's one of a kind," he murmured against her temple. "Like her eldest granddaughter."

His warm tone caused a little triphammer of emotion in her heart. Nora lifted her head and gazed up at him. "I'm going to say something. And please, I don't want you to argue."

"I wouldn't think of it." Not while she felt as fragile as a hummingbird in his arms.

"You're so good for me." When he opened his mouth to respond, she pressed her fingers against his lips. "You said you wouldn't argue." She blinked, forcing back threatening tears. "It's true, Quinn, whether you're ready to believe it or not. And at this moment

I don't know what I'd do if you weren't here with me."

She might feel like a delicate humming-bird, but Quinn knew Nora had the heart of an eagle. She could have weathered this, no matter what the outcome, as she'd managed all the other tragedies in her life. The idea that she valued his presence beside her, that he could bring her strength, made him feel more powerful than he'd ever felt before in his life. As if he could leap tall buildings in a single bound.

It was also terrifying.

"I can't think of anywhere else I'd rather be." It was perhaps the most truthful statement Quinn had ever uttered. Somehow, when he'd let down his guard, when he hadn't been looking, the widow Fitzpatrick had become important to him. Everything about her had become important. Which was something else he was going to have to think about later.

For now, because he was, after all, only human, he dipped his head and touched his mouth to hers.

It was a shimmering whisper of a kiss, soft and tender and as sweet as sunshine through a rainbow. His mouth brushed hers, re-treated, then brushed again, like a butterfly sampling a meadow wildflower. Colors danced behind Nora's closed lids as she allowed her lips to cling.

She trembled as his palms slid over her shoulders and down her arms to her wrists before linking their fingers. She sighed as he traced the tender outline of her mouth with the tip of his tongue. Tension slowly began to dissolve, replaced by trust. And something he might have thought to be love — if Quinn had believed in such an impossible alien thing.

A door slammed downstairs, followed by the sound of Brady's voice. "Nora? Where are you, darling?"

They immediately drew apart at the sound of boots clattering up the stairs. The anxiety Quinn had witnessed in Nora's eyes earlier had been replaced by confusion.

"How do you do that?" she whispered shakily.

"Do what?"

She lifted her hand as if to comb it through her hair, then dropped it helplessly to her side. "Kiss me and make my mind go as clean as polished glass."

"Oh, that." Despite the circumstances, Quinn grinned. "Magic."

CHAPTER FIFTEEN

Broken Wings

The drive to Galway was mostly silent.
Brady, for once, seemed to have no stories to
tell. But that didn't mean they weren't going
on in his head. And from the bleak look in the
man's gaze every time Quinn glanced into
the rearview mirror, he decided that he
wasn't the only one in the car familiar with
horror tales.

Nora, too, seemed to have lost the capacity for speech. She sat erect in the passenger seat, her gaze directed out the
windshield. She was marble pale and would
have reminded him of some statue carved
from the smooth white stone had it not been
for her hands. She seemed incapable of
keeping them still, for they fluttered in her
lap like wounded birds. Sometimes she
twisted them together until the knuckles
turned white or dragged them through her
hair. Every so often she pressed her fingertips against her eyelids.

Finally Quinn reached out and captured

one of those hands in his. "It's going to be all right." He squeezed comfortingly before putting their joined hands on his thigh. "Fionna's going to be all right."

For the first time since she'd gotten that horrid phone call from that *Irish Times* reporter five years ago telling her about Conor's accident, she felt absolutely lost.

She looked at Quinn. "You can't know that for certain."

"True. But although I've never claimed to be the least bit psychic, I feel it in my bones. And besides, Kate said the same thing."

"I know." Nora bit her lip and turned to stare unseeingly at the front window again. "That's the only thing that's keeping me from screaming."

By the time they reached the Galway airfield, Quinn had already called the hospital twice. Both times they'd learned nothing, although a news bulletin broadcast on Radio One over the Mercedes radio did relate that the bomb had damaged the parking garage and nearly the entire street-level floor of a Derry department store. The number of injured were stretching local hospitals to the limit.

Since the single flight of her life had been aboard a prop plane from Shannon to Dublin with Conor, Nora was momentarily startled out of her fear and depression by the sight of the chartered private jet.

"You've booked us our very own plane?"

Quinn shrugged as the trio walked across the tarmac. "It seemed easier. And faster."

"It must have cost you a fortune."

Another shrug. "My accountant keeps telling me I've more money than I can spend in several lifetimes. Might as well make use of it."

Wondering what it must be like to have so much money it had lost its importance, Nora waited beside her still-silent father while Quinn introduced himself to the waiting pilot and the two men discussed the flight plan for the brief trip to the north. Kate had finally gotten through to someone who could give her some information, and called them on Quinn's cellular phone with the welcome news that Fionna's injuries were considered minor.

More hopeful than she'd been since leaving the farm, Nora boarded the plane with Quinn, her father and the pilot.

"Oh! It's as luxurious as a fine city hotel," Nora breathed as she stared around the roomy interior that reminded her of the Shelbourne. She and Conor had stayed there on their wedding night before going on to London where he had a race the next

299

morning. At the time she'd been certain that a palace could not have been fancier.

"It'll do," Quinn said. He glanced at her. She was still too pale. So was Brady. Quinn wondered what his chances were of getting either of them to take a brief nap. The jet had two bedrooms. "Perhaps you should lie down —"

"No." She shook her head, her tone firm. "I'm fine." She turned toward her father. "But, Da, I think a rest might do you good."

When her father lifted his head, Quinn realized where Nora had gotten her habit of jutting out her chin. "What kind of man would you think I'd be? Sleeping while my mam may be lying in some hospital bed dying?"

"Gran's not dying. The doctor told Kate her only injuries are a broken wrist and possible concussion."

"She's not a young woman," Brady argued. "A concussion could be serious. And then there's her heart . . ." He pressed a weathered hand against his own chest. "Oh, Jaysus."

Quinn caught the older man as he sank to his knees.

"Da!" Nora knelt beside the biscuit-colored suede chair Quinn had lowered her father into. "What's wrong? Should we be having the pilot call the doctor?"

"I'm fine." He patted the back of her hand. "I just got a little light-headed, darling. I think it's the airsickness."

"We haven't taken off yet."

"Anticipation is a fearsome thing," he countered. "And besides, that long drive made me a wee bit dizzy."

Nora gave him a long probing look, damning the storytelling ability that made her father such a gifted liar. The color was coming back into a complexion that had momentarily been the hue of putty.

Horribly torn between a need to be at her grandmother's hospital bed, to see for herself that the doctor had told Kate the truth about Fionna's lack of life-threatening injuries, and concern for her father, Nora glanced up at Quinn.

"Your call," he murmured.

She worried an unlacquered thumbnail with her teeth as she tried to make the critical decision.

"I'm the father of the family," Brady stated firmly. "Which means I'll be the one to make the decision. And I say we're wasting time arguing when we could be in the air on the way to Derry."

Nora couldn't remember the last time her father had stood his ground about anything. Although there'd never been a day in her life that she hadn't loved him, there had been times when the thought had crossed her mind that Brady Joyce was a bit weak. Since the idea seemed disloyal, she'd always put it away. But now, for the second time in two days, she was witnessing a spark of the man Eleanor Joyce had fallen in love with.

Still troubled, Nora looked up at Quinn. "We'll be going to Derry."

His brief nod told her he would have made the same decision. "I'll tell the pilot."

Before he left the lounge, Quinn reached down, caught her chin in his hand and smoothed his thumb over her downturned lips. "Everything's going to be fine."

And although it didn't make any sense at all, because it was Quinn telling her this, Nora chose to believe him.

After all the fuss about Brady not wanting to rest for fretting about his mother, Nora was stunned when he refused to enter the hospital.

"You can't be serious!" She stared at her father in disbelief. "Surely you can't be telling me you've come all the way to the North with me only to sit outside the hospital where your own mother may be dying?"

"Nora." Quinn was standing beside her next to the hired long black car that had been waiting for them at the Derry airfield. The car her father was still inside. He reached out a calming hand. "That's not what Kate said."

She whirled on him. "Don't you be telling me what my own sister-in-law told me," she flared. Fear and anxiety conspired to fuel the temper she usually managed to keep well banked. "This is family business."

And you're not family. Quinn read her unstated message loud and clear.

"You're right." He lifted his hands in a gesture of surrender, but didn't budge. "I may not be family, but I can tell this is hard enough on your father. Don't make it worse."

"Of course it's hard on him, having Fionna in hospital." For the first time since he'd met her, her eyes were as hard as stones. She leaned into the long black limousine. "Well, let me tell you something, Da," she said. "It's a lot harder having your mam die on you without so much as having an opportunity to say goodbye. Or being able to tell her how much you love her . . ."

Her voice cracked and she turned away for a moment, drawing in a ragged breath that told Quinn she was not thinking of Fionna right now but of her own mother.

He watched with admiration as she

straightened her shoulders. And her resolve. Then turned back to her father. "You need to get out of the bloody car and come in with me. Now."

Brady's eyes were suspiciously shiny, but his jaw remained firm. "You've no right using such a tone with your father, Nora." He looked past her up to Quinn. "Would you be doing me a favor, lad?"

"Of course," Quinn said, earning another daggerlike glare from Nora.

"Take my daughter in to see her grandmother. And tell Fionna that I love her."

"Da —" Nora started in again.

"Consider it done." Quinn cupped her elbow, pulling her away from the limo. "Come on, sweetheart. We'd better get in there before Fionna starts roaming the halls interviewing patients in search of Bernadette miracles."

"I don't believe this." She shook her head, her face a study of frustration and sorrow. "You've disappointed me before, Da," she said quietly. Painfully. "But never so much as you have this day."

With that indictment ringing in the air, she shook off Quinn's touch, turned and walked past him, headed toward the glass doors.

Quinn paused. "I'm sorry," he told Brady.

The older man only waved a weary hand. "Nora has a right to her feelings. And later, after you come out and tell me that my mother is her typical hale-and-hearty self, I'll be enjoying the fact that for the first time in years, my daughter has someone to lean on. Believe me, Quinn, witnessing her surrender the reins of total control of the family, even for an afternoon, is worth being the target of a few hasty words spoken out of fear."

Quinn gave Brady another, longer look, realizing he may have underestimated the man. "I'll take care of her."

Brady leaned back against the rich black leather seat and closed his eyes. "Of course you will."

Nora was arguing with a gray-smocked reception clerk when Quinn caught up with her.

"Let me," he murmured, stroking her arm. "Hello." He flashed his best smile at the pink-faced twenty-something woman seated behind the computer screen. "I'm Quinn Gallagher. And this is Nora Joyce."

He told himself the only reason he'd omitted her married name was that it complicated the matter unnecessarily. It had nothing to do with the reality that, all logic aside, he was still jealous as hell at the idea of her having belonged to any other man.

"We'd like the room number of Fionna Joyce. She was brought in shortly after the bombing."

"Are you from the authorities?"

"No. We're family."

"Visiting hours aren't until this evening."

"I understand." Another smile, warmer than the first. A hundred-proof grin designed to entice. "And I realize that if you allow everyone to broach the rules —" Quinn's friendly gaze settled momentarily on her name tag "— Ms. Barry, the wards would be chaos, rather than the well-ordered places I've no doubt they are in a hospital with such an exemplary staff.

"However," he said, tightening his fingers ever so slightly on Nora's arm when he sensed her opening her mouth to resume arguing, "we've come a very long way. From Castlelough, and —"

"From Castlelough?" The woman, whose expression had remained one of bureaucratic boredom, despite Quinn's attempt at charm, suddenly perked up. "Did you say your name was Gallagher?"

"Quinn Gallagher," he agreed.

"You're the American novelist."

His answering smile suggested she was, indeed, the brightest woman in all of Northern Ireland. "Guilty."

"I saw all about the movie they're making out of your book in Castlelough on the television news." Her eyes narrowed as they slid back to Nora. "Are you one of the movie people, as well?"

"No, and I don't see what any of this has to do with —"

"You'll have to excuse Ms. Joyce's impatience," Quinn cut in smoothly. "She's been frantic about her grandmother. Mrs. Fionna Joyce," he reminded the clerk as he inclined his head toward her computer screen, which was currently flashing brand names of prescription drugs as a screen saver.

"Joyce." She began tapping away obligingly on the keyboard. "Is Fionna spelled with one *n* or two?"

"Two," Nora supplied with a very unNora-like curtness.

"Here it is. Room 625." Ignoring Nora, the clerk turned her attention back to Quinn. "She's had a cast put on her wrist and is going to have to remain overnight for observation," she reiterated what Kate had already told them. "You'd best keep your visit brief. This is a teaching hospital and it's almost time for evening rounds. The doctors get very annoyed when their presentations are interrupted."

"We'll be in and out before anyone even

knows we've been here," Quinn promised. "Thank you, Ms. Barry." Taking Nora's elbow again, he began leading her toward the bank of elevators. "You've been a true angel of mercy."

"Angel, ha!" Nora said tightly as the steel gray doors closed behind them. "Since when do angels undress men with their beady little eyes?"

"I didn't think you noticed," Quinn said smoothly. "As upset as you were about your dear old granny."

"I *am* upset about Gran!" Her lips trembled even as her eyes flashed. "I'm also upset about the way you seem to have taken over my life like some rich, jackbooted Yank storm trooper."

"I see." He watched the numbers flash in orange lights above the door. "Are you referring to my driving you and Brady to Galway? Arranging for a private plane so you wouldn't have to waste precious time in the terminal waiting to be packed onto a commercial flight like a sardine in a can?

"Or the car, perhaps. Did you find the limousine a wee bit ostentatious for your humble Irish country tastes?"

Nora couldn't help it. His gently teasing tone smoothed the ragged edges of temper, calmed her nerves and soothed the fear that had been bubbling away inside her like acid.

"This isn't the way it's supposed to work," she murmured. Like him she was watching the numbers flash by. "You're supposed to be the nasty one. And I'm supposed to be the one jollying you out of your moods."

"Believe me, sweetheart, you'll undoubtedly have plenty more opportunities to do exactly that. And although I'm not against a bit of role reversal, I'm going to have to put my foot down about tonight."

"Tonight?"

"I promised you dinner," he reminded her as the elevator reached the sixth floor with an electronic ding. "And rich, jackbooted Yank storm trooper that I am, I have every intention of taking you out for the best meal in Derry."

Not giving her an opportunity to argue his renewed plans, he ushered her out the open doorway. By following the numbers and arrows posted on the wall, he found the way to Fionna's hospital room.

Nora was more than a little relieved when she saw her grandmother sitting up in bed watching the television bolted to the wall.

"Shouldn't you be lying down?"

"It's too difficult to watch the telly that way," Fionna said with a great deal of calm for someone who'd just survived a bombing.

"But you've been hurt."

" 'Tis barely a scratch." She lifted her wrist, encased in white plaster. "Though I worry this will be troublesome when I knit. I tried to talk the doctor into using one of those stretch elastic bandages, but you know how stubborn folks are up here in the North."

"Not at all like folks in the South," Nora said dryly. "At least you agreed to stay the night."

"Oh, I'll not be spending the night. I suspected Quinn would be bringing you, and since this room is a great deal more comfy than the crowded emergency department downstairs, I was willing to let them check me in while I waited.

"Mrs. Murphy and I have been passing the time watching the scenes of the bombing and lamenting the foolishness of men."

She tilted her bright red-gold head, which seemed strangely dusted with white powder, toward the occupant of the other bed in the room. The middle-aged woman's leg was held up in the air by a system of pulleys.

"Were you injured in the blast, as well?" Nora asked the woman politely.

"Oh, I was, indeed. Blew me right out of my shoes, it did. Broke my leg in three places." She scowled. "And to think it had taken me all day to find a pair of pumps to go with my new Sunday dress. And now they're gone."

"They were a lovely navy," Fionna divulged. "With white trim. Of course we wouldn't be lamenting them if anyone had been seriously hurt."

"Aye," Mrs. Murphy agreed promptly with a nod of her snowy head. "And isn't that a miracle?"

"The police are reporting the major damage was done to the parking garage," Nora said.

Fionna sighed. "I suppose that means I've lost my lovely automobile."

"We can always buy you a new car." Nora sat down on the edge of the bed and took hold of her grandmother's hand. "What's important is that you — and everyone else shopping in the store — are all right."

"There is another good thing."

"What's that?"

"I was having the devil's own time finding anyone to wait on me." Her grandmother's wicked grin reminded Nora a great deal of Brady's. "So I hadn't yet paid for your new blazer."

They shared a laugh. Then Nora sobered. "Da's downstairs waiting in the car. I tried to talk him into coming in with me, but . . ."

"Well, of course he couldn't do that."

"How did you know?"

"Isn't Brady my son? And doesn't a mother know what disturbs her child, just as you know what upsets your own dear Rory?" Fionna turned toward Quinn. "Brady was born at home. In the same bed you're sleeping in, Mr. Gallagher."

"I hadn't realized that."

"Well, of course you'd be having no way of knowing. It was my bed at the time. Mine and my darling Patrick's. When Brady and Eleanor married, it was passed down to them. As it was passed down to you, Nora, when you and Conor wed."

"Da said at the time it made more sense, with Mam gone, for him to be taking the single."

"That's true enough. But part of the reason he gave it up when you married was that it was too painful for him trying to get a decent night's sleep in the bed where he'd spent so many years with your mam. The very same bed where dear Celia should have been born."

"All the rest of us were born at home," Nora explained to Quinn.

"As have all the Joyce babies," Fionna agreed. "For as long as anyone can remember. But your mother's pregnancy with

Celia was a difficult one. Which is why the doctor arranged for her to have her baby in hospital at Galway, instead of at home."

And the Galway hospital was where her mother had died. Nora began to understand why her father had refused to leave the limousine.

"But this isn't the same hospital," she said.

"No. But hospitals are much the same the world over, darling. And the memories are probably too difficult for your dear da to handle."

"Oh, God." Nora shut her eyes. "I was so hard on him."

"He understood you were upset," Quinn assured her.

"Of course he did," Fionna agreed with her usual brisk manner. "And no harm has been done. I'll just be getting dressed now and we'll leave here, and —"

"No," Nora said swiftly. Firmly.

"What did you say, darling?" Fionna looked up at her as if she'd just spoken a foreign language.

"I said no." She folded her arms across her chest. "I'll not be giving Da another reason to hate hospitals by checking you out early, then having you drop dead because of some terrible fatal head injury."

"The only thing wrong with my head is

313

that I can still hear that explosion going off in it." She grimaced as she combed her fingers through the lank strands. "And my hair is in frightful need of a washing. It's full of plaster dust."

"It won't do you any good to argue, Gran." Nora heard a flurry of activity behind her and turned to see a group of white-jacketed doctors standing in the doorway. "Well, it appears it's time for rounds. We'd best be leaving."

"But, Nora —"

"We're in the doctors' way." Having sensed her grandmother gearing up for a battle, Nora was more than a little relieved at the timely interruption. She bent down and kissed Fionna's cheek. "Sleep well. We'll be back in the morning to fetch you home."

"Traitor," Fionna muttered, nevertheless kissing Nora back. She looked up at Quinn. "Thank you for getting my granddaughter here so promptly. I trust you'll be taking good care of her tonight, as well."

"I'm going to do my best."

"Aye. I've no doubt of that." Fionna tilted her face, offering her cheek to him. "Now give me a quick kiss and get back to my son before he worries himself into an early grave."

She wasn't his grandmother. But as he did

as instructed, Quinn felt a strange jolt of some strong, almost familial emotion. He covered it smoothly.

"You're a remarkably brave woman, Fionna Joyce." He took her uninjured hand and, in a gesture that seemed to surprise everyone in the room, including himself, lifted her fingertips to his lips. "And although I'm no expert on miracles, I have to wonder if your pull with Bernadette might not be the reason everyone in that store managed to survive the bombing."

"Faith, I hadn't thought of that." The elderly woman's eyes lit up. "I'll have to be doing some investigating after I get out of here."

"You'll be coming straight home to the farm as soon as you're out of here," Nora insisted. "You can always write up your report from there." Her voice and her expression gentled. "The children are worried, Gran. Although they've been told you're all right, they're going to want to see you back home safe and sound for themselves."

"You wouldn't be trying to make me feel guilty now, would you, Nora?"

"Me?" Nora flashed her first genuine smile of the day. "Would I be doing such a thing?"

Fionna laughed. "You're definitely your

father's daughter, Nora Fitzpatrick," she called out as they left the hospital room.

Brady sat alone in the back of the limousine, thinking he should be making a close study of the fancy car. He doubted there were many in Castlelough who'd ever seen a limousine, much less ridden in one. Wouldn't they want to be hearing all about it? The tale should be good for several pints at the very least.

The problem was, he couldn't concentrate on the sparkling Waterford crystal vase in the ever-popular Lismore pattern, or the fine leather seats, or the bar with champagne on ice or even the television.

He closed his eyes and pressed his fingers against his closed lids so hard he saw stars. But it wasn't enough to rid his mind of the profound disappointment on his daughter's face as she'd walked away from him.

CHAPTER SIXTEEN

You Touched Upon My Life

Her grandmother's words stayed with Nora all the way back down the hall and during the seemingly interminable elevator ride to the street floor.

"I owe Da an apology," she murmured finally.

"He doesn't need it." Quinn smoothed at the lines furrowing her forehead. "Brady's your father, Nora. He loves you. He understands you were under a lot of stress."

"I should have realized . . ."

"You're not a mind reader. And just because your mother died doesn't mean you now have to be in charge of the entire world, sweetheart," he said as they walked out the double glass doors of the emergency department.

He stopped on the sidewalk and, forgetting his lifelong aversion to public displays of emotion, took her in his arms and pressed his lips to the top of her head. "You've already done more than your share to pick up the reins of the family. Brady realizes that."

Nora wasn't accustomed to being comforted. And although she was frightened by how good it felt to have Quinn's strong arms around her, to have someone to lean on for a change instead of being the one everyone leaned on, she allowed herself to cling. Just for a minute.

"I owe you so much," she murmured into his shirt. "The way you arranged for Kate to stay with the children. For the driving. The plane. And the fancy black car." She looked up at him, her eyes moist. "For everything." *For being you,* she thought, but did not say for fear of chasing him away. "I don't know how to thank you."

"Don't worry." He flashed a wicked grin as he flicked a finger down the slope of her nose. "We'll think of something."

As with everything else in this country, Quinn's dinner did not go according to plan. Instead of a romantic dinner for two in Galway, he was forced to watch as Nora and Brady treated each other with a strained politeness that set his nerves on edge.

They'd begun with a bottle of champagne, appropriate, he'd said when he'd ordered, to toast Fionna's surviving the bombing virtually unscathed. Nora and Brady had obediently clinked glasses, but their expressions remained as stiff as department-store mannequins.

Time after time he attempted to start a conversation, but the uncharacteristic silence kept hovering over the table, through the smoked-salmon first course, the excellent lamb entrée, and now it appeared that dessert would be ruined by the downcast mood, as well.

Unaccustomed to failure, Quinn decided to give it one last shot. "So, Brady," he said, leaning back in the brocade covered chair, "have you ever considered writing your stories down?"

"No, I haven't."

Quinn resisted the urge to grind his teeth. "May I ask why not? It certainly seems there'd be an audience, especially with all the Americans boasting Irish ancestry."

"Not all Americans are interested in their roots," Nora said quietly.

"True. But I'll bet enough are that your dad could earn a bundle if he only took the time —"

"It's not the time." Brady's voice held no more enthusiasm than Nora's. "Writing my tales down would offend my belief in the oral tradition."

"Da's already turned down offers from

publishing houses in Dublin and London," Nora divulged with a bit more strength.

"And New York, too," Brady reminded her.

"Aye." She smiled for the first time since they'd entered the five-star hotel dining room. "The poor man was quite put out that he'd flown all the way across an ocean only to be sent back home again empty-handed."

When she named the famous publisher, Quinn said, "You actually had the man come here? From New York?"

"It was his choice," Brady explained. "Didn't he choose not to believe me when I'd already told him no in a letter? And all those phone calls?"

"His wife heard Da at the Puck Fair and tape-recorded some of his stories," Nora said. "When she returned home, she played them for her husband, who was quite impressed."

"There are probably thousands of writers who'd sell their souls for an offer from that house."

"A soul's a high price to pay for success," Brady said.

"I was speaking metaphorically." Quinn had almost forgotten how seriously religion was taken in this country. Wasn't a centuries-old religious conflict the reason Fionna was lying in a hospital right now?

"Of course you were, lad. And you're right. Many at The Rose called me a fool for turning down such a generous offer. But I've given the best years of my life to the oral tradition. It didn't seem right to sell out a belief. Even if it would pay for a new roof."

"And that prize bull John Kavanagh was wanting to sell us," Nora reminded him without reproach. She turned back to Quinn. "Da's never approved of writing the stories down. He insists they're meant to be told, to be passed down from generation to generation."

"That's commendable," Quinn allowed. "Although I'll have to admit I'm glad not everyone feels that way."

"Oh, books are lovely in their own fashion," Brady said, a bit more lilt in his brogue. "But what's right for one is not always right for another."

"True."

"Da's been asked to perform at the heritage center at Ardagh this summer," Nora revealed with unmistakable daughterly pride. "That's the village where Saint Patrick consecrated Saint Mel as bishop."

"Aye, and that's an important enough historical event," Brady allowed as he reached into his pocket, took out a pouch of tobacco and began filling his pipe. "But I was thinking I'd be telling the story of Una Bhan."

"Oh, Da." Nora frowned. "That's such a sad tale."

"Aye, I can see how some might view it that way. But others might have a different opinion. And won't it give me an opportunity to sing, as well." He turned to Quinn. "Not that I'd be wanting to boast, mind you, but there are those who say I've a fine tenor voice."

"You've a grand voice," Nora said. "And, of course the fact that your favorite version of the song runs forty-five verses wouldn't have anything to do with you choosing that particular story."

" 'Tis a long tale. It needs to be told in its own time."

There was another pause as Brady looked expectantly at Quinn.

"Of course I'm going to bite," Quinn said, leaning back in his chair and taking a sip of his after-dinner brandy. "I'd love to hear it."

"Well, now, since you asked . . ." As the older man lit the pipe, the flare from the match danced merrily in bright blue eyes that once again reminded Quinn of a leprechaun. "In County Roscommon, there's a lovely lough that spreads wide and serene on the upper Shannon River. In the very center of the lake, there's a lonely island —"

"Castle Island," Nora interjected.

"Now who'd be telling this tale?" Brady asked.

Nora's answering grin revealed that things were back to normal. "You are, Da."

"And isn't that what I was thinking?" He huffed out a breath, leaned back and puffed on his pipe. "Well, to continue my story, Castle Island was, for many centuries, the seat of the MacDermotts.

"Now I tell you that there was a fair and handsome daughter named Una, who attracted the love of a man named Thomas Costello, who went by the nickname Tumaus Loidher, which is Irish for Strong Thomas. There was, in Ireland at the time, no man with the strength of Thomas Costello. Indeed, he was so strong that when he was only a lad, about seventeen years or so, a bully — a man who'd already killed a great many people — came to the town of Sligo and challenged the entire county to put forth a man to wrestle with him.

"Well, as it so happens, Thomas had come to the town with his father's brother and they watched as the bully hurled man after man to the ground. In those days, you see, the unfortunate city would be forced to support the champion.

"Against his uncle's wishes, Thomas volunteered to wrestle, but his uncle refused again and again until finally he grew weary of the young man's beseeching and gave him permission to fight.

"There was a gasp from the people gathered, because they feared that such a young man would surely be killed. Young girls and women wept, and it's said that even Thomas's own uncle had tears on his face.

"But Thomas knew he was stronger than the people thought. Indeed, the muscles in his arms were as firm and hard as iron, so when the match began, he grabbed the bully before the man could get hold of him and squeezed. Now everyone, especially Thomas, was puzzled when the champion didn't fight back. But then, when Thomas released him, the man fell back, stone-cold dead, don't you know, his back broken. And that was the first of many heroic feats Thomas Costello performed.

"But that is neither here nor there — there are so many stories about the grand deeds Tumaus Loidher performed that if I were to begin relating them, I'd never cease — and I must be getting on with my story before Nora complains that I've gotten side-tracked again."

"I wasn't going to say a thing," Nora insisted.

"And aren't you a fine polite girl."

Quinn watched as Brady beamed at Nora, causing her to smile back.

"As I was saying, Thomas, who was much beloved by the people, fell in love with the fair Una MacDermott and she with him. But Thomas was not a rich man, and the MacDermotts were a family of property, don't you know, and MacDermott had already chosen a wealthy man for his daughter to wed.

"And then of course, there was that other dilemma I must tell you, which I forgot to tell you before, that the Costellos and MacDermotts had taken opposing sides during the Cromwellian upheavals, like Irish Capulets and Montagues, you see, and there was no way MacDermott was going to allow his family to be linked with the one who'd lost out in the Cromwellian settlement.

"Una was heartbroken and when she fell ill of lovesickness, her father finally allowed Thomas to visit her, but when MacDermott continued to withhold his consent to a marriage, Thomas grew angry and rode away, swearing never to return if he was not recalled before crossing the Donogue River to his own home.

"He tarried for a long time in the water, hopefully awaiting a messenger from his fair Una, but finally, after being taunted by a servant for surrendering his pride to a woman, he drove his horse up onto the bank. He was scarcely on dry ground when a messenger did, indeed, come from Una, entreating him to come back to her.

"But Thomas was known throughout the land as a man of his word, don't you see, and he'd given his vow not to return once he'd crossed the river."

"Pride goeth before a fall," Quinn murmured.

"Aye. You've spoken the sad truth. And Thomas was a fearsome prideful man." Brady gave a regretful shake of his head. "To pursue the story further, 'twas after this regretful day that grief and melancholy settled hard on poor Una. She died of a broken heart and was buried on Trinity Island in Lough Key.

"Thomas swam his horse to that very same island every night to lament their tragically lost love, and during those lonely nights, he composed the passionate tormented poem he called *Una Bhan*, or *Fair*

Una, as it's also known by some. And then, his own heavy heart broken, as well, he died and, as he had requested, was buried beside the darling love of his life.

"And it was soon after that an ash tree magically grew out of Una's grave. And another out of the grave where Thomas Costello had been laid to rest, and they inclined toward each other like lovers, and kept growing until the branches entwined like a bower over the two sweethearts who were finally together at last.

"And if you go to Lough Key today, you'll see poor MacDermott's castle still standing amidst the tangled thickets of briers, wrapped in ivy and creepers, looking for all the world like Sleeping Beauty's castle, awaiting young Tumaus Loidher to return and bring it back to life again."

"Great story," Quinn murmured, lifting his glass in a salute. A man who'd written tales of banshees, ghost stallions and lake serpents could appreciate the story of an ill-fated romance and a castle awaiting rebirth. "A tragic tale of man's flaws of pride and prejudice."

"Aye, I've always thought so, as well. But you'd be overlooking the most important part. The part about two lovers reunited after death." There was something in his

327

voice, something deep and profound that made Quinn wonder if the older man could be thinking of his own lost love.

"You're not only a splendid storyteller yourself, Quinn Gallagher," Brady suddenly declared, his mood lightening once again. "You're a good and generous fellow, getting me talking so as to help ease the pain I've been suffering all day."

"I enjoy hearing tales. And yours was a good one."

"It's a fine tale, sure enough. But that doesn't take away from the truth that you're an equally fine man."

He'd been called many things. But *good* and *generous* had never been words used to describe him. Uncomfortable with the personal turn the conversation had taken, Quinn declared the evening at an end by calling for the check.

In a quirk of bad timing, The Chieftains were appearing in Derry's concert hall, and members of the group had booked all the suites in the hotel. The other top hotels were booked as well, but fortunately Brenda had proven her usual efficient self, managing to reserve adjoining rooms for Quinn and Nora, and one for Brady on the floor below.

Remembering what Laura had said about the gossip concerning his relationship with

Nora Fitzpatrick, he decided that Brenda booking Nora's father on a different floor had not been a coincidence.

When they retired to their respective rooms, Quinn found the comforter turned down, a piece of minty chocolate on the pillow and the radio tuned to some local station that specialized in "easy listening." The work of the unseen maid was, Quinn thought, the first familiar thing he'd experienced since stepping off the plane at Shannon.

He loosened his tie, unbuttoned the top two buttons of his white dress shirt, kicked off his shoes and was eyeing his door between the room and Nora's. Feeling like a nervous groom awaiting his bride, he was trying to decide whether he should knock or just take the bull by the goddamn horns and go in when the door suddenly opened and Nora stood there, still in the somber heather gray dress she'd worn to dinner.

Tension whipped through him like a whirlwind. He didn't speak. Amazingly he couldn't. On some distant level Quinn found it ironic that, after having wanted Nora since that first drunken moment he'd stepped out of the back of Sergeant O'Neill's patrol car and seen her standing in front of the house, backlit by the yellow porch light and looking like an ancient Celtic goddess, he now couldn't move to take what she'd come to offer him.

As if possessing the ability to read his mind, she smiled. Faintly. Softly. And he felt the iceberg encasing his heart crack a little more, as it seemed to do whenever she was near.

"Da made you uncomfortable tonight." Her throaty voice proved devastatingly potent. "When he called you a good and generous man."

She'd come to know him well. Too well. "Your father has an overactive imagination."

"Aye." She closed the door behind her. And did not look back. "He does, indeed. But like all *seanachies,* he's a student of human nature." She crossed the room to stand in front of him. "Why is it that a simple statement of truth should make you turn the color of ashes?"

"Now it's you with the wild imagination." His hand felt abnormally heavy as he lifted it to stroke her hair. The fiery waves felt like silk beneath his palm. He knew her skin was even softer.

"Oh, I've always been the practical one in the family. Ask anyone." She went up on her toes and pressed her lips to his. "You are a good man, Quinn Gallagher. No matter what you say."

The touch of her mouth caused a painful thrumming in his loins. He'd wanted her, all right. But now that he was on the verge of having her, Quinn realized that wanting was too simple for what he was feeling. Music drifted from the bedside radio, soft and dreamy.

"I just realized that as pleasant as dinner was," he said, "we missed an important part of our evening."

"And what would that be?"

"I'd intended romance." He touched her hair again and looked down at her while she looked back up at him, both paused on the brink of something that had seemed inevitable from the beginning.

Her eyes were wide and innocent, and if he hadn't known better, he'd have thought she was yet untouched, as if waiting for him.

"I want to dance with you, Mrs. Fitzpatrick."

"Why, that sounds lovely, Mr. Gallagher."

He took her easily into his arms, his fingers spanning her waist, her hand resting lightly on his shoulder as they swayed to the romantic ballad.

His body was hard against hers, his breath a soft breeze against her temple. It surprised

Nora that despite the difference in their heights, they seemed to fit well together. The tenseness that had gripped her body and heart since the argument with her father, the anxiety that had had her nerves screeching when she'd dared to open that door between their rooms slid away as she surrendered to the romance of the music, of this one stolen night. Sighing her pleasure, she lifted her arms and linked her fingers together behind his neck. Her eyes drifted closed.

Her soft curves were pressed against him in a way that made him ache. He nuzzled her neck and breathed in the scents of the same white soap and herbal shampoo he used in the shower every morning. There was also another faint fragrance that reminded him of Irish druids dancing in fairy rings. In the rain.

"You've changed your scent."

"Aye." Her eyelids fluttered open ever so slightly and in them he saw unmistakable desire. "I bought a bottle of ridiculously dear perfume at Monohan's." Her smile was one of contradictions, managing to be both shy and vixen-alluring at the same time. "I was hoping to seduce you." Her fingers stroked the back of his neck, playing with the dark hair that nearly brushed his collar.

"If that was your plan, you're succeeding admirably. And you definitely could have pulled it off without the new perfume." He touched his mouth to her temple. "But I like it, just the same."

"I'm pleased. Since I bought the body lotion and powder, as well. It took such a long time to spread it on this evening, I was afraid I'd be late to dinner. Although I wash my skin every morning in the shower, I never realized how much I have."

The idea of Nora wearing nothing but perfume and powder licked at his desire, causing it to flame higher. He drew back a little. "You know I want you."

"Aye. That's what you've been saying. From the first."

"The thing is . . ." Hell, her body was practically melting against his and the fingers stroking his neck were driving him to distraction. He stopped moving to the music and captured both her hands. "The thing is, you're an intelligent woman . . ."

"What a lovely thing to say. And although it's a fine compliment, I think I'd rather, just for tonight, that you tell me how beautiful I am." Her hands were shackled in his, but that didn't stop her from pressing her smiling lips to his throat. "And how much you want to go to bed with me."

"Oh, Christ." The words, and the groan, were ripped from somewhere deep inside him. "My point is . . . and I do have one," he managed to say on a gasp as her tongue dampened his hot flesh, "is that a decent intelligent woman like you shouldn't be here like this. You deserve a man who can give you what you need."

"And if I need you?"

The softly spoken words were part question, part request. Never had Quinn had more difficulty drawing air in and out of his lungs.

"Dammit, Nora, you should take off running." Her lips felt like a brand, making this the hardest thing he'd ever done. "While you still can."

"Oh, Quinn." She shook her head, her eyes shimmering with a host of complex emotions. "Don't you see?" She skimmed her mouth over his jaw, until it was a mere whisper away from his grimly set lips. "It's too late for running."

The touch of her soft succulent mouth against his was like a spark against dry tinder. "Too late," Quinn agreed roughly as he hauled her against him. "For either of us."

CHAPTER SEVENTEEN

Towards the Mist

Quinn released her hands, but only to grab her hips, lifting her against him, thigh to thigh, chest to chest, greedy lips to lips as he half carried, half dragged her to the bed.

Sweep the widow Fitzpatrick off her feet, he heard Laura's voice echoing through his heated mind.

And wasn't he doing exactly that?

Unable to remember when he'd felt so free, Quinn laughed as they landed on the double mattress in a tangle of arms and legs. Her hair wound around them, wrapping him in fragrance. He kissed her, a long deep wet kiss that made him quake from within.

"God, you're sweet." His hands dived into the silk strands of her hair and pulled her mouth back to his. "And potent. I've never been with a woman who can make me as drunk with a single taste as you can."

"And I've never been with a man who made me feel like the type of woman who could make a man drunk." She dragged her mouth away and lifted her head. "It's a fearful feeling."

"Ah, sweetheart." One hand smoothed its way down the back of her dress in a reassuring gesture while the other delved beneath the gray skirt. When he realized she wasn't wearing the expected panty hose, but stockings that ended with a border of lace high on her porcelain-smooth bare thigh, Quinn felt his blood begin to boil.

The feel of his hand on her skin made her stiffen ever so slightly. "It's okay," he crooned. "You don't have to be afraid." His palm edged higher. "I'd never hurt you."

He knew that was a lie even as he said the words. For he *would* hurt her. He could only hope that someday years from now, when she was happily married to some easygoing Irish farmer who adored her and the children they would undoubtedly have together, Nora would forgive him for tonight.

"It's not you I'm fearful of, but me. Of how you make me feel." He felt her soft sigh against his mouth, felt her body relax as he continued his caressing touch up her leg. "And you've had so many women . . ."

"None like you." Easy words, designed to trip off the tongue as they had in so many similar situations. But never had Quinn meant them more than he did at this moment.

"I'm afraid of disappointing you."

He couldn't help himself. He laughed at that as he rolled them over on their sides. A rough lust-edged sound that was half groan. "Honey, I've already told you — if there's one thing you can't do it's disappoint me."

"I'm not very experienced."

"Don't worry. I am." In contrast to the sexy lace at the top of her stockings, her panties were white cotton. The type, Quinn thought, as he slipped a finger beneath the elastic leg band, a former would-be nun might wear. But hearing her soft moan as he stroked her intimately, knowingly, he reminded himself that she'd left the convent a very long time ago.

"You'll see, Nora," he murmured as he continued stoking the fire between her legs. "You'll be perfect." Her eyes were huge as they looked up into his. But in them he read absolute trust. "We'll be perfect together."

Nora had never known her skin could be so sensitive. Never known desire could be so sweet and so strong at the same time.

"Quinn —" His mouth drank from hers, swallowing what she'd already forgotten she'd been intending to say. "I need . . ." Her voice was weak. Slurred. "I need . . ."

"I know." And to prove he did, indeed, understand her ragged plea, he used his thumb on the vulnerable nub hidden in her slick folds.

It was as if he'd reached into the sky, pulled down a sparkling white-hot star and touched it against her ultrasensitive flesh. Nora gasped, then trembled as release shimmered through her.

"Oh," she said on a sigh, as the brilliant sensation ebbed, "that was lovely."

"Lovely is good." He planted a trail of lingering kisses down her throat. "For starters."

"Oh, I couldn't. Not again." Once was an event in itself. Something to celebrate when she could think again.

"Wanna bet?"

His grin was rife with masculine satisfaction as he began to unzip her dress. He wanted to rip it off her, but because he was determined to savor, not just for her, but for himself, Quinn forced his touch to remain slow and gentle as he lowered the zipper tooth by metal tooth.

Not surprisingly, given what he'd guessed about her upbringing, she'd turned absolutely passive. After he'd peeled the somber wool away, she lay on her back again and closed her eyes, offering herself up like some early-Christian martyr.

At any other time such lack of participation from a woman would have irked him.

Tonight, because it was Nora, it made Quinn smile. It also made him all that more determined to prove to her exactly how satisfying sex with the right partner could be.

Her bra was cotton, as well, and took only an instant to unfasten. He tossed it aside, where it fluttered onto a nearby chair like a white dove.

The way he'd opened her bra with such a clever deft touch reminded Nora yet again exactly how much more practice he'd had at this, and yet again she fretted that she'd prove a disappointment to Quinn. But then his mouth was on her breast and all her worries fled, blown away by the hot winds of desire.

"You're going to have to tell me what you like, love," he murmured as his tongue soothed the tingling flesh. "This first time."

"I don't know." Her eyes remained closed, her long lashes, which he suspected had never known mascara, looking like threads of gilt silk against her cheeks.

"We'll take it one step at a time, then." His tongue drew slow wet lazy circles around her breast from the tip outward. "Do you like this?"

"Oh . . . aye." Nora felt herself opening to him, like a flower unfolding its petals to the warmth of the morning sun.

"Good. Let's try the other one."

His mouth, his hands, somehow managed to be both tender and rough at the same time. When his sucking caused a corresponding tug deep in her womb, a warmth that spiraled outward, all the way to her fingers and toes, needs rose again, so strong and insistent Nora thought she might go mad with the wanting.

No longer passive, nor pliant, she strained against him in a mute desperate plea for relief. She would have begged, had she been capable of coherent speech, which she wasn't, but fortunately that proved unnecessary as he whipped off her panties and cupped her heat.

It was wonderful. Terrifying. Thrilling. He showed her what passion could be, found secret points of pleasure Nora had never even known existed.

When he dug his fingers into her hips and lifted her against his mouth, she was shocked and suffused with momentary shame, tried to close her legs and pull away. But Quinn was relentless, holding her tight, feasting on her as if she were succulent ripe fruit. Guilt proved brief, washed away by rising desire that pounded inside her like a tidal wave.

His tongue stabbed into her dewy feminine cleft; his teeth nibbled at tingling flesh.

Nora moaned from the ache, gasped from the forbidden pleasure. Her breath had clogged in her throat, and when she tried to catch it to cry his name, she couldn't.

Just when she was certain she would surely drown in such swirling heated depths of feeling, her body convulsed and she was swept away on the dizzying crest of a turbulent tide.

Watching the uncensored passion move across her face, Quinn found himself wishing that they could just stay here hidden away in this room forever.

That idea sent shock waves ripping through him, so strong that for a fleeting second he wondered if another bomb had gone off nearby. He'd never been a man to think about staying in one place, being tied down to one woman. He'd been emotionally on his own all of his life, and that was the way he liked it.

But dear Lord, she was so incredibly unbelievably sweet. Unable to concentrate on any tomorrows when his body was so caught up in the grips of today, after stripping off his clothes and putting on the condom he was never without — no bastards or shotgun marriages for Quinn Gallagher — he lowered his body over hers and felt the sizzle of hot flesh against flesh.

"Nora." He brushed her tousled hair back from her face. "Look at me, sweetheart." He touched his lips softly to hers. "I want to see your eyes." He wanted to watch the flare of passion when he took her over the edge.

She made an inarticulate sound. As if rousing from hypnosis, she slowly lifted her lids, her eyes glowing like rich green meadows shimmering beneath the sun after an afternoon rain. She was at this moment the most heartwrenchingly beautiful woman he'd ever known. And she was his.

Quinn nearly froze at the power of the possessiveness he was feeling. But then she smiled at him, a soft sweet smile, and it took his breath away and clouded his mind.

He linked his fingers with hers in what was, oddly, the most intimate gesture of the night. Fighting the urge to thrust into her, he eased his tip into her silky heat and felt her tense again.

"Just relax, sweetheart." Sweat beaded his burning flesh. Every muscle in his body was quivering from the strain of holding himself back. "I promise not to hurt you."

"But you're too —"

"Shh. It's going to be all right, Nora. Just relax, baby." His lips plucked at hers, soothing, enticing, as he ruthlessly checked his passion. "It's going to be so good."

"Oh, aye," she breathed as her body began to adjust to accommodate him.

"That's my girl. Lord, you feel good, sweetheart." He began to fill her. Slowly. Inch by throbbing inch. "You're so tight. So warm." He rubbed his cheek against hers. "So wonderful."

She gasped when he plunged the rest of the way into her. Then she sighed, a soft shimmering breath of sheer pleasure. With his eyes on hers, he began to move, slowly at first, then faster, his thrusts hot and driving.

The sounds of the traffic from the street below faded away, replaced by the thunder of pounding hearts. And although he couldn't understand the Irish words Nora was whispering in his ear, her meaning, as her hands stroked his sweat-slick back and cupped his buttocks, pulling him deeper inside her, were all too clear.

Responding to instincts as ancient as her mystical homeland, Nora matched his driving rhythm as he took her higher and higher, to where the air seemed to sparkle with a diamond-bright brilliance.

Nora tumbled first, calling out his name as she flew over the edge. Seconds later, fingers linked, his mouth on hers, Quinn took the fall.

★ ★ ★

Magic. As he lay on his back looking down at a sleeping Nora in the pink, pearly predawn light, Quinn decided that was the only word that could possibly describe the night they'd just spent together.

As good as the first time had been, the second had been even better. Once he'd managed to overcome her initial physical shyness, she'd turned incredibly responsive, surprising herself, he thought, with her ability to experience passion. Surprising him not at all with her generosity in returning it.

It should have been enough, Quinn thought. At least for one night. Especially after the grueling day they'd had. But he'd found himself waking up sometime around four and wanting her all over again.

It had only taken the touch of his mouth on her lips to awaken her. The touch of a palm to a breast to bring her to full arousal. She'd been as wet and willing as he'd been hot and hard, and Quinn knew if he lived to be a hundred, he'd never forget the sight of her pale skin gleaming like pearls in the moonlight as they'd rolled over the bed.

Now she was curled against him like a kitten, her fiery hair spread across his chest. There was none of the wanton who'd bucked like a wild horse beneath him, no sign of the woman whose cries of pleasure he'd captured beneath his mouth. She looked as pure as a vestal virgin, reminding Quinn that it had been that enticing blend of innocence and sensuality that had attracted him to her in the first place.

And while his first response had been sheer lust, things had changed between them. First had come admiration and respect. Then affection. And now . . .

What? Quinn was shaken by how appealing the fantasy of staying right here amidst these tangled sheets with Nora for the rest of his life was.

She murmured something inarticulate in her sleep. Then smiled. When she pressed her mouth against his bare chest, his penis instantly responded, hardening to granite.

The woman had him thinking foolish thoughts. Impossible thoughts. It was only sex, he reminded himself as hunger pooled hot and heavy again in his groin. Friendly sex, maybe. But that was all it was. That was all he would allow it to be.

As if his thoughts had infiltrated her sleeping mind, Nora's eyes fluttered open and she smiled up at him. "Good morning."

"Morning." Because the warmth of that uncensored smile pulled dangerous cords, he made his tone inappropriately gruff, and his expression returned to its earlier scowl.

A more cautious woman would have heeded the warning. But having shed the last of her caution in the arms of this man, Nora refused to let him ruin the gilt-edged pleasure that lingered from their magical night together.

She brought her hand to his cheek, ignored the tensed muscle there and stroked her fingers downward to circle his grimly set lips. "You lied."

"About what?"

"You told me not to expect pretty words. But unless this room is haunted, it must have been you telling me all those wonderful things last night." She paused, then, "Unless you didn't mean them?"

Quinn swore as he watched the anxiety chase away the joy in her lovely eyes. *You really are a bastard, Gallagher.* In an attempt to protect his own heart he'd been unreasonably cruel. He'd acted like his son-of-a-bitch father would have undoubtedly behaved under similar circumstances.

"Of course I did." He dragged his hand down his face and reminded himself he'd known from the beginning that getting involved with this woman would prove to be trouble. But such delicious trouble, he considered, remembering the taste of those sweet, succulent lips.

"I'd never lie to you, Nora. I meant every word." He stroked her shoulders in a gesture meant to soothe, even as the touch of her silken skin aroused the hell out of him. "You were incredible. Better than incredible." And because nothing had changed and he was still eventually going to hurt her, Quinn decided he owed her the absolute truth. "I've never before felt the way I felt last night."

"I've never felt that way, either." The color he'd grown far too fond of stained her cheeks. Cheeks that bore the faint marks of beard burn. "I never knew I could fly, but you showed me I could." Her smile spread slowly, gathering him into a silver snare as she brushed a light kiss against his mouth. "And it was a glorious feeling."

Her body was morning warm and Nora soft. "Talk about your glorious feelings." He rolled her onto her back, covered that inviting body with his.

Laughing with feminine delight, she combed her fingers through his hair and began to move beneath him in a way designed to kindle smoldering sparks.

How did she do it? He was already burning up. Quinn was debating whether they had time to do this right, when the shrill demand of the phone acted like a splash of icy water.

Nora froze beneath him. "What if it's the hospital?" Her voice, sultry and musical only moments earlier, was a ragged thread of sound.

"It's probably just your father checking on what time we're meeting for breakfast." Biting back a curse, he reached out and grabbed the receiver. "Yeah . . . Hi, Brady." He slanted Nora an I-told-you-so look. "Nora? Why would you be asking if I know where Nora is?"

Quinn experienced a twinge of pride at his newfound talent for answering a direct question in the roundabout Irish fashion, which was, of course, no answer at all. He was also amused by the way Nora's face was suffused with embarrassed color.

"She's probably in the shower," he suggested. "That's undoubtedly why she didn't hear the phone . . . Sure, I'll give her a few minutes and ring her myself. Then we'll meet you in the restaurant downstairs in thirty minutes."

That settled, he hung up and grinned at her. "Good thing videophones are still a thing of the future."

"Don't you be teasing me, Quinn

Gallagher." Nora slid out from under him, reaching at the same time for the blanket that had slid to the floor sometime during their energetic night. "My heart nearly stopped at the idea of you talking so casually to my father while lying on top of me naked as the day you were born."

"That bothered you?" He arched a brow, enjoying the way she was trying to wrap the blanket around herself as she stood beside the bed. As if he hadn't already seen — and tasted — every inch of her luscious body. "Fine. Next time you can be the one on top."

She laughed at that, an explosive sound of released tension that pleased him for having been the cause. "Sure, and you're a bad man, Quinn Gallagher."

Her words, meant in jest, struck a bit too close to home. "I believe that's what I've been trying to tell you."

The humor left her face and her eyes. "Quinn . . ."

"Don't be fooled by pretty words said in the heat of passion, Nora. There's still nothing pretty inside me."

She met his warning look with a calm one of her own. "You said you wouldn't lie to me, Quinn. But that's the biggest lie of all." She paused, seemed on the verge of saying something else, then apparently changed her mind. "I'd best be getting into that shower you told my da I was taking, if I'm to be ready for breakfast in thirty minutes."

With that she surprised him by dropping the blanket. Then walked out of his bedroom with an amazing amount of dignity for someone wearing only her pride.

This time, instead of a Celtic goddess, Nora reminded Quinn of an Irish queen from the olden days when the Joyce clan ruled over parts of the West. In fact, just before she closed the connecting door between the rooms, he almost imagined he could see a bejeweled crown perched atop her regal head.

CHAPTER EIGHTEEN

Last Night's Fun

Concerned as she was about her grandmother, Nora didn't quibble when Quinn dropped her off at the hospital with the excuse that he had some business to attend to and would pick her and her grandmother up in an hour or so. In truth, she was a bit relieved he wasn't coming to Fionna's room with her. She feared that were her grandmother to see them together so soon after their passion-filled night, she'd know that they'd been together in that intimate way.

She needed time away from him. Time to think about what she was feeling. And just as important, time to figure out what to do about what Quinn was feeling. She knew he'd come to care for her; although he might not be ready to say the words, the tenderness underlying his passion had assured her she was not the only one experiencing something unique. Something special. Something that felt remarkably, wonderfully, like love.

That thought warmed the very cockles of

her heart as she chatted with Fionna, who had, predictably, been telling the entire staff about Sister Bernadette saving so many lives — and Mrs. Murphy, who was more than pleased to have a new audience to hear tales of her six grandchildren.

If Nora had been concerned about making idle conversation with Quinn on the trip back to Castlelough after sharing such passion, she needn't have worried. Fionna and Brady talked all the way to the Derry airport, on the flight to Galway and back to the farm in Quinn's Mercedes.

Listening to Nora's grandmother relate the adventure of her near-death experience at the hands of the bombers, Quinn realized Brady had inherited his talent for story-telling. Fionna may have married into the Joyce family, but she was quite a *seanachie* herself. When that thought got him thinking about his own Gallagher roots, the familiar pall came over his heart. But strangely, this time it didn't feel quite as dark. Or as cold.

After they reached the farm, Fionna insisted that she didn't want any special attention paid to her. Nevertheless it was apparent that she was definitely in her element as she sat propped against the pillows in her oak frame bed, telling the tales again to John, Mary, Kate and the younger children. Nora's brother Michael was there, too, having returned home from Kerry as soon as Kate had contacted him about the bombing.

"It's too bad school is nearly over," Rory complained.

"And why is that, darling?" Fionna inquired.

"Because it would be neat if you could come tell the story to my class."

"Ah, now don't they have more important tales to be hearing than those from an old lady?" Fionna said with the blatant false modesty that reminded Quinn yet again of her son.

"It's a fine tale, Mam," Brady assured her on cue. "You'll be wanting to tell it at The Rose as soon as you're back on your feet."

"Which will be tomorrow," Fionna insisted with a toss of her chin that this time reminded Quinn of both her son and granddaughter. "I'll not be staying in this bed like some elderly invalid."

"You'll be staying in bed until Dr. Flannery says it's all right for you to leave it," Nora insisted firmly.

"You're a darling girl, Nora. But I'm more than half a century older than you. So you've no cause to be telling me what I can and cannot do."

The gauntlet had been thrown down. The air had thickened with the aura of impending battle.

Blithely ignoring the contest of wills taking place in the cozy crowded bedroom, Brady turned to Quinn, who was standing in the doorway. Quinn had been watching the scene from a distance, as if through a plate-glass window, which was the position he'd assumed most of his life.

"Why don't you go out to your automobile and retrieve those packages you bought?" Brady suggested.

"Good idea." By the time Quinn returned, followed by Maeve, who'd come down to the car with him, the tension in the bedroom had been replaced by anticipation.

"You bought us gifts?" John asked, his eyes widening at the shopping bags of gaily wrapped packages.

"These are for the others," Quinn said. "Yours is still in the car, John. I didn't want to cart the box all the way up here only to have to take it back down again for unpacking."

Nora was looking at him as if he were a stranger. "This is what your alleged business was this morning?"

She'd seen him moving packages from the trunk of the limousine into the Mercedes, but at the time she'd been so busy tending to Fionna she hadn't paid any real attention. And when she had mentioned them on the drive home, he'd merely shrugged and said something about computer supplies.

"Aye." He grinned at her and handed her the first package. "I started out to replace your blazer that got ruined in the blast. Then, well, I just got a little carried away."

"I should say so," Fionna said dryly as her wren-bright eyes swept over the bags and boxes. "I doubt if Father Christmas has ever shown up at this house with so many gifts."

"Oh, it's so soft!" Nora had opened her package and was running her palm over the lovely emerald green blazer. She was wearing a prim white blouse and a gray tweed skirt; Quinn watched her slip into the blazer and decided he'd been right. Jewel-tone colors definitely suited her.

"It's cashmere. There's something else in the pocket." Quinn told himself that he shouldn't be so gratified by her expression of pleasure. But dammit, he was.

Nora drew a sharp breath as she found the small square gray velvet box. Surely he wouldn't be buying her a ring? Only a foolishly romantic woman would be expecting such a gesture of eternal commitment after one single night of pleasure.

Unfortunately, since Quinn's arrival in Castlelough, she'd discovered she was, indeed, a foolishly romantic woman. Her heart was pounding like an Orangeman's drum. Positive everyone else in the room could hear it, especially given the way they all seemed to be holding their breaths, she slowly opened the lid.

"Oh, they're pearls!" Mary exclaimed as she viewed the pair of earrings over her sister's shoulder.

"They're lovely." Exquisite, actually. But at the same time, not too flamboyant to wear to town or even to church. Nora looked up at Quinn. "And surely far too dear."

He shrugged. "They weren't that expensive. Besides, they reminded me of you." For discretion's sake, considering that nearly her entire family was packed into the small bedroom, Quinn didn't mention that the pearls had made him think of the way her skin had looked in the silvery moonlight.

"Thank you." Her warm gaze promised a more personal expression of her gratitude later.

Quinn handed out the rest of the gifts he'd had such a surprisingly enjoyable time buying. Despite the excited buzz of conversation around him, he was having an increasingly difficult time keeping his mind off the idea of Nora wearing only those pearls in her earlobes and her new scent all over the rest of her, in his bed.

Reassured that Fionna was, indeed, not gravely injured, the family gradually drifted from the room. As Quinn left, as well, intending to take Nora out for a drive to some distant secluded glen, Michael stopped him outside in the hallway.

"I should be thanking you for taking care of my grandmother and sister," he said.

If he hadn't been introduced earlier, Quinn never would have guessed that this huge man with the weathered face and large work-roughened hands was Brady's son. Only his hair — unruly curls that were black as night as opposed to Nora's and Fionna's bright red ones — suggested his family roots.

"It was my pleasure. And I didn't do that much."

"More than any of us could have done," Michael said, looking at Quinn in a measuring way that he suspected big brothers had been directing toward their kid sisters' lovers since the beginning of time. "It eased Nora's heart to have someone to take care of things for a change. And for that I'm grateful."

"Again, it wasn't that big a deal." Uncomfortable talking about the woman he was planning to get naked with as soon as possible, Quinn opted to change the subject. "She said you have a farm not far from here."

"Aye. About sixty acres split into sections scattered here and thereabouts. I grow mostly oats and barley for feed, with potatoes for sale and for the family. Kerr's Pinks, which, unlike the more usual Golden Wonders, don't break up after a good boil and bring a better price at the market." He tacked on this last with obvious pride. "This year I put in sugar beets, as well. And of course, there's the peat."

"I've seen the peat bogs. And the stacks beside the cottages and stores. I was hoping I'd have an opportunity to see it cut."

"As it happens, I'll be doing that this week. If you'd like to come by on Wednesday, you can observe the process. Then afterward, perhaps we can have ourselves a pint and a chat."

About Nora. The man didn't say the words out loud, but he didn't need to.

"I'd like that," Quinn said, not quite truthfully. The novelist who considered everything grist for the writing mill was looking forward to seeing the Irishman engaged in a centuries-old task. The man who was sleeping with this muscular giant's younger sister was not at all eager to get into a discussion about intentions. "But I insist on helping."

"Fine. We begin work about dawn. Nora will be able to give you directions." He put on his wool cap, tugged it almost to his calm blue eyes, turned away and headed toward the stairs. Quinn watched him leave, then deciding to face this latest little problem on Wednesday, headed down the hall to Nora's room.

Quinn wasn't surprised when, despite the gruff way he'd treated her this morning, she immediately accepted his invitation for a drive. After all, as Kate had pointed out and he himself had witnessed firsthand on more than one occasion, she was not one to hold a grudge.

"That was very sweet of you to buy everyone all those gifts," she murmured as they drove down a winding narrow dirt lane lined on either side with gray stone walls. "Mary's going to look like a fairy-tale princess in that lovely dress."

It was white tulle, studded with seed pearls and crystals that should prove a stunning foil for her pale skin and dark hair. "She seemed to like it well enough," he said, enjoying the memory of the teenager's stunned look as she'd opened the white box with the gold script from one of Northern Ireland's most exclusive stores.

"She adores it. And I truly believed she was going to faint when you told her that you'd arranged for Parker Kendall to escort her to the May dance."

Parker was an actor, a current teenage heartthrob who was playing the part of a university student who joins forces with Shannon McGuire to rescue the Lady's baby.

"However did you get him to agree to such a thing?" Nora asked.

"It wasn't that difficult. I just promised him my tickets to the Lakers' home games."

"The Lakers?"

"A Los Angeles basketball team. Since I moved up the coast, I'm not using them, anyway, so it wasn't any great sacrifice."

"I see." Nora wasn't certain, but she suspected that very little in Los Angeles came cheaply. "It was a remarkably kind thing to do."

"Actually I like the idea of that jerk Jack getting his comeuppance," Quinn countered. "I almost wish I could be there to see it."

"The sisters sent home a note asking for volunteer chaperons. If you really mean that —"

"No way." Belatedly realizing she was only teasing, Quinn chuckled. "I've never claimed to be bucking for sainthood, sweetheart. And agreeing to chaperon a bunch of hormone-crazed teenagers has got to earn bonus martyr points."

She laughed with him. Then sobered. "I do have one little worry."

Her father was right. Her concern for everyone she loved was both blessing and curse.

"What's that?"

"What if Parker Kendall proves even more dishonorable than Jack? After all, he is a handsome young man, and coming from California . . ."

She made his adopted state sound like a modern-day Sodom and Gomorrah. Which, compared to the still-strict moral tenets of rural western Ireland, it probably was.

"Don't worry, I took care of that."

"Oh?"

"I warned him that I'd rip off a vital part of his anatomy if he so much as touched anything he shouldn't."

"Surely he didn't believe that?" She glanced over at him, viewed his glowering countenance and managed a faint smile. "I suppose he might, after all."

"Absolutely." Quinn's wicked grin wiped

away the scowl and had Nora smiling back.

"Rory and Jamie were wild about the outer-space toy figures. I fear we'll be battling aliens around the house for weeks. And Celia's been wanting Bridal Barbie for ages, but I had to keep telling her we couldn't afford it."

"I figured it might replace the martyred Saint Joan."

"You knew about that?"

"Rory told me. Actually I found it rather inspired."

"You would. Since burning saints at the stake is probably something you might put in one of your books," she countered easily. "And of course Maeve looks dashing in her new collar." If she hadn't already fallen in love with him, this gift alone would have made Nora tumble.

It was Kelly green plaid with a shamrock-shaped brass tab engraved with the dog's name. A foolish gesture, perhaps, but Quinn couldn't imagine not taking something home for the huge wolfhound who'd become his shadow.

"She probably would have preferred a new bone," he said. "But there weren't any butcher counters at Austin's Department Store."

"It was a lovely thought just the same."

Nora smiled, then slanted him a serious look. "You realize I should make John return his gift."

"Why?"

"Because it's far too much. People will talk."

Quinn shrugged. "So let them."

He figured he and Nora were probably already a major topic of conversation in Castlelough before today. And although he'd given up caring what people thought about him years ago, he still had to admit to a feeling of pride that people believed Nora was his.

"The kid's going to need a computer at college, Nora. In America, it's a traditional graduation present."

"Perhaps in America. But not many Irish families can afford such a gift."

"That's because not every family is generous enough to open their house to a Yank who had a helluva good time buying one." When he realized she wasn't smiling, he tried a different tack.

"Your brother's a smart kid, Nora. He works hard, obviously keeps his nose to the grindstone more than most his age, and he's got an admirable goal."

"It was after our mother died that he decided to become a doctor," she revealed quietly.

"I kind of figured that might be the case." Quinn knew better than anyone how the loss of a mother could change a kid's life. In his own case, he'd often thought he owed a great deal of his success to working his ass off trying to prove to the world — and himself — he wasn't anything like his alcoholic loser parents.

"Competition to get into medical school is tough," he went on. "Surely you're not going to deny him every opportunity to gain an edge?"

"No. I wouldn't want to be doing that." She sighed as the all-too-familiar Catholic guilt kicked in. "You're a very persuasive man, Quinn Gallagher. It's certainly not difficult to believe you've Irish blood."

Although it still wasn't his favorite topic, Quinn didn't find the topic of his heritage as threatening as usual. He did, however, decide it was time to change the subject.

"I'm glad you like the earrings." He reached out and touched one with a fingertip.

"I love them. So much so that I'm not even going to complain again about the cost."

"Now you're getting the idea." He almost wished he'd also bought the emerald ones that matched her eyes. But, he suspected, there was only so much this frugal farmer's daughter would accept as a gift. "By the way, there's another present in the back seat."

She reached around and retrieved the gold-and-white shopping bag from the rear seat. "Oh, my saints!" Nora lifted the froth of black lace and silk from its bed of tissue paper. "I can't imagine wearing such a revealing thing," she murmured as her fingers caressed the silk.

"Fine. I'll just take it back, and —"

"You'll be doing no such thing!" She hugged the teddy to her breast. "It's stunning, Quinn. Thank you."

"You're welcome." She was getting better at accepting gifts and compliments. Which made Quinn want to keep giving both to her. "Just don't go getting too attached to it," he advised. "Because believe me, you won't be wearing it for very long."

Because she had no answer to a statement that was both promise and threat, Nora said nothing.

Quinn placed his hand between them, next to hers. The contrast between his tanned flesh and her own pale skin stirred a vivid memory of how that hand had looked against her breasts. Breasts that had begun aching for his touch.

She slipped her hand beneath his.

He linked their fingers together.

And, as foolish as some might find it, Nora thought she'd swoon from the pleasure of such a simple touch.

After a while he turned onto an even narrower road, which led to a secluded glen that bordered a small lake, and cut the engine. It had begun to rain, draping the car in a slanting gray curtain.

"How did you know about this place?" she asked.

"Hey, scouting out a place to park with your girl is an old American tradition."

He'd called her his girl. Joy sang through Nora's veins as he turned toward her. Closing her eyes, she lifted her face and waited to be swept away.

The touch of his mouth on hers was feather-light and utterly sweet. His lips brushed hers once, twice, then a third time, tasting, teasing, tantalizing.

"I've been going crazy all day," he murmured, "remembering your taste." He nipped the side of her neck, then soothed with the tip of his tongue where he had bitten. "Remembering how perfect you felt in my arms. How perfectly I fit inside you."

Her bones were turning to water. She could barely lift her hand to his cheek. "I've been remembering that, too," she whispered, her fingertips trailing down the side of his face as if she was memorizing his features by touch.

When he caught hold of her hand and pressed his open mouth to the inside of her wrist, her blood began to heat in her veins.

He ducked his head again. This time his mouth took hers in a sumptuous heated kiss that turned everything to soft-focused slow motion. It could have lasted minutes, hours or an eternity. Time seemed suspended as Nora's entire world narrowed down to Quinn's thrilling lips.

She felt drunk. Drunk with desire, dizzy with need. He'd spent the long and wondrous night teaching her the magic a man and woman could make together, and now she was going to wield it like Merlin's sword, using its power to make him as crazy as he'd made her.

She turned in his arms, and as her avid lips and agile hands moved over him, Quinn realized that somehow, when he hadn't been looking, last night's eager student had become the master. Need rose like a wild beast inside him, snarling, snapping, clawing for freedom.

"My God, Nora . . ." He reached for her, but she was faster, pulling his cotton sweater over his head, somehow managing to keep just out of touch in the close confines of the car. She shrugged out of the new blazer and tossed it into the back seat.

"Not yet." She laughed, a deep throaty sound that could have come from one of her pagan ancestors out to seduce a king. Needing to touch, to taste, he began ripping off her clothes, even as she tore at his.

"It's my turn," she murmured as her tongue teased a dark nipple, causing Quinn to groan. Her lips skimmed down his taut belly and he had to bite back the sharp curse. "You made love to me all night. Now I want to make love to you."

His breath clogged in his lungs, and his heart battered against his rib cage so painfully Quinn wondered if he was about to have a heart attack. When her hungry lips moved even lower and she took him into her mouth, Quinn decided that if he did die at this moment, it'd be worth it.

"I want to be inside you." He reached blindly for his jeans, but reading his intention, she plucked them from the floor of the car and took the foil package from the front pocket.

"Is this what you're looking for?" Her smile was seductive as hell, giving Quinn a very good idea of how Eve must have looked when she was holding that bright red apple just out of Adam's reach.

"Nora . . ." The warning growl reverberated from deep in his throat.

Appearing blithely unthreatened, she tore the package open, then slowly smoothed the condom over his stone-hard erection as he'd taught her last night, protecting them both.

Just when he thought for certain he was going to embarrass the hell out of himself by exploding beneath her erotic touch, Nora lowered herself onto him.

The feel of her, tight and hot and slick, was all it took for the animal in him to burst free. Quinn could practically hear the chain snap as she began riding him like a woman possessed.

Last night her flesh had gleamed like pearls. Now, bathed in the faint glow of the sunset valiantly shimmering through the gray mist, her skin appeared golden, as if she were a goddess, created by a master alchemist.

Grabbing hold of her waist, he dug his fingers into that damp glowing skin and surged upward into her. He watched her as they moved together, counting her orgasms, reveling in the range of emotions that moved across her flushed face in waves. Quinn loved the way she could feel so much. Loved that he was the one who made her feel it.

He'd already passed last night's personal

best when she stiffened, shuddered, then collapsed against him as every inch of her body began to tremble.

Only then did Quinn surrender fully to the beast. With one last mighty surge, he gave in to his own mind-blinding release.

CHAPTER NINETEEN

Moving Hearts

The rain had stopped, revealing a line of purple dusk stealing its way across the reed-rimmed lake. A planet burned on the horizon; the first stars appeared. Although vaguely aware of the possibility of discovery by some evening fisherman, neither Nora nor Quinn were in any hurry to move.

As she slowly recovered, Nora touched her mouth to his chest in a soft tender kiss. "I love you." It was barely a whisper, but Quinn had no trouble hearing it in the hushed stillness. The words reverberated around the car and inside his head like bullets, as if she'd just fired a very lethal gun.

"Nora . . ." He ran his hand down her hair, "I don't know what to say."

She lifted her head, her eyes warm and a little sad. For a fleeting instant he thought he detected a bit of pity in those rich green depths. "You don't have to say anything. I didn't tell you so you'd feel obliged to say the words back to me, Quinn. Love isn't something you can plan. Or demand in return. It just is."

She lifted a hand and smoothed the lines carving canyons between his dark eyes. "It's a gift," she said soothingly. "Like the ones you bought for all of us in Derry. Since I couldn't possibly afford anything so fine, I'm giving you one of the only things I have of any value."

Her heart. Her goddamn warm, generous, loving heart.

"What if I don't want it?" He told himself that his deliberate gruffness was for her sake, not his.

He braced himself for tears and was surprised when she laughed, instead. "It's too late." She touched her smiling lips to his tightly set ones. "I've already given it away. Even in America it must be considered bad manners to return a gift of the heart."

"Nothing's changed," he warned.

Nora didn't answer. There was, after all, Quinn thought grimly as they dressed, no need. Because they both knew that was a lie. The biggest he'd ever told.

Trying to brush her tangled hair into some semblance of order, she looked into the rearview mirror. When she saw the flush in her cheeks, the edgy excitement in her eyes, and her swollen lips, Nora was certain that her entire family would know exactly what she and Quinn had been doing.

And amazingly she didn't care.

"Does this mean you've changed your mind?" she asked as he turned the key and put the car into gear.

"About what?"

"About taking that lovely bit of black lingerie off me tonight."

That provocative question was all it took to make Quinn hard again. Wondering if perhaps Kate wasn't the only witch in the family, Quinn shook his head.

"You might be able to make me crazy, sweetheart, but I'm not stupid. Besides, I still have places I want to take you."

Because he needed to touch her again, to make contact, no matter how slight, he reached out, took her hand and squeezed. The crooked grin he slanted her as they drove away from the lake revealed all of the rich affection he was feeling for her and none of the turmoil. "Magic places."

A visitor can't travel to the west of Ireland without being aware of peat. During his weeks in Castlelough, Quinn had seldom been out of sight or smell of it. He'd drive past the straight black banks cut into the green hills, the piles of neatly stacked sods leaning against stone walls. Slabs of black buttery peat were piled up beside every house, cottage and shop, drying for use as insulation and fuel for the hearths.

"We've good peat in our bog," Nora's older brother assured Quinn as he led him across the hills toward the black field overlooking the sea. Michael was wearing an unbleached Aran sweater, a thick pair of handwoven tweed trousers and boots. Since Quinn had no idea what one wore to go bog cutting, he'd opted for jeans and a black Oakland Raiders sweatshirt. Fortunately Michael had supplied him with boots.

Maeve loped on ahead of the two men, happily flushing out rabbits in the field. The dog had been waiting at the foot of the stairs for him this morning, wagging her tail, eagerly awaiting further developments. Since Rory would be at school all day, Quinn didn't have the heart to leave the eager wolfhound at home.

"A week's worth of cutting should last the family through the coming winter," Michael said with satisfaction. "The peat's three to four meters deep in most places."

"And steep," Quinn observed as he looked a very long way down to a narrow beach where a trio of fishermen in yellow oilskins were hauling their curraghs down to the water.

"Aye. And that's a strange thing. It used to be that such steep cliff land wasn't thought to be good for all that much. Farmers value the flat fields for grazing, you see. But that was back in the days when a man could only get land by inheriting it or marrying into it."

"And now?"

"And now, because of all the blow-ins — Yanks and Europeans who dream of a country life without having any idea what it's like to live on a farm — the steep land is becoming worth more than the flat. For the view, don't you know."

His dry tone suggested he considered such blow-ins, as the Irish tended to call anyone who couldn't trace their ancestry back at least two centuries, "eejits."

"It is a terrific view," Quinn held his breath as Maeve planted her huge paws on the very edge of the cliff and began barking at wheeling sea gulls.

"That's true enough. And at least there are some who appreciate it. Which makes them who actually move here better than our own city people, who are buying up the farmland for investment but would never set foot on it themselves. Men who couldn't grow a single potato in a tub of manure."

"I suppose speculators grabbing up land has been going on forever," Quinn suggested. "Back home everyone's concerned about the farmers being forced off the land by big conglomerates and economics."

"I've been reading about your farmers. I'm especially interested in their modern milking methods. And Nora's thinking about joining the cheese guild. I've also met a few who come to the country tracking down their family roots. Farming's never been easy. Too much depends on luck, Mother Nature and God's whims. But I've lived in the city, and now, like the wayward prodigal son, I've returned home. I won't be leaving again. This is the only life I want."

Quinn thought about Yeats describing the country people of Ireland as passionate and simple. Passionate, Michael Joyce was. About his land and, Quinn knew, his family. He also suspected, that like the rest of his family, the man wasn't nearly as simple as he first appeared.

Michael took off his cap and combed his fingers through his curly black hair as he looked over the fields. "People around here think of land as something they belong to. Not the other way around."

"People such as Nora, you mean." Quinn decided there was no point in beating around the bush.

"Aye." Her brother gave him a warning look. His blue eyes turned crystal hard. "I care for my sister, Mr. Gallagher. A great deal."

"Call me Quinn. And we have that in common."

"I also can't see her being happy living in Hollywood."

"Actually I live in Monterey, which is on the California coast south of San Francisco," Quinn corrected mildly. "But I get your point. And that's another thing we agree on."

"So you'll not be asking her to leave Castlelough with you when you go?"

"No." This was one of the few things — the only thing — Quinn was very sure about where Nora was concerned.

Although Quinn wasn't certain Michael was totally happy with that answer — since they both knew that either way she was going to be hurt — he appeared to be satisfied. Or, more likely, Quinn thought, he'd just as soon drop the personal conversation. Nora's brother seemed less gregarious than Fionna, Brady or even John, a man more comfortable working with his hoes and cows than discussing family matters with a stranger. Quinn couldn't blame him.

They set to work, cutting through the black peat with wing tipped spades, which Michael informed Quinn were called slanes.

"You have to cut the steps," he explained, demonstrating by cutting a trio of steps in the peat. "Tradition has it that Saint Columba got tripped in a bog hole one day and was so furious he laid a curse on all those who didn't cut three steps so he could get out."

"Do you believe that?"

"Now, I can't say whether I do or not," Michael mused, rubbing his chin. "But there's no harm in cutting them just the same."

Although cutting the turf proved easy, considering it had the consistency of butter, the lifting of the sods, which each weighed about twenty pounds and was rough as sandpaper, proved to be hard back-straining work. And although he'd put away a huge breakfast of scones, black pudding, bacon, fried potatoes, smoked salmon and scrambled eggs, by the time the sun was directly overhead, Quinn was starving. He was also extremely grateful for the brown bread, cheese and meat pie Nora had insisted he take along in Rory's knapsack, despite his arguments that after that herculean breakfast, he wouldn't be able to eat again for a week.

They stopped for lunch and sat enjoying the view — miles of beach to one side and blue-tinged mountains to the other, the stuttering golden sun, dew on the grass, even a rainbow to add a perfect touch. Back home in California, developers would probably be willing to commit murder for the opportunity to put a resort and glass-walled restaurant on the site.

The ancient romance he'd found to be part of the country lingered in the wisps of fog floating past like silent ghosts. Down below, children were climbing over rocks on the shore.

"They're gathering seaweed," Michael said when Quinn pointed them out. "Probably to fertilize their family plots. Those roped-off places are mussel farms. The fishermen dangle their ropes into the water, and at the end of the summer, they pull them up and the mussels will be clinging to the ropes, just waiting to be thrown into the pot." He glanced at Quinn. "It's a shame you won't be here in August. Castlelough puts on quite a mussel fair."

"I'm sorry I'll miss it," Quinn answered, surprised that it was the truth.

"It's a fine time. There's traditional music and storytelling, and free tastings on the street. Mussels are evil-looking things, but they taste good served up with butter and lemon. Nora uses garlic." He grinned. "Gran complains it's not traditional, but I've noticed she always manages to eat her share."

"Your sister's a great cook."

"She is that. There aren't very many good places for tourists used to fancier fare to eat around here, so Brady's been after her to open a bed and breakfast after John goes off to university. But of course the farm takes up a great deal of her time, so she's been putting him off."

Returning from her morning of chasing rabbits, Maeve sat down on her haunches beside Quinn, cocked an expectant ear and whined. He tossed her a piece of cheese and watched as she snapped it up in midair, swallowing it in one gulp.

Nearby, mangy donkeys climbed over rocks and sheep hung picturesquely from the cliffs. "You'd think they'd fall off," Quinn said.

"Oh, that's been known to happen," Michael allowed. "Just last fall one of my best ewes leaned too far over the edge to reach a bit of grass and tumbled down onto the rocks and was washed away. Sheep," he said dryly, "are not the most intelligent of animals."

They continued eating in companionable male silence broken only by the caw of a raven, the cry of gulls, lowing of cows and the distant bleating of sheep.

"I know a man in Connemara — Patrick Gallagher," Michael divulged. "His mother has a book with the names of all the family members who emigrated over the years. Perhaps, if you'd like —"

"I don't think so." Quinn cut him off in the same way he had Fionna, when the elderly lady had first suggested he might have family in Donegal. "Gallagher's a common enough name. It doesn't necessarily follow that we'd be related."

"Well, you have a point." Michael gave him a thoughtful study as he drank his tea from an insulated cup. "However, you have the look of him. The two of you could be brothers."

Quinn was vaguely interested in spite of himself. "I suppose he's a farmer, too?"

"Aye. A bit of a one. Connemara's hardscrabble land, not as productive as this," he said with a wave of his hand over the emerald and black fields. "So, his family has always supplemented their income by distilling *poitin*."

"Figures I'd have relatives who're boot-leggers," Quinn muttered.

"It's a fine traditional occupation," Michael corrected him. "And one of the few true examples of Irish entrepreneurial spirit."

"It's also illegal."

"For the most part, although now hasn't the government licensed some for selling to tourists in the duty-free shops?"

"I've tasted Kentucky moonshine." Quinn paused to throw Maeve another piece of cheese, which she wolfed down. "White Lightning, they call it." He didn't think he'd ever forget the burn going down.

"That's well named. John L. O'Sullivan called our *poitin* a torchlight procession down your throat," Michael said approvingly. "The best — like that the Gallaghers are known to make — can warm up the insides of a man like a peat fire on a cold December day. The worst —" he shook his head "— could stiffen a tinker."

"Don't they get raided?"

"From time to time. But mostly the Garda turn a blind eye since they have so many relatives in the business themselves. And even when they do hold their raids for the newspapers, the word has usually already gotten out, so they don't manage to catch many people." He pointed to a small green speck out in the ocean. "See that island?"

"Barely."

"It's where some lads from Dublin once tried growing marijuana. It took the Garda so long to blow up their rubber raft, the growers had time to row out around to the back of the island, harvest their crop and get away."

Quinn laughed as he was supposed to. He decided that Michael Joyce had inherited some of his father's storytelling talent, after all.

After loading the turf into the cart, they took it back to the farm, where they stacked the rectangular sods into small pyramids designed to catch the wind, which would speed the drying.

"We did a good day's work," Michael said. "We probably cut a ton." He gave Quinn an appraising look that suggested he was thinking he might have misjudged the rich Yank's capacity for hard physical work. "You'll sleep tonight," he predicted.

"If I don't die first," Quinn said on a laugh as he rubbed his sore back.

"Poor man." Nora's smile was both teasing and sympathetic at the same time. She was straddling his hips, her palms massaging his aching back. Everyone else had gone to sleep, and the house was as still as midnight. "I should have told Michael to go easy on you."

"And have him telling everyone in The Rose that the Yank is a wimp? No way," Quinn muttered as her clever fingers worked on getting the kinks out of his left shoulder. "Lord, that feels good."

"I'm glad." She moved downward, pressing along either side of his spine. "Cutting peat's miserable work. I'm surprised you could stay awake through dinner."

So was he. Quinn decided not to admit that there'd been more than one time when he'd found his lids growing heavy and had feared falling face first into his bowl of chowder.

"I had an incentive."

"Oh?" The soothing hands were at his waist. "And what would that have been?"

Her voice had turned saucy, her hands, as they moved even lower, anything but soothing.

"You." He rolled over, taking her with him. "I kept thinking of you wearing this." He ran his palms over the cobweb-thin lace that barely covered her breasts and watched with pleasure as her nipples hardened.

Experiencing a miraculous renewal of energy, he snagged a satin ribbon strap with his teeth and lowered it off one fair shoulder.

"Quinn." Her soft sigh of pleasure as his lips skimmed over the fragrant white skin belied the objection he suspected she'd intended. "You've had a long day and you have to be at the lake tomorrow for the filming."

"They'll never miss me if I'm late."

In the beginning the idea that he was superfluous had irked him. He'd always known that writers were not exactly at the top of the Hollywood hierarchy, and the past weeks watching his objections get overruled and the actors, even Laura, objecting to lines of dialogue had pricked his ego.

But since his time in Ireland was running out, Quinn was more than willing to surrender the reins of control fully to Jeremy Converse in order to spend every possible moment with Nora. Take the money and run, his agent had always said. As usual she'd been right.

"But surely you're too tired —" Her voice was smothered by his mouth as he kissed her.

He slipped the other shoulder ribbon down. The top of the teddy was now clinging precariously to the tips of her breasts. It would take only the slightest nudge to send it the rest of the way.

"The day I'm too tired to make love to you, sweetheart, is the day you'd better have Castlelough's undertaker start measuring me for a casket."

That said, he trailed a lazy finger down her breast and sent the lace skimming to her waist. Another quick flick of the wrist and he'd unfastened the snaps between her legs.

Then, as the moon rose over the velvet meadows, Quinn slid gloriously into her.

Ever since Sister Mary Francis had read the story of Christ curing the leper to the first-form class at Holy Child School, Rory had become obsessed with lepers. He'd sit in the chapel during Benediction at the end of the day, and while the other kids squirmed in their seats and risked being cuffed in the back of the head by one of the nuns, Rory would stare up at the stained-glass window depicting the miraculous event and think how terrible it would be to be a leper.

The dread stayed with him during the father-and-son trek, billowing in his mind like a turf-fire spark escaping a chimney and blazing through a thatched roof. Even the relief he felt when he discovered that Jamie's da was still in Dungarven — which meant that he wouldn't be here getting drunk and mean and spoiling things — or the pleasure in showing off the American to his mates could not warm the chill that had wrapped its icy fingers around his heart.

The trekkers had been equipped with the appropriate equipment courtesy of a generous donation from Father O'Malley's wealthy brother Brendan, who owned a sports-equipment store in Waterford that sold everything from hurling bats and balls — *sliothars* — to fishing tackle. The pup tents he supplied were large enough for a single man, or two small boys, which is how Rory came to be sharing one with his cousin.

"Jamie, you must look at this," he hissed, grabbing his cousin's arm. Rory was sitting in the tent after the supper and singing, staring at his lobster-red face in the compact mirror his mother had sent along, insisting he'd need it to brush his hair on Sunday morning.

"Look at what?" Jamie said sulkily.

He'd been in a sour mood the entire trek. Although it was nice to see Mam smiling again, and he understood it was because Da wasn't around yelling and punching walls with his huge meaty fists, it was embarrassing that he ended up the only boy in the class without a father, or someone to act as a father, on the trek. Even Daniel O'Kelley's father, who was a deacon and had never missed a morning mass for as long as anyone in Castlelough could remember, had come along for the adventure.

"I've got it!" Rory said. "See?"

"Got what?"

"The leprosy." Rory pointed the torch up at his face, giving him the threatening look of a devil. Or perhaps an evil sorcerer.

"People in Ireland don't get the leprosy."

"Perhaps that's because we're not told about them," Rory suggested. "Perhaps they're sent away to leper colonies before anyone can learn about it." He picked at the loose skin. "See?"

"That's sunburn, you daft eejit. Your face saw too much of the sun today, that's all."

"But it always begins with the nose." Rory wiggled his own nose, which felt less rigidly attached to his face than usual. "First the peeling. Then before you know it your nose falls off. And your fingertips, as well." He held up his hand palm inward in front of him, looking for signs of decay.

"It's sunburn," Jamie repeated. "Now will ya turn off that bloody light and shut up so I can be getting to sleep?"

Within minutes the soft snores coming from the other sleeping bag told Rory that

Jamie was sleeping soundly. But Rory lay awake long into the night, moving his hand to his nose every few minutes, checking. Worrying.

He kept picturing the chapel window, and the statue of the Virgin Mary who stood guard over the playground at school. The statue that showed her bare toes peeking out from beneath her blue robe and her horribly chipped nose. Although Rory knew the damage had been done when Tommy Doyle had accidentally hit the statue with the ball during an energetic hurling match, for the last week, every time he'd looked at that statue, all Rory could think about was that was what leprosy looked like.

He lifted his hand to his nose — just to check — and screamed when it came off in his hand. A hand that was dripping off him like wet seaweed. He shook it, shocked as he watched two fingers go flying. The sound of laughter behind him had him whirling around, and he was suddenly face-to-face with hundreds of rag-clad people, men, women, children — it was impossible to tell which, since all their features were oozing down their faces like custard that had yet to set.

They were laughing and pointing their leprosy-torn fingers, and when he tried to run away, they took off after him, their rags and their putrid flesh flapping.

He didn't wake up until he was out of the tent, standing in the darkness beneath the razor-edged shining slice of a moon, his chest heaving, the pajamas his mother had insisted he wear soaked with sweat.

He moved as quietly as he could to the tent nearest his, slid open the zippered front and slipped inside. "Mr. Gallagher?"

Quinn had always been a light sleeper. Probably, he'd once thought, because for the first seven years of his life he'd never experienced a night when his parents' fights hadn't kept him awake. He'd also learned to wake up fast in order to have half a chance to escape his father's brutal fists. That was why the faint whisper instantly jerked him from the erotic dream in which he'd been making love to Nora.

"Rory?" He blinked, focusing on the small form huddled beside his sleeping bag.

"I had a dream that lepers were chasing me."

"Leopards?" Quinn wondered if Rory knew how fortunate he was that his nightmares were born of fiction. "Don't worry, kid, there aren't any leopards in Ireland." Understanding night fears all too well, he unzipped the bag, folding it back. "But it's damn cold out tonight. Why don't you climb in with me for a while?"

Rory didn't need a second invitation. "Not leopards," he said, his voice a bit steadier. "Lepers."

A bit of fright from the nightmare lingered, like fog not yet burned off. But as he cuddled closer, Rory felt comforted. It was good to have Quinn in his life. Almost like having a da.

That thought was the last to slip through his mind before he drifted off to sleep.

Lepers. Jesus Christ, what had put that thought in the kid's mind? Looking down at this small imaginative boy Nora had carried in her womb, Quinn realized it felt good to have Rory here with him. It was almost, he thought, like having a son.

That idea gave birth to another stir of something that felt frighteningly like love. And as Rory slept the sleep of innocents, it was Quinn who now found sleep an impossible target.

CHAPTER TWENTY

The Mills Are Grinding

As Nora had feared and Quinn had expected, their budding love affair quickly became grist for Castlelough's eager gossip mills.

Except for those times he'd spent with Brady at The Rose, when his enjoyment of the old man's company and tall tales allowed him to lower the barricades a bit, Quinn's aloof aura had kept most of the other Castlelough residents at a distance. Being linked with Nora, who was obviously much beloved in the village, had changed all that.

Farmers driving their milk and cream to the dairy waved greetings to him as he drove from the farm to the lake each morning, as did the housewives hanging their sheets out to dry in the fragrant spring air. The Irish members of the crew all seemed more friendlier than usual. One of them, a caterer brought in from Kinsale in County Cork to provide lunches for the cast and crew, had even admitted to having a roaring crush on Nora in high school.

"But her heart belonged to Devlin Monohan back in those days." There'd been an air of lingering regret in the handsome young man's voice. "It's a lucky man you are, Quinn Gallagher," he said, telling Quinn nothing he hadn't already figured out for himself.

As soon as class got out in the afternoon, Rory and Jamie would arrive on location, each day bringing more and more of their schoolmates with them until the wardrobe mistress had laughingly dubbed Quinn the Pied Piper of Castlelough. There'd been a time when no one, with the possible exception of Laura, would have so openly teased him. But then again, Quinn was forced to admit as he laughed along with the others, that was before the trip to Ireland. Before Nora.

He was sitting on a moss-covered rock — eschewing the canvas chair with his name stenciled on it that he'd always found pretentious — revising some dialogue for the afternoon's shooting, when a tall reed-slender man in a black cassock came walking toward him. He recognized the parish priest, Father O'Malley.

Quinn's only experience with Catholicism was when he'd turned fourteen and been placed in a Catholic home for nine months. The man and woman had been nice enough, he supposed, albeit harried from trying to control eight children — three of them adopted and the others fosters like him — under the age of sixteen. All the children of school age had received a parochial education with nuns and priests who'd possessed a flair for discipline and a taste for corporal punishment.

"Good day to you," the priest greeted Quinn easily.

"Afternoon, Father," Quinn responded.

Appearing oblivious to the coolness in Quinn's tone, the priest sat down on a nearby rock. "I've been meaning to get out here to see what all the excitement's about," Father O'Malley said, looking around at the commotion with interest. "But the May day celebrations have been taking up a great deal of my time."

"I imagine it's a tricky balance, juggling the Church's celebration of the Madonna with a day lifted from Celtic mythology."

"Ireland has always required a balance of beliefs." The priest ignored Quinn's sarcasm. "Didn't Saint Patrick understand that all too well? You, yourself, in coming down to this lake today, had to pass by a burial site thousands of years old, and right in our view are the stones of a castle dating back to

Norman times. It's impossible *t*
where in this beautiful tragic co
out stumbling over tangible ren
our overlapping layers of human h.
belief. A wise man keeps that in mi.

Although the priest's tone had re.
mild, Quinn felt sufficiently chast
"Touché," he murmured, looking at u
brooding dark castle ruins. "That's a very
pragmatic view. Do you also believe in the
Lady?"

The priest's eyes drifted past the crowds
of villagers, beyond the crew, to the glassy
blue water. "I believe in the Immaculate
Conception, the virgin birth, the Resur-
rection, the Holy Spirit and myriad other
mystical unseen things. I also believe in di-
nosaurs, the Ice Age, the Milky Way and
life on faroff planets. That being the case, I
wouldn't be one to say that the Lady
couldn't exist."

It was as typical a roundabout Irish answer as Quinn had heard since his arrival.
He laughed and felt himself relaxing. Something he seemed to be doing more and more
often.

"As much as I've been curious about the
filming, it's you I really came here to see,"
the priest divulged.

"Oh?" Quinn braced himself for a lecture

his lust having put Nora's immortal at risk.

"I've been wanting to thank you for taking Rory Fitzpatrick on the father-and-son trek. It was a kind and generous thing to do."

Quinn shrugged, uncomfortable as ever with a compliment that was at such odds with how he'd always seen himself. "I had a good time. It wasn't any big deal."

"Ah, but it was to Rory. And to Jamie O'Sullivan, who has himself his own cross to bear, I fear."

Quinn was even more uncomfortable discussing people whose lives had nothing to do with his own. At least that was what he kept telling himself. With lessening degrees of success.

"Kate O'Sullivan should leave her husband," Quinn said. "While she still can."

The priest sighed. His eyes were touched with sadness. And the same frustration Quinn was feeling himself. "I pray every night that God will give her the strength to do what she must to keep herself and her family safe."

His gaze drifted over the lake again. "I see you've gotten John and Mary work on the film."

"Just as extras, after school." Since she'd scraped the heavy makeup off her face,

Nora's sister had, as he'd suspected, turned out to be a beauty. And although thus far Mary had only appeared in group scenes, the camera loved her in a way that had made her pale poet's face jump out of the crowd.

Watching the dailies last night, an uncharacteristically excited and optimistic Jeremy had immediately decided to give her more scenes this afternoon, making Quinn wonder if the attention would cause the teenager to give up her plans to become a teacher and pursue acting, instead, and if so, if Nora would blame him. He also decided to have another little warning chat with Parker Kendall about keeping his hands off the middle Joyce daughter.

"They seem to be enjoying themselves immensely," the priest said. "And of course the attention has to be beneficial to dear Mary. Especially after what Jack Doyle's been putting her through this past month." It seemed there was little in Castlelough that escaped Father O'Malley's sharp eye.

Quinn was wondering if the priest had finally worked his way around to the subject of Nora when he suddenly stood and brushed off his black cassock. "Well, I have a meeting with the ladies' guild about the maypole, of all things. There seems to be some dissension among the ranks concerning the colors of the ribbons and the flowers for the May crown. I've been called in to cast the tiebreaking vote."

"I don't envy you that, Father."

"I have my own trepidations, as well. Any prayers for my surviving the meeting unscathed would be welcome." His blue eyes twinkled as he held out his hand. "I've enjoyed our chat, Mr. Gallagher. Perhaps we'll be seeing you at mass with the family one of these fine mornings before you leave Castlelough."

"I've enjoyed talking with you, too, Father," Quinn said. He did not add that if the priest was waiting for him to show up inside a church, he'd definitely learn the meaning of eternity.

"Well, well," Quinn heard the familiar female voice behind him drawl after O'Malley left. "Surely that couldn't have been Quinn Gallagher I saw passing the time of day with a man of the cloth."

"He was curious." Quinn refused to rise to his former lover's teasing challenge. "About the filming."

"Well, he's certainly not alone there." Laura's eyes skimmed the surrounding hillsides. "The crowd gets bigger every day. It's a wonder anything is getting done in the village."

"It's not every day the circus comes to town." One of his few pleasant childhood memories was when Clyde Beatty had brought his growling lions and roaring tigers to Dunsmuir, California. Quinn had gotten up before daybreak to go down to the railroad yards to watch the circus crew unload the animals from the boxcars. Later that day he'd managed to sneak into the tent to see the dazzling show.

"Especially this village. Why, there are times I feel as if I'm in the cast of *Brigadoon*. I doubt if it's changed all that much in two hundred years."

"Change isn't always for the best."

She patted his cheek. "Watch out, darling. If you're not careful, pretty soon you'll find yourself trading in your computer for a milking machine."

"That's ridiculous."

"Not as ridiculous as the crew taking bets on whether or not you'll be on the plane with us back to the States."

"I'll give you a tip," he all but growled, irritated yet again that his private life was providing so much fodder for public consumption. "Put your money on me sticking to the original itinerary. The day after this film wraps, I'm out of here. On my way home."

Even as he said the words, Quinn found himself wondering why the idea of leaving Castlelough — and Nora — held scant appeal.

Part of the reason was, of course, that he didn't have a home. Just a house. And a leased house at that. There wasn't a single person or thing, not even a cat or parakeet, waiting for him to return from Ireland.

But since arriving at the Joyce farm, for the first time in his life he had something that had begun to feel a lot like family. Something that, whenever he thought about it, scared him to death. Because he wasn't the family type. How could he be, coming from what he did? he asked himself silently as Laura sashayed back down to the lake to shoot a pivotal scene with Kendall.

Later that evening he and Nora were finally alone again, parked beside the little nameless lake in what Quinn had come to think of as their own private place. Even though he told himself that he was getting too damn old to be making love in the back seat of a car like some horny teenager, he understood her reluctance to make love to him under the same roof as her family. It would be different if they were married. But since that was out of the question, this was the only solution.

"Lord, I'd love to spend the night with you again." He was holding her on his lap, nuzzling her neck. In the pale silvery moonlight, her skin appeared as white as swan feathers.

"I know." She turned her head and kissed him on the mouth. "And I'd like that, as well, but —"

"It's okay." It wasn't her fault that the fever he'd felt for her from the beginning hadn't burned off. That the more of her he had, the more he wanted. "I didn't want to make you feel guilty."

She laughed at that. A light musical sound he knew he'd still be able to hear in his head when he was a hundred. "Ah, but isn't that what we Catholics do best?" she asked, punctuating her self-deprecating words with quick sweet kisses. "Feel guilty?"

"Speaking of Catholics, I had a little chat today with Father O'Malley," Quinn said with more casualness than he felt.

"Oh?" She tilted her head back and looked up at him. "Was it about us?"

"No." He ran a soothing hand down her back. "I think he just dropped by to see the filming." He did not mention the priest's comment about Rory. And not wanting to spoil a lovely spring night, he didn't bring up Kate's problem, either. "But it got me thinking . . ." He combed his hands through her hair, pulling it back from her face. "Does what we do bother you? Do you feel guilty about being with me this way?"

"Of course not," she said promptly.

"Yet you refuse to let me make love to you in your bed. Where we could wake up in each other's arms."

Nora took heart from the fact that he'd used the *L*-word. Perhaps not in the context she wished for. But at least he was no longer referring to what they did as just sex.

"I'm not ashamed of what I feel for you, Quinn. Nor of how I share my love for you." Having already admitted to loving him, Nora refused to back away from the word, even if it was obvious it still made him uncomfortable. "But John and Mary are at a dangerous age. I don't want to set the wrong example."

She'd turned so damn earnest he wanted to kiss her again. And that was just for starters. "You know they don't believe that we're running into the village every night for ice cream," he said.

"I know. But what they suspect and what they know are two different things. And although I admit that makes me a bit of a hypocrite, I can remember being that age well enough to know that I wouldn't have understood the difference for what I was feeling for Devlin back then to what you and I have now."

It was the second time today he'd had Devlin Monohan tossed up at him. And it was two times too many. Disliking the way just hearing the man's name could make him jealous, Quinn decided it was time to change the subject.

"Did Kate tell you about our plans for tomorrow?"

"No. She's been so busy getting ready for the horse sale at Clifden, we haven't had time for a proper sit-down talk."

"I thought I'd tag along with Brady."

"To Clifden? Why?"

"I'd like to see Connemara. And both Kate and your father assure me that I haven't truly experienced Ireland without attending a horse fair. And, more importantly, I thought it might be a fun way to spend the day with you."

He felt her reaction before she'd said a word. Her body, warm and soft, turned to ice and stiffened. "I'm sorry, Quinn." Her strangely tight tone said otherwise. "But I won't be going to Clifden with you."

"If tomorrow's inconvenient, Kate says the fair lasts for three days —"

"Not tomorrow, or the next day, or any

day." There was no mistaking the resolution in her expression or her voice.

He was about to point out that there would be music and entertainment, races — including a steeplechase — and wasn't her own father going to be telling his tales, when Quinn suddenly remembered that her husband had died riding in just such a race.

"Tell me about your marriage."

"My marriage?" She stared at him. "Why would you be wanting to know about my marriage?"

"Because, Mrs. Fitzpatrick, I want to know everything about you." *And I can't help wondering if you still love the man you chose to give your virginity and your heart to,* he tacked on mentally.

Nora looked out the windshield at the glassy lake draped in moonlight. "Conor was handsome and —" she paused as if carefully choosing the correct word "— charismatic. He had an energy that seemed to capture everyone in its force field. And a smile like a brilliant summer sun." She sighed, a soft sound that Quinn had no trouble hearing in the stillness of the night. "I never knew anyone who wasn't bedazzled by him at first meeting."

The jealousy that Quinn had reluctantly come to recognize suddenly had claws, forcing him to wonder yet again why he kept reacting so strongly to the idea of Nora loving another man. Especially one who'd been dead for five years.

"And were you?" He played with a curl that had fallen across her cheek, tugging it straight, then watching it spring into a coil again. "Bedazzled?"

"Aye." Her reminiscent smile caused the claws to dig a little deeper.

"Then it was a good marriage?"

"Of course." He thought he saw a faint shadow like a veil of fog move across her expressive eyes. "We never fought. Not ever." She said it with a forcefulness that made him suspect she was lying.

"That's admirable. And a little amazing." He didn't call her on the lie. But he wasn't quite able to keep the challenge from his voice.

"Well, we may have talked hard from time to time," Nora allowed. "Like all couples we had our differences. But we never went to bed angry."

"Now that I believe." He ran his hand down her bare back. "I can't imagine a man staying angry with you in his bed."

"What a lovely thing to say." Her smile, while not as bright and open as usual, still made his heart turn over.

"It's the truth. And if you'd rather I spend tomorrow with you —"

"No. Kate and Da are right. You should be going to the fair. Just mind you keep your hands in your pockets or you'll find yourself buying a horse. And meanwhile I'll have that lamb you never got the chance to sample waiting for you when you get home."

There it was again. That word. That damn, seductive, terrifyingly appealing word. *Home.*

"The lamb's definitely an incentive, Nora, my sweet. But I'd rather have *you* waiting for me." He skimmed a palm over her breasts and felt great satisfaction at the way her nipples pebbled at the seductive touch. "Naked. Hot." Quinn's searching hand trailed lower. "Ready."

"Always," she breathed with not a little wonder as he captured her mouth with his, lowered her onto the seat and took them both back into the mists.

Situated along Ireland's rocky western coast, Connemara was part of the province of Connaught. In the seventeenth century Oliver Cromwell had given the Irish the choice of exiling themselves from the profitable midland farms "to hell or Connacht." The families that had stayed had managed to eke out a living on the rocky soil, only to nearly be wiped out by the famine years of the late 1800s.

As he drove through the treeless landscape past the lakes, waterfalls and crystal creeks interspersed with rock-strewn open spaces and flat brown, black and golden turf fields trimmed with gorse and heather, Quinn found himself once again enchanted by the panorama of sea and sky, land and bog.

The buildings scattered across the wild moorland provided as much contrast as the landscape. He'd pass a snug whitewashed, thatched-roof cottage that reminded him of Nora's farmhouse, only to turn the corner and find himself face-to-face with a manor house turned bed and breakfast, a castle or the remains of an ancient stone fort.

"Aye, this is the back of beyond, even for Ireland," Brady agreed when Quinn mentioned that, except for random glances of habitation, the only signs of life were the sheep and goats on the rocky hillsides, the only sound the trill of a bird floating on the salt-tinged breeze. "But it's lovely, just the same. . . .

"That's Croagh Patrick." Brady pointed toward a dark cone of a mountain jutting up in the distance. Pewter clouds draped the top of the peak. "Legend has it that that's where Saint Patrick got God to grant him the right to judge the people of his adopted land on Judgment Day.

"Every year on Reek Sunday in July thousands of pilgrims climb the mountain — some even barefoot, mind you — to celebrate mass and commemorate the blessed event." He slanted Quinn a look. " 'Tis a shame you'll be missing the amazing sight."

Quinn wasn't fooled for a minute. He knew this was Brady's roundabout way of asking the same question Michael had alluded to, the one the crew had been betting on — whether he was returning to America or staying in Ireland with Nora.

"I'd like to witness that," he said. "But I can't see them changing the date on my account. . . . So, have you made the climb?"

"No. Although I have spent several pleasant hours in the pub at the foot of the Reek toasting with some of the best and creamiest stout in Ireland those who've returned. But those who've made the ascent say that on a clear day, which unfortunately isn't all that often, the view from the peak is enough to convert the most hard-hearted pagan."

Having felt the effects of this country on his own heart, Quinn didn't doubt that in the least.

The unofficial capital — Connemara — sheltered at the head of Clifden Bay, backed by the brooding peaks of the Twelve Bens and pierced by the spires of the Protestant church and Catholic cathedral, was an arresting sight. It was also familiar.

"Aye, it's a popular postcard," Brady agreed. "Thank God that divil Cromwell was too stupid to understand the beauty of this land or we'd have been pushed off our country altogether and now be living beneath the sea."

"Like the Lady."

Brady laughed and agreed.

Although the land surrounding the town may have seemed deserted, it appeared everyone for miles around had arrived for the horse fair and weekly market. There was an amazing selection of items from local vendors — ancient leather-bound books, newer paperback romances with pastel covers promising stories of happily-ever-afters, wool goods echoing the heather shades of the surrounding moors, exquisite hand-tatted lace, vegetables, woven baskets and jewelry, including Tara brooches and Claddagh rings — a heart clasped by two hands and topped with a crown — displayed on black velvet trays.

"It was a Joyce who first designed that

lovely ring," Brady informed Quinn.

"Really?" None of Quinn's guidebooks had mentioned that little bit of Galway history.

"Now, would I be making up such a thing when it's so easy to document? I suppose you'd be knowing that the Joyce family was prominent in the affairs of Galway City?"

"One of the Fourteen Tribes of Galway," Quinn answered. That much he had learned.

"The first bearer of the family name in this country was Thomas de Joise, a man of Norman Welsh descent, who married the daughter of one of the O'Brien Princes of Thomond in 1283 and settled in the far west of Connacht. It was their son, Mac Mara, who subsequently married into the powerful O'Flaherty family, and his descendants went on to rule the territory until the seventeenth century."

Once again Quinn marveled at the way the Irish could make a seven-hundred-year-old story seem relevant to their own lives. Once again, he thought of the Joyce blood — the blood of kings — running through Nora's veins and compared it to his own.

"At any rate," Brady continued, "William Joyce was captured by the Barbary pirates. It was during his imprisonment in Algiers that he learned a trade as a silversmith, then went on to create the Claddagh ring. The same symbol of abiding love that I gave to my own dear Eleanor on our wedding day. The same one that will be handed down to Nora on her wedding day."

That seemingly offhand statement captured Quinn's immediate attention. He looked up from the gold bracelet embossed with Celtic designs he'd been considering buying for her.

"I don't understand. The ring is handed down from mother to daughter?"

"Aye. In some families that's the tradition."

"But if your wife had already died when Nora married Fitzpatrick . . ."

"Ah, I can see the way your mind is going," Brady said with a knowing nod. "And the truth of the matter is that Eleanor didn't want Nora to be given the ring on that day. Because she didn't believe the marriage would last."

Quinn wasn't about to ask Brady how he knew what his deceased wife wanted. "I thought they had a good marriage."

Brady rubbed his jaw. His expression sobered. "Let me be putting it this way . . . would you be knowing the difference between a widow and a wife?"

Quinn understood it was not as simple a

question as it appeared. "Why don't you tell me?"

"A widow knows where her husband is spending the night."

The two men exchanged a look. "Fitzpatrick may have been a hotshot steeplechase rider," Quinn said, "but he was a damn fool."

"Aye." The older man nodded. "I've often thought so, as well." He gave Quinn another long look and seemed on the verge of saying something else, something even more intimate, when a voice called out his name, causing him to turn. A man was walking toward them, his stride long and self-assured. "Why, isn't it Devlin Monohan," Brady said with obvious pleasure.

"We've met," Quinn muttered, still not at ease with the idea of Nora having been in love with this handsome Irish veterinarian.

The two men shook hands, each silently measuring the other as they'd done that first time on the beach.

"It's a pleasure to see you again, Mr. Gallagher," Devlin said. "I was sorry you and Nora were unable to attend my mother's party."

I'll just bet you were, Quinn thought, suspecting that while his presence wouldn't have been missed, Nora's undoubtedly had. "It couldn't be helped," he said.

"I was pleased to hear that Fionna escaped injury. Terrible thing, the Troubles," Devlin said with a regretful shake of his head before turning back to Brady. "I hope you're planning to tell the tale of Queen Grace this afternoon?"

"Grace O'Malley was pirate queen of Connacht," Brady informed Quinn. "If the stories are to be believed —"

"And surely there's no reason not to," Quinn interjected with dry humor.

"Aren't you getting the idea now, Quinn Gallagher," Brady said with obvious approval. "As the story goes, there wasn't a seaside castle in all of Connacht that didn't pass through Grace's hands at one time or another."

"My favorite tale is when she got out of bed right after giving birth," Devlin said.

"Aboard ship," Brady said, again for Quinn's sake. " 'Twas at sea, on her corsair, that Grace felt the most at home." He turned back to the man who might have been his son-in-law. "But continue your story, Devlin, lad. For my guest's edification."

"If you're interested," Devlin said to Quinn.

"I've yet to find anything about your country that doesn't interest me," Quinn answered truthfully.

Devlin gave him another of those brief measuring looks before continuing. "Well, although I'm not the storyteller Brady is, it was in the midst of battle and Grace could hear that the tide was turning against her, so she grabbed a blunderbuss from one of her men and shot the captain of the enemy ship dead. This rallied her troops and they fought on to victory."

"I'd expect nothing less."

"Grace was the scourge of the Elizabethans, that was for certain," Brady said. "Fighting them at every turn and winning most of the battles. Even so, Elizabeth — the first one — offered to confer the title of countess on her after a furious conflict with Connacht's English governor."

"To encourage her to stop her piracy," Quinn guessed. "Aye. And didn't our Grace turn the offer down, informing the English Protestant monarch that she was already a queen in her own right."

"For all its alleged chauvinism, this country certainly seems to have its share of strong women," Quinn said.

"Aye," Devlin and Brady said in unison. And as all three of them fell silent, Quinn suspected that, like him, the others were not thinking of Grace, or the warrior queen Maeve, or even the mythical Lady, but of Nora.

Quinn found the day every bit as informative and enjoyable as Kate had promised. His only regret was that Nora wasn't there to share it with him.

" 'Tis a fine thing you did, Quinn Gallagher," the older man said as they drove back to the farm at the end of the day.

Quinn glanced up into the rearview mirror at the trailer that had been hitched to the back of the Mercedes. "Nora warned me to keep my hands in my pockets. But when you told me that Rory's seventh birthday is coming up next month and how much he's wanted a horse . . ."

"Oh, he has, indeed. But of course Nora always insists that it's too dear. So it looked as if the poor lad was going to grow up to be the only boy in all of Ireland without a pony."

Although he knew that was a blatant exaggeration, Quinn couldn't deny that he was looking forward to seeing the kid's face when he got a look at the bay mare.

"Monohan said she was gentle." Although it had grated, just a little, since he knew nothing about horses, Quinn had felt it only prudent to ask the vet for his professional opinion.

"As a lamb."

"I wonder what Kate wanted."

Nora's sister-in-law had actually paled when she'd seen what he'd done and had hurriedly told him that, after she'd seen to the selling of her own stallion, it was imperative they talk. But when he'd gone to look for her later, he couldn't locate her in the teeming crowd.

"She undoubtedly wanted to congratulate you," Brady said quickly. A bit too quickly, Quinn thought with a little niggling of suspicion. "But whatever it was, it will surely keep until tomorrow."

"I suppose that's true." Quinn remembered what Nora had told him about God making plenty of time. Then smiled at the thought of how she was going to react when he arrived home with Rory's horse in tow.

CHAPTER TWENTY-ONE

Treat Me Daughter Kindly

Nora came out the kitchen door when she heard the Mercedes pull into the driveway. "What is that?" she asked, staring in seeming disbelief at the trailer hitched behind the car. Her expression was far from pleased.

"A present for Rory," Quinn said, another tinge of suspicion dulling the self-satisfaction he'd felt earlier when he'd slapped hands with the robust Clare farmer who'd sold him the mare. "I know it's a little early for his birthday, but —"

"A horse?" Her voice rose. Hectic color stained cheeks as white as rice paper. "You bought my son a horse?"

The others had gathered in the driveway behind her, their expressions ranging from Fionna's regretful one to Rory's wide-eyed disbelief. Maeve, who had run out of the kitchen behind Nora to greet him, began barking loudly in the direction of the trailer, even as she hovered behind Quinn.

Ignoring the wolfhound, Quinn decided

this was simply a repeat of her reaction to his giving John a computer. Obviously Nora was uneasy accepting such an expensive gift. "Brady mentioned that Rory's been wanting a pony, and I realize you're going to feel the need to complain —"

"You're damn right I'm going to complain," she cut him off with a furious wave of a hand that was visibly trembling. She turned on her father, fists at her hips. "How could you do this, Da? Knowing how I feel? How I've always felt?"

"Now, Nora," Brady began cajolingly. "You know I love you with all my heart, daughter. And I truly appreciate all you've done over these past years to keep our little family together. But you're wrong about this."

"Wrong about what?" Quinn asked, feeling as if he'd just walked into a movie during the second reel. Obviously he was missing an important part of this latest story.

"Mam won't let me have a pony," Rory offered on a voice thick with building tears. "Because of how my da died."

Hell. That was what he got for giving in to impulse, Quinn blasted himself. He should have thought of that. And even though the idea hadn't occurred to him, Brady damn well should have warned him.

"Nora, believe me, I didn't know. If I had —"

"I'll be hearing no ifs." Her face had hardened to stone. Her eyes were frost. "Nor will I be putting my son at risk. The horse goes back."

"Now, Nora," Brady said again, "you know that a Castlelough's man's handshake is as good as an oath."

"Quinn is not a Castlelough man."

"True enough. But I was the one who introduced him to Johnny Keane in the first place."

"Then you're the one who can take the horse back."

"I'll not be doing that." Brady raised himself up to his full height. "I understand the fear that struck your heart the day your husband died. But you're not being fair to your son. The lad's Irish. Irish boys need horses. It's as simple as that."

Nora lifted her chin and folded her arms. "Now there's where you're wrong." She turned to Quinn. "I realize you didn't mean any harm, Quinn. But Rory's my son, and I'll do what's best for him. And for now I'd appreciate it if you'd take the horse to Kate's until I can arrange to have it returned to Mr. Keane at first light tomorrow."

"Mam!" It was a wail. Quinn looked at

419

mother and son, one's eyes brimming with tears, the other's as hard as the stone walls separating the Irish fields, and damned himself for having created such an impossible situation.

She turned to her distraught son, crouched and stroked a hand over his dark hair. "You know my feelings on this, Rory, darling. And although I don't expect you to understand now, someday, when you have a boy or girl of your own —"

"I don't want a boy or girl of my own." He jerked away, his freckles dark against a face as pale as his mother's. "I want a horse. And if you won't let me keep this one, I'll never be speaking to you again!" With that threat hanging in the air, Rory spun on his heel and ran back into the house, slamming the kitchen door behind him.

Quinn decided to try once more. "Nora, I'm truly sorry."

"I believe you." Her voice was as flat as her gaze. "But the damage has already been done. Now I'd appreciate it if you'd just get that beast out of here."

"It's not a beast," Brady insisted. "Didn't Devlin say she was a fine and gentle mare?"

"Devlin?" Obviously this betrayal cut deepest of all. "Devlin was in on this, as well?"

"I asked his professional opinion," Quinn explained. "It seemed like a good idea at the time."

"And wasn't that something, all the men in my life deciding they knew what was best for my son." Her voice clogged. "I swear, Da, I've half a mind to take the children and move to Galway."

"Now, darling, you wouldn't want to be doing that," Brady cajoled.

"Please, because I don't want to say things we both might always regret, I don't want you to say another word. Not now." As if afraid she'd break down in front of her family, she turned away and began walking toward her car. "I'll be taking a drive. And when I get back, I'll not be wanting to see any sign of a horse on this farm."

With that she was gone. Leaving Quinn feeling like the Grinch who'd stolen Nora's happy family.

"I guess I'd better take the mare over to Kate's," he said to no one in particular.

"I think that might be the thing to do for now," Fionna agreed. "Nora's always been a strict mother, but fair. But she does have a sore spot when it comes to horses."

"It's one she needs to get over," Brady continued to insist doggedly. "It's not right for the boy to be denied a horse just because of his mother's unreasonable fear."

"Not that unreasonable," Fionna told her son. "And you had no business using Quinn to get round her that way."

"True." He turned toward Quinn, regret etched into every line in his face. "And I'm sorry for my little intrigue. But I truly thought that once Nora actually saw how happy your gift made her son, she'd relent."

Since the older man's usually ruddy complexion was an unhealthy shade of gray, revealing his own stress with this situation, Quinn decided that no good would come from backing Nora and Fionna. He also realized that, contrary to conventional wisdom, the widow Fitzpatrick could hold a grudge, after all.

"She'll calm down," he said, wanting to offer some words of assurance to this man who looked every year of his age. He looked even worse, Quinn thought, than he had outside the Derry hospital where his mother had been taken.

"Aye." Brady nodded, a bit more strength in his voice and his spirit. "And when she does, I'm grateful she'll have you to turn to. You're a good man, Quinn Gallagher. I only hope you'll be able to forgive me for today's little scheme."

"You're Rory's grandfather. You did what

you thought was in the boy's best interests. Nora will understand that once she has time to think about it." Out of the corner of his eye, Quinn saw Fionna shepherding the other children back into the house. "Would you like a drive to The Rose?"

"No." Brady shook his head and managed a smile. " 'Tis a lovely evening. I think I'll just sit here and enjoy the sound of the crickets for a time."

Quinn was torn between staying with the man he'd grown fond of and getting rid of the mare before Nora returned from her drive. "If you're sure you'll be okay . . ."

"Don't you be worrying about me, lad. I'll be as fit as a fiddle. The day an Irishman can't handle a redheaded female's temper is a sorry day, indeed."

Deciding that he'd only insult Nora's father by pressing, Quinn climbed into the Mercedes, started the engine and began to drive away, trying to ignore the small desolate face he saw looking out from an upstairs window.

As he watched the car and trailer drive off down the road, Brady decided that after the day he'd had, a drink and some convivial company was definitely in order. Unfortunately his mam's car had been blown to

423

smithereens in Derry, and Nora had the other.

"I should have taken Quinn up on his offer," he muttered up at the star-spangled sky. On the other hand, perhaps an evening walk was just what he needed to lift his spirits the rest of the way.

Wisps of fog rolled in from the sea like silent ghosts, wrapping him in a cool mist. Although the village seemed a bit farther away than the last time he'd walked from the farm, which was, he realized, probably five years earlier, he managed to keep up a brisk pace, proving to himself yet again exactly how wrong that pup Flannery was. Why, his heart was as strong as ever. Probably as strong as the fool doctor's himself, Brady decided as he approached the stone bridge crossing the river into Castlelough.

"What the feck?" The bridge, dating back to the time when the town was first founded, had stood in the same spot for centuries. But no more. Strangely, it had disappeared. "Now how is a man expected to get to his favorite pub?"

"I'll be giving you a ride — for a gold piece," a voice hidden deep in the thickening fog, offered.

Brady peered into the mist and thought he saw the faint glow of a lantern from somewhere on the water. "And what would the likes of a poor farmer such as meself be doing with a piece of gold?" he asked.

"Check your pocket," the voice suggested helpfully in Irish.

Thinking the man was obviously daft, Brady nevertheless did so — only to humor him, he told himself — and was surprised when his fingers closed around the coin. "Where in the divil did that come from?" he asked.

"Magic," the man said on a rusty cackle.

He held the lantern aloft, allowing Brady to get a good look at the boatman sitting in the old-fashioned canvas curragh favored by traditional west Irish fishermen. His grizzled face looked older than the Joyce family fields; the stump of a pipe disappeared into a beard as white as the snow that occasionally muffled the island.

"Is your curragh sound?"

"And hasn't it been taking passengers across this river since before you were a twinkle in your da's eye, Brady Joyce?"

Brady was not all that surprised the man knew who he was. After all, he'd acquired a bit of fame in his lifetime. The strange thing was that Brady didn't recognize the boatman. He would have bet a year's worth of pints he knew every man in the county.

That thought in turn gave birth to another — he was thirsty. And he certainly wasn't going to be getting a pint standing here on the bank of the river talking.

He handed over the coin and climbed into the small shallow boat. A moment later he found himself engulfed in fog so thick he couldn't see his hand in front of his face. The cold dampness seemed to be seeping its way through his wool jacket and trousers, all the way to the marrow of his bones. He saw a light from what he took to be the far bank and assumed the welcoming glow was coming from The Rose's windows. Perhaps, he thought, as the chill deepened, he'd forgo the Guinness tonight for the warming comfort of some whiskey-laced coffee.

"It won't be long now," the boatman assured him from somewhere in the swirling gray mist as he rowed toward the light.

"Jaysus!" Brady exclaimed when he saw the figure standing on the bank, surrounded by a light as bright as the gilded halos painted over the heads of all those saints on the curved ceiling of the Immaculate Heart Church.

"Not quite," a blessedly familiar voice said with the hint of humor he'd always adored. "And not yet."

While he was accustomed to talking with his wife on a daily basis, Brady had not seen her since they'd lowered her casket into the rich loamy earth. Amazingly she appeared as she had the day they'd married, her hair as black and shiny as a raven's wing, her cheeks blooming like roses in the snowfield of her flawless complexion, her white dress enhancing curves he still caressed nightly in his dreams.

She held out a slender hand as the boatman docked. Rising slowly to his feet, Brady held out his own. When their fingers touched and he felt the spark shoot through him like summer lightning, Brady realized this was no dream.

Although he would not have thought it possible, the shimmering light surrounding her glowed even brighter, engulfing him as he gathered her into his arms.

"Ah, my love." Eleanor sighed as she twined her slender arms around his neck in exactly the same way she had on their wedding night so many years ago. "I've missed you so."

And as her lips touched his, warming him in a blissfully familiar way that Irish coffee never could, Brady realized he wouldn't be going to The Rose tonight. Because after all these years of loneliness, he'd finally rediscovered heaven. With the one true love of his life. His beloved Eleanor.

Alone in her bed in the upstairs of the farmhouse where she'd been raised, Kate was jerked out of yet another restless sleep by the feeling that something was wrong. At first she thought Cadel might have returned from his cousin's in Dungarven, which couldn't mean anything good. She lay in the shadowed darkness, willing her startled heart to be quiet, and listened, as she had night after night ever since the misty dreams had begun.

But all she could hear was the scrape of a tree branch against her window, the sigh of the wind in the chimney, the distant unceasing murmur of the sea and the creaking sounds of her house.

When she failed to hear the painfully familiar noise her drunkard husband made stumbling into furniture or clomping up the stairs, she began to breathe a wee bit easier. Climbing out of the hand-carved tester bed she'd been born in, she drew on her robe and went across the hall and checked on her daughter.

Brigid's hair gleamed like wildfire in the starshine streaming in the window, and her rosebud mouth was curved in a smile, suggesting happy dreams. The sight of such childish innocence brought a smile to Kate's own lips as she bent down and brushed the top of the toddler's bright head with a kiss.

Next door, in the room that had once been Conor's, she found her son also sound asleep. But his sheets were twisted in a way that suggested he'd been restless as well. She untangled him from the bed linens as best she could without waking him, removed the toy laser-light sword Quinn had brought him from Derry that was making a lump of his pillow, kissed him as she had Brigid, then tiptoed out of the room.

Stopping in the hallway at the top of the stairs, she stood stone still and listened again. Nothing seemed amiss in the house. Yet, unable to shake the continuing feeling of unease, Kate returned to her bedroom and stared out the window into the night. Wondering. Worrying. Waiting.

The house was dark when Nora finally returned from her drive, which had included a long contemplative time spent at her secret place at the lake. The solitude and the mystical presence of her surroundings had calmed her restless mind, as they so often did, allowing her to think more clearly.

Although she dearly loved her family, it hadn't been easy taking on her mother's role at such a young age. When she'd first returned home from the convent, everyone was so devastated by Eleanor's death, she'd buried her own feelings of loss and tried to provide an atmosphere of calm support, even though deep inside, her heart was shattered. Looking back, Nora realized she'd given them all the mistaken impression that she was unsinkable. That whatever the problem — from a broken doll to a dead husband — steadfast practical Nora could handle it.

But heaven help her and God forgive her, she thought as she cut the car engine, she was so very weary of handling things.

She went into the house, finding the note her grandmother had left on the kitchen table assuring her that Rory had gone to bed like the good little lamb he was, and that she'd said a prayer to Bernadette to ease the pain between mother and son.

Wishing she possessed the unwavering faith Fionna seemed to have in the martyred nun, Nora read on. "Although I've gone to bed as well, darling," her grandmother had written in that spidery script that still held a vestige of the penmanship method taught by the Sister of Mercy nuns, "if you should feel the need for conversation when you return home from your drive, feel free to wake me."

Knowing the offer came from the heart,

Nora opted against seeking out whatever comfort Fionna might be able to offer. The regrettable truth was, as she'd sat beside the moon-gilded waters, she'd taken a long hard look at the fear that had been part of her for such a long time, and realized that although she'd always prided herself on being a good mother, she hadn't been fair to her son.

Although Conor had been a great deal older than she, Nora could recall stories of Mel Fitzpatrick — his paternal grandfather — taking him riding before he could walk. Everyone in the county always said that Conor had been born to the saddle. And wasn't his blood running in his own son's veins? How could she have let the dread that had put such a stranglehold on her keep her from understanding Rory's lifelong dream for a pony of his own?

She owed her son an apology. And, she'd reluctantly accepted, a horse. As she'd driven home, she'd decided that if he'd managed to fall asleep after the emotional evening, she'd wait until morning for the long-overdue conversation. But now, standing alone in the dimly lit kitchen, she changed her mind.

"No time like the present," she murmured as she turned off the light Fionna had left burning for her and left the room, headed upstairs.

Rory's door, like all the others along the darkened hallway, was closed. Nora entered the room, feeling the usual surge of maternal emotion she felt whenever she watched her son sleeping.

"Rory." She leaned over the bed, instinctively reaching for him in the dark. On some distant level she found it odd she couldn't hear his breathing. "Wake up, darling. Mama has something she needs to tell you." Her hand touched the pillow, stuffed with feathers from hens that had ended up on the table. It was strangely cold. "Rory?" Reaching out, she turned on the lamp on the nearby nightstand. When she saw the empty bed, icy fingers clenched her heart.

Quinn heard her drive up. Heard her enter the house, and after a few moments, come upstairs. He'd been waiting up for her, but when he heard the faint squeak of Rory's door across the hall, decided to give her an opportunity to make things up with her son before they had their necessary talk.

He was prepared for her continued censure. After all, there wasn't anything she could call him that Quinn hadn't called himself while driving the mare over to Kate's farm. A conversation with Nora's sister-in-law, filling him in on a few more of the details of Conor's death — including the way he'd lingered in a coma for three long months — had left him feeling even guiltier.

Although it was an unpalatable idea, he belatedly realized that he'd bought the horse as much for himself as for the boy. It was more than a little obvious that, while certainly not poverty-stricken, the family lived mostly hand-to-mouth. He'd gotten off on playing the rich American, bestowing gifts like some bountiful Santa Claus.

He'd let her blast him for as long as she needed, he'd decided as he'd tried, unsuccessfully, to work on his new novel while waiting for her to return. Then he'd agree to everything she might say.

And then, if he was lucky, since he'd already determined she possessed a kind and caring nature, she might even be willing to forgive him. And if he was very, very lucky, perhaps she might even be willing to make the argument up in his bed.

He'd begun to fantasize about all the things he wanted to do with her when his bedroom door burst open and he saw her standing there, her face impossibly pale.

"It's Rory." Her eyes were as wild as an escapee from an asylum; her complexion that of a wraith. "He's gone missing, but I called Kate, thinking that he might have followed the mare to her farm, and she found him in the barn, with the mare."

He was out of bed in a shot. "Give me two minutes to throw on some clothes and we'll go get him."

"I was hoping you'd say that."

As he pulled on a sweatshirt and jeans, Quinn acknowledged that Nora was capable of handling the matter of a runaway boy in her own brisk, effective manner. But that didn't stop him from being immensely relieved that after what he'd done, she'd want him with her. Obviously Kate was right. Nora was not a woman to hold grudges.

"Rory isn't the first boy to run away from home," he assured her. Hadn't he done exactly that too many times to count by the time he'd reached Rory's age? Unfortunately the sheriff's deputies, or cops, or social workers always took him back to his parents. "And he won't be the last."

After jamming his feet into his boots, he gathered her into his arms and pressed his lips to her temple. She was as cold as ice. And trembling. "Come on, sweetheart, let's go bring your son home."

"It's all my fault," Nora murmured five minutes later as she stared out the windshield of the Mercedes. She wasn't seeing the rain that had begun to streak down the curved glass, only the stricken look on her son's young face when he'd run back into the house earlier.

"I've never been one for assigning blame," Quinn said mildly. "Personally I've always thought it a waste of time. But if someone has to be at fault, it's me for bringing the damn horse home in the first place."

"Perhaps you should have asked me," she allowed, clasping her hands more tightly in her lap. "But I've been unnecessarily rigid."

"Stop the presses and notify the pope." He reached out and took hold of one of those rigid icy hands, linking their fingers together in a companionable way. "It seems that the allegedly saintly Nora Fitzpatrick isn't quite ready for beatification, after all."

Despite a bit of fear that remained after finding her son's bed empty, and her regret for having exchanged such harsh words with both the son and father she loved, Nora smiled. She thought about telling Quinn once again how good he was for her, but knew he'd dismiss her words, and her feelings, just as he had in the past.

"And isn't that a shame?" she murmured mildly. "Just when I'd gotten so used to wearing that pretty gold halo."

His answering laugh was rich and warm and slipped beneath her skin, into her blood, melting away the last of the lingering ice.

Kate was waiting outside the house for them, standing in the spreading glow of the porch lamp, a flashlight in her hand.

"He's in the barn. I found him there asleep and I was going to wake him, but since you were on your way, I thought I'd be leaving that up to you." She turned to Nora. "She's a fine mare, Nora. Sturdy, with a sweet disposition, and from the papers Keane gave Quinn, she comes from a good bloodline. I'll be more than happy to take her off your hands."

"No." Nora shook her head, her answer surprising Quinn. "Brady's right. Rory's entitled to a pony, and we'll be keeping her. But I would appreciate it if you could board her until I can get the barn ready for her." There hadn't been a horse in the barn since Conor's accident.

"I'd be happy to." Kate's approving smile as she handed over the flashlight hid the feeling she had that something wasn't right. When she'd first gotten the call from Nora and had found Rory in her barn, she'd hoped the boy's running away was what she'd been sensing. But if that was the case, why was she still feeling this vague unease? "Your son and the mare — and Maeve of course — are in the first stall."

And that was where they found him, curled in the straw, his arms wrapped around Maeve's neck, using the huge dog for a pillow. The wolfhound looked up at their arrival and gave a welcoming thump of her thick tail.

"Rory." Nora crouched beside her sleeping son and stroked his hair. "Darling, wake up."

His eyes fluttered open. When he saw his mother, he tensed and tightened his hold on the black, white and gray dog.

Seeing the tracks of tears on his cheeks and the dread in his eyes, Nora bit her lip to keep from crying herself. "Rory, I'm sorry. I've tried my best to be a good mother to you, but —"

"But I can't have a pony," he interrupted flatly.

"No. I mean, no, that's not right. What I'm trying to tell you is that I was wrong about the pony. Your father was a great rider, Rory. All the Fitzpatrick men have been. It's only natural that you'd inherit their love of horses. And Kate assures me this is a very nice mare."

"Oh, she's better than nice!" Rory said quickly. "She's the best mare in all of Castlelough. The best in the county, even."

The horse, standing at the far side of the

stall, nickered softly in apparent agreement.

"She looks as if she may be the best in all of Ireland," Nora said, and watched as her son's small, earnest face lit up. "And I think we owe Quinn a thank-you for such a glorious early birthday present."

"Aye." Rory looked up at the man standing beside Nora as if viewing some ancient king come back to life. "Thank you. It's the best gift ever. Even better than the Millennium Falcon model."

Quinn laughed, feeling unreasonably lighthearted as he bent down and lifted the boy into his arms. "Believe me, Rory, me lad," he said, "it was my pleasure. Perhaps one of these days, before the filming is over, your aunt Kate will lend me one of her horses and we can go riding together."

Rory glanced at his mother. "I think that sounds like a lovely idea," Nora agreed. "Perhaps the three of us could go together. And of course Maeve, as well," she added as the dog stood up and executed a long blissful stretch.

Rory's grin was a flash of white in his smudged face. "That's the best idea you've ever had, Mam."

As the thin arms twined around his neck, bringing with them the pungent aromas of horse and hay and six-year-old boy, Quinn forgot to worry when he found himself silently agreeing with Rory's assessment.

After being assured that the mare could be brought over to the farm as soon as a stall was ready and the paddock fence repaired, Rory slept in the back seat of the car on the way home.

As Quinn carried him upstairs and they tucked him into bed together, Nora's unruly heart couldn't help thinking how good it felt to be with Quinn this way. How right. So right, in fact, that she didn't hesitate going across the hall into the room that had been hers.

"I owe you an apology," she said softly so as not to wake the family who'd managed to sleep through the entire adventure. "For taking off on you that way."

"I deserved it." Because it had been too long since he'd kissed her, Quinn lightly touched his lips to hers. "I already knew about Conor's accident of course." He considered it personal growth that he could say his long-dead rival's name without choking. "But after Kate filled me in on the details, I understood why you flew off the handle."

"I was so afraid for Rory." Luxuriating in the comfort of his strong arms, Nora was as emotionally, physically and mentally exhausted as she'd ever been in her life.

"Believe me, sweetheart, I know something firsthand about fear." He skimmed his mouth up her cheek and was rewarded by a shimmering sigh. "But although I've never been a father, I also know that kids are amazingly resilient." Quinn considered sharing some of his own past as proof of that claim, then allowed himself to be distracted by her hands slipping beneath his sweatshirt to stroke his back. "You can't wrap Rory up in cotton batting and keep him tied to your apron strings forever."

His mouth returned to hers. Tasting. Teasing. Tormenting.

"Even if they are very nice apron strings," he alleged, untying the apron Nora had forgotten she'd been wearing when she'd left the kitchen to confront him so many hours earlier.

"We'll have to be very quiet," she whispered. Remembering how he'd made her cry out in the car, Nora wondered who she was warning. Quinn? Or herself?

"As mice," he whispered back as he pulled the emerald green sweater over her head in one smooth deft movement. Scooping her up with the same ease he had Rory earlier, he carried her the few feet to the bed.

That was the last thing either Quinn or Nora was to say for a very long time.

CHAPTER TWENTY-TWO

Tears on the Heather

Nora awoke to the sound of larks singing in the meadows. She opened her eyes and found herself staring straight into Quinn's.

"Good morning," he murmured. He brushed some sleep-tousled waves away from her face. "Have I told you that waking up with you in my bed could easily become my favorite thing to do?"

Enjoying the warmth of his gaze and the feel of his hard body pressed so close to hers, Nora smiled. "Mine, too," she admitted.

"We're going to have to talk about this." He cupped her cheek with his palm, the sensual desire she'd witnessed in his eyes turning as serious as she'd ever seen it. "About me." His thumb traced a melting trail around the mouth he'd spent most of the night ravishing. "And you." His free arm drew her even closer. "Us together."

Hope was a snow-white dove, spreading its sun-gilded wings to take flight in her romantic's heart. "Aye." Her lips parted and her body began that now-familiar slow melt.

"Later."

Quinn had given up wondering why it was that he couldn't get enough of this woman. He'd have expected, especially after last night, he'd be too exhausted, not to mention sexually satiated, to want to start things up again. And it wasn't just his body, he realized as he felt the familiar hardening in his loins. If it had been merely sex, he could have handled it. But his mind wanted her with an identical fever. Not to mention, Lord help him, a heart he'd never been aware of possessing.

Allowing himself one long deep kiss that left him aching, he pushed himself out of the warm bed. "I'm going to take a cold shower before Rory comes bursting in to make certain he didn't dream last night." The way she was looking at him — at the part of him that inevitably hardened whenever she was anywhere around — made him groan.

"You realize, of course, if you keep looking at me that way, we're going to risk having what could be a very embarrassing moment."

"I know." She sighed. And then smiled. "I just can't seem to help myself." She hitched herself up in bed, not bothering to catch the sheet as it slid down to reveal rosy-tipped breasts he could still taste.

"You're a truly beautiful man, Quinn Gallagher." Her warm gaze drank him in, missing absolutely nothing. "I think Michelangelo must have had you in mind when he sculpted *David*."

Make that a very long cold shower, Quinn decided. "Remember last night? When I suggested you weren't going to make sainthood?"

"I remember everything about last night." Her satisfied smile reminded him of the one with which Vivien Leigh's Scarlett had lit up silver screens all over the world after having been thoroughly ravished by her husband. "Absolutely everything."

"I'm finding it more and more difficult to believe you were ever in the convent."

"I'm finding it difficult to believe, as well." If she'd had even a glimmer of the thoughts the sight of Quinn's magnificent naked body could invoke back in those days, she would have been forced to spend all her waking hours on her knees on the stone floor of the convent chapel.

"You're not only far from a saint. You're a witch." His muffled laughter rumbled in his chest even as the ache deepened in his groin. "If you'd been alive during the Inquisition,

443

sweetheart, the Church would have burned you at the stake."

His control was nearing the breaking point, and before he gave in to the urge to drag Nora into the shower with him, Quinn left the room.

Nora was relieved when it seemed that Brady was going to sleep in. Relieved, but not surprised. After their argument he'd undoubtedly gone off to The Rose, where he could tell everyone what a hardheaded, heartless woman his eldest daughter had turned out to be.

No, she admitted as she went through the motions of preparing her family's breakfast, that wasn't fair. Brady had never been one to air their dirty laundry in public, and he was also not one to say negative things about anyone. Let alone his own family.

Didn't everyone in the county agree that Brady Joyce had a spirit generous enough for a dozen men? Which was why, she considered later, as she waved the children off to the crossroads to catch the bus, he'd dared to risk her wrath by standing up to her about Rory's need for a pony.

"I'm going to have to apologize to Da," she said to Quinn as they sat at the kitchen table.

Fionna had just taken off, this time to nearby Casla, where she was scheduled to be interviewed on Raidio na Gaeltachta, the Irish-language radio station, regarding her frightening experience in Derry. Claiming no desire for personal fame, she'd explained to the others that she'd only agreed to the interview because it provided a perfect opportunity to spread the message of Bernadette.

Quinn covered Nora's hand with his. "He understands you were upset."

"Just the same, I owe him the words."

Reminding himself how important words were to the Irish, Quinn knew that he owed Nora more than a few words himself. Words he'd never spoken aloud to any other person. Words he'd never thought he'd be wanting to say to a woman. Words he still wasn't certain he had the right to say to her. As much as he wanted to believe in a future, having spent an entire lifetime expecting the worst, he couldn't quite allow himself to look forward to a happily-ever-after future.

Feeling his nerve waver, Quinn decided that, since he'd already waited this long, a few more minutes wouldn't matter. The one thing he didn't want was to have Brady come downstairs just when he was trying to tell Nora he'd fallen in love with her.

He got up from the table and refilled his coffee cup. "How late do you think he'll sleep?"

"I don't know." She glanced up at the clock and frowned. "He's usually up and about by now. Perhaps I should go check on him." Before she could stand, the phone rang. Since Quinn was already on his feet, he said, "I'll get it," and went into the parlor.

When Quinn didn't return right away, Nora guessed it was Kate calling about the mare. Indulging herself a bit longer, she poured more tea and added cleaning out the stall to her mental list of today's chores.

"I suppose Rory will be expecting his pony waiting when he returns from school today," she said when Quinn returned to the kitchen. "I'd best be getting things prepared for her —" She stopped. "Quinn?" His face was as grim as she'd ever seen it.

"It's Brady."

"Da?" She glanced past him toward the parlor. "On the telephone?"

"No." He raked his hand through his dark hair, looking as if he'd rather be anywhere on earth right now but in Nora Fitzpatrick's cozy kitchen. "It was about your father."

"Oh." She still couldn't understand the problem. Weren't people calling all the time

446

hoping to book Brady and his tales for their event? "Well, I suppose this settles it." She stood up. "I'll just go upstairs and —"

"He's not upstairs." Quinn crossed the room and wrapped his arms around her, holding her so tightly she could barely breathe.

She tilted her head. "What do you mean? Of course he is. Haven't we been waiting for him to come down so we could have our talk?" She'd been as nervous as a barn cat in a roomful of rocking chairs waiting to hear what Quinn had to say.

"Sweetheart." His tone was as rough as a gravel road. He cupped her face between his large strong hands and, looking up at him, Nora saw the love she'd been hoping and praying for. But something else, too. Sympathy? Pity, perhaps? "Your father's dead." When she flinched, his fingers stroked her cheeks in a way meant to soothe, rather than arouse.

"Dead?" Surely that couldn't be her voice? Nora thought, hearing the unfamiliar high fractured sound.

"He was found on the road just this side of the bridge by a farmer who was taking his cows to his field this morning. The doctor says he'd probably been there since sometime last night." Quinn took a deep breath.

"It was his heart. Dr. Flannery says he would have gone quickly."

Nora felt the blood literally drain from her face. "I don't believe that!" She tore away from him and raced blindly out of the kitchen and up the stairs.

She ran down the hallway, past Rory's door, past her own, past Mary's and John's and Fionna's, finally flinging open the door of the small room tucked away beneath the eaves. The bedroom her father had moved into after Nora had wed Conor, claiming that they should have the couple's room, after all.

The narrow iron bed had not been slept in. Nora stared disbelievingly at the lace spread that had been a wedding present to her parents from an elderly Joyce aunt. It was as smooth and unwrinkled as it had been when she'd put it on the bed after changing the sheets yesterday morning.

White spots, like snow crystals, began to swirl in front of her eyes. On some distant level she was dimly aware of Quinn coming up behind her. Of him putting his arms around her shoulders, pulling her close, murmuring inarticulate words that could have been Greek for all the meaning they held for her.

The blizzard increased, blinding her while

turning her blood to ice. Then Nora Joyce Fitzpatrick, who'd never fainted — not even when she'd gotten word that her husband's stallion had failed to clear that stone wall somewhere on the far distant rocky coast of Breton — surrendered to the darkness.

Brady had always been a man to honor tradition. That being the case, his death set into motion a ritualized series of events, beginning with a home wake, never mind that such things had passed out of fashion, killed by the influence of modern Catholicism.

Since he was a popular person, known to one and all as kind and generous, the small house became packed with friends from all over the county. Even with some who'd not known him personally but felt moved to join all those gathered at the farm not to mourn Brady Joyce's passing, but to celebrate his remarkable life.

Guinness and Jameson flowed like water, stories were traded, each one more outrageous than the previous, but none, everyone agreed, told with quite the flair Brady would have shown.

Nora moved through the gathering as she had since first regaining consciousness in Quinn's arms: on autopilot. Although she managed to smile at all the right times and remembered to thank the women for their gifts of food and the men for sharing those joyous memories, she could not stop thinking about her father dying all alone out on that lonely dark road with her angry threat to move to Galway — which she hadn't really meant — ringing in his ears.

"It wasn't your fault," Quinn told her yet again after he'd gone upstairs and found her sitting vigil beside Brady's bed. Although she'd agreed to the wake, she'd put her foot down at the idea of her father's body lying in the center of her parlor all night surrounded by merrymakers.

Although a part of Quinn found the core belief of the wake — that it guarded the deceased's soul from the devil until internment — a bit ghoulish, he could understand the concept. And there was no denying that, with the exception of Nora — who was proving inconsolable — the wake seemed to bring the family comfort.

Indeed, there was something strangely reassuring in the idea that death was simply one more part of the life cycle. "A necessary phase everyone must pass through before achieving immortality," said Nora's brother Finn, who'd come from Australia.

"My words killed him." Her voice tolled like a funeral knell in the quiet bedroom. It was nearly dawn. A pink pearlescent glow offered the promise of a new day.

"His heart killed him," Quinn repeated what everyone had already told her. Again and again. Unfortunately it appeared that no amount of arguing or well-meaning words of consolation could ease the guilt that had taken hold of her gentle heart. "Dr. Flannery said he'd recommended a bypass months ago."

"Dr. Flannery should have said something to me."

"Brady told him not to. And even out here in the back-of-beyond west, doctor-patient privilege has to be respected."

Her eyes were bleak and uncharacteristically empty, the purple smudges beneath them evidence of a lack of sleep. "If I'd only known, I could have done something."

Mindful of the way father and daughter had parted, Quinn, like everyone else in the family, had been treating Nora with kid gloves. Now he began to wonder if perhaps that had been a mistake.

"What could you have done?" he challenged mildly, pulling up a wooden chair to sit beside her. "Hit him over the head with a shovel and drag him into the hospital for the operation?"

"No, but —"

"Perhaps you believe you could have changed his mind? Made him see the light of his folly, so to speak?"

She sighed at that idea. "Da was, in his fashion, a hardheaded man."

"And nearly as stubborn as his lovely daughter," Quinn said, taking her hand and lifting it to his lips. When she tried to tug it free, he tightened his hold. "Face it, sweetheart. Although he might not have always acted like an adult, your father was a grown man. Capable of making his own choices."

"I can't believe it was truly his choice to die alone out on that road." Words clogged in her throat, and emotions burned at the back of her eyelids in the form of unshed tears. "Without his family around him."

Giving up on retrieving her hand, she turned her gaze back to the bed. How strange it was, she considered, to see such a vibrant man lying so still and quiet. Brady Joyce's presence had always energized a room, bringing with it a golden sparkle that made the air around him as heady as French champagne. Now he reminded her of a porcelain statue hidden away in a church niche.

"At least he had a family." Concern for Nora, as well as frustration at his inability to get through to her, had Quinn trying again.

"People who loved him unconditionally. Without hesitation."

As he had come to love her. Unfortunately, before he'd had the chance to share that astounding little news flash with Nora, they'd gotten that telephone call and all Quinn's plans had flown right out the window. There'd be time later to tell her how he felt about her — about the entire Joyce/Fitzpatrick clan — he'd kept reassuring himself over the past two days.

After all, they were going to have a lifetime together. If Kate could be believed, several lifetimes, some of which they'd already experienced. And even if Nora's sister-in-law's reincarnation theory proved false, Quinn found himself more than willing to buy into Fionna's belief system. Now, as the day of the funeral slowly, inexorably dawned, he decided that an eternity spent with this very special woman would definitely be no hardship.

Despite the sorrow of the moment, Quinn considered the fact that this warm and generous woman had fallen in love with him the single miracle of his life.

In the midst of death, we are life . . . Finn's words, spoken during the funeral mass, kept ringing in Nora's ears as, still keeping with tradition, Brady was carried on his last journey by his sons and closest friends. Although the day had dawned a soft one, Mother Nature — or ancient Celtic weather goddesses — had cooperated, too, causing the rain to cease before the mourners left the old stone church.

Michael was at the front of the casket, Finn just opposite. Finn had come to resemble their father so closely Nora had heard parishioners say how looking at the priest was like looking at Brady Joyce himself thirty years ago. John had been assigned the other corner, and at Fionna's request, Quinn served as the fourth pallbearer. Other men of the village filled in the middle spaces, taking turns as they slowly made their way along the road to the cemetery overlooking the sea.

Looking at her younger brother in his somber dark suit, standing nearly as tall as Michael and a head taller than Finn, Nora was struck with how close John was to becoming a man. As she followed behind, with her grandmother, her sisters and her son along with Kate, Jamie and Brigid, she was reminded yet again that the family would soon have to say farewell to another, although John's parting, thankfully, wouldn't be permanent. But she knew that once he went off to university, he'd change. The family would change.

She sighed as she glanced over at Mary, clad again in the unrelieved black she'd mostly abandoned after her little midnight chat with Quinn. Everything was changing. Sometimes, it seemed, too fast. This time next year, Mary would be gone, as well, hopefully to school rather than marriage.

And as if Nora didn't have enough to worry about, just when her concerns regarding the testosterone-driven Jack had begun to lessen, her sister had returned from the filming at the lake with the announcement that she wanted to be an actress.

Nora still hadn't made up her mind how she felt about that, and although she'd intended to ask Quinn more about the movie business, her father's death had prevented them from having any private time to talk about anything personal.

"Are you all right?" she asked Fionna, who was walking beside her. Although Nora had suggested her grandmother ride in a car to the cemetery, she'd insisted on making her way on foot with the others.

"As well as can be expected under the circumstances, I suppose." She did, indeed, look remarkably hale for her age, despite the sorrow that had created new lines in her face. "It's not right, outliving your child."

Nora's dark and guilty thoughts flitted immediately to Rory. "How do you bear it?" she asked, unconsciously reaching out to take her son's hand.

"Faith," the elderly woman answered without hesitation. "I keep reminding myself that's not my child in that wooden box. My darling Brady is in heaven with his own dear da. And his poor little brother Liam and his sister Katherine, as well."

Liam, Nora knew from family history, had died of a burst appendix shortly after a twelfth-birthday celebration at the beach. At the time, his pains had been tragically misdiagnosed as too much cake and ice cream. Nora's aunt Katherine had died peacefully in her sleep the previous winter.

"And, of course," Fionna added, "most importantly, he's finally reunited with his darling Eleanor, which should be cause for celebration here and in heaven."

Although Nora hoped her gran was right, she couldn't stop the barrage of self-recriminations.

They reached the gates of the cemetery where Castlelough residents had been laid to rest for more than five hundred years. Weaving their way past lofty high stone

Celtic crosses adorned with bas-relief twining interlacings and spirals and ponderous gray tombstones, some of the names and dates worn away by wind and weather, they continued beneath mercurial gray clouds to the Joyce family plot.

A grave had been opened for Brady beside that of his wife. When she saw the marble stone he'd bought so recently waiting to be set into place, Nora had to choke back a sob.

The men set the casket on the ground and came to stand with the rest of the family. Although he was still concerned about Nora, Quinn took heart that when he put his arm around her waist, she did not move away. That she felt like stone beneath his touch was less encouraging.

Finn concluded the graveside service, speaking as he had during the mass in Irish, which to Quinn's untutored ear was incomprehensible. As soon as the gathered had made the obligatory sign of the cross, Fergus, Brady's longtime pub companion, stepped forward and began to sing.

It was a song like none Quinn had ever heard. Performed solo and without accompaniment, the elderly man's voice actually became an instrument in itself, the lyrics and meter as fluid as the curling lines carved into the surrounding crosses. Fergus stood as still as those silent stones, his gaze directed over the cliff, looking out to the sea. Or, Quinn thought, toward eternity.

Below them a herd of white horses suddenly appeared from the mist to gallop through the frothy white surf at the sand's edge, looking like the ghost stallions from last year's book.

While the Irish lyrics rode the breeze like sea birds, wheeling, diving, climbing even higher into the salt-tinged air, the singer's expression remained absolutely detached from the obvious emotional content of his song.

Quinn was obviously not the only one enthralled. Tears streamed unashamedly down female cheeks, and a few male ones, too, as the mesmerizing singing continued, constantly changing, seemingly improvised variations on a theme.

And then, suddenly, without any warning whatsoever, the plaintive tune ended, and the spell was broken.

"Lord, that was amazing," Quinn murmured to Nora, who'd continued to stare at the gaping dark hole all during Fergus's performance.

"It's *sean-nos* singing," John volunteered when his sister failed to respond. "It's mostly the old men out here in the west, who speak the language more naturally — not just learning it in school — who know how to do it properly. But it's becoming popular among the young, too. I have a friend who's been taking lessons and hopes to make his living performing with a group."

"My son and Fergus occasionally performed together," Fionna informed him. "At fairs and weddings and the like."

"That must have been something to hear," Quinn said, wishing too late that he'd thought to film — or at least tape-record — Brady telling his stories. "Brady with his tales and Fergus with his singing."

"Aye. There were quite a few times when they paid for the seed potatoes. My son may not have been much of a farmer. But in his own way, he supported his family as best he could."

Quinn heard another choked sound from Nora. Unlike most of the others, her eyes remained dry, and he wondered at the battle she must be waging within herself to rein in her tumultuous emotions so tightly.

They drove back to the farm, Quinn sitting on one side of Nora in the back of the undertaker's limousine, Rory on the other. Somehow she managed to carry on a conversation with her young son, agreeing that yes, the flowers had been truly lovely, yes, wasn't it fortunate that Brady had thought to buy that lovely marble headstone, and yes, wasn't the singing the loveliest anyone had ever heard Fergus perform.

She was saying all the right words, answering at all the right times, but when he exchanged a glance with Kate, who was sitting with her children on the seat opposite them, Quinn knew they were thinking the same thing. That Nora's mind — and her heart — had disengaged.

If he'd hoped to get an opportunity to talk with her any time soon, the crush of people who'd returned to the farm for the after-funeral supper forestalled those plans. Quinn found himself constantly being cornered by villagers wanting to know all about the filming.

Had he seen the Lady? Did he believe in her existence? And even occasionally, though not nearly as often as in America, how much money could a person make from writing one of those books? They were all questions he'd been asked numerous times, and under normal circumstances, he wouldn't have minded the constant interruptions. But these were far from normal circumstances.

Once, when he ducked into the kitchen to retrieve another platter of ham at Fionna's request, he'd found himself cornered by a woman who introduced herself as Mrs. Sheehan and informed him that her butcher shop had just gotten in a nice supply of French pâté.

"That's good to know," he answered obligingly, wondering why she felt moved to share this bit of information.

"I just thought you'd want to keep it in mind," she said, glancing across the room at Nora, who was nodding in seeming agreement to something Father O'Malley was saying. Quinn, who'd come to know her well, could tell that her mind was somewhere else. Back at the cemetery? Or, dammit, he thought with building frustration, back on the road where Brady had died alone?

"In case you and Nora will be planning a formal wedding supper," the woman tacked on.

Quinn could only stare at her, not that surprised by her mention of a possible marriage, but at her inappropriateness in bringing up the subject on the day Nora's father was buried.

"Or perhaps I should be discussing this with Nora," she suggested, looking as if she was about to do exactly that.

"No. I'll discuss it with her at a more opportune time."

When he tried to move away, she sidled back in front of him. "I could be getting fresh pheasants, as well."

He was wondering if he was going to have to resort to physical force when Kate suddenly appeared by his side. "I was hoping, Quinn, you could help me carry in some trays from Mrs. Duggan's car. I hurt my wrist riding yesterday," she lied blithely, "and the trays are quite heavy."

"No problem." Nodding a brisk goodbye to the now-frowning Mrs. Sheehan, Quinn made his escape. "If you weren't a married woman and if everyone in Castlelough wasn't here to witness it," he murmured after they'd left the kitchen, "I'd kiss you, Kate O'Sullivan."

"You definitely had the look of a man who needed rescuing. Mrs. Sheehan is a bit of a harridan, but I suppose she means well enough."

"She was trying to sell me pâté. For my wedding supper."

"Ah." She looked up at him. "And does Nora know about this yet?"

"The goose liver? Or the wedding?"

"You're definitely an Irishman, Quinn. I swear you're getting better and better at avoiding a direct answer. What would I be caring about pâté? What I'm curious about is whether or not you've proposed to our Nora."

"It's complicated," he said, hedging.

She followed his gaze across the room to where Nora was now talking with Brendan, from The Rose. "Love usually is," she remarked sagely. "But when it's right — as it is with you and Nora — it's well worth the risk."

Concerned that if she could see in all the dark corners, she might warn Nora against him, Quinn was grateful when someone on the other side of the room called out to her, effectively forestalling his need to respond.

Finally the crowd began to disperse. Unfortunately Nora seemed to have disappeared, as well.

"The last I saw, she was in the parlor, with Devlin Monohan and his fiancée," Fionna, who was wrapping the multitude of leftovers in white waxed paper, told Quinn when he went searching for her.

"Devlin's already gone," Mary offered, looking up from cutting slices of breast off a roasted hen. Her eyes were weary and red-rimmed. "About twenty minutes ago."

"Did you try upstairs?" This from Sheila Monohan, who'd stayed behind to help with the cleaning up. "She looked as if she might have had a headache. Perhaps she decided to have a little lie-down."

Unfortunately that suggestion proved to be as fruitless as the others.

"It's my guess she's gone to the lake," he told Kate after learning that Nora had asked her sister-in-law to stay at the house with the children for a time.

"She's always found comfort there before," Kate agreed.

"Will you stay with the kids until I can bring her home?" Quinn did not find it at all unusual to be asking such a question — as if he'd assumed the role of the man of the house — until he saw her faint smile.

"Of course." Her eyes filled with affection. "All night, if need be. And tomorrow, as well, if it comes to that. You're a good man, Quinn. Nora's an extremely fortunate woman to have you in her life."

"I'm the fortunate one." He plowed a hand through his hair, worried that guilt may have caused Nora to believe she didn't deserve a second chance at happiness. Even more worried that he still might do something to screw up what they had together. "I just hope I can get through to her."

"If anyone can, it will be you." She went up on her toes and kissed his cheek. "Good luck."

"Thanks." Taking hold of her shoulders, he kissed her smooth fragrant cheek in turn.

"I wouldn't object if you'd burn a candle, or do a few twirls with your daughter in the circle of stones, or whatever you druid witches do to cast your love spells."

She laughed at that, a rich throaty sound that lifted a bit of the gloom from the day. "And didn't you already cast your own love spell, Quinn? That night you first stepped into Nora's parlor?"

She patted the cheek she'd kissed, rubbing at the faint smear of pink lipstick. "Now, you'd best be getting to your lady. And don't worry about Nora's car. We'll send someone to fetch it."

As he drove down the twisting narrow road to the lake — to Nora — Quinn tried to remember a time when he'd been more nervous and came up totally blank.

Chapter Twenty-Three

Dreamers and Believers

Nora sat alone on the bank of the lake, looking out over the black satin water, thinking back to the time she'd been in this private place with Quinn and explained to him the old Irish saying, *ciunas gan uagineas.* Quietness without loneliness.

Well, it had certainly never been more quiet. There wasn't even a nighttime breeze to sigh through the reeds or ripple the glassy waters. There were no cheerful clicks of crickets, no deep croaks of bullfrogs calling for their mates. The clear April night was almost eerily still. But for the first time in her life, Nora felt absolutely devastatingly alone.

She reached into the pocket of her black dress and pulled out a small smooth stone inscribed with ogham. Kate had given her the stone this morning before Brady's funeral mass.

"It's a wishing rune," she'd explained as she'd curled Nora's fingers around the black stone. "I know you feel as if you've left

466

things unsettled with Brady, Nora. If you open your heart, this stone will help you contact him."

In truth, Nora hadn't really believed that at the time, but not wanting to hurt her sister-in-law's feelings and knowing the gesture was born out of love, she'd slipped the stone into her pocket and promptly forgotten it.

Not surprisingly Kate hadn't been the only one to offer Nora some gift of the heart. Once they'd returned to the farm after the interment, her grandmother had pulled her aside and offered a gilt-edged holy card depicting a pretty young nun with gentle loving eyes.

"Pray to Sister Bernadette," Fionna had urged. "Open your heart, Nora, darling, and Bernadette will make a miracle."

"Open your heart," Nora murmured now as she drew her knees up to her chest and rested her cheek on them. Pain was an anvil, pressing down on her chest, crushing that aforementioned heart. "And doesn't that sound simple?"

It should have been. Hadn't her mother told her that her strength — and her weakness — had always been her generosity of spirit? Her willingness to let her emotions overrule her head, even when it could lead to heartbreak?

She closed her eyes and pressed the hand

holding the rune hard against her breast, as if subconsciously hoping it could melt the ice that seemed to have filled all her empty places.

"Oh, please." The whispered words were part plea, part prayer.

When she heard a sound, like footfalls on wildflowers, Nora opened her eyes again and looked up. The moon was rising, casting the castle that brooded over the lake in a ghostly silvery light.

"Da?" When her father suddenly appeared, walking out of the moonlit mist, looking as he did when she'd been a girl, Nora was certain she must be hallucinating. Hadn't she read that a lack of sleep combined with emotional distress could play havoc with your mind?

"It's not your imagination, Nora, darling," the wonderfully familiar voice assured her. "It's your prodigal da."

He was bathed in a shimmering light that made him look as if he was surrounded by dancing moonbeams.

"Oh, Da," she said, barely managing to push the words past the painful lump that had taken up residence in her tight throat. "I'm so sorry."

"Now what would me favorite girl have to be feeling sorry for?"

"For losing my temper." She sniffled just as she had that long-ago day she'd fallen off her pony for the first time. "For saying those dreadful things to you."

"Now didn't I know you were upset?" he asked blithely. "And wasn't that because of my own foolishness in the first place, thinking I could trick you into getting Rory a pony?"

"I'm keeping the mare."

"I know." His grin shone like a beacon in the dancing silvery light. "I do believe the Lady's going to be having to put up with a rival for your son's attention."

Nora smiled at that. "Aye. I believe you're right." Then she sighed and shook her head. "If only I'd agreed sooner, we'd not have exchanged hard words, and you'd not have been walking all the way into the village to The Rose, and —"

"Nora. Darling." His voice wrapped around her like a warm woolen shawl. "You're taking too much responsibility on those lovely young shoulders again. I love you, daughter. You were my joy from the moment you were born, the light of my life. And ever since my dear Eleanor passed on, you've been my anchor, just as your mam was before you.

"But as God has taught us, Nora, to

469

everything there is a season, and a time to every purpose under heaven."

"A time to be born, and a time to die," she murmured the familiar words. The passage from Ecclesiastes had always been a favorite of her father's, which is why Finn had chosen to recite it to the mourners who'd gathered at the hilltop ceremony this morning.

"A time to weep, and a time to laugh," Brady continued, his voice ringing out over the hillsides as if he were telling a tale to the multitudes. "A time to mourn, and a time to dance."

"I don't want to argue with you, Da," Nora countered softly. "But I don't really feel like laughing right now."

"Ah, but you will, Nora. And that's the point of my wee tale. I wept like a babe after your poor mother died —"

"I didn't know that."

"Well, didn't you have enough to deal with? Without having to see your da bawling his eyes out and keening into his pillow every night so as not to wake the rest of his family?

"But my children are now almost grown, all but Celia, and I have not a single doubt that you and Quinn will raise my youngest daughter as if she's your own dear girl.

Everything's all settled now, don't you see? You have a fine man you love . . ."

"I do, indeed." Her voice was a little stronger.

"And isn't that obvious to anyone with eyes? And, to continue my point, that very same man loves you back —"

"He hasn't said that."

"Jaysus!" The exclamation was expelled on a hearty laugh. "Isn't it bad enough you interrupt your poor old da when he's alive? Can't you be letting him finish a sentence after he's passed on? It seems, if my memory isn't failing me, that Ecclesiastes mentions something about a time to keep silence."

Despite the grief that had taken hold of her heart these past days, Nora found herself smiling back at him. "I'm sorry. Of course I want to let you finish."

"Well, now, as I was trying to say, before I was interrupted, Quinn Gallagher might not have said the words out loud yet. But it's obvious you're holding his heart in your hands, darling.

"And although I'm not overly fond of admitting I could be wrong about anything, mind you, I'll have to say that I misjudged the Yank. He's a good man, Nora. He'll make you a good husband. And a fine father for the children."

"Aye. You know that, Da. And I know that. I believe even Rory and poor dear Maeve understand it, too. But that doesn't change the fact that Quinn's still planning to leave Ireland next week."

"Now don't you be worrying about that. The pope will be taking back Saint Patrick's sainthood before Quinn Gallagher chooses a lonely life in America over a full and loving one with my eldest daughter here in Ireland. Can't I recognize a lovestruck man when I see one, having been one meself?

"The point to my little narrative, Nora, is that you can begin building your own family now. And I'm finally free to be with my own darling Eleanor, don't you see."

He smiled again, that dazzling infectious smile that everyone had always said could charm a leprechaun out of his pot of gold. "I love you, daughter. I always have and I always will."

Tears clogged her throat, filled her eyes. "I love you, too, Da. And I always will."

"Slan agat," he murmured as he bent to kiss her cheek.

"Slan leat," Nora answered her father's final farewell in the language of her roots. Her heart.

And then he faded away, like misty morning fog. Just when Nora thought Brady was truly gone for good, something drew her gaze to the far side of the lake. It was her parents walking hand in hand over the moonlit velvety hills.

She touched her fingertips to her cheek, felt the lingering warmth and knew that her father's visit had been no hallucination.

A time to every purpose under heaven. With her father's words ringing in her ears, Nora buried her face in her hands and finally allowed herself to weep.

When he saw her sitting in the moonlight, rocking back and forth in the age-old rhythm of mourning, Quinn made yet another new discovery. A heart really could ache.

She was weeping into her hands. Although the sobs were silent, from the shaking of her shoulders, Quinn could tell they were violent. He put the blanket Kate had sent along with him on the ground, sat down beside her and without a word pulled her into his arms. He found it encouraging that she came willingly, without a struggle. Wondered how it was that he found her trust even more amazing, and humbling, than her love.

"That's it, baby." He stroked her hair as she buried her face in his shirt. Drew her closer, kissed the top of her head. "Let it all out."

Nora clung to him unashamedly and allowed her tears to flow. Although her father's words of reassurance had helped ease her feelings of guilt, the pain of loss remained. A deep gaping wound she was all too familiar with, having suffered it twice before. Once when her mother died, then when she lost Conor, who, despite all his faults, a part of her — the young idealistic teenager who'd married the west's most dashing man — would always love.

But she was no longer that starry-eyed virgin bride fresh from the convent. She was a woman. A woman who'd had a child. Who'd kept her family together during bad times and good. A woman who'd suffered heartache and survived, like a piece of handblown Castlelough crystal hardened by its time in the flames.

She was a woman who loved. A woman who was loved, she thought as she ran her hands over Quinn's wide capable shoulders, by a remarkable man. A man who, despite his protests to the contrary, possessed an infinite capacity for caring.

When she was finally cried out, drained of anguish, tumultuous emotions exhausted, she pulled away — just a little.

"Your shirt is soaked."

"It'll dry." He brushed at her wet face with the back of his hand. "Feeling better?"

"Aye. I am." She managed a faint smile at that and cuddled closer again, luxuriating in the feel of his arms around her. "When you were researching the Lady, did you discover the Celtic concept of *Samhain*?"

"What we call Halloween?" Quinn had no idea where this conversation was headed, but glad that she was finally talking again, he would have followed it anywhere. "Sure. It's summer's end, supposedly the time when the veil between the living world and the dead is the thinnest."

"Do you believe it's possible for that veil to part and allow the dead to communicate with the living?"

Quinn thought about what Father O'Malley had told him about believing in myriad mystical unseen things. "I believe anything's possible. Especially when you're talking about people with strong spirits."

"Like Da."

"Yeah." He continued to stroke her face, thinking that he'd never known a woman with skin as soft as Nora's. When that idea had him wanting to touch her all over, Quinn wondered what kind of guy could even be considering seducing a woman on the day she'd buried her father. "Like Brady."

"He came to me." She tilted her head back and looked up at him. Lingering moisture still shone in her eyes. "Here, at the lake. To tell me he loved me."

With his gaze on hers, he cupped her cheek in his palm. "That's certainly an easy thing to do."

A flare of surprise leaped into her eyes, a spark that quickly turned into a warm pleased glow. "Would you be saying what I think you're saying?"

Quinn shrugged carelessly. "Now wouldn't that depend on what you'd be thinking?" His smile spread slowly as his fingers slipped into her hair. "But if you're thinking that I was telling you that I love you —" he bent his head and touched his lips to hers "— I suppose you'd be correct."

The words Nora had longed to hear were like a prayer against her lips, the soft tender kiss a promise. She sighed and felt the last of her tension draining away as the feather-light caress of his fingers at the nape of her neck made her muscles go lax.

"I love you, Nora Joyce Fitzpatrick." His deep voice thickened with quiet seriousness. "More than I could have ever imagined possible."

"More than you wanted, I'd be guessing."

He laughed at that, the explosive release of tension scattering ducks from the reeds at lake's edge. "A helluva lot more than I wanted. More than you should have wanted." The laughter died suddenly, as if turned off at a tap. His eyes turned serious. "You realize, of course, that I'm not a good bet. I've no idea how to be a good husband or father."

"You've been wonderful with Rory."

"He's a great kid. But I'm afraid I'll let him down. Afraid I'll let *you* down."

"That couldn't happen."

"You sound pretty sure of that. Considering you don't know anything about me."

She framed his frowning face between her palms. "I know that you're a generous decent caring man. I know that for some reason you don't believe that."

"For good reason. You keep making me out to be better than I am. I'm just a man, Nora. With more flaws than most."

"Well, of course I understand you have flaws, Quinn. I'm not a naive schoolgirl like Mary, after all." She sighed. "But I suppose I can get used to sleeping with a man who's out of sorts until his second cup of morning coffee and who steals the bedcovers."

"You're not taking this seriously, dammit. And I do not steal the covers." Actually, if she wanted to get technical, the only two nights they'd spent together the sheets and blankets had ended up on the floor.

"I'm afraid you do." Another sigh. "Which makes me wonder what I'll be doing for warmth once winter comes." She looked up at him through her lashes, in a blatantly flirtatious way that made him want to laugh and ravish her at the same time. "Perhaps you'd be having a suggestion about that?"

"One or two. Both of them having to do with us providing our own heat."

She smiled at that. "Ah, and didn't I know you were a clever resourceful man, Quinn Gallagher?"

He'd feared it would be harder. Worried he'd have to struggle to get past the barriers he'd watched going up since they'd gotten the news of Brady's death. Now he realized that it was Nora's own vast capacity for love that caused those walls to come down before they'd been completely erected.

Quinn wondered if his life would have been different if he'd met this woman when he was younger. Would her stunning ability to feel so strongly, to care so deeply, have saved him all those cold and lonely years? Probably not, he admitted, recalling some old lyrics his mother used to sing about not knowing what you had until you lost it. In his case, Quinn considered, he hadn't had a clue that anything was missing from his life until he'd discovered it. Discovered Nora.

He'd been like a man alone in the desert. A man who, having suffered through that arid time, could now fully appreciate the cool fresh taste of an icy spring bubbling up in the oasis.

And speaking of tastes, it had been far too long since he'd drunk from her lips.

"I don't want you to take this wrong." He reached for her wrist, then lifted her hand to press a kiss to her palm. "But I want to make love with you."

The touch of his mouth against her flesh was like a brand. "Why would you worry I'd be taking that idea wrong? I think that would be in order after a declaration such as you've just made."

"It's not exactly been your usual day."

"True enough. But I've already lost someone I love." She turned their hands and kissed his knuckles. "I'm not about to risk letting you get away."

She was the most incredible woman he'd ever known. And amazingly she was his.

"How did I ever get so lucky?" he murmured in honest wonder.

"Oh, now that's an easy one to answer," Nora said on a silvery breathless laugh that made him think of fairies singing. "Mam sent you to me."

She was so wonderfully warm. So soft. So perfect.

"I love you." He kissed her long and lingeringly as his fingers began working their magic on the pearl buttons that ran from her lace collar to her hem. "Love you." He pressed his mouth to the pulse at her throat and felt her blood hum. "Love you." The more he repeated them, the easier, the more enjoyable the words proved to be. "And now that you've shared that little bit of Irish magic with me, I've decided that I love your mother, as well."

Her skin tasted like honey. Her lips were like a banquet after a long fast. Quinn knew he'd never get enough of her. Not if they were granted a thousand lifetimes together.

They knelt in the center of the blanket, undressing each other slowly, in unspoken agreement not to rush. Quinn reined in his impatience — for himself, as much as for her. Nora tested the limits of her weakening restraint — for herself as much as for him. It was a night of promises, of pledges both spoken and unspoken. A night to remember. To cherish.

Gradually, as the moon rose in the cloud-scudded sky, casting its mystical glow over the landscape, murmured words of love became shimmering sighs. Soft moans. Hands that had lingeringly explored warming flesh moved faster, harder, over curves and hollows. Lips that had tantalized earlier now tormented, capturing stuttering breaths from lungs.

"I want you." Quinn's fingers dug into her hips, as his eyes locked on hers, which were huge and bright with a flame of hunger equal to his.

"Then take me. Now," she gasped as she struggled to fill her lungs with air.

"Not just for now." He slid into her so easily they could have been created one for the other. "For eternity. Forever.

"Aye." Her lips skimmed over his face, her hands pulled him closer, deeper. "Forever."

As the moon rose higher in the black velvet sky, passion soared, taking Nora and Quinn with it.

Much, much later, as he held her in his arms, luxuriating in the aftermath of passion, Quinn viewed a flash out on the glassy waters of the lake. He told himself that the fleeting glimmer of green was merely a trick of the moonlight.

CHAPTER TWENTY-FOUR

Let Down the Blade

Despite her lingering sorrow over her father's death, Nora discovered that Quinn's admission of love for her brought a whole new dimension to her life. For the first time in years she felt as young and giddy as a schoolgirl, yet the happiness brimming in her heart was definitely that of a woman. The shooting for the movie was winding down, and although there seemed a never-ending list of chores to do on the farm — including getting the barn ready for Rory's mare — she spent those days at the lake, watching the filming, all too aware that Quinn looked decidedly in his element among those beautiful confident Americans. She also couldn't help noticing that he seemed terribly close to Laura Gideon, but was surprised when the stunning actress treated her with genuine warmth.

"Will you miss it?" she asked him softly as they lay together in bed. Although she still didn't want the children to know they were sharing a room, Nora no longer had the will-power to spend the night alone when the man she loved was sleeping next door.

"Miss what?"

Where to begin? Despite his assurances, she worried about asking him to make so many major changes to his fast-paced American life-style. Would he honestly be happy living on a small farm in west Ireland? Away from the bright lights of the world he was accustomed to?

"Hollywood, for one thing."

"Not in this lifetime."

He'd already determined that the movie business wasn't for him. There were too many delays for what he found ridiculous reasons, too many compromises made on a daily basis, too much emphasis on marketing the story rather than worrying about the message of the tale. The only reason he'd agreed to write the screenplay in the first place was to maintain control over a story he cared a great deal about. Unfortunately control had proved to be an elusive thing in Hollywood.

"The only good thing about working on this film was meeting you."

"What a lovely thing to say."

"It's the truth." He ran his hands over her bare shoulders and down her arms. "I love the idea of living here in Ireland with you.

And the family." He wasn't about to admit that every so often, when he wasn't looking, old fears would attack, like a skeletal hand reaching out from under the bed to grasp at an ankle. His life had changed. Quinn assured himself several times a day. He'd changed.

Nora's heart fluttered. He was doing it again. Heating her blood, melting her bones. "I love that idea, as well. Although it's a shame a famous man such as yourself is going to be writing his best-selling novels in a barn."

He shrugged. He'd written his first stories during his stint in the navy, scribbling away in his bunk, lost in the world of his characters while a noisy shipboard life went on around him. Quinn figured Rory's mare would undoubtedly prove a much quieter roommate than a bunch of sailors.

"I'm only going to be using the tack room until my office gets built." They'd designed it together, a traditional cottage with a thatched roof situated on a piece of green meadow overlooking the standing stones between the Joyce and O'Sullivan land and the sea beyond. Quinn knew writers who'd kill for such an imagination-stimulating location.

"Oh, that reminds me. Robert Duggan

brought by some paint samples today. I left them in the kitchen."

"You can get them later." He snagged her wrist as she went to climb out the bed.

"But you'll be wanting —"

"To hell with the paint. White's white. I don't want to waste the night trying to detect some imperceptible difference between Swiss Coffee, French Cream and China Mist. Let Duggan pick whatever he wants." He paused. "Because what I want right now is you."

Nora turned back into the arms of the man she loved. The man who, just as her father had predicted and her mother had promised, loved her back.

"I want you. too." And as she lifted her face for his kiss, Nora's carefully planned argument for Swiss Coffee immediately fled her mind.

It was the day before May Day and the household was in an uproar. The postman had been bringing greeting cards all week for Celia, who was preparing to receive her First Holy Communion. And if that long-awaited occasion wasn't enough, Mary had, indeed, been chosen queen of the May Day dance, which raised the anxiety level of the sixteen-year-old girl several notches.

As she baked the cakes for the party that would be held after mass at The Rose, Nora assured Mary yet again that their mother's jade earrings were perfect with her new evening gown.

"Aye. Much more flattering than the gold hoops." As Mary left the room to one more time try on the lovely dress Quinn had bought her in Derry, Nora heard a squabble break out in the parlor. "Celia, Rory, stop that bickering this minute!" she called out.

Celia had proven insufferable all week, lording the money that had come in all those first communion cards over her nephew. And Rory, who was growing impatient waiting for his horse to arrive, had been uncharacteristically short-tempered.

"The girl's certainly all puffed up with herself," Fionna muttered from her seat at the kitchen table where she was staging her battle plan to confront the bishop on the steps of the church immediately after tomorrow's mass to celebrate the Virgin. "When I suggested she give some of her money to the missionary fund, she began rattling on about a Barbie playhouse."

"I suppose when you're seven years old, dollhouses are more appealing than saving pagan souls," Nora said mildly. She glanced at the stack of colorful flyers scattered over the top of the table. "Are you certain you want to confront the bishop in such a public place?"

"He won't answer my letters." Fionna uncapped a black felt marker and began printing tall block letters on the placard she intended to take to the church. "And he's been stalling for months. This way he won't be able to duck the issue."

Nora glanced over at Quinn, who was peeling potatoes for dinner. She still wasn't accustomed to a man in the house. Especially in her kitchen.

"If you intend to run out on me, today would definitely be the day to do it."

"Not on a bet." His grin was as warm as buttery summer sunshine and made her heart feel as light as the helium balloons she'd ordered from Monohan's Mercantile for Celia's communion celebration tomorrow.

She smiled back, so in love sometimes she thought her lips would freeze into the foolish grin she saw on her face whenever she passed a mirror. "Did you happen to have an opportunity to speak with John?" she asked quietly so as not to garner Fionna's attention.

"While we milked the cows. And he promises to behave in the future. But it's really not that big a deal, sweetheart."

She'd gone into John's room to put away

some laundry this morning and had discovered him downloading photographs from the Internet. The women, clad merely in the rosy flesh they'd been born with, were supposedly, according to the caption, Babes from Britain. Both Nora and John had momentarily frozen; as the suggestive photos flashed onto the screen, she hadn't known which of them was more embarrassed, her or her brother.

"I don't want him getting into trouble," she said firmly. "He has his entire future ahead of him." A scowl darkened her face and furrowed her brow. "A future that hopefully does not include any Knockers from Nottingham," she muttered, remembering all too well the heading above one particularly well-endowed platinum blonde.

"It's not so different from a kid sneaking his first illicit look at *Playboy*. All boys do it, Nora." The brown potato skins were flying into the sink. "Just like all teenage girls probably check out romance novels searching for the sex scenes."

She felt the color rise in her cheeks as she thought back to those forbidden books so many of the postulates — herself included — had nervously giggled over after the sisters had turned off the lights in the convent dormitory.

"Mary has a best friend, Deidre McMann, who's about to become a mother. The father is a college boy. Or was until he had to quit school to work on his parents' farm to support his new family."

"John's a bright kid. And a responsible one. You did a good job raising him these past years. I think it's time to relax and let him take responsibility for his own life, let him make his own choices."

"I know." She sighed, thinking of the fateful choice Kate had made when she'd been John's age. "But I do worry."

"Of course you do." He leaned over and dropped a light kiss on her lips. "That's what I love about you."

Love. It was, Nora thought, allowing him to ease her concerns, the most glorious word in any language.

The following day, as Nora watched the processional of little girls dressed up like brides of Christ in lacy white dresses and sheer pearl-studded veils, she thought Celia looked like an angel. Only the little girl's white knuckles, as she clutched the rosary from Fionna and the new white missal Quinn had surprised her with this morning, revealed her nervousness.

Later that evening, when Mary came downstairs dressed for the dance and looking as beautiful as a movie star, Nora thought once again how many things had changed. Some for the worse. She couldn't help wishing her da had been here to see his two daughters looking so lovely today. But then again, she considered, he probably had been watching. Along with her mam.

That thought, and the memory of their last conversation by the lake, comforted her.

As she watched Parker Kendall pin the orchid corsage on Mary and saw Quinn fix the young actor with a steely protective warning gaze, she realized that most of the changes — and all of them having to do with this man — had definitely been for the better.

Much later, as she lay in Quinn's arms floating on the ebbing tide of spent passion, Nora said a silent prayer of thanksgiving to God, her mam and da, and even any of Kate's ancient Celtic gods and goddesses who might be listening, for bringing such a special, loving man into her life.

Nothing in Quinn's life had ever come easy. He was also Irish enough to feel superstitious about enjoying such uncommon domestic bliss. Which is why, despite his love for Nora, despite the way he was beginning to feel like a true member of her extended family, he couldn't help continuing to feel a lot like Sydney Carton's tragic character in *A Tale of Two Cities*. The question was not *if* the damn blade was going to drop. But *when*.

It was the day after May Day, the day before he'd been scheduled to return to California. The day before he'd planned to leave Ireland — and Nora — forever. As he hooked up the horse trailer to the Mercedes, which he'd already arranged to buy, he was amazed at how much his life had changed in four short weeks. How much *he* had changed.

"Talk about magic," he murmured as he drove to Kate's farm to pick up Rory's mare. The country, the family and most of all Nora had definitely done a number on him.

Thinking of how excited Rory was going to be when he returned from his trip to the village with Nora and discovered his pony in the stall, Quinn experienced a feeling of satisfaction that was downright paternal.

He moved on to thinking about having more children. Not that he wasn't already beginning to think of Rory as his own, but the idea of making babies with his beloved redhead was more than a little appealing.

Picturing Nora round and ripe with his child had Quinn smiling as he knocked on Kate's door. The grin instantly faded as he viewed the woman standing in front of him.

Her face looked as if someone had used it for a punching bag. The flesh was bruised and swollen, unattractive shades of blue and purple. One eye was shut, her upper lip split open. When he saw the purple marks on her neck — an unmistakable imprint of Cadel O'Sullivan's fingers — a cold fury swept through him.

"Where are the kids?"

She looked surprised by that question. "They went with Nora into the village. She promised them ice cream."

"Then they weren't here when the son of a bitch did this to you?"

"No." She closed her good eye for a brief moment. "Thank God."

"I'll call Fionna," he said. "And have her track down Nora and keep the kids while I take you to the hospital."

"No!" Kate backed away and held up her hands as if warding him off. "I'll not be needing to go to any hospital."

"I don't think you're in a position to judge that." His eyes skimmed over her, noticing that she wasn't exactly standing upright. "There's a good chance you could have a cracked rib or —"

"I'd know if that were the case. I'll be fine, Quinn. Really, I just need a little lie-down and —"

"You need a helluva lot more than that, dammit." Furious at Cadel O'Sullivan, frustrated by Kate's continuing denial and concerned for her safety, he dragged a hand through his hair and considered his options. Despite the fact that Kate handled thousand pound horses every day, she was a slender woman who barely came up to his shoulder. It would be a simple matter just to lift her and carry her out to the car.

The problem with that plan, dammit, was his reluctance to use bodily force. Especially since she'd already suffered too much at the hands of her brutish husband.

"At least come with me to Nora's. Where the family can keep you safe."

She seemed to consider that as she gave Quinn a long look. "All right. Let me just get my bankbook. It's upstairs."

Although he didn't want her to stay here an instant longer than necessary, he nodded and came into the house, leaving the door open so he could keep an eye out for O'Sullivan. When she turned around to leave the room, the first thing that caught Quinn's attention was the gingerly way she was walking, which wasn't, he decided grimly, all that surprising. And then he saw the blood on the back of her flowered cotton skirt.

"Wait a minute." He caught her arms,

carefully, gently, first one, then the other, and eased her down into a chair, noting her grimace. Strangely, rather than muddy his thoughts, his icy rage made his mind as clear as Castlelough crystal. He could kill O'Sullivan. Without hesitation. Without an iota of remorse. "The bastard raped you, didn't he?"

She looked away in embarrassment. And, he suspected, shame. "A man can't rape his wife."

Quinn's response to that was brief and vulgar. Then he said, "All right. We'll skip the hospital. But I'm calling Dr. Flannery to meet us at the Joyce farm and examine you. It's important he collect evidence so you can press charges."

She sighed wearily and shook her head, looking decades older than the twenty-six Quinn knew her to be. "You're not in America now, Quinn. Things are different here. And even if I'd be wanting to admit to Sergeant O'Neill what a foolish woman I've been to marry such a violent man, he wouldn't go rushing off to arrest Cadel."

Quinn crouched beside the chair, struggling with his gut-wrenching emotions. "Dammit, this isn't about what you did or didn't do, or whether you made a mistake by marrying the guy, or staying with him after discovering what he was really like.

"It's about a short-tempered bully who gets off on hitting women and kids whenever he feels like it. There's nothing you've done to deserve this, Kate."

Her face pale as paper behind the bruises, she'd turned away, pretending interest in the framed painting of three times British Grand National winner Red Rum hanging on the opposite wall. Quinn put his fingers gently on her chin and turned her face back to his. "You don't deserve it."

She closed her eye again. "I suppose you're right. And I'll see Dr. Flannery, but I still won't call in the Garda. This is a family matter, Quinn. I want to keep it that way."

"Fine." And since he was almost a member of the family, Quinn was more than willing to take the matter into his own hands. "Now, where's the bankbook?" He made his tone sound calm, almost conversational, designed to conceal his intentions. "I'll go get it. And whatever other personal belongings you want to take for yourself and the kids."

"The bankbook's taped behind a photograph of Jamie and Brigid on the wall in my bedroom." She went on to describe where he could find the other things she'd be needing for the brief stay at her sister-in-law's.

As he entered the bedroom that looked as if it had been attacked by a horde of vandals, Quinn realized what had set Cadel off. The man had undoubtedly come back looking for money. Money Kate seemed recklessly willing to risk dying to protect. Stepping over the clothes and drawers that had been pulled out of the bureau and dumped onto the floor, he retrieved the blue bankbook, determined to get her out of here as soon as possible.

Forty minutes later she was lying in the small bed Nora had so recently vacated, sipping a cup of stout tea that a concerned but briskly efficient Fionna had brewed for her, waiting for the doctor to arrive.

"I don't understand why you called Michael," she said to Quinn.

"I have to go into the village and I'm not about to leave you and Fionna here alone in case your husband comes looking for you."

"Ah, isn't that just like a Yank," she murmured with a flash of the wry humor he'd come to admire and enjoy. "Rushing in to play John Wayne."

"It's a dirty job." Despite the circumstances, he grinned down at her. "But someone's got to do it."

She laughed, as he'd meant her to. Then immediately sobered. "You're going after Cadel, aren't you?"

He considered lying, then figured she'd obviously hear soon enough. "Yeah."

"I'm not your responsibility."

"You're family," he said simply. "And family takes care of its own."

He heard the sound of tires crunching on gravel and went downstairs to let in Michael Joyce, who was followed by Dr. Flannery. The doctor, Quinn thought, didn't look old enough to have graduated from high school, let alone medical school. Quinn wondered if that meant he was getting old and decided it probably did.

That idea brought up another. That his worst fears — of being too much like his father — were about to be realized. Had it been only this morning that he'd foolishly believed he'd be lucky enough to grow old with the woman he loved? Now there was the unpalatable likelihood that once again, a brutality was about to cost him any chance at happiness.

But this was no time to be worrying about himself. He'd deal with the fallout of what he was about to do later. First he had a score to settle.

CHAPTER TWENTY-FIVE

Hard Times

It was raining when Quinn arrived in Castlelough, and not a soft rain, either, but a thick gray drizzle that matched his grim mood. An anger he'd forgotten he could feel was surging through his veins. Memories poured back, filling his mind like smoke, memories of his father's beatings, his mother's screams, that horrifying night a nine-year-old boy had leaped onto a brutal man's back in a futile attempt to stop an assault that had ended with the bottle of gin coming down like a sledgehammer on the back of his mother's head.

He could hear the thud as clearly now as when it had happened — a dull muted sound like a melon falling out of the refrigerator and smashing onto the floor. He remembered the blood — so much of it, pouring out of the back of her poor broken head, turning her blond hair crimson, staining his hands as he tried to staunch the flow, drenching his shirt as he'd knelt beside her and held her close like a broken doll. Salty tears had poured down his face, even though his father had always whupped him harder whenever he'd cry, calling him a faggot sissyboy.

And so, by age nine, Quinn had come not to expect anything good from life. He'd always been suspicious of anything that came too easily. Such belief had allowed him to distance himself from reality during the harsh years that had followed his mother's brutal murder.

He'd developed his own defense system — never trust, never let anyone get too close, always be prepared to end a relationship if it threatened to become personal. The tactic had worked just fine for years, allowing him to secure his feelings beneath a thick layer of seemingly impenetrable ice.

The one thing he'd never counted on was coming to Ireland and meeting a woman who possessed her own personal blowtorch.

He was going to have to tell Nora about his past, he realized. Let her know exactly what kind of man she'd be marrying. And if she changed her mind, well, hell, he'd get over it and move on. The way he always had. No harm, no foul.

As he pulled up in front of The Irish Rose,

Quinn wondered when he'd become such a goddamn liar.

The buzz of convivial conversation stopped the instant Quinn opened the oak door. It didn't dwindle, table by table, bar stool by bar stool, but ended abruptly. Nearly every eye in the pub was on him. The sole exception was Cadel O'Sullivan, who was sitting in his regular spot at the end of the long bar, hunched over a bottle of Bushmills malt.

"O'Sullivan." Quinn's low voice was like an alarm siren in a room so atypically quiet it would have been possible to hear a toothpick drop.

Kate's attacker looked up, his gaze as flat and cold as a snake's. "Well, well," he said scornfully, tossing back a shot of the whiskey while meeting Quinn's stone-hard eyes. "If it isn't the rich Yank who's been screwing our women. What the fock do you want, Gallagher?"

"I want to talk to you. Outside. Where we won't risk breaking any of Brendan's furniture."

"Ah." The cruel mouth twisted in a smirk. "So, it's a fight you'd be wanting to start up with me, not a conversation at all." He filled his glass from the bottle and tossed back another long swallow.

"I'd say you're the one who started the fight," Quinn said with a reasonableness he was a long way from feeling. "When you decided to treat Kate like a punching bag."

A low murmur spread across the room. The cold smile was instantly replaced by a dark scowl. "You'd be having no right interfering in the personal business between a man and his wife."

"Even if I felt that way, which I damn well don't, I figure I'm entitled. Since your wife is Nora's sister-in-law, and I'm going to be marrying Nora."

"So the boys have been telling me." The smirk was back, testing, taunting. Quinn couldn't decide whether Cadel O'Sullivan was the stupidest man he'd ever met or merely had a death wish. "Weren't we all sitting right here discussing the interesting fact that only a month ago, the widow Fitzpatrick was going to have to leave her farm for the city?"

He gave a wink that was rampant with sexual innuendo. "Looks as if lifting her skirt and focking a rich Yank solved that little problem."

Quinn saw red. Literally. It swirled in front of his eyes like his mother's blood so many years ago. The next thing he knew he was pulling Cadel from his bar stool.

"You have exactly two seconds to apologize," he ground out. "And then I'm going to kill you."

"It'll take a better man than you to do that, Yank." At the same time Cadel spat in Quinn's face he shot a mean right jab into Quinn's gut.

The meaty fist was like a cudgel. Quinn felt his bones rattle, the breath leave his lungs. The scarlet veil in front of his eyes darkened. And with a mighty roar, he was on the Irishman, his balled fists pounding, bare knuckle against bone, left, right, left, right, each blow landed for Nora. For Kate. For Jamie and Brigid.

Onlookers scattered, rescuing pints as they scrambled to the edges of the room to watch the fight. O'Sullivan might be bigger, but his strength was brutish, unschooled, his blows random and unplanned.

"Come on, O'Sullivan," Quinn taunted, "you can do better than that." He feigned to the right, dodging a wild roundhouse punch. "I guess you're a lot more used to beating up defenseless women and children than you are taking on someone closer to your own size."

His opponent's answering roar was like a wounded lion. He lowered his massive head like a buffalo and charged, butting Quinn in the ribs, which caused them both to fall to the hand-pegged floor in a tangle of arms and legs.

They rolled over and over, landing random wild blows, any boxing technique Quinn might have learned during his days in the navy lost in the heat of the escalating battle.

Cadel managed to push himself unsteadily to his feet long enough to pick up a chair, lift it high, then bring it down in the direction of Quinn's head. It landed on his shoulder, instead, then a booted foot slammed into the ribs the Irishman's thick head had already pounded. Grabbing it, Quinn managed to pull the giant down for second time.

"She's not worth this trouble," Cadel taunted yet again as he aimed a left uppercut at Quinn's jaw. "Didn't Conor Fitzpatrick tell everyone that his wife should have stayed in the convent for all the good she was in bed?"

A muffled *oof* escaped his split lip as Quinn landed a blow on the brute's nose. The sound of bone breaking was followed by a string of curses as crimson blood gushed. "Or maybe the woman's picked up a few tricks since then." He swiped at the blood with the back of his hand and just barely managed to evade the follow-up blow. "Maybe, when I finish here with you, I'll pay a little visit to the farm and try out the red-haired little slut meself."

Quinn had been trying, with lessening success, to keep some faint vestige of control on his temper. But the vulgar threat caused the last thread to break. Hatred he'd spent a lifetime trying to ignore exploded inside him, like red-hot lava bursting forth from a volcano. He straddled O'Sullivan, forced him onto his back and began pounding. And pounding. And pounding. His fists fast and brutal.

He had no idea when the bloodthirsty calls of encouragement turned to cries of concern. He remained unaware of Brendan placing the emergency call to his cousin, shook off the hands that grabbed at his sleeves. All Quinn knew was that this man represented everything he'd ever hated in his life, and he was not going to stop until he'd achieved revenge.

For his mother, for Kate and for a nine-year-old boy who'd tried his best to save a life and had never forgiven himself for having failed.

In the end it took five of them — the bartender, Brendan's cousin, Sergeant O'Neill, and three other strapping men whose strength bespoke a lifetime of cutting hay and peat, to drag this Yank, who seemed to have gone berserk, off the nearly unconscious bully.

"You'll be killing him," the bartender told Quinn.

"That was the idea." Quinn bent down, put his bloody hands on his knees and drew in a deep breath, realizing his error when his ribs burned.

"Nora would never forgive me if I had to put you away in jail for manslaughter," the sergeant said. "We'd best be getting you to the car so I can drive you to casualty and have you seen to."

Quinn wanted to object to that suggestion. Intended to object. Unfortunately he failed to see O'Sullivan stagger to his feet. A blow like a boulder falling from a cliff landed against the back of Quinn's head. His already wobbly knees gave out. Then everything went black.

"You can't be serious about this." Nora watched, stunned as Quinn emptied out the dresser, literally throwing clothes into the suitcase.

"I'm sorry." Christ, talk about an understatement. The problem was, there were absolutely no words for what he was feeling. Nothing he could say that would make either one of them feel any better. "I tried to warn you." Sweaters tumbled on top of briefs, socks tangled with jeans. His shirt was spotted with blood, some his, some O'Sullivan's, but Quinn wasn't going to take time to change. "I told you I wasn't any good for you."

"That's not true." She was not going to resort to tears, Nora vowed, even if she thought that the age-old feminine ploy might get him to change his mind. She didn't want him to look back on this day and believe he'd been trapped.

"You *are* good for me." She wanted to touch him even more than she needed to weep. Nora resisted both urges. "What you did in The Rose for Kate —"

"I almost killed a man."

"No!" She shook her head. "You wouldn't have done that, Quinn."

"I would have. If they hadn't pulled me off him."

"You were angry. At what he'd done to Kate. And rightfully so. There's been many a time I've wished Cadel O'Sullivan dead."

"You just don't get it, do you?" He stopped on his way to the bathroom to retrieve his shaving kit and turned toward her, his dark eyes as bleak and empty as a tomb. "We're not talking about wishing, Nora.

We're talking about me pounding a man to a bloody pulp with my fists."

"You weren't the only one doing the hitting." She reminded him of the lump on the back of his head and the cracked rib the X ray had revealed. "And you didn't start it."

"Every man in that pub knew I didn't go there to have a conversation with O'Sullivan. I went there to beat his goddamn brains out."

"Which would be difficult to do, since I don't believe he has any."

He shook his head, ignoring the pain that hit like lightning behind his eyes. "You're not taking this seriously, dammit."

"Of course I am. I take it seriously indeed when the man I love, the man who says he loves me," she said pointedly, "tells me he's walking away from what we've made together."

"I do love you." The one thing he refused to do was lie, even though it might have made it easier on both of them. "More than I ever thought possible. And I know, if I live to be a hundred, I'll never feel about any other woman the way I feel about you."

"Not that I'd want to be arguing with you, Quinn, but you have a strange way of showing such love."

"I know it seems that way." His head was spinning. Deciding he'd better sit down —

just for a moment before he fell down — Quinn sank onto the mattress.

"But believe it or not, it's because I love you that I'm leaving. Before I end up hurting you. Or Rory. Or one of the other kids. I'm a violent man, Nora. I come from violent bloodstock. I thought I could overcome my past. I thought I *had*."

He dragged both hands through his hair, flinching as his fingers brushed against the lump Cadel had raised with that heavy bottle of Murphy's stout. "Obviously I was wrong."

"No." On this point, Nora was very clear. "I have no words to tell you how sorry I am about your mother."

He'd told her his life story while she'd driven him back to the farm from the hospital. Since the doctor had refused to release him if he intended to drive with a head injury, Quinn had reluctantly allowed the casualty-department nurse to call Laura, who'd followed in the Mercedes. His former lover was now waiting downstairs in the front parlor to take him to the inn until tomorrow's flight back to America.

Nora had kept silent during the telling of the horror tale, and Quinn knew he'd never forget the sight of those silent tears falling on the slender hands gripping the steering wheel.

"What happened to you when you were

just a lad was every bit as much a crime. No child should have to suffer so, Quinn. And it breaks my heart that you had no adults in your life to protect you from such brutality." She pressed crossed hands against that tender saddened heart. "As you protected Kate and Jamie and Brigid today."

He knew where she was going. And didn't buy it. "What I did — using violence to respond to violence — isn't the answer."

"Not under usual conditions. But perhaps it's the only thing a man like Cadel understands. It will be a long while before he raises his hand to his wife again."

Those words caught his reluctant attention. "She's not staying?"

"No. But although we have divorce now in Ireland, it's not an easy thing. Even in the best of circumstances, with parties agreeing, it takes five years of separation. Which doesn't matter to Kate," she said sadly, "since she's understandably in no hurry to get involved with another man."

"She deserves better."

"Aye." Nora sighed and wondered again what might have happened if only she'd been able to convince Kate to write that letter to Andrew Sinclair so many years ago. "She does, indeed."

"And so do you."

"So we're back to your misguided belief that you're not good enough for me?"

"Doesn't it always come back to that?" Wasn't that why he'd tried like hell to stay away from this woman in the first place? "Did I tell you I saw some distant cousin of mine at the horse fair?"

"No." She'd been waiting, but he'd remained silent on the matter. "But Michael mentioned he'd introduced you to a Gallagher he knew from Connemara."

"Patrick Gallagher. A farmer. And bootlegger."

"Well, now, making *poitin*'s not such a crime in that part of the country," she said, misunderstanding the acid in his tone. "Well, of course, it is a crime, but —"

"I know." He lifted a hand that felt as if it weighed fifty pounds.

It was more than the fight that had him feeling dead on his feet, Quinn knew. He'd certainly had his share of brawls in his younger days, and they'd never left him so wasted. And it wasn't just that he was older. It was, Quinn thought, because he was so emotionally drained. He felt as if he'd slashed his wrists and let all his feelings drain out with the blood.

"Michael already explained all that. My point was, that looking into his face was like looking into a goddamn mirror."

"The Gallaghers I've known over the years have always had strong features. And didn't Gram say that she grew up with a boy in Donegal who had the look of you? That's not so unusual, Quinn."

"I suppose not. But the point is, that got me to thinking about bloodlines. My bloodlines."

It took her a moment. And when she understood what he was saying, Nora's heart lurched so painfully she was amazed she was able to keep from crying out.

"Oh, Quinn." She knelt beside him, her hand on his thigh, her green eyes as pained and earnest as he'd ever witnessed them. "You're not like one of Kate's horses. Like the mare you bought Rory. You're a man. You have free will, the intelligence to make choices. Just because your father was a cruel and brutal man . . ."

"Who used his fists to settle arguments," he reminded her pointedly as he looked down at his knuckles, skinned and swollen from connecting with the bones in O'Sullivan's face.

"No." Her hair flew over her shoulders in a brilliant cloud as she shook her head again. "Don't you see he was like Cadel? Just a bully who finally met his match?" She lifted his hand and pressed her lips against the injured flesh. "You're nothing like either one of them."

How he'd wanted to believe that! "I can't take the risk."

"And isn't that for me to be deciding?"

"No." It was his turn to shake his head. Firmly. Resolutely. "It's not easy raising children. One day Rory, or one of his brothers or sisters, if we were to be that lucky to have them, might do something to piss me off. Something that might cause me to strike out instinctively.

"Or perhaps you and I might have an argument. You can be a hardheaded woman sometimes, Nora, and —"

"I know. And I'll be trying to work on that."

"And you also have a habit of interrupting when a man's trying to make a point." Although Quinn could find little humor in this discussion, the memory of her doing the same thing that night in Derry when Brady was trying to tell his tale, that night they'd made love for the first time, almost made Quinn smile.

"It's a foolish point," she muttered.

"Not so foolish." He looked down at their hands, still linked together. He brought her hand to his lips. "I truly do love you, Nora. And if I ever lifted a hand to you, I'd want to kill myself."

"You'd never do such a thing."

"You can't know that. For certain."

She lifted her chin in that way that always made him want to kiss her silly. "Aye. I do. Because I know you, Quinn Gallagher. I'd stake my life on that."

"Don't you understand? That could be exactly what you'd be doing." This time he did smile, but there was not an iota of cheer in it. It was, Nora thought, the saddest thing she'd ever seen. Even sadder than that thin white scar she now knew had been caused by his father's belt buckle.

"No." He released her hand and pushed himself to his feet. "I'm not going to take the chance. I'm not going to let you take the chance."

That said, he gave her one last look fraught with so many emotions Nora couldn't begin to catalog them all. But none of them was the slightest bit encouraging.

"I do love you," he stressed yet again, wanting her to remember that one vital point. "I always will."

With that he was gone. Out of her bedroom. And her house.

Laura, who'd been waiting downstairs, paused in the parlor as Quinn walked out to the Mercedes. "I'm sorry," she said to Nora.

"I know." Nora never would have thought

she could feel a kinship with such a glamorous movie star. But then again, ever since the Americans had come to Castlelough, she'd experienced a host of unfamiliar unexpected emotions. "But it doesn't change things now, does it?"

"Believe me, honey, he'll be back," Laura assured her. "Quinn can be a son of a bitch, but he's smart enough to know when he's hit the jackpot." Her judicious gaze measured Nora from head to foot. "And although I would have bet the farm against it when we first hit this place, you turned out to be the treasure at the end of the guy's rainbow."

That said, she flashed a smile that never failed to bedazzle her fans and left the farmhouse, then climbed into the driver's seat of the Mercedes.

Nora stood in the doorway as the car drove away, watching until it turned the corner and disappeared behind the stone wall separating her farm from Kate's.

He'd said he was leaving to keep from hurting her. The ragged pained sound that escaped her tightly set lips was half laugh, half sob. Didn't he realize he'd done exactly that? Couldn't he understand that he couldn't have wounded her heart more if he'd taken down one of those antique swords from the wall of The Rose and slashed her heart to ribbons?

Covering her face with her hands, Nora finally gave in to the tears that had been threatening since she'd arrived at the hospital and discovered that the man she loved had retreated into his dark and icy shell. She had no way of knowing that as Laura drove toward Castlelough, Quinn couldn't stop himself from believing that he was leaving the best part of his life behind.

CHAPTER TWENTY-SIX

Find a Way Home

Quinn was gone. Back to America. Rory sat in his secret wishing place and related the sad news to his best friend, who, now that the movie people had left Ireland, was free to stop hiding beneath the water.

"I thought he was going to be my da," he told her. He sighed. "He seemed to like me well enough. At least he let me in his tent with him on the father-and-son trek. And he bought me Splendid Mane."

Rory did not have to explain to the Lady that he'd named the horse after the one that had belonged to Manannan mac Lir, the ancient Gaelic god. The original Splendid Mane was said to be swifter than the spring wind and, as was befitting the patron of sailors, traveled equally fast over the waves of the sea as he did over land.

"I wouldn't think a man would be buying a pony for a boy he didn't love. But Jamie says perhaps he had so much money it didn't seem like such a special thing."

Rory sighed again, drew his knees up to his chest, wrapped his thin arms around them and looked out over the darkening blue water. Beside him, Maeve whimpered. Rory could tell that she missed the American almost as much as he did.

A pony is a very special thing, the Lady assured him.

Rory wasn't as surprised as he'd been the first time she'd spoken to him. But this time her words didn't ease the worry that had been heavy on his heart.

"I wish he hadn't left," he said again. And sighed yet again. "Mam's been crying a lot. Just like she did before the Americans came. But I don't think she's worried about moving away from the farm anymore. I think she misses Quinn, too."

He looked up at the Lady, lines of concern etched into his freckled forehead. "I've been worrying that perhaps I did something to make him go away."

He couldn't think of what that might have been, but hadn't Tommy Doyle's da left when Tommy had gotten the cancer? Rory had heard his grandfather Brady remark that Brian Doyle just couldn't deal with so much trouble, but after Tommy had come back from Dublin, bald, but cured, his da still hadn't returned.

"Perhaps some men aren't made to have families," he said, repeating what his grandfather had told him about Mr. Doyle. "Perhaps, if it weren't for me, Quinn would have married Mam. And she'd be happy. Like she was before he left to go back to California."

The American leaving had nothing to do with you, Rory Fitzpatrick. The Lady's golden eyes rested on him reassuringly. *Doesn't he have some of his own ghosts to calm before he can be making a family? You must be patient. He'll be back.*

That said, she turned and disappeared beneath the water without so much as a ripple, returning to her kingdom beneath the waves.

"Quinn will be back." Rory poured milk from the pitcher into the glasses that Celia had set on the table.

"Oh, darling." Nora turned from the stove, trying to decide whether it was kinder to let her son continue to believe this or to dash his hopes with cold reality so he could move on with his young life. So they could *all* move on. "I wouldn't be counting on that," she said gently.

"He'll be back." Rory's expression was, as it had been for the past two weeks, confident. "The Lady told me he just had some ghosts to get rid of first. Before he could be part of the family."

Nora's first thought was that it wasn't so strange that a boy who talked to a lough beastie could so readily accept the idea of ghosts. Her second thought was to wonder how Rory could understand so well that the man he kept insisting would be his father could have been so haunted.

"I don't know what to say to that," she said honestly. Having never lied to her child, she wasn't about to start now.

"You don't have to say anything, Mam." He finished pouring the milk and put the pitcher back in the refrigerator. Then he flashed a grin. "We just have to be patient. The Lady promised."

Half a world away Quinn sat on the deck of his rented house, looking out over the ocean. The white-capped water reminded him too much of Nora. But then, he thought grimly, everything reminded him of the woman he'd left behind in Ireland.

"You realize, of course, that this is getting boring."

He glanced over at Laura, who was sitting beside him, her bare feet up on the railing, long tanned legs displayed to advantage in a pair of brief white shorts. "Sorry I'm not a better host."

"Oh, don't apologize." She took a sip of the fumé blanc and smiled sweetly over the rim of her glass. "I've always admired your overachieving spirit, darling. And the way you've been behaving ever since we left the 'auld sod' is by far the best example of a pity party I've ever seen."

His only answer to that was a succinct curse. He took a long drink of the iced tea he'd made himself stick to the past two weeks, fearing that if he started drinking he might never stop.

"Why the hell don't you just go to her?" Laura asked, not for the first time. "Instead of continuing to make the two of you miserable. Not to mention that poor kid — he's got to feel deserted."

Quinn didn't want to think about Rory. It was bad enough picturing the boy every night while he was trying to sleep, the image of that open freckled face flashing with all the others he'd betrayed in some kind of bizarre slide show in his mind.

"I explained all that." It hadn't been easy to open up to her, to share that story of his life yet again. But he'd needed someone to talk to. And amazingly Laura was turning out to be a good friend.

"I know." She sighed and shook her head. "And I think it's about the most ridiculous excuse for walking out on a woman I've ever heard."

"That's your opinion."

"True enough." She put her feet back onto the deck and stood. Figuring she was going into the house to refill her empty glass, Quinn turned back toward the view of the sun-spangled water, which while admittedly magnificent, was the wrong damn ocean. He let his eyes drift closed.

Suddenly he heard a loud smack and felt a sharp sting on his cheek. He brought his hand to the burning skin and looked up at Laura.

"What was that for?" he asked without rancor.

"It was a test." Smiling, she raised her hand and delivered a slap to his other cheek. "You might call it a kind of scientific experiment. Of nurture against nature, so to speak."

"I have no idea what you're talking about." Although on some distant level he thought he might.

"I hit you," she pointed out unnecessarily. "And you didn't hit me back."

"Hell, of course I didn't." Oh yes, Quinn considered grimly, he could definitely see where she was headed with this little bit of amateur psychology.

"Isn't that interesting?" Again she slapped him, this time with enough force to turn his head. "You'd think a man with such violent genetic tendencies would feel the need to strike back."

"Laura, this isn't going to work."

"Oh?" She arched one perfect blond brow. "And why not? I thought you told me that you couldn't stop yourself from beating up that thuggish wife-abusing Irishman?"

"That was different."

"How exactly?"

"You're nothing like O'Sullivan."

"Now there's a news flash." She folded her arms. "Neither, would I venture a guess, is Nora Fitzpatrick. Or her son. Or, for that matter, any of the other children."

When Quinn didn't — couldn't — answer, she put her hand on his arm. "You'd never hurt them, Quinn. Not in a million years. I know it. And I know that deep down inside, you know it, too."

"Then you know a helluva lot more about me than I know about myself."

"Your instincts weren't even there. Your hand didn't even make a fist. I watched," she said when he glanced down at his hand, as if to check out the assertion firsthand for himself. "You allowed your sadistic son-of-a-bitch father to control the first thirty-five years of your life. You're too damn smart — and Nora is too special — for you to allow him to control the next thirty-five."

The idea of spending those years with Nora was admittedly appealing. Terrifyingly wonderfully appealing.

"I'll think about it."

She smiled, patted his cheek, which still bore the imprint of her fingers, then kissed him. "Why don't you do that, darling?"

Quinn Gallagher was a remarkably intelligent man. Which was why it was such a surprise to Nora that he could be so stupid about something so basic. So important.

She'd tried to be patient, tried to give him time to realize the mistake he'd made, but with each passing day, she feared that the walls that had begun to crumble during his time in Castlelough would begin going up again. Higher, this time. And thicker. Until there'd be no way to breach them. Which was why, three weeks after he'd left Ireland, as she lay alone in her bed — the bed that now seemed heartbreakingly empty — wearing the T-shirt Quinn had left in the laundry, she realized what she had to do.

She was going to have to go to America

and convince him that they were perfect together. And then, she considered, she'd tell him that she was willing to leave Ireland and live in California with him.

"I understand it won't be easy," she told her family as they sat around the table after Sunday mass. "John, I understand that you'll not be wanting to change your plans to go to university. Nor should you."

"He'll be all right," Fionna assured her. "I'll be watching out for him. And he can always come and visit you and the rest of the family in California. It's not as if your new husband won't be able to afford the airfare," she said dryly.

Nora turned to her grandmother, refilling her teacup. "Are you certain you don't want to come?"

"I've lived more than eighty years on this farm, darling. My roots are sunk too deep into the peat to transplant. And then, of course, I'd not be wanting to give up my Bernadette campaign just when I've finally piqued the Vatican's interest."

The letter from the Congregation for the Cause of Saints had arrived in yesterday morning's post. By evening Elizabeth Murphy, who considered her postmistress job to be akin to town crier, had spread the word throughout not only Castlelough, but

also the entire county. Even Bishop Mc-
Carthy had been seen on the nightly news
agreeing with the lissome blond interviewer
from News One that this was, indeed, a red-
letter day for the parish.

The newscast had also featured an interview with a beaming Fionna, who'd been
videotaped standing beside the Mercedes
that had arrived at the farm a week after
Quinn's departure. The same Mercedes
Quinn had driven during his visit to Castlelough. The one he'd somehow arranged to
have painted with bright murals depicting
the life and times of Sister Bernadette.

"But you can be sure I'll be coming to
America for the baptism of all those beautiful babies I expect you and Quinn to make
together," Fionna promised.

Although just the thought of leaving her
beloved grandmother made her heart heavy,
Nora couldn't help smiling.

"And you, Mary?" she asked her sister. "I
realize you might find it difficult to be
leaving your friends in your last year of
school. If you'd like to stay —"

"No." Mary shook her head. "Though it's
true I'd rather stay here, in Castlelough,
there's something to be said for going to
California, too. Perhaps Quinn can help me
find movie work."

That was not Nora's favorite subject. But she was also relieved that she wouldn't be leaving Fionna to deal with Mary's teenage angst.

"What about Splendid Mane?" Rory asked. There was no doubt he was willing to go to California if that was what it took for them all to be a family. But he hated the thought of leaving his horse behind.

"Kate says we can get papers for your pony to join us in California. And I'm certain there will be some stables somewhere nearby where we can board her."

It wouldn't be like having her right outside the door, where he could walk out whenever he wanted and give her a carrot or lump of sugar. But, Rory figured, weren't the nuns always saying that God appreciated sacrifice?

"I think that will be just fine, Mam," he assured his mother, who was looking at him with obvious concern. She hadn't quite gone back to the laughing smiling woman she'd been when Quinn had been living in the house. But at least he didn't hear her crying anymore when he got up in the night.

"I promised Peggy I'd send her a Malibu Barbie from California," Celia piped up.

Knowing how close the two girls were and understanding that the move might prove difficult for her youngest sister at first, Nora laughed. "I think that's a lovely idea. So long as she can resist any more stake burnings."

It was the night before she was to leave for California. The plan Nora had come up with called for her to go first, then send for the rest of the family once she'd settled into Quinn's house. And his life.

And now, although it wasn't easy, she was saying the farewells she'd been putting off to last.

"You tell that Yank of yours," Michael said, his voice unusually gruff as he hugged her goodbye outside his farmhouse, "that if he doesn't make an honest woman of you, he'll have me to answer to."

She laughed as she was meant to. "I'll tell him." Her voice cracked and tears welled up in her eyes as she clung to her older brother. "I love you, Michael. And I'll miss you something terrible."

"We'll have our visits."

"Aye." Her voice didn't sound any more enthusiastic than his. Why was it, Nora wondered, that life always seemed to demand a person make such hard choices? "We'll come home for Christmas."

"Now that will give me something to look forward to," he promised.

They shared another hug. Then, dashing away the tears she couldn't keep from trailing down her cheeks, Nora drove to Kate's.

"I'll miss you," Kate said as she handed her a cup of tea. She'd taken down the Beleek, which was usually only used for special guests and celebrations.

Since her separation from Cadel, Kate had begun to bloom like a parched Burren wildflower whose roots had just tapped into an underground stream.

"No more than I'll be missing you." Nora's eyes welled up again and she knew she'd never be able to get away without another flood of hot tears. She took a drink of tea, swallowing past the lump in her throat. "But I promised Michael we'd be back for Christmas."

"We'll take a day shopping in Galway," Kate said. "Think of the fun we'll have seeing how much of your rich husband's money we can spend."

Even as Nora laughed, she felt the first tear escape and begin trailing down her cheek. "And it's not as if we're living in the nineteenth century," she insisted. "There are phones, after all. We'll be able to talk almost as often as we do now."

"Of course we will." Neither woman mentioned that the vagaries of the Irish phone system — especially out here in the west — made that proposed scenario highly unlikely.

"I'm so happy for you." Now it was Kate's eyes that had turned suspiciously shiny. "Quinn's a wonderful man, Nora."

"Aye."

Neither brought up Quinn's fistfight in the pub. The fight that had brought Cadel O'Sullivan's abusive behavior into the open, exposing it to the bright light of day in a way the villagers could no longer ignore. As if realizing that to stay in Castlelough would result in a lifelong shunning, Cadel had returned to Dungarven. The letter Kate's lawyer had sent him had suggested strongly that he not think about returning unless he wanted criminal charges pressed against him. So far the ploy seemed to be working.

They talked some more. Cried some more.

"You're going to have such a glorious family," Kate said as they exchanged hugs.

"I know." Nora gave her sister-in-law a watery grin. "I just wish you could meet a wonderful man like Quinn."

"Perhaps someday I will. But in the meantime I think I'm going to enjoy having my little brood to myself."

As she walked to the car, after having exchanged one last hug, Nora realized that finally Kate would be all right.

Kate stood in the driveway, watching the taillights disappear around the stone wall. She dashed at her tears with the back of her hands. Then smiled as she thought of something even her sister-in-law didn't yet know. Nora was carrying Quinn's child.

After a sleepless night, during which Nora felt like a young girl anticipating Christmas, she was pacing the parlor, waiting for her brother to arrive to take her to the airport. Her suitcase, which had been packed for two days, was sitting beside the front door.

"Where is he?" she asked for the umpteenth time. "If he doesn't hurry, I'll be missing my flight."

"Now, darling," Fionna soothed as she looked up from her knitting. She'd found a pattern for an infant's Aran Isle sweater that would be the perfect gift for Quinn and Nora's first child. "It's not that late yet. You still have plenty of time to get to the airport."

Nora glared at her watch, wondering if it was broken. She'd swear the hands hadn't moved since she'd last looked at it. "That's the trouble with the Irish," she muttered. "We have no sense of punctuality."

Much to her annoyance, her family's only reaction to her was laughter.

"If he doesn't arrive in the next two minutes, I'm going to call Dennis Murphy to come with his taxi and take me to Shannon."

"And wouldn't that cost a pretty penny," Fionna observed.

"It doesn't matter how much it might cost," Mary said. "Because our Nora's going to be rich after she marries Quinn."

Her nerves horribly on edge, Nora turned on her sister. "That's not the reason I'm marrying the man." Hadn't she heard Eileen Donovan mutter just that very same accusation to Nancy McCarthy while the two women had been comparing hair coloring in the cosmetics aisle at Monohan's Mercantile?

"Of course it's not, darling," Fionna agreed. "Why, anyone can see that you and your Quinn are soul mates."

"Aye," Mary said quickly, as if not wanting to part on an unhappy note. "I hope if I'm still unmarried when I'm your age, I'll be lucky enough to find a man like your Quinn, Nora."

"Thank you." Understanding that her sister was trying to make amends for her incautious words, Nora decided not to take offense at the way she'd made her sound positively ancient. "That does it. I'm going to call Dennis and —"

"Oh, here he comes! Finally!" At the sight of the car turning into the driveway, she grabbed her suitcase and flung open the front door.

"It's not Michael," John said. The entire family stood in a little group by the door, watching the dark gold sedan, which was a long way from Michael Joyce's battered old Fiat.

"Oh my." Fionna lifted her hand to her throat and met Nora's gaze over the top of Rory's dark head.

"Do you think . . . ?" Nora couldn't get the rest of the words out. It was too much to hope for.

"It's Quinn!" Rory shouted as they all watched the man climb out of the driver's seat.

Nora felt suddenly warm all over. As if she she'd just flown too close to the sun. She ran toward Quinn, who lifted her off her feet and spun her around, kissing her as if it had been a lifetime and not just three weeks that they'd been apart.

"I was coming to you!" she said between kisses.

"I know. Michael told me when I called him late last night from New York." His lips blazed a trail of fire up her smiling face as Maeve bounded around them like a crazed puppy, yipping a canine welcome. "He promised not to let you get on the plane."

"I was ready to kill him."

"Why don't you kiss me again, instead?"

"Oh, aye!" The kiss sent streamers of dazzling sunshine through Nora. But it was his next words that caused her glowing heart to take wings.

"I've come home."

EPILOGUE

The marriage was held in the circle of stones overlooking the sea. Nora's brother Finn returned again from Australia to perform the ceremony and, just as at Brady's funeral, it seemed as if the entire village had turned out. Even Maeve was in attendance, sporting the shamrock collar Quinn had bought her in Derry and a wreath of spring flowers Celia, Rory and Jamie had woven around her furry neck.

And that wasn't all. As Nora walked toward Quinn, following Mary — whose fresh-faced beauty drew appreciative murmurs from the congregation — and Kate, looking resplendent as her matron of honor, down the path of blazing pink fuchsia petals Celia had strewn, she felt a soft caress against her cheek. Nora knew that, although some might claim it was only the breeze blowing through the spring leaves of the oak trees, her mother and father had joined the family gathered together at her wedding.

"They're all here," he murmured, revealing that Nora was not alone in her thinking. "The Joyces, the Fitzpatricks, even the Gallaghers. And all the ancients, going back as far as time. They've all shown up to celebrate this day with us, my love."

"Aye," she whispered back, her eyes glistening with tears of joy.

And although Nora knew medical science would insist it to be physically impossible yet, as she repeated the age-old vows to love, honor and cherish, she felt the child she and Quinn had made together — the first of a new generation — stir in her womb.

Quinn slipped the gold Claddagh wedding band depicting two hands joined over a heart, the same ring that had belonged to her mother, onto Nora's finger.

"You may kiss the bride," Father Joyce announced with obvious brotherly pleasure.

"Now there's an idea," Quinn said, earning a laugh from those standing close by.

As the sun set over the water in a glorious blaze of ruby light, he lowered his head. An audible sigh of pleasure could be heard rippling through the gathered throng as their lips touched for the first time as husband and wife. Then, hands linked, Nora and Quinn Gallagher walked out of the magical circle of stones into the arms of their family.

It was twilight, that mystical time when the world seems suspended between day and night.

Patrick Driscoll and Peter Collins had been fishing for the past hour with little luck, when suddenly, right in front of their boat — close enough that they could have reached out and touched her emerald green scales, they were to say later that night in The Rose — the magnificent lough beastie had risen from the glassy cobalt blue depths.

And if that t'weren't amazing enough, Peter Collins told the eager audience, they could have sworn that the Lady was smiling.